I0747156

ARIEL

Zorica Gojkovic

The Time of Light Productions

Print ISBN: 978-1-947168-04-6

eBook ISBN: 978-1-947168-05-3

Library of Congress Control Number: 2025902746

The Time of Light Productions

Book Cover Art by Paul Youll

Book Cover Design by Ronnie Jensen

In memory of my father, Miodrag Gojkovic,
who was a big reader and enthusiastic about any new innovation
and technological advancement.

Chapter One

Palladium, their starship, was a building vessel, and although large, carried only a small crew for maintenance work on Laurus. It was constructed of a translucent alloy with psychic reception sensors. Its colorful walls emitted healing energies. Ariel imagined from a distance their ship looked like a child's toy, all color and light.

The hallways glowed amber today. Ariel hummed as she walked to her design studio. Once in a while, she timed the clicking of her white boots to her humming. Today was a big day for her new world design. She smiled, performed a little jig, and bounced along.

At the studio, she waited for the door to open, then stepped into a bright spacious room. The crystal transducer shimmered in the center. Equipment clicked and whirred. In the back, giant screens displayed worlds she had designed.

She scrunched her nose. The scent of orange permeated the studio. On the table in front of her lay breakfast dishes. And orange rind. She shook her head. She'd come in early to work and forgotten, yet again, to clear the table.

She gathered everything up, carried it to the recycler and ordered a mug of hot chocolate from the food dispenser next to it. At the beep, she picked it up and called for music. Drums and guitar blasted through the studio. She sashayed her way to the workstation, careful to move only the lower part of her body.

At the desk, she set the mug down, spun several times singing loudly, plopped into the chair, powered up the station and brought up Argos, her latest world design.

Brilliant colors, diagrams, numbers filled the big screens. Holographic forms set up all around. She tilted her head, squinted and smiled. She'd designed a beautiful world.

"Let's get to work," she told herself, pulled off her boots, unzipped her blue work suit a little and tightened the blue topaz clip holding her hair. She took a big swallow of hot chocolate, sweet and delicious, and pulled herself closer to the desk.

The intercom blared.

Ariel jumped, inhaled and pushed a button. Darius, the New Worlds Project Coordinator, appeared on the screen, his dark eyes tight. Long gray and white hair hung in strands around his face.

"Ariel." He sounded surprised to find her in the studio. "What's that racket?"

"Ah, yes. Sorry." She switched the music off.

"That's better. Some not-so-good news, I'm afraid."

Ariel tilted her head. A line appeared between her brows.

"Got another call just now. This one from the engineer. They're finding problems with Argos." Darius looked at her, his lips a flat line. "I know this is a little late with the meeting coming up, but thought I'd let you know."

"What? But that's impossible." Ariel sat straighter in her chair. "What kinds of problems?"

"Argos' overall energy emission."

Ariel looked at Darius for a long moment, feeling her heart pounding in her chest. "But that can't be. I've checked everything endless times." She did not make mistakes. Her world designs always easily passed building requirements.

Darius nodded. "Of course. I understand. Just telling you what they're saying so you're prepared. I'll see you in an hour." His dark eyes softened. "Hopefully this can easily be resolved."

He waited a moment.

She gave one slow nod.

And he was gone.

Ariel stared at the blank screen. How extraordinary. That never happened. No mistakes ever existed at this late stage of world design.

She thought a minute then focused on Argos, grew still, took in the whole of it. Beautiful. It was her most ambitious design to date. If everything went right and the committee approved, they would start to build her world.

But now? A mistake at this stage? How was that possible? Of course, she'd gone over the design hundreds of times. There were no mistakes.

But she checked again—design parameters, species blueprints, energy emissions, looking for anomalies, then entered hyperawareness, a state of high alert combined with psychic perception that allowed her to scan deeper and faster.

No mistakes.

She sat with hands in her lap, listening to the roar of the equipment, smelling the scent of orange. Then blinked, noticed she wasn't breathing and started to take slow deep breaths. She swiveled to face the crystal transducer, closed her eyes and absorbed the emitting healing energies.

After a while she felt her shoulders let go. She took a big breath, turned back, looked at the Argos data. What could she do?

Her whole body tightened.

Something was very wrong.

She shivered, ran sweaty palms down her thighs.

Chapter Two

Ariel walked into a conference room loud with conversation and smelling of coffee. Some of the crew sat at the triangular table in the center. Others stood by the food dispenser, holding mugs, talking and laughing. At the perimeter, tall crystal transducers shimmered rose-colored healing light.

She clutched her console, a 5-D portable computer, with sweaty hands and looked for a place to sit, her legs like rubber. She lifted a hand in greeting when she saw her friend Max. He smiled, winked and went back to his console. He wore his usual white robes, his long brown kinky hair and beard the usual scraggly mess.

Darius sat at the head of the table, fingers interlaced, looking straight ahead, his face tight. As New Worlds Project Coordinator, he was the interface between the ship's building mission and the Earth Council.

Ariel found a seat, sat down, lips compressed, stomach tight. She wanted to know what the problem was. And dreaded knowing.

The Earth Council members started to arrive one by one in holo form.

Those standing drifted to their seats.

The room became quiet.

"All right," Darius began. "As you all know, we are here to

review Ariel's new world design, Argos." He looked around the room. "I've been informed there are some issues. So, let's see what they are and if we can quickly resolve them." He swiveled his chair to face Brandon, the planetary scientist, "Brandon, why don't you start?"

Brandon straightened up. He was in his thirties with an open innocent face and neatly combed short brown hair. With delicate pink fingers he activated 5-D modeling and Argos data sprang to life for all to see.

Ariel watched, eyes wide, throat tight.

"A beautiful world," Brandon said with admiration, "But with some problems." With his stylus he pointed to various pieces of data. "You can see here Argos' energy emission far exceeds safety limits. Early sentience would produce too much energy. Eventually this excess would lead to Argos' self-destruction and would threaten our very own existence." He shook his head, "And worse. .."

Those who knew this already sat silent, looking down at the table. Others gasped, looking at each other in disbelief.

Ariel sat frozen in shock. She saw that the data was accurate. Saw Brandon was correct. But it made no sense. It couldn't be right. Her heart thundered.

After Brandon, other scientists presented their data.

It didn't take long to see that Argos had a big problem.

Silence. Whispers expressing incredulity. Heads shaking. Someone cleared his throat.

"Ariel, do you have anything that might explain this?" asked Darius.

Ariel shook her head, lips compressed, managed to say, "I don't understand how this could have happened." She glanced at the rose transducers. Shook her head. "No, nothing to add right now."

Silence.

Ariel swayed, felt herself traveling inside, moving away, the scientists, the room, everything fading until all she could hear was the loud buzz of inner silence.

From a great distance she heard Tom, their systems engineer, a younger man with red hair and fair complexion, say, "Of course, if we were able to move Earth to a new dimension immediately, we could use this excess energy to do it. We'd be out of here and this sector would continue safely without us."

No one said anything.

They had known from the moment they became Creators that this dimension could sustain only so many of their built worlds. Energy in the universe had to remain in balance. Worlds emitting energy had to be balanced by worlds absorbing energy. Managing energy was their biggest challenge. They knew this from the beginning and immediately set about finding a way to transport Earth to a new dimension. Without success.

Darius turned to Varian, a gray elder on the Earth Council. "Any Gateway progress?" The Gateway was the portal to other dimensions. They needed to find the Gateway before they could move Earth.

Varian looked down at his hands, shook his gray head and looked up. "Nothing." All-out effort had been made to find the Gateway right from the beginning, but there had been no advances since Andreas and Vivian seemed to come close to finding it.

Ariel looked at the blurry faces around her, shifted in her chair. It wasn't possible she had made this kind of mistake in designing Argos. Yet the scientists showed she had made such a mistake. Everything in her head conflicted. Thoughts, calculations bumped into each other, creating chaos.

Max was tapping his stylus, looking at her. His eyebrows went up. Ariel shook her head, lips compressed.

It came to her she'd done no research on the Gateway herself, not in a long while. It wasn't her job. She did it because there weren't enough people who could. It required a facility in teleportation that most humans did not have and a whole set of other skills besides. It was one of the reasons they'd made little progress. Then there was that hollow empty feeling of missing her parents, Vivian and Andreas.

Whir of equipment. Clicking. Whooshing. A soft tinkle from the transducers as they switched frequencies.

They had no choice. They had to create, build worlds. That was the New Earth Prime Directive. Since the Destruction, they had committed to being Creators. It was the only way they knew how to survive as a species.

"Early sentience would have given us such an energy boost," said Darius, his voice sad, filled with regret. "But of no use if we don't have the Gateway." He compressed his lips, looked around the table.

Ariel felt her entire body begin to shake, vibrate. Something inside her exploded in frantic rebellion. A voice boomed inside her.

Argos must be built!

She lurched from the power that coursed through her. Her chair screeched across the floor.

Heads turned her way.

She sat in a thick mist and could not move. Vaguely she realized they might be wanting to read her thoughts and struggled to put up her psychic shields. She was burning up. Small wisps of hair stuck to her forehead and cheeks. She lifted her hand and wiped the sweat. Again, the force shook her.

They are wrong! Argos must be built! The voice boomed inside her.

Ariel grabbed and held onto the table just in time not to jerk violently again. She suppressed a gasp. No one must know these rebellious thoughts. No one on the New Earth had ever defied its laws and rules.

She trembled hot jittery shakes, struggled to sit upright. She hoped no one noticed, hoped her psychic shields held. She worked hard to make her face neutral, forced herself to take deep breaths. She noticed wet spots under her armpits and squeezed her arms closer to her body.

Through the fog she heard Darius say, "We don't want to repeat our history." He leaned back in his chair and put his hands in his lap. "We don't want to create anything worse than what we have already experienced." He closed his eyes, and everyone knew to do the same.

They entered group consciousness and reviewed Earth history. Ariel, again, as many times since she was a little girl, vividly saw the entire human history—bloody tribal battles, hellish screams of the tortured, rubble and fires blazing entire countries, miles and miles of ashes once forests, grotesque genetic failings—a world turned hell, a point of no return.

The darkness seemed complete, having burned itself out in bitter angry embers, the life force thin in those few that remained awaiting their end. Waiting. A long wait with nothingness. Gloom and despair. But it did not come. Instead, came a Light. Filling them all with a new vision. At first barely visible, but as they latched onto it with their last breath, it became brighter, giving them hope. They ran toward it, hungry for life, and it became bigger, informing them, leading them, loving them until they were strong enough to vow never again to forget, never again to repeat that which had already been done.

They carved into their psyches that violence leads to death, greed leads to destruction, fear leads to hell. They accepted that technology is technology, and human biological organisms as existing in a natural world, and the only recourse was to honor nature, to support the unfolding of that which was inherently natural to all humans.

At the moment of the Light, the few remaining humans knew their oneness with the Universal Being, knew that the only way out of this hell was to keep that knowledge, knew themselves to be co-creators with the Great Universal Consciousness, understood that the only Life they had was to create, to expand, and in that creation and expansion was the ever-unfolding Life of the Universe. And it was Love.

This became their Prime Directive, guiding all their actions, all their decisions.

So the slow rebuilding began. It took thousands of years to develop psychic abilities to the level where each human had tremendous power and tremendous control. It took thousands of years to organize and consolidate that power so they could become Creators—design and build their own worlds in the same way they were designed and built by their own Creator.

All the energy and creativity of every New Human became engaged, in some way, towards this creative expression and co-creation with the Great Universal Being. And the species they created, they hoped, would one day, as they themselves had done, achieve superconsciousness and become Creators themselves. Thus the ever-expanding life of All That Is would unfold in its infinite variety, power and creativity.

Ariel shivered, as she always did when they all remembered their history. It reminded them all. It kept them on track. It was built into their psyches to review regularly and never forget.

At completion, they were all calmer, quieter and in harmony. They all knew Argos would have to be aborted and were silent.

"Project Argos is terminated pending irrefutable evidence countering current scientific findings or thus far unknown variables," concluded Darius, his voice flat. It was a glorious design of a world. It would have been a joy to watch it, like a precocious child, reach for the heavens and into its own unique expression.

There was a momentary silence, then Darius adjourned the meeting.

The Earth Council vanished. Loud chatter broke out, chairs screeched, everyone gathered their materials, discussing Argos and the Gateway.

It was over. Ariel breathed a sigh of relief. She looked toward the door, pushed her chair back and got up, her legs weak, shaky. She grabbed her console and moved as fast as she could. She heard voices talking to her, but they all blended into a big noise. She heard Max's voice calling after her something about dinner.

Chapter Three

She forced her legs to move. Hurry! Just get to the studio. Echoes of the voice thundered through her, making her uncoordinated, taking up all of her mind. She focused hard to stay upright, to keep walking. What was happening to her? She swayed. A little further. Just get to the studio.

Her face began to spasm. She wanted to cry. She tightened her lips, her jaw. Almost there. She kept pushing, seeking sanctuary, reprieve, a moment to understand all this.

At last, her studio. She slid through the door and let out a big sigh as it closed behind her. She stood, legs trembling, eyes closed, breathing jerky breaths. Calm down. Calm down. She made herself inhale a big deep breath, exhaled slowly, then walked to the workstation. She dropped the console on the desk and collapsed into the chair. She felt her face start to change again, put her head in her hands and allowed herself to cry.

After a long while she sat up straight and reached for the box of tissues, took a handful, wiped her face and blew her nose. What happened back there? Her brain didn't work, felt like slush. She blew her nose again and looked around, relieved the meeting was over, relieved she was alone. The crystal transducer glittered and hummed. She blinked at the flickering giant screens displaying her worlds, her entire body buzzing.

She sat for a while feeling numb, then pushed herself up, legs trembling, and managed to get to the food dispenser. She ordered a big mug of hot chocolate and was never more grateful for its sweetness.

Back at her desk, she pushed her boots off and sat for a long time drinking hot chocolate. What happened to her? No answers came. Her brain was slush. She looked up at all her worlds. She loved them. She tightened her lips not wanting to cry again.

She forced herself to breathe evenly. What to do? She put the mug down and brought up the Argos design. She had to check again. She moved steadily through all layers of the design, strangely clear-headed. After a while she gave up.

Nothing different from when she last checked. And completely different from what the scientists found.

She picked up the mug and swiveled back around to face her worlds.

Argos must be built! The voice boomed.

She jerked with the shock of the energy, spilling hot chocolate, trembling, burning up, sweat beading up on her forehead. She blinked, breathed quick shallow breaths. Her heart pounded.

Then it passed. What was happening to her? She put the mug down, reached for tissues, wiped her forehead, wiped the spilled hot chocolate from her suit and chair, then got on her knees and wiped the floor.

Nothing made sense. This crazy inner order to build Argos when building Argos would destroy them. That was absurd.

It would pass, she told herself. It had to pass. She sighed. Her shoulders slumped. It would not pass. She knew it would not pass.

She sat in misery she had never known in her entire life. The New Humans had control of their emotions. Something they developed immediately after the Destruction. And here she was, completely out of control.

What to do?

She pushed herself up and shuffled toward the giant Laurus screen. Thousands of strands of color pulsated continuously. This was Laurus' foundation as a world. Data flickered around the screen, reporting detailed information on every facet of Laurus. They would be there in a few weeks for maintenance work, and she had a lot to do to prepare.

Ariel focused, visually inspected Laurus, then entered hyperawareness and quickly assimilated the data. Everything was going as it should. She lingered on the psychic exploration of Laurus, on each one of its inhabitants, knowing each intimately, loving every tiny part of her creation with so much passion it was a wonder to her.

She came out of hyperawareness surprised she could even enter hyperawareness given her condition. A small hope arose in her that she was getting better. She walked around to the other side, to Demete, the very first world she designed. The dominant species was a wispy organism whose existence primarily revolved around sound. Ariel switched to hyperawareness and quickly scanned multiple layers of their condition, the crystal transducer assisting and focusing her psychic energies.

They were unfolding beautifully, slowly attaining sentience, expanding, starting to create simple things for their world. One day she hoped they would attain superconsciousness and become Creators. Hopefully without the useless suffering humans had endured.

She returned to the present. The crystal transducer pulsated healing energy, and she took it in. There had to be an answer to

Argos. There had to be an explanation for what was happening.

She walked back to the workstation and sat with elbows on the desk, chin in hands, and looked at the Argos data. Then she switched to simulation mode. There was Argos pulsating in and out of physical existence, deftly operating in the physical and non-physical band of existence, a perfect blend of sound, light and color, a perfect interweaving of millions of diverse species. Pain coursed through her body. Not to build this world. It was unbearable.

She tightened her lips and swallowed the pain, shut down the Argos data and brought up the Laurus data. There was work to be done for the changes they needed to make once they were there. Could she do it given her mostly mushy brain, not think about Argos for a while?

She became aware she had been sitting in front of the Laurus data seeing nothing. She focused and tried again. She leaned closer to the screen, deciphering information. After looking at it for a while, she again realized she wasn't registering any of it. She leaned back in the chair and reached for the mug of hot chocolate. Cold. She sighed. Guess she'd have to wait to work on Laurus.

She looked down at the mug. Earth travel standard, white and plain. She'd have to design a set of more cheerful mugs for the dispenser.

Her stomach growled, and she looked up. She was hungry. Get something to eat, if she could eat, wash, get some rest.

She shut down the workstation, picked up her boots and console and headed for her quarters. Maybe tomorrow answers would start to appear. She tightened her lips, feeling a heaviness in her stomach.

Chapter Four

Ariel pushed away the breakfast plate and sat at the kitchen counter with her head in her hands. Nothing had changed since yesterday. That powerful sense that Argos must be built was exactly the same. She groaned. And those dreadful convulsions! How could she be around anyone?

Soft guitar music drifted through her quarters. The food dispenser and recycler hummed to her left. On her right sat the fireplace with shelves of Old Earth pottery and utensils; this part of her kitchen especially designed for her Old Earth cooking experiments.

She got off the stool, carried the dishes to the recycler then shuffled to the sleeping quarters and into golden morning light—a simulation she designed to feel like she was back home on Earth where her bedroom faced east.

To the left, the crystal transducer sparkled and hummed at the small workstation. The garment dispenser and recycler to the right. Her bed a heap of green rumpled covers in the middle.

She stood with her hand on her stomach. What to do? Everything inside her had been run through a grinder, hurting and confusing.

After a while she looked over at the workstation and held her breath. The green light was not on. No messages. She exhaled, relieved. She didn't have to talk to anyone.

What did she have to do today? She thought a minute. Nothing urgent.

She stepped over to the bed, pushed thecovers back and sat on the edge.

What will she do about this mess she was in? Obviously she couldn't build Argos. She couldn't go around having fits. She sat there a good long time, occasionally shaking her head. No answers. Then stood up, pulled the bedding into place, and went to wash up.

She was combing her hair in front of the mirror, then froze. Two strange cobalt eyes looked back at her. Her eyes. But she did not recognize them, recognize herself. She looked at this stranger for a while, then with deliberate precision placed the comb down on the counter. She was in trouble. She had to do something. She had to find herself. Get back to the Ariel she knew. She exhaled, tightened her lips. Maybe if she got away from the ship for a while, think, sort this out. At that thought a surge of energy ran through her and she leaped to the garment dispenser and searched for something to wear.

She was tying the strings of a blue woolen gown that had just come out when the intercom went off. She crossed over to the workstation and answered. Max's smiling face with messy hair and scraggly beard appeared.

"My dear, why a face so dour it threatens to sink a thousand worlds?" Max's shoulders shook with laughter, his soft brown doe eyes shining with mirth. "If you were any more serious, the species you design would simply die from premature aging before it ever reached superconsciousness."

She looked at Max, eyebrows raised, waiting. He was enjoying himself immensely, but today was not good for the banter they usually relished.

"Have you ever thought of smiling once in a while, Ariel?" Max continued.

Ariel shifted from one foot to the other, lips compressed.

Max's eyes widened, waiting for her response.

Ariel mustered up the energy and played along, mimicked an exaggerated laugh, shook her head side to side: "Max, Max, my worlds may stand the threat of dying from premature aging, but yours stand the risk of shattering from sheer jocularity. I'd say you have something to worry about yourself."

"No. I don't think so." He shook his head, imitating her. "A world exploding out of existence because of laughter! Just think how much energy that would yield! That's a positive yield!" Both of his hands came up in emphasis. "Much more exciting than living out your last breath in ever-contracting morose self-reflection," he finished, a smug smile of satisfaction punctuating this conclusion.

"Ha!" exclaimed Ariel, "Given your abilities in math, you've probably calculated that yield wrong. Check again and get back to me," and she pretended to reach for the button to shut down communication and was needled by the thought that that was the reason Argos was rejected.

Max went on hurriedly, "Hey! Wait! I think I know the cause of this little problem of yours." His brows up, he pretended to wait for Ariel's full attention. "Maybe, just maybe, you're stuck in the Old Earth Middle Period and it's not yet reached you that humanity's evolved from that narcissistic state you seem to be wallowing in. Hah!" And he laughed again.

"Oh, stop it, Max! Are you calling about dinner?"

"Ah, Ariel, your psychic powers are only exceeded by your beauty," and his hand crossed the screen in a flourish.

Ariel smiled, waiting for him to finish. Instead, he continued.

"Off for a little psychic vacation into the past, are you, wearing that blue gown? Will you be back in time for dinner?"

"Yes, I'll be over later."

"Oh, and I have a little surprise for you," Max clasped his palms under his chin in childish delight.

"Max, really, no need to go through the trouble of creating a surprise."

"I will please the mistress of time travel in a way only another New World Designer can," said Max, winked, and was gone.

Ariel shook her head. What a clown. She loved Max, his lack of guile, his boundless creativity in designing new worlds. She wondered what he'd think of what was happening to her, wondered if she should even tell him or how much. They were best friends from way back and she trusted him completely. Though this was something entirely different.

She returned to the garment dispenser and searched for ankle boots, found a nice brown leather pair, then found a brown wool cloak with a hood. They came out with a beep.

She reached to pick them up when she became aware of her sister's presence back on Earth. She looked up. Frowned. Another interruption. She focused a little more and understood that Miranda wanted to talk to her. Should she call or wait until she got back? It could be important.

She walked back to the workstation, sat down and called Miranda. She didn't want to have to worry about her while away.

"I understand the decision was not to proceed with Argos." Miranda's pixie face and short gold curls filled the screen. Her blue eyes looked intently at Ariel.

"Yes, too big a risk."

"Are you doing all right?" Miranda's mouth twisted in concern.

"Not happy, but I'll design other worlds. How are things at the Horse and Buggy Enclave?"

"The mare is due in a couple of weeks."

"Yes?" Ariel already knew that and was waiting for Miranda to say why she wanted to talk to her.

"Where are you going dressed like that? To visit your little friend Marion?"

"Yes. I've not seen her for a while. Thought I'd take a break from everything and go for a visit."

"Good, good." Miranda nodded repeatedly, but Ariel saw the small tightening around her eyes. She could not detect Miranda's psychic shields, yet was certain Miranda had them up. What was she hiding? So unlike Miranda to hide anything. She felt a small wave of worry pass through her. She looked closer at Miranda, but could not decipher what might be going on.

"When you can, please come see me."

"Anything important?"

"Oh, nothing that can't wait. In any case, we need to go see Mom and Dad. We haven't seen them in quite a while."

"All right. I will come as soon as I can." She leaned closer to the screen, "Mom and Dad all right?"

"Yes, yes. Just come by when you can. I have to go now." She waved and was gone.

Ariel stared at the blank screen. That was abrupt for the gentle Miranda. Ariel sat for a moment contemplating what this might mean. Hmm. But obviously nothing very serious otherwise she was sure Miranda would have told her. And she's right, they did need to see their parents. Ariel felt a tightening in her stomach, feeling guilty for not visiting them more often.

After a minute she went back to the garment dispenser to finish dressing.

When she was done, she looked at herself in the mirror and was satisfied. Well, a little tall. Well, a lot—if she was really honest with herself, for where she was going, but so far she'd gotten away with it. She looked the perfect wife of a successful man in the trades. A little money, her clothes said, but not too much.

She stood for a minute thinking what she needed to bring and remembered the basket. She went to the kitchen to get it and noticed the bowl of coins and coin purse next to it, took a handful of coins put it in the purse and tied it around her waist. It was always good to have a basket and look like you were on some errand like everybody else. And she needed coins if she wanted to buy anything at the market.

That taken care of, she turned down the lights, stood still, entered hyperawareness, focused her energies on the location fine tuning the year, day and time and slowly dissolved to appear near the town of Eventon, England, Old Earth Middle Period, 1289.

Chapter Five

Ariel held suspended outside Marion's cottage amidst morning autumn splendor. Hills wet from the night's rain glittered in the golden sun. Puffs of white mist drifted in the valleys. Cooking fire smoke seeped through the thatched cottage roof, floated upward and dissolved. Not far from the cottage bleated a few penned-up sheep. Farther down, a path led through the forest to Eventon.

She saw Marion on a rise of earth in the back of the cottage tossing grain to cackling chickens. Her brown gown was tucked in the belt at her waist. She was muttering words of encouragement to the chickens. Then she looked toward the path leading into the forest and made a face. All that cold mud, she was thinking, Ariel sensed. And she had to trudge through it to get to the market in Eventon.

Marion tossed the last of the grain, wiped her hands on her apron, pushed her skirts back, and picked her way through the mud to the cottage.

Good. She's going to the market. She teleported down the road toward Eventon to wait for Marion.

When she was far enough away, she looked around, saw no one, materialized and gasped as her boots sank into frigid mud. She shivered, raised the hood and pulled the cloak tighter around her.

She turned in a circle looking for a way into the forest, spotted an opening and weaved through to the trunk of a fallen oak. She brushed off the leaves and sat down. She looked around, satisfied. This was a good place to wait for Marion.

The smell of the raw morning air, earth and decaying leaves entered her lungs and her entire body woke up to the vibrant life around her. Argos seemed far away now, though that horrid tight feeling inside her persisted. She was afraid of the attacks, afraid of what might happen next. She took a breath, determined to put it aside and just enjoy being here. She took another breath, relaxed. Listened. It was quiet and still except for the occasional rustling of leaves in the gentle breeze and the twittering of a bird now and then. She closed her eyes.

So good to be away from the ship, from the New Earth. None of that thick presence of the New Earth psychic grid here. She could let her thoughts and feelings drift freely with no worries as to who might be listening or whom she might effect. No need for psychic shields here. A good place to rest.

The New Earth was an enormous, complex, powerful web of psychic energy, which was regulated and enhanced by numerous crystal transducers. Each person daily contributed psychic energy to the whole. That energy was then enhanced by the small crystal transducer in each residence. Enhanced, it was then directed to the larger local transducer, enhanced again, then delivered to the enormous central transducer where it was enhanced, refined and distributed for use on various projects. It was this energy that in part powered Palladium and enabled them to build worlds.

Drops of water fell on her nose. She opened her eyes, smiled, brushed them away and closed her eyes again. She exhaled and sent her awareness through the earth and trees and hills, drifting freely, resting deeply.

Thoughts of Argos appeared and she made the effort to let them pass through her, relieved she didn't need to put up psychic shields. Miranda's face appeared, faded. Max.

She felt her body let go, worries of the past days drop away. A wonderful calm began to permeate her entire being. She rested.

After a long while she sensed Marion approaching. She opened her eyes and smiled. She gathered her skirts and basket and stood up. It was a good decision to come here for a little break from everything. She was fairly confident the attacks wouldn't come for a while anyway.

She weaved her way back to a road that was much brighter, now that the sun was higher in the sky, and set out slowly to give Marion time to catch up.

Argos entered her mind. She shook her head, let the thought go and focused on the rustling leaves and breathing deep refreshing breaths.

"Lizzie, Lizzie!" she heard Marion call, turned around, waved and waited.

Marion came running, her little basket swinging, her black hair and brown cloak flying behind her. "Lizzie!" she called out and bounced to a halt in front of Ariel, splattering mud over both of them. Lizzie was the name Ariel used when she came to visit. Marion had a big smile on her face her blue eyes, almost violet, sparkled, her cheeks pink from the chill.

"God morgen, little Marion." Ariel smiled and put a hand on Marion's shoulder. "You're an industrious little girl if you're headed for the market this early."

"Oh, yes," Marion said matter-of-factly, "You're going to the market, too?" Hope and joy in her voice.

"I am, so we can walk together and chat."

At that, Marion did another skip and another splatter.

They started down the road, making their way around puddles and mud and deep furrows made by carts and wagons, the tall oaks on each side of the road looming like powerful guardians.

"And how is everything with you and your mother and baby John?"

Marion was still skipping beside Ariel, splattering mud. "Gooood."

"I am happy to hear that. And what's your business at the market today?" she asked, knowing Marion liked to think of herself as a grown-up at the age of ten.

She had befriended Marion one day about a year ago when she was on a research trip to the Old Earth Middle Period. She was at the market when she heard crying, went to inspect and found a little girl tugging at her gown in anguish. Through sobs, she learned that her father had just died, her mother sick and about to have a baby. Besides just feeling the little girl's bewilderment, when she had looked deeply into Marion, she found a beautiful spirit and felt instant kinship with her.

She had taken her by the hand, led her aside, bought her food and talked to her until she had calmed down. She made up the story that she was in the next village and that, of course, she'd see her again. So she'd been coming back, helping in as many ways as she could.

Marion looked up, her eyes wide with excitement. "I have four eggs to sell!" Four eggs made a lot of difference here. It took a lot of work just to stay alive. And even with all that effort, you were lucky to live past thirty.

"Your chickens are very good indeed," said Ariel, focused and reinforced the protective shields she had placed around the cottage.

The level of help Ariel offered was in accord with New Earth's rules. If you traveled to the past, small influences were fine, big interferences unacceptable. But most of her people weren't interested in teleporting to the Old Earth anyway, so this had never been an issue.

The sun was coming up higher, shining through the trees and beginning to dry the mud. It would make it easier for Marion to walk back home. Ariel looked down the road. There was no one, peasants with carts having gone earlier to set up stalls at the market.

"And what are you buying at the market today?" Marion asked, looking up at her.

Ariel thought quickly. "Ah, the usual supplies for Philip and me and a few spices." Philip was her made-up husband and they had a made-up life in a village south of Marion's hamlet. Ariel hoped nothing ever happened where this would need to be verified.

Marion nodded. "When I sell my eggs, I will have enough to buy my baby brother little shoes." And she bopped up and down, splattering mud again. "I saved coins. I think I have enough. He's starting to walk and needs shoes."

Ariel listened carefully and scanned Marion, gently boosting her overall energies.

"I can get you a pair of shoes for baby John," said Ariel.

Marion stopped bopping and looked at Ariel, "You can?!"

"I can. And when you sell your eggs, you can buy something else."

There was silence. Marion swung her basket back and forth.

"My cousin works in leather," Ariel improvised quickly, "I'm sure he has lots of scraps and can make a little pair."

Marion wrapped her arm around Ariel's waist, "You are so nice."

Ariel stroked Marion's head. "I'll come by the cottage and bring them when they are ready."

She looked at Marion, "How big are his feet, show me?"

Marion stopped, pushed the basket into the crook of her arm, held up both hands and looked at her fingers, gauging the distance. "This big, I think," she glanced at Ariel.

Ariel nodded, "Yes, he can make a pair that size."

Marion started skipping again and sang, "Little shoes, little shoes for little John."

Ariel smiled, savoring Marion's unabashed delight.

It was turning out to be a beautiful sunny day. The mud steamed in the heat of the sun. Ariel had warmed up walking. She pushed down her hood, threw back her cloak, and shifted her basket to her other arm.

"Lord Charles has gone to the Crusades," Marion said, relating local gossip. "Did you know? I wonder if he will come back. Lord George didn't." These were the local nobles. The Crusades were still absorbing a lot of men. Marion always chatted about what was going on in these parts, and Ariel listened attentively. It helped her gauge the safety of Marion and her family and advanced her own detailed research of the period.

They chatted and continued the long trek to the market. Argos came to mind and darkened everything inside her. She looked up at the golden trees, breathed. She'll find the answer to this. She must.

Chapter Six

E venton market was buzzing with activity in the brilliant morning sunshine. Women carrying baskets pushed their way to stalls, tables and tents. Loud voices bartered, dogs slithered around legs sniffing for scraps, children raced screeching with laughter. Men jammed carts through the crowd, shouting warnings. The air was thick with smells of sweat, animals, dung, mud, cooking and ale.

Marion wedged herself between a woman selling candles and a woman selling yarn. She laid her basket on the ground and pushed back the cloth to show her eggs.

"You all settled there?"

Marion nodded and looked around at the milling crowd.

"All right. I'm off to make purchases. I'll be back later."

Marion looked up, "I'll have sold my eggs by then and then I can go around the market, too."

"That's right."

Ariel smiled. She planned to savor every minute here. She liked being with these people, her ancestors. They were of earth and moved with unselfconscious ease.

It was messy going through the mud, her feet cold, but Ariel made it to every vendor, smelling apples, handling yards of fabric, admiring pottery. She watched jugglers, listened to the sad sounds of rebec and flute. She drank a nice, strong ale from a tankard. Periodically she tuned into the thoughts of the people around her. Mostly they were about things that needed to be done, people they cared about, their animals and crops. This felt light and easy on her compared to the thick complexity of the New Earth. And the sudden complexity of her life—the reality of her present situation rushing into her consciousness. She felt the heaviness of it and deliberately pushed it aside. Later. Now she would enjoy this.

When she had gone through the entire market, she stood and thought if she wanted to do anything else. She returned the empty tankard. She was ready to go. Then she remembered. She had to purchase something as a show of having really shopped at the market—in case Marion asked.

She wove through the crowd to the stall where she had seen a man selling spices. She haggled about the price because that's what you had to do and she didn't want to stand out, and purchased ginger, cinnamon and cloves for tardpolane, a spicy dried fruit pie, her next baking experiment, then headed toward Marion to say goodbye.

"One more egg to sell," greeted Marion, and looked from side to side at the passing people.

Ariel started to say, "Marion..." to say she was leaving when there was a commotion. Voices grew louder.

They both turned and looked in the direction of the disturbance. The crowd was moving all in a throng. Ariel tried to find the cause of the ruckus and spotted a man slicing through the mass in a great hurry. She saw him because he was a whole head taller than the people around him.

Voices grumbled and called out obscenities at the inconvenience of being pushed aside. She wondered where he was going in such a hurry. She kept watching, saw the top of his head stop, disappear, then reappear atop a horse. He had long black hair, a short beard and now rode directly towards where she and Marion stood.

She looked down and saw Marion looking up at her. "What are they doing?" She couldn't see the man.

"Just a man trying to get through. He looks in a big hurry."

The man was coming closer, making rather slow progress as the people pushed and shoved trying to get out of his way.

He wore a black tunic and a short black cape. His face was tight with determination. He looked directly in front of him, intent on getting through. Black leather gloves held the reins.

Then abruptly he slowed down, hesitated, wavered, as if he'd forgotten something. He looked down at the reins, very still, then lifted his head and looked around the crowd, his brows squeezed together. When his eyes met Ariel's, he reined in. He sat completely still and looked at her. His face a power of concentration. His eyes were such an unusual blue, Ariel gasped. Reflexively, she stepped back, bumped into someone behind her, came out of her daze, collected herself and stared back.

He looked hard for another second, his jaw clenched, then turned his head and was in motion again, his long black hair glistening in the sun.

Ariel exhaled, blinking.

"He is ever so handsome, Lord Richard is," she heard Marion say in a wispy voice. "I wish I was old, then I could marry him." She looked up at Ariel, "Don't you think he's handsome?"

Shaken, Ariel thought quickly, then nodded, "A true knight," was what came to her to say.

"He's not a knight," protested Marion, "He's a physician. He even sees poor people. He helped my father when he was sick."

Ariel looked down at Marion. Helped her father? No physician at this time helped the poor, only the wealthy. How unusual.

Just then a smiling short woman with a broad face wobbled up, bent over Marion's basket, lifted the remaining egg, handed her a coin, said, "There you go, deary," and was off.

Marion looked at Ariel, "I've sold all my eggs!" and clapped her hands. "Let's walk through the market." She bent down, picked up her basket and pulled Ariel's skirt. "We need honey," and she pushed through the crowd, pulling Ariel behind her.

Ariel had wanted to say goodbye but was now following Marion, unsettled by what just happened. She could still feel his eyes on her. The blue of a very hot flame. Who was he? Why did he look at her that way?

"Cart coming through!" a man yelled and jolted Ariel out of her reverie.

They stepped out of the way and Ariel took the opportunity, "I have to go, Marion, but I'll be by your cottage soon with baby John's shoes."

Marion formed her mouth into a pout, looked down, shifted from one foot to the other, then looked up and smiled. She put her basket down and wrapped her arms around Ariel's waist.

Ariel bent down and hugged her. "You take care of your chickens. I know everything will be fine. I'll be back to see you soon."

Marion let go her embrace, "Thank you. It will be a surprise when I get home bringing honey."

"Yes, it will." She patted Marion's head, pinched her cheek, "Off you go, and I will see you soon with the shoes."

Marion picked up her basket, turned, waved, and disappeared

into the crowd.

Ariel looked after her then headed down the main road leading out of town carrying her basket. She wanted time for contemplation and deeper rest. Then her mind turned to the man. Who was this Richard with eyes that were on fire, a physician who helped the poor?

She looked behind her to see if she was far enough away so no one could see her teleport and kept walking.

Such power and cogency. Very unusual. She wondered what he was seeing in her.

The road took a turn to the left, and she was out of sight of the town. In the distance she saw rolling hills with patches of thick crimson and gold leaves.

She stopped and scanned for a secluded spot where she could think things through and teleported.

Chapter Seven

She landed in a large sunny meadow of tall grasses, gnarled oak trees and large boulders. All around lay low hills glistening in the autumn sun.

Ariel smiled. Her shoulders relaxed. She closed her eyes and absorbed the sleepy peace. A gentle warm breeze caressed her face. A perfect place to think through her problem. At that, her face darkened, and a knot formed in her stomach. She tightened her lips and looked around for a place to sit. On a rise, she spotted a large boulder sitting in the sun.

She lifted her skirts and pushed her way through the wet grass. By the time she reached the boulder, the bottom of her gown was wet, and her boots and stockings soaked. She shivered. She would wear a thermal suit under her gown next time. Never mind this business of wearing what the natives wore. Just too uncomfortable.

She stepped around the boulder to the sunny side, put down the basket and sat down. She pulled off her boots and stockings and laid them out to dry, then spread her skirts to dry. She leaned back. The boulder was warm. She relaxed, closed her eyes and listened to the drowsy sounds of life around her, the swish of the grass in the breeze, the buzz of insects, the occasional flapping of birds' wings.

The man at the market burst into her mind and shook her into alertness. Those extraordinary eyes and that strange look. How puzzling. She shook her head and pushed him out of her mind, though reluctantly. She had to focus.

A raven flew by, and she watched it land on a branch of a distant tree.

She leaned back on the boulder and was lolled into a deep sense of well-being. Everything was all right in all the worlds. She breathed deeply, enjoying being here.

After a while she sighed. She had to get to work, try to sort out this Argos problem. She thought about a good approach then closed her eyes, inhaled the sweet smell of grass drying in the sun, shifted her body to get more comfortable, entered hyperawareness, accessed deep resources of her memory and began a methodical search—every detail of the Argos design. After a thorough checking, double checking and cross-referencing, she discovered nothing unusual. Her design worked perfectly and did not reflect the findings of the scientists who had the exact same data.

She frowned, opened her eyes and looked around. The sky was a perfect shade of vibrant blue. All was still except for the buzzing of something small flying by. She had no explanation for how she could have designed a world that could not be built.

She took some breaths and rested. Deep memory access took a lot of energy.

The attacks. That booming voice that Argos must be built. Where did it all come from? What was the source? What propelled them?

She focused and initiated a scan of herself. She had to be stable enough to do a deep search for the source that was booming inside her.

First she checked bodily processes, then her mental and emotional condition. After a while, she was complete. She was calm enough and stable enough to do the deep search.

She entered hyperawareness. First, she checked to see if anything in her thinking made her biased in regard to building Argos. Of course it was her world and her love and she wanted to see her species come to life, but that was natural. She searched for other motives, something she was not aware of in her normal consciousness. After a comprehensive exploration, she discovered nothing and went deeper.

She spread her awareness outside herself and scanned for any energies that would be influencing her, any unusual, foreign energies. She pursued every thread of energy she could identify, examining it from every angle.

After a long search, she opened her eyes, exhaled and frowned. She found nothing that emitted strong influence in her direction or that affected her simply by its presence. There was no source, no reason, and seemingly no way to alter this imperative that Argos must be built. She uttered a deep low groan. What was she going to do?

The sun was high in the sky. She was hot. She pushed her cloak back, then turned the boots upside down so the bottoms could dry. She turned the stockings, rearranged her skirts to dry the still wet parts.

She considered the implications of this inner command that Argos must be built. It went against all the rules and laws of the New Earth, against her people, against a harmony and peace that had now existed for thousands of years. Her head snapped up at the loud screech of a bird flying by. She felt so alone, so separate, locked in this madness. And very clearly she heard again, a soft voice now, commanding that Argos must be built.

Ariel gasped with dread. Here it was again. Her legs shook. She wrapped her arms around them trying to make them stop. Her body trembled. It felt like she was being shaken by something not her. She was breathing short shallow breaths, took a big inhale and a big exhale trying to calm down. Now she was cold. And she was sweating.

They were back, the voice, the shakes. Ariel looked down, her shoulders slumped. She was at the mercy of some force greater than her, greater than her will. She was on the verge of crying again.

She looked up at the hills shimmering in peaceful sunshine as if there was no trouble in the world at all, and here inside her was unbearable inexplicable turmoil.

With trembling hands she pulled her boots on, cold and damp, pushed herself up to stand, her legs weak and uncertain, brushed dried grass and dirt from her gown and staggered down the hill.

At the bottom of the hill, she stopped, closed her eyes, looked up and let the sun warm her face. What was she going to do? She pushed through the grass, thinking.

This, that was commanding her, could it be a new type of energy, a new kind of energy coming from Source, the Great Light? She stopped and considered. That was one possibility she hadn't thought of. Could be. Why not? Not that she had experienced it herself, but in New Earth history such events had taken place. Powerful forces had come in taking them in a completely new evolutionary direction. Though they were very rare since the Destruction. They had carefully stayed on a constructive evolutionary course.

She reached down and pulled a blade of dried grass and chewed on it. She swished through the damp considering this possibility, no longer caring about the wet and cold. She stopped, threw away the dried grass, closed her eyes and accessed all stored information she had about unusual, unexplained new energies coming into the human experience since the beginning of the New Earth. She found a few incidences. All of them were experienced by the Elders whose job was to stay alert to such new energies—all of them preceded by significant unmistakable signs and all of them small, but significant, corrections in their development. She was not an Elder. Unlikely she'd be receiving such a directive. In any case, there were none of the early signs. And no Elder went through traumatic New-Earth-defying laws and rules, as she was experiencing. Besides, as a species, they were doing fine. There had been no fork in the road to force a decision about which way to go. There had been no serious problems that were outside their experience to handle. No, this was something different. She let out a low growl of frustration. Dead ends everywhere.

Her head felt like it would explode. She reached up and massaged her temples, relieving some of the pressure. What else could she do?

In the distance she saw the sky had turned gray. Looked like more rain was coming.

What about asking for help? Is there anyone she could tell about what she was experiencing? Maybe Darius. She could open it up to the Earth Council. She considered this for a minute and knew the answer. If she was to bring this up to the Earth Council, she would be treated as the first anomaly in New Earth history. She fit none of the descriptions of sick patients. Her urges went in direct opposition to everything: scientific data, the Earth Council, New Earth Prime Directives. She would be held for observation and analysis for who knows how long and who knows how many and what kinds of tests. And she could not let that happen.

She was left with the distillate: Argos must be built.

She exhaled, then laughed a strange laugh that had the quality of broken glass.

But how? How could Argos be built? She laughed again. It took all of New Earth to build Argos, as it did with all the worlds they built. It took all the resources of the New Earth and all of its people. So how could Argos be built? She laughed again at the complete absurdity of the idea and started back up to the boulder.

What could she alone possibly do? She felt small, overpowered by this demand, overwhelmed and scared. She was relieved she was here alone and free to feel all of this and think all of this and not have to bother with psychic shields.

She sat looking down at her trembling hands, shoulders slumped, feeling completely miserable. No answers. No solutions.

After a while, the sun warmed her. She relaxed, became sleepy and comfortable, for a while forgetting everything. Then she felt something move inside her. She sat up alert. It spread slowly throughout her being. Her eyes were wide with wonder. She nodded her head. It was crystal clear. She understood.

She knew what to do!

It continued to well up in her, becoming solid, certain, filling her with strength and power.

The heaviness pressing down on her began to lift. She could breathe again.

She relaxed against the boulder and straightened her legs in front of her.

She had her answer.

Gently, afraid she'd lose the pristine clarity that organized all of her being into a powerful coherence, she gingerly re-explored this new idea and the concomitant feelings. Yes, it all fit. It was all of a piece. No further questions. Only action.

She blinked at the newness, the novelty of such an astounding denouement. Her body felt light. Her brain freed up.

She breathed deeply, relaxed her shoulders. She let it all settle in her, like sediment drifting back to the river bottom after turbulence.

She knew what she had to do.

After a while she looked up. The sky was the color of Richard's eyes. She gasped. He was back in her head! Intruding! She frowned. Who is he? Why was he invading her mind? Yes, that look was intriguing, but... She looked in the direction of the market. Where was he rushing? She shook her head. Not wise to be curious about a man from another time. Stop. It did not matter. He did not matter. She had work to do.

Chapter Eight

$\mathbf{A}$riel dropped the coins back in the bowl in the kitchen and filled the empty spice jars with ginger, cloves and cinnamon she had purchased. They would add to the authenticity of the flavor when she made tardpolane. She put the basket back on the shelf and looked around. She felt more like herself for the first time since the meeting. The comfort of the vision was strong with her, the purpose clear.

The man Richard accosted her mind again. She sighed, smoothly pushed him aside and made for her sleeping quarters.

At the workstation she found a few messages from the crew expressing their regret about Argos and hoping she was doing all right. Some of them invited her to dinner. All in all everything was as it should be. She was not needed anywhere and nothing urgent had come up. She thought about all that had happened in Eventon. She felt calm. The clarity was there about Argos. She shifted in the chair. Should she tell Max about what happened? What about that strange man Richard? She felt her stomach tighten. It's all too new.

She got up, went to the garment dispenser, took off her gown, placed it in the recycler and dressed for dinner in a roomy ice-blue tunic, cream pants and lilac boots. It was niggling her, should she tell Max? It felt good not to feel that intense roaring push of energy to build Argos. The calm clarity felt good. But where did it all come from? She took a breath, decided not to think about it just now, picked up the brush, combed her hair and let it fall around her shoulders. She noticed the lines on her face had diminished and her eyes were bright. At least she looked a little better.

She put the brush down and went to see Max. Approaching his quarters, she announced herself psychically. She sensed Max's mirth and smiled. It would be good to be with her friend.

The door slid open, she stepped in, screamed and jumped back. At her feet was a hologram of sharp, snow-peaked mountains. She'd walked in on top of a virtual mountain peak—Max's new floor.

"My surprise worked!" Max glowed. He stood, hands on hips, a huge grin on his face.

Ariel's hand was on her chest. She exhaled. "Very nice, Max."

"Come in, come in!" he boomed.

Ariel kept her head up and stepped into Max's cluttered sitting room, which was no longer a sitting room. Long tables piled with gadgets, cords, dials, beakers and who knows what else lined the wall, partially blocking the ship windows.

"Taking full advantage of the ship's design capabilities, as usual. Why am I surprised?" Ariel laughed, now holding her stomach, which was still turning somersaults. Palladium was designed for creative people with features that permitted easy change of décor.

"Someone has to keep you on your toes," said Max. He was wearing his usual white robes but apparently a new set fresh from the garment dispenser. His long brown hair was combed and neatly tied back. He looked rather handsome.

Max pivoted on his heel, his robes swishing, and walked away toward the control panel. "It will change in a second."

Ariel waited for Max, making sure she did not look down. "Whatever you're cooking smells delicious."

He glanced back at her, "I've done my best. Over this way," Max pointed toward the kitchen. "I was working on Dahlame and wondered what it would be like to look at everything from the top of a mountain, as a consistent perspective, a kind of on-the-edge perspective, you might say, hence the floor experiment." Dahlame was the new world Max was designing.

Ariel nodded into his back, "What have you discovered?"

"It makes me think differently, as you might expect. That's the point after all, right? You'll see when I'm further along."

They walked into Max's kitchen, a dim-lit cozy cave with brown and beige rough walls. In the center burned a small fire, a bubbling pot suspended over it. Two wooden bowls and two wooden spoons sat next to it. Thick cream fur rugs lay all around the fire. Soft sounds of flute and drums filled the air.

He motioned to Ariel to sit. "Now, for our dinner." He stood rubbing his hands together. "But first, anything to drink?"

"You still have your caveman decor."

"Oh, nothing like human beginnings. Boundless potentiality. Anything could happen!"

"Not bored yet?"

"Not yet. It's inspiring, you know."

Ariel pulled off her boots and sat down crossing her legs. The rug felt soft and warm.

"The stew's almost ready. Dinosaur nails sautéed with garlic, falcon's wings delicately seasoned and eyes of sturgeon softly boiled," Max grinned.

Ariel groaned.

"Oh, come on, cheer up. It could have been... ah, ah..."

"I think you've done your worst, Max. Can't beat that, can you?"

She wondered if he was telling the truth. Could be. Max occasionally traveled to the Old Earth, way to the beginning, and brought stuff back with him.

"All right. Something to drink?" he asked again.

Ariel shook her head. "Later."

Max sat down across from her and stirred the pot. "It will be done soon."

It was warm and pleasant in Max's cooking area. Ariel relaxed. She liked it when Max cooked her dinner.

"How was the visit with Marion?"

"Good. They're doing fine. The baby is starting to walk and I promised to bring shoes for him," and she told him about the visit to the market, then remembered the incident with the unusual man and felt uneasy. She thought about it and decided not to tell Max.

Max was nodding. "Good. You had a good visit." He scratched his beard, "What about Argos? How do you feel?" He looked closely at her, his face serious.

Ariel shook her head, "It was crushing."

Max nodded, "I thought it would be. I am really sorry."

They were quiet for a while listening to the music.

"What went wrong? Do you know? How did you miscalculate like that?"

Ariel shrugged. "That's the problem. I did not miscalculate. My data shows Argos can be built. There are no mistakes. I've checked and re-checked. But then, the scientists look at it and they show different results. Same data, different conclusions."

Max's eyes widened, "But how is that possible?"

Ariel looked and Max and kept looking. Should she tell him what happened? She wanted to. But she also didn't want to involve him. And she was afraid of what he'd think of her and her plan.

"Ariel," Max leaned toward her. "Are you all right?"

She nodded. "It's been a hard two days."

"Yes. I can believe that. I don't know how I'd feel if I've put everything I've got building a world only to have it rejected." Max shook his head.

They were silent for a while thinking about that, the fire casting erratic shadows and light on their faces.

She made up her mind, looked up and said, "Max. I have to tell you something."

Max sat up straighter and waited, "Yes? What?"

"Just listen, please. This will sound strange, but just listen, all right?"

Max tilted his head, his brows came together, then nodded, "All right," his voice tentative.

Ariel sat straight up. "This is what happened. As all the engineers and scientists were demonstrating why Argos can't be built, this booming voice inside me said it *must* be built."

"What?" Max's brows came up. He shifted on the rug. "What do you mean must be built, what kind of voice?"

Ariel exhaled, "I don't know. Nothing's made sense since the meeting." She felt she was about to cry and put her hands over her face.

Max got up, rushed around, sat down and wrapped his arm around her.

She managed not to cry, turned toward Max and told him everything that had happened since the meeting, except what she planned to do. When she was done, they were silent. The stew bubbled, issuing puffs of steam. Max leaned forward and gave it a stir.

"A strange booming voice. A directive. That's a lot." He pushed up, walked to the automated kitchen and came back with a wooden board of thick slices of dark bread. He set it down beside the pot and sat down opposite her.

The music had changed and soft gentle sounds of lyre filled the room.

"Argos must be built." Max shook his head, "And you're certain. How very unusual. Have you thought this through?"

"Of course. It's why I went to Old Earth, to think."

Max waited for her to continue.

"I got an answer, but it does not make sense."

Max nodded.

"I am convinced that indeed Argos must be built. That's the answer I got. It has to happen."

Max was silent for a while. "But how? We can't force them to build Argos." He adjusted his robes and shook his head. "You're right, it doesn't make sense. And certainly not after what the scientists have said."

Ariel watched the flames dance around the pot. Should she ask him to help? She was not sure she could do it alone. Finally, she made the decision, "I know. It's why I want to build a prototype, a small model." She took a big breath. "I was hoping you'd help."

"What?!" Max shook his head, his brows raised, his mouth open. "But you can't do that! It's not allowed."

Instantly, they both put up their psychic shields.

"I know." She bit her lip. "I know it's crazy."

There was silence except for the sound of the lyre and the simmering of the stew.

"If we were to do anything like this..." he shook his head. "No. Absolutely not. We'd be in all kinds of trouble if we tried anything like that."

Ariel nodded. Saying it all out loud sounded way worse than just thinking it. She looked at Max, "I sound like a deranged person, right?"

"Obviously!"

After a long while Max said, "Prototyping would certainly yield a lot of information. It would explain the discrepancy between my data and this command to build Argos, and the scientists' conclusions."

"In secret!" Max inhaled in a loud hiss. "No one's done that before."

"I know."

Max had his fist under his chin, index finger on his lips, thinking.

Ariel watched the stew bubble.

"We'd put everything in jeopardy, our careers, potentially entire New Earth..."

Ariel nodded, feeling her whole body tightening in fear, aware of the magnitude of this consideration.

Max finally moved, stirred the pot and ladled out a bowl and handed it to Ariel, "Not exactly early human victuals, as promised." He filled his own bowl, "But then I see this is not a good time for more surprises."

"Thanks, Max."

Max stood up and came back with two glasses. He handed one to Ariel. "A little refreshment."

Ariel hesitated.

"It's fine. Just some apricot juice."

Ariel took it, sipped. "Oh, nice. Like having a fresh apricot. Thank you."

Max sat down opposite her again and ate his stew. Ariel followed suit, taking a small spoonful to start. Pasta shells, chunks of some kind of meat, carrots, basil. She was relieved. "This is delicious, Max."

"Hard to believe the team was wrong, but..." he shrugged, "I suppose there could always be a first." He bit into a chunk of bread, and crumbs scattered on his beard.

"I don't think they are wrong. Something else is going on. I don't know what it is. But I am clear it must be done, and that in doing this we will find out why the discrepancy."

Ariel watched the flames change colors on the cave wall, amber, yellow, rust. "I feel like I've walked into a bad dream. This has all been so strange."

Max nodded, "Yes, hard to take in."

Ariel took a bite of the dark bread, hardy and grainy, perfect with the stew.

"How were you thinking of doing it?"

Ariel caught her breath. He's thinking about it. She put the bowl down and leaned toward Max, "I thought I'd build a prototyping area in my studio. I have a rough idea of the phases. I need to work out the details."

Max's head moved side to side, his lips pursed, "You'll need a lot of stuff to build with no guarantees."

Ariel held both palms up, shrugged her shoulders. "Whatever is needed."

"And when will you find time? We're almost to Laurus." He took a big gulp of his juice.

"I'll just have to work it in with the other projects." Before they could implement changes on Laurus, a lot of detailed work had to be done.

"And if I were to help, and I'm not saying I will, what did you have in mind for me to do?"

Ariel's hopes went up. "The holo/material replication." As simple as this sounded, it was an enormous undertaking just for the two of them.

Max nodded. She could see him thinking, running through all the things he would need to accomplish this. He nodded again.

They talked this through for a good long while with psychic shields firmly in place.

Ariel felt little flutters in her heart, like little earthquakes. She took one long deliberate breath. It looked like she was moving forward now. Deep from the center of her being emerged a steel resolve, rippling outwards through her entire body. She felt solid and strong. She picked up the glass and drank the sweet nectar.

Max looked at her closely, a puzzled look on his face. "I do see that something big is going on," he chuckled. "Heck, it's only our careers at stake. Only the New Earth. No big deal." He shook his head, "It is my fate to experience the vicissitudes of design life." He laughed again, shaking his head.

Ariel felt a small hope in her heart. She raised her glass, "To the designers' fate."

"I haven't said yes." Max gave her a mock stern look.

Ariel's shoulders drooped.

"I will let you know. Doesn't mean we can't toast." He raised his cup and smiled, shook his head, "To the mysteries of the universe!"

"To the mysteries of the universe," said Ariel.

Chapter Nine

Ariel pushed back from the desk, stood up, stretched and yawned. Her eyes felt like they had broken glass in them. It was late. She'd gotten a good start on prototyping Argos. Maybe she should get some sleep.

The transducer shimmered. The big screens flashed, showing fresh updates from her worlds.

No, she wanted to do a little more at least. She shook one leg then the other and stretched again, then massaged her temples, took deep breaths and felt a little more awake.

She hadn't heard from Max yet. What if he said no?! Now that she had started prototyping, she didn't think she could build the prototype alone. There was just too much to do. Her lips tightened, her stomach lurched. No. She couldn't start thinking that way. She had to believe he'd help. She sighed and relaxed.

The time at the workstation showed midnight. She was hungry. She shut everything down, picked up the portable console and headed for the Knife & Fork, the ship's cafe.

Crystal chandeliers sparkled in an old-fashioned dining room with thick green carpet of pink roses and heavy round wooden tables. Violins played softly. There was no one at the Knife & Fork. Ariel was not surprised. Not at this time of night.

On the counter sat covered plates with meals prepared during the day, ready to be heated in case someone wanted a freshly prepared meal instead of one from the dispenser.

Ariel looked at the selection, chose a plate of chicken, noodles, and something green, heated it up, put it on a tray and walked to a table facing the windows. Outside the cafe proper was a walkway with benches and holographic flowers.

She sat for a minute and looked at the shimmering pink, blue and yellow flowers swaying, as if blown by a soft breeze. She smiled, then ate the chicken. Not as good as right after it was baked, but still tasty.

She thought about the prototyping. She was eager to start working out the details. She stopped eating. Since she'd committed to Argos, she'd not had an attack. This made her wonder again—where did that directive come from? That thought made her fall into an abyss of terror. She froze, sat paralyzed for a second, then started breathing again, took a big breath, exhaled and dug in with her fork. She refused to think about that right now. She had made a decision or rather the decision had been made for her. She'd accepted, and she wasn't turning back. And that was that. She'd take Blossom out, her personal spacecraft, and make a start detailing the prototype before going to bed.

Now that she had a plan, she felt a bit of peace. She listened to the music and enjoyed the chicken. Finished, she deposited everything in the recycler and made for the hangar bay.

Seated in Blossom's pilot chair, she entered hyperawareness and infused the launching procedures with psychic energy. Palladium doors started to open, and she proceeded forward. Blossom hummed a deep sturdy hum as it moved away from Palladium. Ariel shifted back to normal consciousness and accelerated into cool, thick blackness.

She had designed Blossom to be able to get away, explore and be alone—a beauty, sleek, fast, luxurious and comfortable. The center was a thickly carpeted lounging area with an abundance of blankets and pillows in pink, peach and green. A step up from the lounging area, around the perimeter, were other amenities and the necessary transducer and basic workstation.

Far enough away from Palladium, Ariel set Blossom to coast, pushed out of the pilot chair, walked to the food dispenser and got a cup of hot chocolate. She picked up her console and stepped down to the lounging area.

She moved pillows and blankets around, then sat down with legs extended, comfortable and pleased to be on Blossom. A million stars beamed around her through the transparent craft. She relaxed. These infinite spaces comforted her.

She took a swallow of hot chocolate. Max crossed her mind. She tried to convince herself again that he'd help. Though it worried her about involving him. She sighed.

She took another sip of hot chocolate and considered how to proceed and was whammed with an explosion of fear. Fear. No, terror! She was terrified. What was she doing building a prototype? Jeopardizing her people? What about her own life? What if she died? What about Max?

She put the cup down, breathed short hard breaths. She was going into the complete unknown. The first New Human to wander off from the whole! She wrapped her arms around herself, cold and scared. Her neck was stiff, her jaw tight, her eyes big. The loneliness of Blossom now suffocated her.

Stop! She had to stop these thoughts! She shook her body, let out a long breath and moved her head side to side, inhaled a deep breath, then let it out slowly. No, she would not, she would not succumb to fear!

She pounded her outstretched legs on the floor and felt her own solidity again. She clapped her hands together and shook them out. She put her head back and let out a loud lion's roar.

The inner directive was clear. The decision was made. She knew what she had to do. Fear would not stop her! The unknown would not stop her!

She clenched her jaw in determination and turned on her portable console. It whirred awake. She sat for a minute listening to it hum, listened to Blossom hum, then called out, "Music," and gentle notes of harp and oboe filled Blossom. Beautiful. She let out a long breath. Her shoulders relaxed.

She pulled up the Argos phases she'd already created and began to detail what needed to be done in each phase and the equipment and supplies needed. A long list of materials, some of them on Palladium, the rest would have to be obtained elsewhere. Meaning a lot of teleporting.

Teleportation was a superior means of travel. Not all New Humans could do it and those who could, did so to various degrees of ability. It had consequences. Done too much, it had side effects— loss of memory, loss of concentration and general disorientation. If the person persisted, they grew worse. Ariel shuddered. She was an expert teleporter, yet this would be another risk. Internally she steeled herself and carried on.

After a long work stretch, she stopped. She was tired, bleary, but happy about the progress she'd made. She looked at the time. Almost morning. She set the console aside, turned down the lights, scooted down into the softness of the blankets, adjusted the pillow under her head and relaxed. She was drowsy and comfortable when the blue eyes sprang into her vision. Her body jolted into wakefulness. That man Richard! She'd forgotten about him. What was he doing in her head again? Clearly he'd interjected himself into her mind through the power of his intention. She was amazed. His concentration was formidable. But why? What did he want?

She turned over on her side and closed her eyes. It didn't matter what he wanted. He simply couldn't be in her mind. She pushed him away and relaxed, feeling the tiredness of the long day and night.

Then she was on Earth, standing at the front door of her house. The azalea bushes by the door were in full bloom. She stood looking at them, pleased with the thick fuchsia blossoms. Something pulled her attention. She turned to see Miranda coming up the path toward her.

A yard away from Ariel, she stopped and extended her hand, "Take it." Her eyes focused on Ariel with powerful intensity. "Take it," she insisted, pushing her hand closer.

Ariel's mouth was open in surprise, eyes questioning. She looked down at Miranda's extended hand and saw her blue topaz hair clip. She looked up at Miranda, puzzled.

"To the unfolding mysteries of the universe," Miranda said, smiled and faded.

Ariel pushed up on her elbow, fully awake. She heard the soft hum of the transducer and saw the flickering lights of the navigation equipment. What was that? She fell back down, breathing hard, looking straight up at millions of points of light in the blackness. A dream? A vision?

Miranda was handing her the topaz clip she had made for her birthday last May. Why? And the intensity and power in Miranda's eyes baffled her. Why the intensity, the earnestness? It was just a topaz clip she already had.

She sat up, reached back and unclipped the topaz clip and looked at it. What's so special about it, outside of course that Miranda made it for her and it was very beautiful? She focused on it, sensed the energies but felt nothing unusual. She reminded herself she had to go see Miranda.

She pushed the blankets aside, stood up and walked around Blossom wondering what the dream could possibly mean. Dream or vision. The man's face flickered through her mind. Ah! She stopped, irritated.

Why were his eyes following her? He was just a man living in the Old Earth Middle Period, nothing more than that. He couldn't intrude on her like this! She shook her head and resumed pacing, the blue topaz clip warm in her hand. She couldn't understand what it meant, if it meant anything. It nagged at her. She clipped her hair again.

She walked to the controls, thinking of going back to Palladium, when Richard's face appeared clear and intense. She stopped. How is it possible that his psychic powers were strong enough to reach her with the distance and the time and everything else in between? He was just a mere mortal on a mere mortal Old Earth. He couldn't possibly have such strong psychic output for it to be reaching her. Psychic abilities this powerful rarely existed on the Old Earth. But he did. He reached her. And his powers were strong enough to reach her.

She started pacing again, shaking her head. She'd have to eradicate him from her brain. With the prototype to build, what did it matter if he had strong psychic powers? She had no time to think about it.

She checked the time on the navigation panel. Four in the morning. She was too awake to go to sleep and too tired to work.

She made her way to the dispenser, ordered a cup of coffee, then continued to pace.

His eyes appeared again, looking hard at her, the blueness cutting like ice. And she saw something else in them. Expectation. He expected something from her, waited for her to do something. She was taken aback by the power and persistence of his presence.

She stepped down to the lounging area and thought about it. She raised the cup to take a sip—could it be something important?! The cup froze midair. This is the second inexplicable thing happening to her! She put the cup down and sat with elbows on knees, head in hands, thinking. Something important?

She stood up, took the cup to the recycler, stood a moment considering, then entered hyperawareness, focused in on Marion's cottage and scanned for Richard.

She found him in a large house just outside town, in his bedchamber. Some chickens were running around in the yard. A stable sat at a distance from the house.

Chapter Ten

He sat on a bench at a long wooden table by the window writing, an inkstand beside him. Two candles, one directly in front of him, the other to his left, illuminated brown leather books and piles of parchment.

Ariel hovered by the door, maintained transparency and watched him.

He started to turn her way, and then he was looking straight at her. His face was still, his lips parted. He watched her with steady eyes. The quill unmoving in his hand. He looked at her a second longer, blinked, twisted to put the quill down, then energetically swung his leg over the bench and walked toward her. He stopped directly in front of her and looked her straight in the eyes.

Ariel froze.

He could see her!

"I've been waiting for you." His lower lip trembled a little.

She was shocked. How could he see her?!

He took one step closer, reached up, touched her hair. His fingers went straight through it. He stepped back, his eyes narrowed, looking at her for an explanation.

She blinked, looked at the fine line of his jaw, the strong delicacy of his nose. The power of his eyes.

He tilted his head to the side and waited for her to explain herself.

She realized there was no use trying to hide and materialized.

"Ah!" He smiled, his smile only making it clear that he did not smile often.

"I didn't think you'd just appear like magic." He laughed.

What?! He was expecting her arrival? She wanted to say something, but her throat was tight. She stood entranced.

His eyes moved down her body, taking in the tight blue suit. When he looked up, she saw amusement in his eyes.

"You're not supposed to be able to see me," Ariel uttered, her voice coming out in a raspy whisper. Ariel chewed on her lower lip. "I did not intend for you to see me."

"You speak. You understand. I understand." His brows lifted. He looked delighted.

She thought about what to say, frantically searched the New Earth rules but was too muddled. She scanned to see if anyone else was in the house, found no one, but sensed a couple of people in the stables and glanced toward the windows. Richard followed her gaze.

"They're taking care of the horses. No one is in the house."

Ariel breathed out.

"Why don't you sit? Be my guest," and he extended an arm toward the bench at the table.

Ariel didn't move. She had to think quickly. What to do?!

He turned back toward her and crossed his arms, watching her closely. He wore a brown tunic and black hose. "I see you are more surprised we meet like this than I am." He pursed his lips.

"You knew. You knew we would meet?" Ariel was incredulous. She looked past him at the bench and started to walk toward it.

He turned quickly and ran ahead of her and started to clear

the table. "Apologies for the mess. Didn't think you'd quite show up like this."

Ariel sat down. "You knew?"

He nodded his head slowly. "Saw it in a dream." He kept nodding, "Long time ago." He was smiling. "Of course, as you can see, I didn't forget."

He made himself comfortable on the bench next to her, his right elbow on the table. "But I've wondered ever since if it was truly telling of the future, or just a fancy." He stopped and looked at her, waiting for her response.

"A dream?"

He suddenly stood up. "A tumbler of ale, perhaps?" he asked, palms up. "In my surprise I am forgetting to be a good host."

Ariel's mouth opened. Ale? Now? He had the presence of mind to be a host? She nodded, "All right."

He headed for the door, then turned to her, "You won't leave, will you?"

He had read her mind, and she was embarrassed. She shook her head.

When he was gone, Ariel thought quickly. I should have gone when he first noticed me. I should go now. I shouldn't be here. New Earth rules specify not to disclose yourself as being from another time. How can I explain this to him? Her mind raced. She squirmed on the bench. She wondered why his eyes looked the way they looked. She wanted to ask him how he could see her. She wanted to know about his dream.

He'll be back soon. Decide! If she left, he'd just think of this as a vision. Maybe. If she stayed... she'd be breaking the rules. She closed her eyes, winced in pain. Decide!

Her eyes went to the embers glowing in the hearth. Smells of earth and fire. Tapestries, brown paneling around his bedchamber. A canopy bed against the wall.

She heard steps. The door opened. At his appearance, gladness filled her heart before she had any chance to decide if she wanted to feel glad or not.

He put the tray down, picked up a tumbler, handed it to her, took the other one and sat down at the other end of the bench. He sipped and looked at her.

Ariel felt her face getting hot and concentrated on holding the tumbler.

They sat in silence for a while.

"Where did you come from?" he finally asked. Then he blinked, looked around. "It's cold here, isn't it?" and was up, moving towards the hearth. "When I am doing my studies, I don't notice much."

He squatted, "I'll have it roaring presently," and layered logs. Flames shot out erratically.

"I did not mean to… it was not my intention to intrude on you like this." She was embarrassed to have come to spy on him.

He glanced over at her, his brows coming together. "But how could I have found you otherwise?" He stood up, wiped his hands on his breeches and walked slowly back to the bench.

"I know this is rather unusual." Ariel looked at him, trying to gauge how he might take the truth.

"How did you just appear?" He straddled the bench and sat facing her. "Where exactly did you come from?" His voice was earnest, his curiosity intense.

The fire crackled loudly, tossing wild shadows about the chamber.

Ariel thought what to say. She turned the tumbler in her hands.

Occasionally she looked at him. She said nothing.

"I know magic," he said, trying to help her along.

Ariel started to say that it's an ability when he interrupted.

"In my dream..."

There was a knock on the door downstairs. They both looked toward the door, then at each other.

Ariel nodded, dispersed her physicality, saw Richard take long steps to the door, then stop, turn around and look at where she was standing transparent, "Come back," he mouthed, and was out the door.

Chapter Eleven

Ariel stood in front of the garment dispenser completely shaken. All she wanted was a quick look into the man's life. And now she was overwhelmed with inexplicable feelings, disoriented, confused. She stared at the garment dispenser screen seeing nothing, then unfroze and ordered clothes for the day. Caught by the blue of his eyes and the unwavering intense stare. How could she get trapped like that?

The dispenser beeped. She pulled out a cream sweater, plain brown pants and brown boots. And his casual behavior at her appearance. She closed her eyes. How can anyone not knowing anything about teleportation—or did he—be so casual about someone appearing in his bedchamber? In 1289? She opened her eyes. Her world was crumbling. Within a short time, her life had turned upside down. She felt lost, adrift, the usual anchors of meaning disappearing. Yes, a quick look to satisfy her curiosity about Richard and look where it got her. She shook her head. And she thought Max's curiosity was out of control.

She dressed then stepped over to the workstation to check in for the day. Every morning she looked for Gateway research updates. Usually there was nothing of significance. Small updates about different approaches they were trying, what they were discovering in the process. And if there was anything new, it was something related rather than actual progress. And that's how it was this morning. She looked at the sparkling crystal transducer. She'll have to do a run herself. She marked that in her mind to do as soon as possible.

She continued the check-in. Nothing about Laurus. That's good. They were on track there. And no personal messages. And nothing from Max. She tightened her lips and felt the small worry knot in her stomach. Perhaps she'll hear from him later today.

She made her bed, fluffed up the pillows, and thought about the day. She was making good progress on Argos, though there was a lot of work. Then the strangeness of her life descended upon her. The disorientation. She was sneaking around building a prototype. She let herself be seen by a man from another time. She stopped, took deep breaths. She must not succumb to fear and guilt. Somehow she must let the man go, hope he forgets the entire incident. With that hope, she knew she was lying to herself. He would not forget. He would not doubt what happened. The best that could happen is that he said nothing to anyone.

In the kitchen, sitting on a stool, she had toast with raspberry jam. She chewed with a resigned reluctance to what her life had become. But she had to keep moving, going forward. There was nothing else she could do.

It worried her that she hadn't heard from Max. The thought that she might not succeed in building the prototype gripped her. And instantly that inner boom, Argos must be built! shook her entire body. "All right," she said out loud, "It will be all right."

She breathed deeply trying to calm down. After a moment, she felt collected. She simply could not let herself doubt. It wasn't an option. She had to stay focused. Give all her energy to building the prototype. Trust that it will all work out. She remembered the vision she had in Eventon, the way she was filled with conviction and the truth of it. Yes, she will stay focused. She will do that. Even though she felt heavy and miserable with the whole of it.

Her body was still trembling. She had to get herself together before she went to see Miranda.

After a cup of mint tea, she was ready. She shut down the workstation, turned down the lights and teleported to Miranda's house.

Chapter Twelve

The morning sun streamed through tall windows flooding Miranda's spacious sitting room in brilliant golden light. Coffee and cooking smells filled the air. Miranda sat at the table by the window bent over working on something. She turned, saw Ariel, and rushed to hug her. "You're here!" She had a big smile on her face. Her blond curls gleamed. She wore a blue top and white pants.

"Yes, and glad to be away from the ship for a while." Ariel looked around the big sitting room with pink and green sofas and chairs, "It's so nice and warm here with the sun coming in." She glanced at the table, "What are you working on?" and walked over to see. Miranda followed.

Purple amethysts, cherry-red rubies, sky-blue topaz, creamy dancing opals and other gems sparkled in little boxes on the table. Wire, pliers and other tools sat to the side.

"I'm making a necklace." Miranda held up a string of small opals and rubies. "For one of my riding students."

"So delicate. Beautiful. She's sure to like it."

Miranda put the necklace down and turned to Ariel, "Have you had breakfast, coffee?"

"I did, thank you."

"I'm so glad you're here." Miranda stood with hands on hips

looking at Ariel. "I was thinking we could go visit Mom and Dad and talk on the way. Then we can go to the Artists Enclave and have lunch. And cake, of course. What do you think?"

"Excellent plan." Ariel looked away through the tall windows at the sunny hills. "I feel bad I haven't seen them for quite a while."

Miranda exhaled, her lips compressed, and patted Ariel on the shoulder, "Let's get going then," and started to walk away, then turned and looked Ariel up and down, "Will you be warm enough? It's chilly out there. I can get you a jacket."

"I didn't think of that. Yes, thank you."

Miranda rushed off and came back wearing a blue jacket and handed a green one to Ariel, "Let's go get the buggy ready."

Soon they were comfortably seated in the buggy with two horses pulling. Vast open country of low rolling hills shimmered gold and red all around them under a vibrant blue sky.

"So good to be here." Ariel inhaled loudly. "Smells wonderful."

"Yes, I imagine, after breathing the ship's air."

The buggy crunched along a narrow gravel road that went on straight into the distance.

"How are you?" asked Miranda.

"I'm all right. A lot of work, as usual. I'm glad to have a break today. How are you? How are things here?"

"All right," Miranda hesitated. "Except for father. He's not doing so well." She turned to Ariel, a frown on her face.

"What? Why didn't you tell me?"

"Well, you know how things change with them, they don't do so well, then get better... I thought that would happen again, and didn't want to worry you. In any case, here you are." She smiled.

"I am glad I came. How bad is it this time?"

"Worse than usual. It's why I wanted us to go see them. I try not to worry, but I am worried."

"Do they know what's going on?"

Their parents, Vivian and Andreas, worked as a team in the search for the Gateway. This included teleporting to various locations that promised an opening to other dimensions that might support Earth. On their last mission, their bodies came back, but that's all that came back. They've been at Melrose, a healing center, ever since. They believed their spirits were trapped somewhere. Teams had been sent out to look for them with no success.

"They don't know. They're just weaker, both of them. But Dad is worse."

Ariel sighed, "Well, at least we know they're doing their best for them at Melrose. I just wish we knew more."

After a while Miranda said, "All these years of not knowing whether they will live or die."

Ariel wrapped her arm around Miranda and squeezed. Miranda turned to look at her, a sad smile on her face.

"I know. It's always there, the worry that one day we'll get that call..."

"Yes. I think about that all the time." She sighed, "And no progress in finding them. If they ever do." She let out a long frustrating exhale making her lips vibrate.

Ariel had nothing to say. It was always there the heavy uncertainty about their parents.

They traveled in silence for a while.

"It's puzzling," said Ariel, "Why is Dad having problems now? Why did they decline significantly now? Why not before? Why not during all those other long years?"

"I wondered about the same thing." She looked around, "But

then I was grateful. It would have been torture to have them be in a really bad state."

"Yes. They've gone through ups and downs since the accident and always recovered. Maybe this is another down, just a really bad one."

"Let's hope."

"I'm glad it's a sunny day." Ariel closed her eyes, leaned her head back and took in the sun's warmth. She sighed. "Maybe they'll be better by the time we get there."

Miranda nodded.

The man Richard came into her mind and Ariel was overwhelmed with misery. So much going on. And now Mom and Dad. So much she was doing she wasn't supposed to do. Should she tell Miranda? She'd feel so much better. After thinking about it, she decided it was not a good idea. Miranda had too much on her mind already.

Ariel listened to the steady hoofbeats of the horses, the crunching wheels. "How much further?"

Miranda smiled, "You're not used to this slow pace. But you would be if you were to live in the enclave for a while."

In the Horse and Buggy Enclave, as in all enclaves, you had to follow the rules of the enclave. The Horse and Buggy enclave was a low-technology enclave, hence no modern transport. Once at the transport node, they could take any transport they wanted, and fast was what Ariel had in mind. She didn't want to get too comfortable. It would be hard to go back to everything.

She looked around, "No houses anywhere. So peaceful."

"Yes, not many people care to live in such an old-fashioned enclave. It's one of the reasons I like it."

Just then a buggy came into view. Miranda slowed the horses

to a stop.

An older man in a brown jacket lifted his hat and called out, "Fine morning for a ride, isn't it?"

"Beautiful," responded Miranda.

He carefully maneuvered past them and Miranda got the horses moving again.

After a while she turned to Ariel, "You're not doing Gateway research, unofficially, are you, Ariel? You're always doing things you shouldn't be doing."

Ariel's psychic shields leaped up. She forced her face to stay neutral feeling terrible guilt. Of course she was looking for Mom and Dad. And it was true. She was doing things she shouldn't be doing.

"I know you've gone over Mom and Dad's experiments many times. I know you wanted to see where things went wrong. But you're not taking any chances, are you?" Her voice rose just a little, her face tightening into a frown.

"Please don't worry. You have enough going on with Mom and Dad."

One of the horses pulled back, spooked as something scurried across the road. Miranda encouraged them on.

She turned and looked at Ariel with sad eyes, "What if I lost you, too?"

Ariel wrapped her arm around Miranda, again, "I know it's been hard for you once Mom and Dad were gone. And I'm away for work... I am sorry. But there is no need to worry. You know I am very careful in all that I do."

"I know, but..." Miranda frowned. She urged the horses who had now slowed down showing interest in the grass beside the road.

Ariel thought for a minute. "I've not had time off for a while. Maybe when we're done on Laurus we can go on a vacation together. It would be nice to be on Earth for a good long while, in my own house having real coffee and real breakfasts and visiting you regularly. Everything's great on the ship, but it's not like being at home."

Miranda perked up. "It would be wonderful to have you around for a good while. And a vacation! Maybe we can go to one of the resort enclaves by the ocean." She waved away something that buzzed past her face. "Do you think you'll be able to get away?"

"I think so. I've not had leave for a long time. Anyway, the timing would be good with a big mission completed."

"When you're close to finishing, we can make plans. All right?"

"Yes, we'll do that. Something to look forward to. It will be fun."

Ariel sat back and fantasized about that time when the madness was over, when her life was normal again. That was pleasant to think about. And a nice vacation with Miranda.

She looked up. The sun was higher in the sky. It was getting warmer. She unbuttoned her jacket.

"How are the children doing with their horseback riding lessons?"

"Great." She turned to look at Ariel, "They are so fearless," she smiled, "And they learn so quickly. Had two more kids sign up last week."

"Wonderful. I love that necklace. And how's jewelry making going?"

"Mmm. I think I'm ready for something new. I've been designing in this same style for a long time now. Something new would be nice." She nodded her head. "Something fresh and different."

"Yes, I understand. Max and I are still in our respective Old Earth early human and middle period modes, but that's sure to come to an end at some point, I suspect. In any case, you're still enjoying it?"

"Yes, but I really am ready for something new. I need inspiration. Something new and exciting," she smiled.

Ariel considered the "excitement" in her own life, wished there was less of it.

"Well, let's try to enjoy the smooth times. Never know what the future holds."

Miranda nodded, "Yes. Good thinking."

At the Transport Node they left the buggy and horses at the stable to be taken care of and boarded a small Sky Taxi to the Melrose Enclave.

Chapter Thirteen

"**S**uch a beautiful enclave," said Miranda looking around, a smile on her face.

Melrose spread before them, an immense park of emerald lawns, white gazebos, sparkling crystals, splashing fountains and winding brick paths. Giant willows leaned luxuriously over ponds with quacking ducks and buzzing insects. Colorful stucco buildings lay scattered on the property. Constructed of bioenergetic material, they aided in rejuvenation for those receiving treatment. Some research was also conducted here.

Their parents' room was spacious and bright with high ceilings and big windows. The walls pulsated fresh green and emitted low-level healing frequencies. It had a strange smell like nothing Ariel smelled before. The smell of absence of time, perhaps.

Vivian sat unmoving in a chair, her dark brown hair tousled. She was wearing a loose blue dress that clearly looked like it was made for someone else and that, also, someone else had put on her. Why it had to always look that way, Ariel did not know, because she knew that, above all, her parents were well cared for.

Andreas lay motionless in a bed by the window, his face blank, his thin hair combed to one side. Wrinkle lines circled his eyes. He looked small. Sunlight fell on his face, but he didn't seem to notice.

Ariel exhaled, everything in her sinking. The sight of her

parents, looking relatively normal, but empty, no matter how many times she had seen them this way, always felt like being stabbed with a knife.

She looked at Miranda, who was looking at her. Her eyes were sad, her lips compressed. She walked over to Vivian, "Mom. I am here," she said and bent down to kiss Vivian on the cheek. Vivian blinked, staring straight ahead.

Ariel kissed Andreas' cool cheek, pulled a chair and sat beside him. He looked paler than usual and more absent somehow, but no other change since she last saw him.

"Looks like he's stabilized."

Miranda nodded. "Maybe we should have checked with the staff."

"No need, really. I don't sense significant change."

She searched for his hand and pulled it from under the covers. It was lukewarm and motionless. Nothing there. She held on, loving him as she had loved him when she was a little girl and she and Miranda had sat on his bouncing knees, their laughter staccato with the bouncing.

Andreas was the one who found her in the family's Crystal Room when they came back from a work trip. Ariel had sneaked away and spent two days learning how to use the crystal transducer, successfully maintaining her psychic shields so no one could find her. She remembered being held in his arms. So much love. Vivian had cried with relief. Ariel was exhausted, hungry and thirsty, but very happy. She had succeeded. She was six years old.

Miranda was combing Vivian's hair. She looked up when she sensed Ariel looking at her, then quickly turned away. Her eyes were shiny.

"I hope he continues to improve," Ariel transmitted.

Miranda looked up again, her eyes sad. She nodded.

I will look for them, Ariel determined, her jaw tightening with resolve. Maybe this next trip. Maybe find them. Bring them back. They won't die this useless death.

"How are you girls doing?" said a cheerful voice. A woman in the green Melrose uniform with curly brown hair stood at the door smiling. "Do you need anything?" She looked from Ariel to Miranda, her hands on her hips.

Ariel and Miranda looked at each other. "Yes," they said in unison.

"A couple of chairs. We'd like to take them out to the waterfalls," said Miranda.

The attendant helped them put Andreas and Vivian in chairs that floated, gave them the controls, and said, "Off you go. Enjoy your visit."

Through a bougainvillea-laden archway they entered one of the many garden spaces spread out on Melrose. A tall pink crystal glittered in the center. Water splashed over it and fell into a pool. Two benches sat on opposite sides. Low trees, shrubs and flowers grew around, creating a private space.

"This is so nice," said Ariel.

"Beautiful."

They sat on a bench with Andreas and Vivian on each side.

Ariel adjusted the pillow behind Andreas' back and tucked in the blanket. His head stayed tilted to the right. Always difficult to see her dad this way.

"I'm glad we're here," said Miranda. She sat on the bench and held Vivian's hand.

Ariel breathed in. "The roses smell divine." She listened to the soft hum of insects for a minute. She heard buzzing, looked around and saw a hummingbird hovering over a pink rose, its green chest glistening in the sun.

They talked to their parents. That's something they always did, pretending they could hear. Ariel talked about work on the ship and Miranda about her life on the ranch.

"Mom, Dad, please try to stay with us longer. Ariel's working on finding the Gateway. She's not supposed to be working on it, but she is working on it anyway. If you try to stay with us, I think maybe, maybe," and she started to cry, "Maybe she will find you, bring you back."

Ariel put her arm around Miranda. "It will be okay, Miranda. Somehow things will come out okay." She tried to believe that. And a part of her did believe it. Things worked out one way or another. Hopefully it would work out in a way where their parents were restored to themselves. But it was hard to believe this. They weren't even sure that Vivian and Andreas were lost, let alone that they could be brought back. As hard as Ariel squeezed to hold them back, the tears rolled down her cheeks. She hoped. She wanted to know her parents as an adult, wanted to know what they were like as people. Now all she had were memories of a young girl.

She flicked away the tears and took Andreas' hand.

Apparently Miranda didn't believe a word she said about her Gateway research. So after a while she added, "Miranda's right. I am working on the Gateway." She tried to avoid feeling defeat with her gateway explorations. After all, entire teams were sent out with no success. "And if you promise to stay just a little longer, I promise I will find you," she heard herself say. Then stopped. Her own conviction surprised her.

She sat up straighter and looked at Miranda who was looking at her, her eyes wide searching, trying to see if Ariel meant this or if this just came out of her as a child's wish, or maybe something to placate her parents—but they couldn't hear, could they?

Ariel shrugged. "I don't know. I guess I'm hoping." She leaned her head back and closed her eyes. The rhythm of the splashing water was relaxing. She sensed the changing light of the crystal move across her lids. She inhaled the sweet smell of roses. She relaxed deeply.

Suddenly the image of Andreas leaped before her. He was looking straight at her, holding out his hand. In it was a key.

Ariel's head snapped upright, her eyes wide open. Andreas sat motionless beside her. Miranda was adjusting Vivian's blanket.

Ariel let go of Andreas' hand and sat up straight.

No residual energies had emanated from Andreas or Vivian since the accident. No psychic footprints of any kind were left behind. They had all searched for traces of energy that could give them information as to what happened, lead them to find Andreas and Vivian. They found nothing.

Now this. Did she imagine it? Her heart was beating fast. She looked at Andreas again. A latent psychic footprint? A vision?

Chapter Fourteen

Ariel's eyes snapped open into total darkness of her sleeping quarters. She was fully awake, completely lucid, her heart racing as if she'd been running, but she'd been asleep. She stared into the blackness taking deep slow breaths trying to calm down. What was it? A vivid dream. A vision? It was very clear, in sharp color. Miranda was handing her the topaz clip. And Andreas was handing her the key. She pushed herself up and leaned against the headboard. Two separate… what were they—dreams, visions? One after the other. She noticed all muscles in her body were tight, ready for action.

She pushed the covers back, called for lights, squinted, blinked when they came on, then leaped out of bed, pulled on her jumpsuit and boots, clipped her hair and rushed to the studio.

Maybe she'll find something. Maybe this was a sign?

She powered up the equipment, noticed her hands trembled. Maybe this is the day. Maybe this is the day she found something.

She pulled up the coordinates Vivian and Andreas left behind, the place they last journeyed in their effort to find the Gateway. They were odd coordinates, going into a kind of embedded depth, not just traveling out of this dimension and into the coordinates of another, but out of this dimension into another and then into an unusual loop. And that's where it all ended.

Next, she pulled up all to-date research on the Gateway, including notes from her last mission.

It puzzled her, as it did everyone else, that they had the coordinates Vivian and Andreas left, yet they were useless. They could do nothing with them.

Ariel brushed back a strand of hair. Obviously there had to be something they were overlooking. There had to be a key that would unravel the whole mystery. She remembered the key Andreas was handing her. She looked up and shook her head. What was the key that would unlock the mystery? If it even meant that.

She pushed off her boots, sat back in the chair, took deep breaths, calmed down, entered hyperawareness and teleported to the exact coordinates left by Andreas and Vivian.

She was in a gray mist of diverse energy fields. She looked for a distinct patch of clear, stable energy that led to other energy systems. She stabilized her position, then started to scan around her, looking for irregularities in the energy field. She examined each frequency looking for an opening, a change in the texture, an inconsistency that might lead out of these coordinates to another place, a door, a gateway through which Andreas and Vivian may have gone.

Vivian and Andreas, according to their notes, had come here, to this exact location many times. Since then, researchers found some interesting things, but no one made it beyond this point. No crack in the thick fabric of energies.

Ariel changed the depth of her probing and continued to scan. After a while she stopped. Nothing. All thick, undifferentiated masses of energy. Then started again, scanning, sensing, continually shifting her focus to see if there was anything at all on any frequency that she might pick up, but it was all the same everywhere, thick, undifferentiated masses of energy.

After a while she could think of nothing else to try, and focused her way back to Palladium.

She sat in her chair shivering. She rubbed her hands together, then wobbled over and got a mug of hot chocolate, then walked on stiff legs back to the workstation and sat down. She turned up the heat. She'll warm up soon. She felt fuzzy and uncoordinated. She blinked and drank the hot chocolate, vaguely looking at screens of her shimmering worlds. The mug warmed her hands, making her feel her body again.

Soon the thickness in her head began to fade. She had stopped shivering. She swiveled toward her desk and made notes.

In minute detail she recorded where she'd been and what she'd found and tried not to be disappointed that this entry was much like every other she'd made. Another unsuccessful mission. She exhaled her disappointment, pushed back from her desk, got another cup of hot chocolate and found herself thinking about Richard.

In the last few days he'd come to mind and she was torn as to what to do. She remembered she'd nodded her head yes when he asked her to come back. She felt bad she didn't have the presence of mind to think about what she was saying. She kept her promises. But what would she do about keeping her promise to Richard? She didn't know. And she didn't want to think about it, not now anyway. She shifted focus and analyzed this last mission.

Not even a slight variation in her findings. It was hard to believe they'd made no headway in finding the Gateway with all-out effort. And the entire Earth depended on it! Andreas came to mind. How much time did she have to find him, if she even could? How much longer could Vivian and Andreas live this way? Why did the

Gateway elude them? Would they even make it as a species?

She pushed back her chair and walked around the transducer, aligning with it, receiving energy and comfort. It clicked and beeped soft, comforting sounds, flashing golden lights. Feeling a little better, she went back to the workstation and pulled up the Argos prototyping project. Maybe she could make some progress on that at least. She frowned, realizing she hadn't heard from Max.

She tried to concentrate, but after a while realized she could not focus. She was still bleary from the exploration and could not shake the disappointment of yet another failed mission. So what did those images mean, the clip, the key? She shook her head, frustrated. And that man Richard was interfering again.

She pushed away from the desk, swiveled and sat staring into space. She was tired and disillusioned. She took a big breath, turned back to the desk, shut everything down, picked up her boots and headed to her quarters.

She walked in and heard a call coming in. She rushed to her sleeping quarters and answered.

"Not up yet, I see," boomed Max, "Did I wake you?"

Ariel exhaled and smiled, "No, you didn't wake me. I was in the studio. Just walked in."

"All right. Are you free? Can you come to my studio?"

"Sure, I'll be right over."

She looked around to see if she wanted to bring anything with her, then pulled on her boots, picked up her console and headed for Max's studio. Maybe today is the day after all. Maybe Max will have good news. She hurried.

"Welcome, welcome," greeted Max and pointed to a chair at the table by the door. "Have a seat." He walked to the food dispenser, "Anything to eat, drink?"

Max's studio smelled funny. Ariel took a quick glance around. Same old cluttered mess she'd rather forget she saw.

"What's that smell, Max?"

"Oh, just a little something I've been experimenting with. Not too bad, is it?"

Ariel crinkled her nose. "Well... no... no nothing from the dispenser, thank you. Feeling a little queasy. Just did a Gateway run."

Max came back, two big steaming mugs in his hands. He placed one in front of Ariel, "This might perk you up a bit. Coffee," and walked around, sat opposite her and took loud slurps of his coffee.

Ariel looked at him, a mild look of disgust on her face. "Slurps, really?"

Max grinned. "I'm the caveman, remember. Anyway, did you find anything?"

Ariel held up her mug, "Thank you. Found absolutely nothing."

Max shook his head, "We're so used to finding nothing that if we actually found the Gateway we might be too shocked to do anything with it. What a situation!"

Ariel nodded then sensed Max put up his shields. She squinted at him and waited.

"I'll help you." He smiled a big smile.

Ariel felt dazed and just looked at Max.

"I'll help you," Max said again, louder.

"Max!"

"I've given it serious consideration. It's important to you. You're important to me. I am curious about the disparity, the voice. I am curious where it will lead. I am interested in building a prototype. And you could be right. Argos may need to be built. We can find out."

Ariel looked at Max. He was adorable. "You are the best friend in the world," she said at last.

Max had a big grin on his face, "It will be fun, don't you think? Oh. And I think it's best we build the prototype here. I have more of what we need…"

"You're right. Thank you, Max," she let out a big breath. "I wish we didn't have to do it in secret. And the chances we're taking…"

"I know. But it will be all right." Max pointed with his chin at her console, "Now, ready to tell me what you had in mind?"

Ariel straightened in her chair, pulled herself closer to the table and reached for her console.

"Just tell me the basic plan so I can start working on it and we can go into more detail another day. All right?"

Ariel nodded. Her body buzzed with energy. And then there was the small knot in her stomach. The unknown. The uncertainty.

Chapter Fifteen

Ariel stood by the garment dispenser waiting. She was dressed in a blue woolen gown with brown cloak and brown boots. Slippers for baby John finally came out and she placed them in the basket. In the kitchen she added a wedge of cheese, a loaf of bread and smoked fish, covered it all with a length of linen cloth and teleported a ways down the path from Marion's cottage.

It was a chilly misty morning. A cutting wind careened through the trees rustling leaves. Ariel pulled her cloak tighter, adjusted the basket on her arm and started toward Marion's cottage. She rehearsed what she would say, reminding herself not to stay too long and possibly create opportunities for suspicion.

Around the cottage, chickens ran clucking. A gray pig burrowed noisily next to the cottage. She didn't see Marion anywhere.

When she was a few yards from the door, she called out, "Marion, oh, Marion," then walked up to the door. A second later, the door flung open and Ariel looked down on a pink smiling face.

"Lizzie! It's you!" Marion screeched. She swung her head to the back and yelled, "Mum, it's the lady from the market!" and pulled Ariel in.

The small, dim cottage was filled with smoke and cooking smells. In the center a fire crackled with a steaming cauldron above it. A rushlight glowed on a small wooden table by the wall. In the back lay sleeping pallets.

"This is my mum, Elisabeth," said Marion, pulling her mother by the hand.

A short, thin woman stood in front of Ariel. A brown scarf covered her hair except for the dark blond wisps that had escaped. She wore a loose brown gown. Her face was gentle with many lines.

Ariel smiled. "I am glad to finally know Marion's mother."

"Her mother, I am," she laughed. "So kind of you to stop by, Lizzie. Marion always talks about you. And now here you are. Sit down, sit down." She stepped over to the table, pulled a stool out from underneath it, and motioned for Ariel to come and sit.

"Thank you," said Ariel and perched herself on the stool, setting the basket on the dirt floor.

At that moment Marion came up carrying a little bundle in her arms, her face shining. "And this here is my little brother John." She held him for Ariel to see. "See how beautiful he is. A good baby."

Ariel looked down at the small sweet sleeping face. She could see why Marion loved her brother so much. He was a tiny light in all this gloom. "He is beautiful, just like you said."

Marion beamed and rocked her brother.

Elisabeth looked at John. She had a small, sad smile on her face. Ariel tuned into her. She was wondering how long she will live, wondering if she'll get to see him grow up. She's not well. She's wondering if he'll even grow up. They need food. Ariel's heart was crushed. So much human suffering for so long in the world before the New Earth. She focused and released healing energies.

Elisabeth reached over and took baby John from Marion. "Let's give our guest some pottage, Marion," she said, then turned to Ariel, "We're just about to eat. You'll eat with us, won't you?" she looked at Ariel hopefully.

"That would be a lovely way to visit." Ariel and picked up the basket beside her and put it on her lap. "I've brought the shoes, and I've brought a few other things."

Marion, who was by the fire stirring the pot, screeched and rushed over. She picked up the little shoes. "They're perfect!" She looked at Ariel. "Thank you. And so soft," she was running her fingers over the little brown slippers and looking up at Elisabeth.

"When he wakes up, we'll put them on him," Elisabeth nodded. And to Ariel, "How kind of you. And look bread and..." she looked at Ariel again. "Very generous and kind."

Marion clapped her hands, leaped to Ariel and gave her a hug. "Thank you! We'll have a feast today!" Then she pivoted and ran to the hearth.

Elisabeth sat down at the table. "Have you come a long way?"

Not a topic Ariel wanted to discuss. "It was not a bad journey, really. How are you getting by here?"

Elisabeth started to talk about their difficulties, but Marion interrupted. "We can eat."

Then Marion dashed back and forth, bringing wooden bowls and spoons to the table. "I am hungry." After she had brought everything to the table, she stood and ladled the pottage for each of them. "I saw him out riding," she smiled, taking a glance at Ariel.

"Who?" asked Elisabeth.

"Master Richard," said Marion, looking at Ariel again in a meaningful way. "Ever so handsome," she giggled.

Ariel shifted on the stool. She looked down at her bowl, thinking fast. How best to guide this conversation away from Richard. She looked up and smiled, then proceeded to take spoonfuls of pottage, a runny liquid with a few roots and grains. She was glad she had brought the cheese and fish.

"Eh, silly girl," chided Elisabeth. "Leave Master Richard alone. He's got enough troubles as is." She looked at Ariel. "You must know Master Richard at that house outside the town. Everyone these parts knows him."

"Uh huh," said Ariel and dipped into the pottage again.

"The way he dashes with that horse of his 'round the countryside, wild and angry." Elisabeth shook her head. "As if the devil was after him."

Ariel searched for something to say, "We all have our troubles," she said at last and felt this was only too true at the moment.

"He's not wild," Marion protested. She was tearing pieces of bread for all of them. "He's," she hesitated, "He's... different," she concluded, pleased with herself for having identified this special quality and come up with the right word.

"Though a good physician he is," continued Elisabeth, "Helped my husband," she said softly. She rocked the sleeping baby.

"But, he is handsome," insisted Marion, a dreamy look in her eyes and a soft smile on her face.

"What nonsense," said Elisabeth, shaking her head.

Wild Richard. She wondered what else people thought of him and felt sad, guessing the cause of his restlessness.

They ate and chatted about the weather, their animals, neighbors and the growing baby. Subtly Ariel used her energies to lighten their burdens. She infused Elisabeth with more strength, helping her body, which, more than anything, was exhausted from work, poor food and lack of sleep because of the baby.

Slowly laughter emerged in their talk and Ariel knew that they would now be better, for at least a while, and that she had succeeded in helping even if in a small way.

Then out of nowhere Marion burst out: "You're different, too." She looked straight at Ariel, a bold, defiant look. "It's like you're not even from around here." Her head was tilted, her eyes squinted in analysis.

Ariel quickly sent up her psychic shields. How could she answer? Then another lie. But what else could she do? "You're right. I'm not from around here. I came here when I married my husband from the county south of here. Things are different there."

Marion nodded, her attention shifting to the little slippers that were still sitting on the table.

Time to go. She stood up, announced her departure and had to watch the smile vanish from Marion's face and Elisabeth's shoulders droop again.

She picked up her basket. And after a lengthy goodbye and promise to be back soon, she was out the door and walking down the path away from the cottage.

Chapter Sixteen

Ariel sat at the table in her studio, tapping her stylus, looking at the door waiting for Max. Her console was open. A cup of hot chocolate sat on the side. Her psychic shields firmly up. Her mouth squeezed tight. Her stomach a big knot. She wanted to get on with it, for Max to already be here.

It was quiet except for the hum of the transducer and the occasional low beep from her world screens. She took a big breath, relaxed and took a swallow of hot chocolate. She thought back on her visit to Marion. She was glad the baby had the slippers and she no longer needed to think about going back, for a while anyway. She could focus on her work.

She sensed Max and sat up straighter. The door slid open and he stepped in.

"Idle, are you?" he boomed, stopped, looked at her closely, then walked around the table to see her better, "Burgundy jacket. And look at all that lace on that blouse!" He bent over and looked under the table, "Indigo pants. Boots the color of plumbs!" He straightened up, "Lovely, lovely, just like an Old World duchess! Are we celebrating?" then stopped. "I guess we are. The commencement of our subterfuge." He laughed simultaneously pulling up his psychic shields tightly.

Ariel smiled, "I was inspired today. Have to admit spent quite a bit of time in front of the garment dispenser. Like it?"

"Love it!" Max walked back around the table pulled out a chair and sat opposite her. He was wearing his usual white robes and his hair was tied back. His eyes were big and shiny. "All right, let's see it, let's see all you've got?"

Ariel started to bring up her notes. She noticed her hands were shaking a little. "Here we go." A 5-D display of the prototyping stages appeared.

Max studied it for a while, his head tilted, "Nice," he said with admiration, "Tell me about it."

Ariel went over the general plan. "Phase one, we build the representative elements of the world. Phase two, we enliven. Phase three, we monitor."

Max's head wobbled side to side in consideration, his lips pursed. "All right." He drew out the *all*.

"Now, this is the tricky part. We need to have all this done before we get back to Earth."

Max nodded, "That doesn't give us much time, especially if we finish updates on Laurus early." He scratched his head, "We may not have enough time to monitor and reach accurate conclusions."

"I know. But that's all we'll have. Have any better ideas?" Ariel looked at him, hopeful.

Max pushed his chair back and walked to the food dispenser punched buttons and the smell of coffee wafted through the studio. He looked at her, eyebrows raised.

"No, thank you. Nothing for me."

Max took a swallow of his coffee and stood thinking. "No. No ideas right now. But I'll think about it." He came back to the table. "Let's hear the rest."

Ariel proceeded with the details. When she was done, Max transferred all the data to his console, then pushed it aside and sat with his hands on the table fingers intertwined. "I guess this is it. How do you feel?"

"Anxious. Scared." Ariel took a deep breath and exhaled through the side of her mouth puffing her cheek.

Max continued to look at her, "But certain?"

She nodded, "I am sure we're on the right track."

"I checked records. Nothing like this is recorded, I mean a situation where a designer designed a world that was off so dramatically. The world designs that were rejected mostly had species conflicts. There was never a world design that gave off such huge excess of energy as Argos."

"Yes, I know."

"I can't help but wonder what all this means, why the disparity, why the voice...?" Max reached out and put his hand on Ariel's. "We'll find out, though, yes?" He smiled, stood up and walked to the screens displaying Ariel's worlds.

Ariel twisted in her chair and looked after him, "Thank you, Max."

After a while Max turned and looked at her, "Before we start, let's think. Are we overlooking anything, anything that would change our approach?"

They were quiet for a while, then Ariel said, "Can't think of anything right now." She put her finger on her lips, "Have to be prepared for anything."

Max shook his head, "Can't think of anything either. We have to be careful. No room for errors. Not enough time and well..." His brows lifted, his mouth twisted in concentration. "It will be difficult keeping this a secret for any length of time."

Ariel stared at Max's back. He'd turned to look at the screens again. What would they do if anything went wrong? What if after all their work, they discovered nothing? What if she was simply wrong? Her hunch some personal quest, after all.

She leaped out of her chair, walked to the food dispenser and got a mug of steaming coffee. She held it with both hands drinking big gulps. She was shaken. Again. She remembered the time she froze with fear on Blossom. She set her jaw. She can't let fear stop her. Onward they must go.

"We will do our very best," she said.

Max stood in front of Laurus.

"What a world you designed when you designed Laurus," he chuckled.

Ariel walked over and stood next to him. A world exploding with brilliant color.

"Beautiful." His head was tilted to one side, he was smiling. "I wonder how they will evolve. If they look so grand now, how much grander might they look when they are more evolved?"

Ariel smiled too. "All the happy moments of my life pulled together into light."

Max looked at her. "I see that!"

They walked back to the table and sat down.

"Argos is different."

Max leaned toward her, "Yes?"

"It's so much deeper than happiness, than joy." She looked off to the side, "It's the as yet unexplored terrain of my innermost being."

Max nodded. "I know that edge." His voice was soft and dreamy. He took a swallow of coffee.

"Yes, that edge, its limitation, its boundary. It's how I know something else is there, something more, something even grander than I had ever felt before, thought before." She paused, "Something beyond my capability to even conceptualize, to even imagine right now. Right now, from where I am, with how I think and feel."

Max put his mug down and held his hands palms together under his chin. "Yes, it's why I create, why we create, isn't it? To know the furthermost edges of our being, those places we knew not even existed, until we worked up the courage to explore there, to that edge where we might fall off, where anything might happen, where anything is possible."

Ariel nodded. "There is always another veil to be lifted, isn't there?" Her voice was soft, tender.

Their eyes held.

The silence around them was complete, encircling them in the tightest of bonds. Their deepest natures were the same. Wanting to know beyond that distant horizon. That edge sharp. Enticing. Irresistible. Unpredictable.

Chapter Seventeen

Ariel clutched the bedcovers around her face, eyes wide open. She was trembling. Andreas' face loomed before her, intense, fierce. She tossed to her side. Then Richard's face jumped at her, his eyes pleading. She tossed over to the other side. Her body felt pricked by a thousand tiny thorns. Max. The deceit. Stealth with Argos.

She rolled onto her back and folded the covers down.

Richard!

Then that strange energy again, pushing, defying everything that was her reality, the reality of her world, her people, the reality of the New Humans. The pressure so intense she thought she'd explode from the contradictions.

And again, something forming inside her, taking shape, that firm resolve again.

She threw the covers aside, called for lights and in an instant was at the garment dispenser getting dressed.

She found him riding in a big valley and appeared at his side.

Richard's head jerked to look at her. His mouth opened in a silent gasp. Then he smiled and pulled back on the reins. "You're back!"

Ariel looked up at him, her heart pounding. He was wearing a black cloak and his hair was a wild tangle from riding.

"Yes, I am back."

He dismounted, and then she was looking straight into those blazing blue eyes and everything inside her was in upheaval. "Hello, again," she whispered.

They stood in tall grass wet with morning dew.

He bowed slightly, reached for her hand and lifted it to his lips, his eyes remaining on hers.

The warmth of his lips on her hand spread through her in slow waves halting all thought.

His eyes moved down, inspecting her clothes, then back up to meet her eyes.

Ariel pulled her cloak tighter, turned and started walking. Richard followed, leading the mare.

"You knew I would be back," she said.

The sun was peeking from behind a distant hill. The valley gleamed with morning freshness.

"Fairly sure," he paused, "Though what I'm not sure of is if I'm dreaming or if I've gone off my head."

Ariel laughed. If only this was a dream.

A dog was racing toward them. "Here comes Bennet," said Richard, "He's friendly."

A black and brown hound wagged his tail, sniffed Ariel and was off again. "Handsome dog," said Ariel.

They walked in silence for a while. Occasionally he turned his head and looked at her as if about to say something, but each time she felt his energy pull back and he said nothing.

At last he stopped walking. He looked down at the reins in his hand then up at her. "Who are you? Where do you come from?" His brows were squeezed together.

She stopped too, looked at him, then started walking again.

How could she explain?

After a while she said, "How did you see me?"

"I sensed your presence and then I looked."

"But I hadn't yet materialized, and you saw me."

He cleared his throat, looked around at the distant hills, the sky, took a quick glance at her, "I can see things."

Ariel felt her feet getting cold and realized her skirts and boots were soaked. She stopped, scooped up her skirts and wrung them out.

He looked down at his own wet boots. "We need to dry out," and pointed with his chin towards the hill ahead of them. "There's a hut up there the shepherds use sometimes." He looked at her, "We can make a fire."

Without saying anything they started through the tall wet grass.

"You're not wearing your blue clothes."

Ariel heard amusement in his voice. She caught his eye and smiled. Her blue work suit was a tight-fitting jumpsuit.

After a good climb, she saw a small hut sitting on top of the hill. Long stalks of broomweed covered it, almost reaching the ground.

"Mistre, back," said Richard, then tied his mare to some brush a distance from the hut.

"Mistre?"

He looked up. "Yes."

Ariel stood looking at the chestnut mare named Mystery. Mystery indeed.

Richard bent down and stepped into the hut. A musty smell of earth burst forth. Ariel waited. After a while, he called her in.

He was stacking logs in the fire pit. "It will warm up fast." He patted a rock next to the fire, and Ariel sat down.

A small black cauldron sat next to the fire pit. On one side was a pile of straw, a brown woven blanket thrown on it. On the other side sat a low table with assorted wooden bowls, spoons and a bucket covered with a slab of wood.

The fire started to crackle, sharp blades of yellow danced furiously.

Richard sat down next to her and held out his hands to the fire.

Ariel pulled her skirts back so they wouldn't touch her skin. Her boots were wet through, her feet cold.

They watched the fire in silence, then Richard asked again, "Where did you come from?"

She looked at him. He looked back. His cheeks were pink from the cold and the fire, his eyes sharp with curiosity.

She had to give him an explanation and heard herself say, "The future." She watched him and held her breath.

She was keenly aware of breaking yet another New Earth rule and felt her chest tighten with anxiety.

He turned to look at the fire and consider this. "How far from the future?"

"About ten thousand years."

He rubbed his chin. "Earth's future?"

Ariel nodded.

"How?" His voice was low. He shook his head slightly, then held up his hand, "No, no need to answer that now. I think I already know."

Ariel watched him watching the fire, saw his mind racing. She held her breath, wondering what conclusions he would reach. She wondered about her reasons for being here: she'd dashed off into the past to get away from the present.

And then of course he had to ask: "Why?"

She could not bring herself to tell him.

It had warmed up. She pulled off her boots and stockings and set them next to the fire to dry. Richard saw her doing it and did the same.

But she had to say something. At least assure him that her presence was benign.

"Seeing you at the market was an accident," she started, "I wasn't there looking for you."

He kept looking at her, his eyebrows raised, waiting for more.

"One of the reasons I can be here is because we have developed our innate psychic abilities to their fullest. All humans have. We've harnessed that power."

She waited and looked to see whether he was understanding. She saw that it was she who was having difficulty with this and that he was waiting for her to be comfortable enough to talk. She decided to go on. "You can imagine the power, the complexity. The New Earth is an enormous web of deliberately directed and controlled psychic energies, and a variety of other kinds of energies." She hesitated, "I come here to rest. And visit my little friend Marion."

"Ah, yes, the little girl. I saw her father..."

The fire crackled and hissed. Richard bent over and put another log on top of it. "There wasn't much I could do to help him."

He was quiet for a while then laughed. "I see. Coincidence we meet."

Ariel sensed some multiplicity in his thinking, but could not identify it.

His eyes sparkled, "Ah, this is the beginning of my real life!"

And he chuckled, a self-satisfied, deep-throated chuckle.

She waited, but he did not elaborate.

The fire had warmed the hut sufficiently, so she pushed back the hood.

She felt Richard watching her, his brows together.

"The pin," he pointed, "Your blue pin."

Ariel reached up and touched her topaz hair clip.

His brows were together and his head was tilted.

"What is it?"

"Hmm." He rubbed his chin. "Strange. Looks familiar." He shook his head as if to let go of the feeling.

After a while she said, "I'm as puzzled by all this as you are."

She reached over to the pile of wood, found a long stick and poked at the fire making it spark. "You should not have seen me, but you did. And here we are."

Richard nodded, took a big breath and blew it out. "All right then," and continued staring at the fire.

Ariel knew that what they were doing was trying to get used to all this. Sitting together, they each hoped the answers would emerge.

After a while he said, "When I saw you at the market," he hesitated, "Well... I felt strange." He shook his head. "I don't know that I can describe it."

"I know," said Ariel.

Richard jerked his head up and looked at her. "Same for you?"

She nodded, her eyes wide. "Came back to find out why."

The fire hissed and popped, dancing golden on the brush hut walls.

Ariel rearranged her skirts so other parts could dry. She looked up.

Richard looked at her, his eyes soft.

Ah, how they go into me. That incredible warm knowing.

"I don't understand. But something... there is something there." He reached up and lightly touched her hair. "If I can just remember."

"I know," said Ariel.

Richard looked at her and nodded, "Yes. Something there."

After a while she asked, "What do you mean you can see things?"

He waved his hand in dismissal. "That's a long story."

Ariel tried to feel into him, but found nothing except a slightly heightened emotion. Wondered how he could shield himself. Obviously it came naturally to him. But how?

"Perhaps if I see you again, I will tell you." His eyes were teasing her, challenging her. "You're not supposed to?" His eyes questioned, "Come back?"

"No. I am not supposed to have," she searched for words, "This kind of interaction with people here."

"But you are. Here we are."

"Yes, we are."

They looked at each other. They knew. Whatever this was, it would take some figuring out.

He shook his head. "And you need to leave now, that's what's on your mind."

Ariel reached for her boots and stockings.

"Your dream." She wanted to know about the dream he had about her.

"When you come back." He smiled.

She stood up, "I have to come back now," she laughed, "Just to hear your stories."

"That is my intent." He stood, hands folded in front of him. "You will vanish, like before?"

Ariel nodded.

"Could you stay here permanently if you wanted to?"

She nodded again, "But it would not be good."

He stood in front of her, his head almost touching the scraggly ceiling, a furrow between his eyes, "Will you be back?"

She smiled, reached up and slowly ran a finger down his cheek.

Chapter Eighteen

Ariel laid in bed, stared into darkness and thought about Richard. She'd broken more rules. She could not control herself. Everything was getting worse and worse taking her further and further away from her normal life. She didn't know lies, secrets, uncertainties could hurt so much, make her life agony. She shook her head thinking what to do, and realized there was not a thing she could do. Everything seemed out of her hands.

She exhaled a resigned breath, pushed up on her elbow and looked at the time. Four in the morning. She grunted. Too early for anything and wide awake.

She turned over a few times, irritated at everything, then gave up, called for lights, walked to the garment dispenser and took her time getting dressed. Maybe she could get some work done since she couldn't sleep. It mattered little how she felt. She stopped and thought about it and realized the only thing she could do was move forward, slog along, take those steps and find out where they led.

In the studio she got a piece of toast with apricot jam and coffee, worked on Laurus, spent a good amount of time on Argos then took a break, yawned, stretched, swiveled to face the transducer and relaxed. She was tired, sleepy, but at least she'd gotten work done and with her mind occupied had a small respite from her troubles.

She started to nod off when the intercom blared. She jumped and turned to find Miranda's smiling face, "How's it going with the Laurus preparations?"

Ariel rubbed her eyes, "Well, good morning. Why aren't you out riding? Don't you ride every morning? Is anything wrong?" She felt her stomach tighten. "Is it Father? Miranda, is Father all right?"

Miranda shook her head, "No, it's not Father. Don't worry. That's one of the reasons I called. Good news. He's improved." She looked down. "Well, back to where he was before, stable. They're both all right at the moment."

Ariel put her hand on her heart and exhaled, "That's good. What's the other thing you wanted to talk about?"

Miranda squinted, "What's that mess on the table behind you?"

Ariel turned and looked. The table was stacked with dirty dishes. Dishes, again! She moved her chair in the way so Miranda could no longer see them.

"What's going on?" Miranda looked closer at Ariel. "Are you all right?"

Ariel smoothed down her hair, "I guess I've been a little distracted," she pulled her mouth into a smile, "And forgetful. Thanks for the reminder. What did you want to talk about?"

Miranda inhaled and didn't say anything for a while, her mouth moving side to side, "Well... I haven't told you, didn't want to bother you really, but I've been seeing this man Sean."

Ariel nodded, her eyebrows raised. "Yes?"

"I met him at Anne's. Remember Anne, my friend from the Artists Enclave?"

"Wait a second. Let me get some more coffee and you can tell me about it." Ariel turned and got herself a cup of steaming coffee.

"All right, go on?" She held the cup with both hands and took big swallows.

"Remember a while ago I went to see Anne?"

Ariel nodded.

"She had a lot of people over to look at her new sculpture, and I met this man. Sean."

Ariel pushed her chair back and put her legs up on the desk.

"I liked him right from the start. He was funny and sweet. We saw each other quite a bit and I don't want to see him anymore," she finished, looking at Ariel with a sad face.

"What?" Ariel leaned closer to the screen, "I don't understand. Why not? Did he do something?"

"No. That's the trouble. I don't know exactly why." Miranda was scratching her cheek. "It's why I called. I feel awful. I can't figure it out."

"Hmm." Ariel exhaled, "It's not like you're talking to someone with experience here."

"I know. What's our trouble with men?" Miranda tightened her lips and shook her head.

"I've been busy designing. That's my excuse."

"Yes," Miranda laughed.

"I know, not a convincing argument," she shrugged. "So what happened?"

"He's been calling." She looked to the side, "But I just couldn't bring myself to call him back. And he's stopped calling."

"I still don't understand." She could not decipher what exactly the problem was here. "Why not?"

"I miss him so much, but I can't call him back." She exhaled loudly her shoulders drooping.

Ariel thought about this for a second, "Maybe it's the obvious,

Miranda. You're scared." She shook her head. "It's new to you. This is the first time you've really liked someone that I can remember."

Miranda nodded, "And we were making plans to have a birthday party. For my birthday! And I never called him back."

"I think you're just scared," Ariel said again.

Miranda sat quietly, looking down. "You think that's all there is to it? I feel silly telling you all this."

"You need to know him better and then you'll probably feel more comfortable. It's all new. That's all."

"Perhaps you're right. I've overreacted, hah?" She twisted her mouth into a crooked smile.

Love pushed you beyond your utmost capabilities. It was a strange feeling of perfect terror and perfect exhilaration. Ariel sighed. She knew that from somewhere. Probably something she read when she was young.

"You just have to get used to having him around, not only the kids, horses and jewelry."

Miranda lifted her arms and combed her hair back with her fingers. "Maybe you're right."

"Give it a chance." She thought of Richard and felt a jolt of energy rush through her body.

"Hmm." Miranda glanced over to the side.

"I am sure you will find many wonderful surprises in getting to know Sean."

"Thank you. Silly hah? Sorry to have bothered you when you're so busy."

"No bother. We don't know much about this stuff. Anyway, I think you should just have fun and see how it goes."

"I'll let you know about the party. If it happens, of course. Meanwhile, you promise to do something fun instead of just working, yes?"

Ariel nodded, "I will try. Thank you for the reminder."

Miranda waved and was gone.

Ariel looked at the blank screen. Richard was in her mind again, the compulsion to see him again. She pushed back from her desk and walked around the studio. The world screens flashed. Why the compulsion? So many out-of-control emotions. She quickly pushed up her psychic shields. Out of control behavior. She stopped, looked down, closed her eyes. Yet she could not help her curiosity. Could do nothing with this thing that was driving her. Stronger than her own will.

She stopped at the table, picked up the dirty dishes and carried them to the recycler, then stepped over to the workstation and shut everything down.

In her quarters, she threw her blue suit into the recycler, washed up and crawled under the covers. She hoped a nap would take away the bleariness in her eyes.

She lay on her side and thought about Miranda. It would be good if Miranda had a partner. She knew Miranda got lonely with her being away so much. Yes, it would be nice if Miranda had someone special of her own.

She adjusted the pillows and thought it was good Andreas had stabilized. She called for music, and soothing sweet sounds of violin filled the room. She'll have to go on another Gateway mission. She thought of her mother and father. They had loved each other very much, worked perfectly as a team, like two beats in 2/2 time. She could hear Vivian's bright laughter, see her sparkling blue eyes. Andreas serious. But always there was amusement in his voice. Where were they now?

Ariel turned over to the other side.

Left somewhere fragmented in some strange dimension? She was tormented by the possibility they might be suffering in some way. And withholding information about the work she'd been doing on Argos from Miranda. She groaned. From everyone. And Richard. She shouldn't have gone to see him that last time. She was curious. He was unusual. She also admitted he was handsome, though she believed herself above such things and sniffed at the thought. She shouldn't have gone. She simply won't go back again. She had to stop. It was unbearable. Her life was all secrets and inexplicable things.

She turned over again, restless. She had to sleep. Had to get some rest.

Richard's eyes were looking at her again.

She pressed the pillow against her face, trying not to see him, trying to make him go away.

Chapter Nineteen

"I was eight years old. A horse threw me. They were waiting for me to die," Richard said. "I was gone from the world for days. But awake inside. Awake in the inner worlds."

He looked at Ariel, brows together, waiting, making sure she understood. He wore a cream wool tunic, the sleeves pushed back, and black hose.

Ariel nodded. She sat on a low stool Richard had brought for her, anticipating her return, trying to recover from the impetuous decision to come see him. He'd waited for her in the hut, built a fire and had a pot simmering on top of it. It was cozy, warm and pleasant.

Richard moved his hand as if to touch her, then stopped. "I am glad you came back. I have been waiting."

Ariel clutched her cloak around her, "I shouldn't be here. I shouldn't have told you who I am," she shook her head. "But I had to come back."

Richard looked at her for a long time. His eyes were sharp with concentration. "There is a reason for our meeting." His voice was low. He said each word with precision, emphasizing the is. "I don't believe this is without purpose."

He picked up the stick next to him and poked at the fire. Wild flames burst hissing and crackling.

"But... I'm not supposed to be here." She felt terrible guilt, breaking all laws and rules, the harrowing tear from her people. How could this possibly have purpose? She realized she was hot, shrugged off her cloak and sat in a green woolen dress.

"You are upset." His voice was gentle. "Let's just give it some time, all right? Understand more. Our meeting was not a coincidence. There is more to it than that. It's why we have to give it time, find out what it is. All right?"

Ariel felt her shoulders relax. She nodded. "Perhaps you are right. Give it a little time."

Richard patted her knee. "All right." He stirred the pot, "It will be done in a bit and we can eat. You are hungry, aren't you?" he smiled.

"Ravenous. But please continue with your story. I want to know what happened."

Richard looked up, his eyes focused on something distant, "I was away from my body, could see it lying there, could see everyone. They could not see me. After a while, a brilliant light came toward me and I was swept up in it. The most glorious white light. It took me on a journey. It showed me this world and other worlds and other beings." He turned and looked at her, "We're not the only beings God made!" He chuckled. "This being, that showed me all this, was all love." He tilted his head, looking off into space, "That I will never forget."

Ariel watched his face, now soft and glowing as he remembered. Many had these types of experiences throughout history but rarely talked about it in those early days.

"When I was back, everything looked different. I knew I was just a small part of my bigger self, and this life a small part of a great big mystery, not real in the bigger reality. Of course, no one else saw it that way. For everyone else this here was as real as anything could ever be." He sighed, "And from then on I was alone. A bystander watching the play of life. Everyone believed all this was real," he motioned with his arm, "Everyone was in it. And I watched."

He looked at the fire, then picked up a log and squeezed it in. The flame blazed, then settled crackling and hissing.

"Difficult. Seeing and knowing things other people can't perceive. Hard for you."

Richard took a big breath and exhaled. "Yes."

He picked up the stick and pushed the log more deeply into the flames.

"You should know that what you were shown is real and true. It's common knowledge where I come from. In fact the New Earth was built on this understanding of reality."

Richard's brows rose. "Someday it will be common knowledge?!"

It seemed to Ariel his entire being lit up when he heard her say that.

She nodded, "And do you know what else? A lot more came from that understanding."

Ariel felt joy leap up in her. Richard knew from experience the most fundamental nature of the universe. This explained so much. She herself now felt lighter.

Richard shifted on the stool, taking quick glances at her, a smile on his face. He stirred the pottage. Wonderful smells issued forth.

"You know," Ariel paused, "I've felt similar things you felt when you came back—in my world, where everyone sees and knows other realities." Her voice was sad.

He looked at her, lips tight, brows together.

She reflected back on her academy days. While all her peers were excited to find partners, she had no interest. Now she understood that it wasn't because she wasn't interested, it was that she longed for something she couldn't explain, that she didn't see in the face or body of any man she met. She still didn't know what it was, but at least now she understood why she felt the way she did.

She continued, "I look into the eyes of my people and feel they're not seeing something. But I don't know what it is they're not seeing. And I'm not sure what I am seeing. But it's something. There is some kind of gap." She exhaled a big sigh having put all that into words.

"You don't feel like you're a part of them?" Richard's voice rose in surprise, "Like you live in a different reality? But how can that be in your world?"

Ariel shifted on the stool. "I don't know. Now that I've said it, I see I've always felt that way. But lately even more so." She paused, looked at her hands, then up at Richard, "There have been unusual developments."

"Unusual developments?" Richard looked at her, his head tilted, his brows together.

When she didn't say anything, he stirred the pottage one more time, picked up a wooden bowl filled it and handed to her. He filled his own bowl, then reached for two wooden spoons.

"Why don't you finish your story first? What happened?" said Ariel.

Richard nodded, "Well, I came back with unusual gifts. I could see things other people couldn't. It's how I could see you. I see a lot of things now. See into my patients."

When Ariel arrived earlier, the first thing he'd said was, "I focused very carefully sensing your return."

"And it's how I appeared in your dreams?"

He got up and came back with a round loaf of dark bread. He tore a chunk and handed it to her. "Yes. Again and again through the years. Never long dreams. Just... the face. It would appear. Of course now I know it was your face."

"But how? With all that's between us?" She looked at the fire, shook her head, then ate the pottage, tasty with chunks of meat, cabbage, carrots and leek. "Good," she mumbled.

Richard continued, "Now that has changed. I no longer think about your face. But your presence. How I feel when I am with you."

Ariel looked at him, full of wonder at what was happening to her.

Soft drops of rain started to fall on the thatched roof as if murmuring secrets.

Richard stopped for a minute listening, then continued, "I learned a lot at university. Reading the Greeks explained much of what I witnessed."

Ariel nodded. "Do you have brothers, sisters?"

"Family all dead. Long time ago." His brow lifted, "Alone at the house." The left side of his mouth went up in a crooked smile.

Ariel felt her face get hot. She looked down at her pottage and stirred.

The rain pounded harder on the roof.

Richard looked up, "It will be a wet ride going back."

He finished eating, saw she was done, and put their bowls aside. "Some sweet wine?" He got up, went to the sack sitting in the corner, rummaged around and pulled out a jug, then two goblets.

"You thought of everything!" said Ariel.

He laughed. "It wasn't hard for a special guest."

He filled the goblets, handed her one and sat down. "What is this Earth like in your time?"

Ariel thought what to say. "So much is different, but the same."

Richard nodded, "And how can you be here? How have things changed so you can be here?"

Ariel lifted her goblet.

Richard turned and looked her in the eyes, lifted his goblet. "A toast."

"All right. To what?" Ariel felt herself fill with excitement as if some momentous decision was innocuously being made.

"To us, of course! What else?"

Without hesitation they clanked and drank. Very sweet with a background of cherry.

"It's simple, I mean about how I could be here. We have learned how to work with the atom. All of us have. And we have developed our innate psychic abilities and harnessed them with our knowledge of the atom."

Richard took a drink. "So, work with the atom has only progressed. The theory did not die?"

Ariel felt warm inside and wanted to touch him, but held back. Instead, she sat sensing him, smelling the raw smell of him mixed with the pottage and smoke and the earth smell of the hut.

"That's right. It was just expanded over time."

A reluctant smile lighted his face. His shoulders dropped. It was as if all up until now he had held himself rigid and now he could relax.

"It is the same with my work." This just erupted out of her somehow.

Richard looked at her, brows together, waiting for her to

explain.

She realized now that she had started to talk about work, she wanted to say a whole lot more but knew she shouldn't. He waited.

"I'm working on a project I'm not supposed to be working on. This project feels the way you do. Feels right. But it's all wrong." And she let out a big breath she felt she was holding since the council meeting.

Chapter Twenty

Ariel stopped at the door to Max's studio and announced herself telepathically. They were ready to move on with the next phase of Argos.

"Come in!" shouted Max, and Ariel stepped into the worst clutter she'd ever seen, and the strained hums of crystal transducers.

"Ah, there you are. Come in, come in."

"Where are you, Max?" Ariel could hear him but not see him.

"Over this way," called Max.

Ariel looked around trying to find a way to Max's voice. It was slow progress. She stepped over cords, tubes, pipes, string, tall equipment she did not recognize, ducked down to avoid curled leaves of strange plants. Max had put up a web of wires across the ceiling from which hung various objects. They obstructed light creating deep shadows here and there. Strange smells. Chemicals, food, heat from equipment that was never shut down. What a mess.

"When are you going to clear this mess up, Max? This is ridiculous."

"I need all this stuff for my projects. Come on, it's not that bad."

Ariel held her console tight to her chest and tried to make herself small so as not to bump into anything.

"I'm almost there. How do you get around in here? And your transducers sound awful!"

Regularly Max overloaded his crystal transducers, breaking their integrity, was given new ones and the whole process started all over again. Once he'd asked for a more powerful model, was told he had to stay within the allowable power for ship models, had raised his hands, said, "C'est la vie!" and continued with the systematic blowouts. They left him alone with the occasional gratuitous reprimand.

She finally stood in front of Max and exhaled. He looked back at her. They both waited. Finally he held both palms up, shaking his head, "What?"

Ariel looked up at his cap.

He reached up and touched it, "Oh, that," and smiled. "An impulse creation." He shrugged his shoulders. He was wearing an old-fashioned jester's cap.

Ariel shook her head and tried to see a chair. It was behind this *thing* almost as tall as she was, with transparent tiles and strings of organic matter protruding here and there. "Can I move this?" She was pointing at the *thing*.

"Sure," said Max, "It doesn't bite."

She started to slide it away from the table.

"It just kills you!"

Ariel pulled her hand back.

"Ha, ha, ha," laughed Max, his shoulders shaking.

"Max!" He'd probably placed it there on purpose to irk her. He always won at these pranks. Thus far. Ariel decided that one day, when all this was over, she'll give Max a surprise that would make all his surprises seem tame. She smiled to herself, pulled out a chair, and looked up at Max.

"It's all right, just push it off."

Ariel brushed off what looked like a sponge and sat down.

Max did a sweep of the arm and cleared a space on the table in front of Ariel, and she put her console down.

"Anything to eat, drink?"

Ariel shook her head. "No, thanks. Had too much hot chocolate already."

She waited while Max walked over to the dispenser. The dispenser buzzed. Max turned around, holding a giant yellow cup with red polka dots, and an oversized donut. She rolled her eyes. She was certain he'd designed all this himself. The donut was three times the usual size.

He bit into it and chewed with gusto. Powdered sugar rode up and down on his beard.

She couldn't resist: "Can't have those in your favorite time period."

He swallowed and took a loud slurp of coffee. "Ah, but just think of how fresh, just how fresh the game is!" and took another large bite.

Ariel gave up this tack, secured her psychic shields and focused, waiting for Max to get to business.

Max walked back to the table, put down his donut and coffee and swept a hand across the chair. Ariel jumped as something crashed to the floor.

Max looked at her and smiled.

He sat down.

Ariel sensed him secure his psychic shields. "How are you?"

"Like I'm carrying a giant load I can't put down." She sighed, "So much to hide. Everything feels so unreal. But at least that booming voice has not come back in a while."

Max nodded. "Seems like that inner directive to build quieted down once you took action." He looked down at his hands, "I know what you mean about the secrecy. That's been hard. But I'm curious. Now that we've started, I am curious what we'll discover. At the very least it will be incredible to see a miniature Argos world."

Ariel nodded.

"I have all aspects of Argos secured for prototyping," Max said. Then he pushed his chair back and stood up, "Come and look at what I've done so far."

Ariel followed through the maze of objects and wondered how Max could keep his robes from getting entangled in all the stuff, especially with the way he moved, total quiescence and then an explosion of movement propelled by some new idea that was so important it required, not only instant, but energetic action. Ariel was glad she was not his partner, but wondered if Max would ever even have a partner. It would take a special woman to deal with Max.

In a corner of his studio Max had set up a dome. Laser beams were in place. A small crystal transducer stood beside it. Their miniature holobio world would be born here. Ariel felt small flutters of excitement course through her body.

"This is excellent, Max!"

He muttered, "Not bad, not bad."

"Where'd you get the transducer?" All transducers had to be signed out.

He winked, "Connections. Back on Earth."

"How'd you list it?" Ariel started to panic.

"Ah," he waved his hand in dismissal, "As usual. Signed it up for another project. No big deal."

Ariel let out a sigh of relief, but wondered.

He stopped, faced her, his voice low, "That's the least of our worries, Ariel." Then he was in motion again, "Come and look at this."

He walked around and began to point to different parts of the model, explaining what he'd done.

At this stage there was not much to see that was recognizable, that had any form. What was present were mostly tiny power centers that were the primary support of the holobio model.

Max rubbed his hands together, "Should work just fine. Just fine."

"Looks that way, doesn't it?" said Ariel. She was pleased. They were making progress. Then she thought of the data they would get that would demonstrate how those magnificent minds were wrong, or clearly show why they were right. Ariel could not imagine it, could not see how the leap would be made. But of one thing she was certain, significant information would emerge, and she hoped it would solve the mystery.

After they both admired the beginnings of the holobio model, they went back to the table.

Max bit into his donut, then slurped his coffee loudly. Ariel was sure he did it to annoy her, so she ignored him. She powered up her console. "All right. Next steps."

"What do you think we'll find when we're done? Can you speculate?" Max was rubbing his hands, his eyes big and bright. "Have you thought about it?"

Ariel nodded. "Yes, a lot."

"And..." He leaned toward her.

"Nothing," she shook her head, "And everything. Imagined all sorts of things." She shrugged and exhaled. "Just want the answer."

"I've searched again through New Earth's history. Found no

record of anything like this ever happening."

"I know. It's what sends me into panic."

Max exhaled, looked to the side, thinking, then turned back and looked at her, "Let's get to work."

Chapter Twenty-One

It was warm and cozy in the kitchen. A small fire crackled. Gentle sounds of guitar drifted through the air.

Ariel donned a blue apron and retrieved the tardpolane recipe on her console. Almonds, flour, sugar, dates, figs, raisins, pears, red wine, eggs, cheese.

She hummed a little. It was good to be in the kitchen baking instead of in the studio working.

Most of the ingredients for the tardpolane had to come from the dispenser, unfortunately, but at least the spices were authentic. She was curious what tardpolane would taste like given these unusual ingredients.

She fetched a bowl to soak the almonds when Richard popped into her mind. She stopped and exhaled. It's been a while since she saw him and had been in turmoil ever since. One moment she'd smile thinking of him. The next moment she'd tell herself she must not go back. A painful confusing mess.

She remembered that early near-death experience he had. It had set him up for a hard life in his world, given him uncommon powers. She shook her head. Difficult to be so very different from the people around you.

She dropped the almonds into the bowl and poured water over them.

And he'd used that experience and his university studies to create a comprehensive understanding of the way things were in the larger reality. Ariel marveled at his abilities.

The intercom toned.

Ariel turned on the screen in the kitchen and saw Miranda's smiling face, "Good morning! What are you making?"

"Tardpolane."

"One of the Old Middle Earth recipes?"

"Yes. It's a bit complicated, but I'm curious to find out what it tastes like. There is a crust involved and a whole lot of different ingredients that go into the crust and then it's baked. How are you? How's it going on the ranch?"

Miranda wore a bright yellow blouse. She was sitting at her jewelry table. The sun was on her. She was shining.

"Everything is great. Sean and I are seeing each other and... and this is the reason I called—we are having the birthday party. I am so excited. Will you come? Can you bring Max?"

"This is good news. I have to check with Max, but I'm sure he'd love a birthday part. How are Mom and Dad?"

Miranda's smile vanished. "They are fine. Their usual fine, that is." She sighed, and her mouth formed into a small pout.

"I know. Always hard these fluctuation," Ariel sighed. "Anything else going on?"

"No. Just getting ready for the party. How about over there?"

"Nothing extraordinary. Just the usual work and preparations for Laurus. Everything's going well," Ariel lied, with firm psychic shields.

"That's good. I will let you know the exact date of the party. We'll have fun. All right, bye," she waved.

Ariel waved back. How wonderful, a birthday party. And to

get away from the ship for some fun! She'll have to check with Max.

She strained the almond mixture, added flour and sugar, made the dough for the crust, divided it into twelve pieces then lined the twelve small tart pans.

She chopped up dried pears, dates, almonds and the rest of the ingredients, poured wine over them, then mixed in the egg and cheese and added the spices. She stirred. It smelled wonderful.

She was grateful the attacks no longer troubled her. She and Max had worked on Argos. Things have been going smoothly except, of course for the persistent feelings of guilt and fear and doubt. Ariel sighed. She could not wait for all of it to be over.

She spooned the filling into the tart pans and placed them in the oven.

She washed her hands, took off her apron and went to call Max.

"Lovely you are this morning, Ariel," greeted Max, "And I smell something baking in the oven." His eyes got big, "I can have some of whatever you're baking, right?"

"Did some psychic sniffing, I see," Ariel laughed, "Of course. When it's done, I'll bring some to your studio."

Max clapped his hands, trying to look like a happy little kid.

"Miranda is having a birthday party. Do you want to come?"

"Of course. A great break from the ship and all those projects," his eyebrows went up, "And by the way, they are going well," Max was nodding, "I'll tell you more and show you upon wonderful-smelling-something delivery."

"All right, see you a little later."

The kitchen smelled divine. Ariel got a mug of hot chocolate and sat at the counter waiting for the tardpolane to finish baking. She wished Richard would stop appearing in her mind. What could happen with them? They could never be together. She suddenly became aware of the fact that she had actually considered being with him permanently!

She groaned. She felt as if she was under the weight of a giant boulder.

And he said there had to be meaning to their meeting. It wasn't a pointless coincidence. Then she remembered. She was telling him about the New Earth. She even began to tell him about Argos! She groaned again. What was she doing?

She took a big breath. All too much. Too many strange things. Breaking all kinds of New Earth laws. If she could just not go see him for a good while. Maybe the whole thing would fade. Maybe then he'd leave her mind.

Chapter Twenty-Two

She found him on the moors with his dog Bennet. His hair was scraggly and wet, his cloak smeared with mud. It was a cold gloomy afternoon, the sky low, thick and gray.

When she appeared next to him, he stopped, looked at her and kept walking.

Her heart lurched. His face was compressed into a horrible darkness.

She hurried after him through the wet grass and brush. Her heart pounded. He'd been thinking. He'd reached conclusions. She was swallowing hard.

Bennet ran up to her, tail wagging. She ignored him and he went off sniffing in the grass.

"What could become of us?" His voice was raspy and low.

It started to rain. Ariel pulled her hood up, tightened the cloak around her.

"Richard! What's happened?!"

"You don't even exist in my world," his voice rumbled.

"What have you been thinking?" She was filled with panic. She was finally facing all she'd tried so hard not to face.

The rain plastered her hair, trickled down her neck, cold, setting off shivers.

"I finally meet the woman in my dreams, the dreams I've had

all these years, and…" he stopped and held his hands palms up, "She is just that! The woman in my dreams!" He laughed a strange sardonic laugh.

"I *am* real," she yelled, but knew what he meant and felt helpless, without recourse.

He walked fast, and she ran to keep up with him.

"All my life I've wandered these hills never feeling a part of them, a part of this Earth. I meet a stranger and I don't feel like a stranger anymore."

"Richard! Listen! Stop! Maybe there is a way. You said…" But a dreadful rising realization inside her said there was no way. She swallowed hard to hold back tears.

They were pushing up a hill through tall grass. Lightening flashed. Then thunder.

He wiped the rain from his forehead. "Except this person I feel at home with is a stranger in my world. In my time!" He shook his head and took big angry strides up the hill.

Ariel ran after him. She put her hand on his arm. He stopped and looked at her.

"My heart's already broken and I've not even begun to know you." His voice cracked. He took hold of her hand.

"I see something, but I also see it cannot be." He looked deep into her eyes, "Cannot be." His voice deep and hoarse. He let go her hand, turned and stormed up the hill.

Ariel breathed hard from the effort of pushing through the tall grass from the misery of it all. She'd come, her heart fluttering with desire to see him. Even though she knew she shouldn't. To this.

He stopped abruptly, again took both of her hands this time and looked into her eyes. "It's best this not continue." He leaned toward her. "Go back to your time." His voice urgent, "Do not come back. Forget." He let go her hands. "I will also forget." His head dropped to his chest. "It will be easier to forget now than later." His face was distorted with pain and the effort of saying this. "It's easier now," he said more quickly, urgently, nodding his head.

Ariel heard him, but couldn't take in what he was saying. His words moved through some heavy fog in her head. She couldn't breathe. He said I should leave. He said I should not come back. She blinked trying to absorb what that meant.

"No, no," she shook her head. But inside she was thinking. He's right. It's impossible and I always knew it.

"It's best." He pierced this idea through her.

"No! No!" and she was backing away. She should get out of here. Now!

She turned and ran. She heard the swishing of the grass behind her as he followed her yelling after her: "That's right. Go! Go and don't come back!"

It thundered loud, long explosions. The rain came down hard, furled by gusts of angry wind.

"I will go," she muttered. "I will go. I will not come back. It's best. Yes. You're right."

She stopped, looked back at him. Rain was flowing down his face.

She tried to hold them back, but the tears came anyway.

"No tears! Go back!" He choked out the words.

She backed away, struggled to focus to make her escape.

He remained standing where he was, hands on his hips. His face hard. His lips a thin line. He was forcing her to leave.

She found the coordinates, looked at his face, saw his lashes flutter. For a second she allowed herself to sink into the blue fire of his eyes so she would never forget, then vanished.

Chapter Twenty-Three

Water dripped all around her, dissolving the mud on her boots making a mess on the carpet. She tried not to move, pulled off the cloak and gown, a soggy bundle of smelly wool, then pulled off the muddy boots. Threw everything into the recycler. Her hair hung in wet strands about her. She shivered, hugged herself, crying. She didn't expect this. But then, did she really know him at all?

She hurried to the washroom, stood under hot water a long time crying, then went back to the garment dispenser and pulled on burgundy pants and a big cream sweater. To be warm again. Tears kept flowing down her face. She made no sound. She should have anticipated something like this. After all, she was thinking the same thing. But she didn't want to. She shook her head, raised her hands and covered her face.

After a while she ordered tissues wiped her eyes and blew her nose. She saw the mud on the carpet, then glanced over at the workstation. The message light was blinking. She considered a moment, then headed for the hanger bay.

Once she was far enough away from Palladium, she set Blossom to coast and sat and cried. She didn't care how loud it was. She didn't care if the New Humans had better control of their emotions. She cried. Her heart was shredded. How could he do it?

How did he have the courage? She breathed hard uneven breaths.

His eyes drifted before her. She'll never forget them. She blew her nose. He was right. It was better to stop it now than later. Better to have avoided bigger pain which was sure to come. How could she have let herself get into this situation? She shook her head. Why was she asking pointless questions? Never had she done anything so foolish that hurt so much. And certainly never had she broken New Earth laws.

She dragged herself out of the pilot seat. Her body was buzzing. She felt weak, drained. She got a mug of hot chocolate. She had to leave it. Leave it all behind her. And fast. She had to focus. Argos came to mind and a dreadful fear swept through her. She had to pull herself together. But not just yet.

She stepped down to the lounge area, put down the mug, arranged pillows, pulled the blanket over her legs and leaned back. Warm and comfortable.

Where could it have led? She could not have moved to Old Earth nor he to the New Earth. She realized the idea had been in the back of her mind all along, she just hadn't wanted to face it. She had all these expectations she did not want to admit to herself. Romantic notions. She sipped the hot chocolate, its warmth and sweetness wonderfully soothing. To have continued to go back and forth would have been madness. In any case no doubt they would have been found out soon enough. Romantic involvements of any kind with those in other times were obviously forbidden. And she'd already broken the rule of disclosing her true identity.

She shivered and tucked the blanket closer around her. She couldn't understand her feelings for Richard. The intensity. The fact that she simply could not stop herself from going to see him. Why? She was weak to have succumbed to her feelings like that.

Was she? She looked back and did not recall being weak like that before, and there were other hard times in her life.

His eyes flashed before her again. She put the mug down and cried again. Never to know Richard. Never to find out what he was really like. To find out why they felt toward each other the way they did.

She wiped her eyes and picked up the cup again.

She'll try. It's best. He said forget. She will try. But not right now. A little later. It was best that way. She had enough trouble as it was.

The amount of energy it took to sustain so much deceit wrenched her body into horrible pain. She shook her head. Never would she have believed she would lie to so many people all at once about so many things. She exhaled. And the constant watch over her own feelings. How much longer could she keep it up?

She was on edge about Argos all the time, anxious in case something went wrong and, of course, in the end—what? What would they find out? Would she be right? Would it all have been worthwhile? Or was she just heading toward disaster and taking them all with her? She squirmed in agony.

How long could she live like this? It was insane for her to defy the Earth Council. Enthralled by Argos, tormented by the unknown.

In this silence, her loneliness was absolute. Her heart crushed.

She slid down, laid on her back and looked at the stars. The darkness and quiet comforted her. She was glad that at least there was a finish date. Maybe. Then again, the way things were going, maybe not.

And Andreas and Vivian, how much longer? She was thoroughly frustrated with her Gateway research. How could so much effort, not just on her part but everybody's, yield nothing?

She pushed back the blanket and stood up. There had to be an answer as to why they were all failing. She walked around Blossom. In some way all of them were simply on the wrong tack. What was the right tack?

She got another mug of hot chocolate.

And Miranda struggling with a new relationship. What would it be like to have Miranda be with someone? What would it mean for the two of them?

"Everything's changing!" she said out loud, "And not much makes sense."

She wanted, just for a little while to forget, to be free of all of this before getting back to all she's committed to and to forgetting Richard.

She put the mug down and focused for a long time. She had to execute this just right for it to work because any mistake would be fatal.

She teleported just outside Blossom and held suspended. Thinned herself out, all atoms. Through which passed the universe. She sank deep into this feeling. Relaxed. Then she spread her awareness out further and further until she felt herself to be everything. Herself as she was, Ariel. And everything. And rested. The blue fire of Richard's eyes flashed for a second.

Chapter Twenty-Four

Ariel looked in the mirror, at her drooping eyes, drooping mouth. She had to let it all go, forget everything. Forget Richard. Forget Argos. Somehow enjoy Miranda's birthday party.

She combed her hair, took a small section in the front, pulled it back to her crown, clipped it with an amethyst clip and let the rest fall in waves around her shoulders. She did a turn in front of the mirror was satisfied and headed for the sitting room just as Max announced himself at the door. He stepped in, a smile on his face. He carried a small blue package. He halted abruptly, looked Ariel up and down. "You look terrific!" Ariel wore a shimmering white unitard, a long diaphanous indigo scarf around her neck. Her feet sparkled in white sandals with large amethysts.

"Thank you, Max." She picked up a large pink package from the sofa. "You look rather dapper yourself, even if on the ancient side of dapper looks." Max wore clean white robes. His hair was combed and glowing, his beard and mustache neatly trimmed.

He performed a small bow. "I'm really looking forward to this. Haven't had a fun break in a while."

"I know. We both need this. Ready for the coordinates to Miranda's ranch?"

They arrived and heard Anne say, "We could go enclave hopping!" Then she turned to Ariel and Max, "Oh, hello!"

"There you are!" said Miranda and rushed over to hug them.

Miranda's great room was filled with lively music. Tall white incandescent vases with strands of glowing colored lights were everywhere. They glittered in the waning afternoon light.

"Happy birthday!" Ariel and Max said in unison. They held out the birthday presents.

"You look beautiful, just like your sister," said Max.

Miranda wore a long gauzy yellow gown with lilac flowers. Her curly blond hair was studded with tiny lilac crystal flowers that shimmered when she moved.

"Thank you, Max. What did you two bring? These packages are heavy," said Miranda. "Sean, can you please help me carry these to the table?"

Anne stepped up. "I was just making suggestions for tonight's festivities, thought we could go enclave hopping. What do you think?"

"That's certainly a possibility," said Ariel.

Miranda was back with Sean. "This is Sean." She extended her hand, pointing to Sean.

"It's such a pleasure to finally meet you, Ariel," Sean said.

His voice was deep and rich. He was medium height with light brown hair neatly combed to one side. He wore a loose linen jacket and linen pants. He radiated health.

"And very pleased to meet you," said Ariel. In his touch she felt wholesomeness. She liked him.

Sean turned to Max. "I understand you're a master trickster." He was smiling.

Max cleared his throat. "This is unfortunate, my secret is out already." He pursed his lips and nodded, "I had plans."

"I am Anne," said Anne and extended her hand to Max. She

wore a long apricot dress with a wide hoop, the latest revivalist fashion. Her blond hair was twisted up on top of her head. Light curls framed her face.

"A pleasure indeed," Max bowed, lifted Anne's hand and placed a kiss.

Anne giggled and blinked rapidly. "Would you like something to drink?" She looked from Max to Ariel, then back to Max. "We have a bottle of champagne open."

"I'll take a glass," said Ariel.

"And one for me," said Max.

Champagne in hand, Ariel smiled and relaxed. She planned to make the most of her time off provided she was successful in not thinking about Richard or Argos. At those thoughts she darkened. Forgetting was not going well. She wasn't sure she could, not the way Richard intended, anyway. Anne's voice burst into her thoughts.

"I've been saying we should go enclave hopping," she said again. "And maybe now that the two of you are here, you can support me in this perfectly grand idea." Her laugh sparkled. "It's still early, we could make a nice circuit, starting with the pub for some ale and darts, here in Miranda's enclave, then to the Roman Enclave for the baths, then in my enclave for dinner. What do you all think?" She looked at Max, clearly expecting him to support her in this notion.

Murmurs of general approval issued all around. "A grand idea it is indeed," said Max.

"Excellent! Then that's what we'll do," said Anne. "Now, Miranda," she turned to Miranda, who stood with her arm through the crook of Sean's elbow. "Why don't you open your presents?"

"Oh, how exciting," said Miranda, turned and headed for the

big dining table piled with colorful packages. Everybody followed.

"Thank you all for coming," said Miranda. She smiled a shy smile. "And thank you for the presents." She turned and unwrapped the biggest package. "An ancient lap harp!" She turned to Ariel, "Thank you! I didn't think to play the ancient harp. I think I might like that." She ran her fingers across the strings, and lovely tinkly sounds filled the room.

"I thought you'd enjoy learning something new," said Ariel. But as she watched Miranda, she sensed consternation. Miranda had a routine she did not like to break, even with learning something new that was fun.

"I thought it might add to your creativity, maybe inspire that new direction you are seeking," said Ariel, not so sure any more about the present. It may end up just being an ornament.

Anne had brought her a set of brushes for the horses with handles she had made and engraved.

Miranda looked up at Anne, "Beautiful! How did you know I needed new brushes?"

Anne stepped up and hugged her, "You are my friend, how can I not know?"

Max had brought her a calibrator for her jewelry, which she was pleased about. Lastly she opened Sean's present.

"A huge opal," she exclaimed and looked at Sean.

"You like it?" He took a step toward her. "I thought you might start a new line of jewelry starting with this opal." He had a big grin on his face.

"What do you mean a new line of jewelry?" Her voice had a slight edge.

He pressed along, "I thought," he looked around at all of them, the red coming to his face. "I thought it might be fun to create a line of jewelry where each stone could be calibrated to the energy of the wearer and designed so that it could augment desired energies at certain times, a sort of mini transducer in jewelry form. You said you were looking to create a new line," he stammered to the end.

They all said something about how this was a fabulous idea. Max especially was enthusiastic. Miranda said nothing. She stared at the opal, then at Sean, her face grim.

Sean looked a little desperate now. "You'll have to do some inner journeying to adjust the frequencies for the gems, but..." he stopped.

For a second they all froze.

Oh, oh, he just crossed the Miranda boundary, interfering in her work, telling her what to design. Let's hope he makes it. She looked deeply into Miranda, but came up against shields firmly in place. How good she is at that. She'd never known. Maybe we were too young before. Maybe before there was nothing much to keep private.

After a moment, Miranda was in motion, "It's very beautiful," she smiled and hugged Sean.

Sean unfroze and moved, a tentative smile appearing on his face.

In the end, they all conceded that Anne's enclave-hopping plan was the best, possibly because everyone was already happy and planning no longer seemed important.

"I'll get the buggy ready," said Miranda and started for the door.

"I'll help," said Sean, set his drink down, and followed her.

Chapter Twenty-Five

The Dog & Duck pub was dimly lit, crammed with people and loud with conversation. It smelled of ale and oak barrels. Thick wooden beams ran across the ceiling and brick walls. Metal chandeliers hung low, holding amber lights.

They stood in a bunch and looked for a place to sit.

"I'll get drinks," shouted Sean, and they shouted back preferences. Sean nodded and pushed his way to the bar.

Max moved, and they all followed, ending up squeezed on a bench against the brick wall. "Maybe we should have gone to the Swan," shouted Anne, "Might have been less busy."

No one responded.

At small tables heads leaned together in animated discussion and sporadic laughter. A few threw darts, tankers in hand. A big fire danced in a big stone hearth.

Ariel sat with a smile on her face. She loved the crowded pub, the lively atmosphere, a balm for her soul after recent events and the lonely ship environment.

"They'll bring the drinks out," said Sean, and they squeezed some more to make room for him.

A cheerful tune started up. Ariel looked to see where it was coming from and located three smiling musicians in the alcove set back from the door. An all-around festive spirit.

Their drinks delivered, they sat back and settled in to enjoy their ales.

After a while Max leaned forward, twisted so he could see them all and yelled so he could be heard, "Love isn't something you can manufacture toward a person," He was continuing the conversation about love they started in the buggy, no doubt because of Sean and Miranda.

Manufacture love? What a ridiculous idea. What was Max thinking? Probably related to some world he was designing—using his famous "new" perspective.

"There has to be something special there, otherwise, what's the point?" continued Max. He took a sip of his ale, leaving foam on his mustache.

"How would you know anything about love, Max?" asked Miranda, "You've not been in any relationship as far as I know." She looked up at Sean.

"That doesn't mean I can't know some things," Max sniffed, though that sniff was mostly lost in the din.

"But how *would* you know?" asked Ariel. "If you've never experienced true love in a relationship, how would you know it is the real thing, that there isn't something superior, entirely different, maybe something you couldn't even imagine?" She was thinking of Richard.

"And what is the purpose of love in a relationship, anyway?" asked Anne. There was an edge to her voice.

"Sounds like you don't have a mate, by the tone of your voice," said Max.

Anne looked hard at him.

"No one can keep up with Anne," said Miranda. "She's just too clever for most men."

Max ignored her, "How can you even ask that, Anne? We all know the purpose. It's what it's always been since the creation of the New Earth—to expand."

Anne shook her head. "Maybe not." She looked down and wiped the perspiring water on her tanker. "Maybe there is more to it than we know, even now." She looked up at them.

"I don't think so," said Sean. "It's the same as it's always been. To be human is to be human always. We still feel all the emotions, grief, rage, hate, hope, frustration, they just don't dominate us, control us. It's all that and also feeling love in a special way towards one person." He paused. "That love is always new. It's why we create, why we're Creators." He picked up his tanker, looked down in it, as if thinking something that he did not want to say out loud.

Miranda looked at him, a smile on her face.

"There are different kinds of love," Max picked up, and so the conversation on love continued with no new insights, a lot of opinions, and a lot of nonsense until Anne shouted, "Time to move on."

Richard was in her mind and Ariel wondered what she herself had really felt, what that feeling really was. She exhaled and slid her way across the bench and followed the others to the door.

Outside, soft shapes of hills rested in pale light of the moon. Miranda lit a lantern and hung it on the bottom of the buggy. They piled in and bumped along to the Transport Node.

"What do you call an Earthling who has lost his crystal transducer?" asked Sean happily.

They considered for a minute, then in unison shouted, "What?"

"An unilluminated human," laughed Sean.

Everyone groaned.

"Silly," said Miranda, poking him.

"All right, listen up everybody," said Anne. She sang the beginning of a song they all knew from childhood:

"Silver moon, silver stars bring delight to our human eyes, fill us with love, fill us with vision, let us prosper and expand in our creation."

She looked at them, "Let's sing harmony."

She assigned them parts, sang each part until they learned it and soon they were singing in harmony, keeping warm snuggled up against each other.

"That was fun," Ariel said and clapped. Everyone followed suit.

After a while Anne said, "When are you going to move out of this snail enclave, Miranda? Look, it's going to take us forever to get to the Transport Node. I'm cold."

"We'll be there soon. Just amp up your body heat a little," said Miranda.

"Such a traditionalist," said Anne. "If it wasn't for the constant expansion of the Prime Directive, you'd probably do nothing but ride your horses. But I love you nevertheless." She wrapped her arm around Miranda and squeezed.

"I like this snail enclave," interjected Sean. "I like the way it smells." He hugged Miranda, "It's why Miranda smells so wonderful."

Anne chuckled, "If Miranda lived on the North Pole in a big oxygen bubble, you'd say the same thing, Sean."

They all laughed. Sean reddened. Miranda giggled.

At the Transport Node, they handed over the buggy to the attendant and stood on the platform debating which kind of transport to take. "It's a glorious night, said Miranda, let's take the SloT?" This was an open sky taxi.

"It's just too cold!" said Anne, hugging herself. "Of course, you're warm." She looked at Miranda and Sean who had their arms around each other.

"It's Miranda's birthday," said Max, "Let's take the SloT.

"We'll warm up at the baths," said Ariel.

On SloT Ariel positioned herself behind Max as the speed of the cab picked up and the cold air rushed at them. She started to adjust her body temperature then stopped. She did not want to fuss with the effort. So, she'll be cold for a while. She was having a good time and wanted to leave all effort behind, at least for tonight.

The stars were all out now and glistened clear in the sky. It was cold, but the air smelled of fresh grass and earth and night. They slid through creamy darkness and dark shapes of hills and the occasional cluster of twinkling lights of people's homes.

Soon they were at the Roman Enclave in the big steamy echoing hall with a giant pool. The sliding roof was pulled back, the lights turned low, the stars sparkling bright. Tall blue columns rose around them. It was warm and pleasant.

A few people were in the pool. They joined them, swam laps. Sean would launch Miranda from his shoulders, and then they would both disappear. Anne and Max were diving.

Ariel swam leisurely laps on her back and looked at the stars. What a beautiful night. Anne had a great idea about coming here.

Eventually they all ended up in the hot tub. "Even if we do find the Gateway," Sean said, "There is still the big job of moving Earth. That will take years."

The conversation had turned to what's preoccupied them all their lives, the urgent need to find the Gateway.

"It is curious," said Miranda, "That we've not been able to find a way." This was the New Human refrain. The same conversation over and over.

Ariel, upon hearing their comments, wondered if they, as a species, had become too arrogant without noticing. Creators of new worlds, travelers in space and time, accomplished teleporters many of them. Maybe they needed to be reminded they were still mere humans, still learning, that still there was the Universal Consciousness that was beyond any of their ability to imagine—its love and power. She thought about pride and felt guilt about her own prideful actions in assuming she knew what was best for Earth in building the Argos prototype. She forced herself to let go of the thought, slid deeper into the water until only her head remained and enjoyed the hot water moving about her. She closed her eyes.

"Well, if we don't find a way, it's poof Earth, poof evolved humans!" said Anne.

"That won't be for hundreds of years," said Sean.

"But we don't know how long it will take for us to find the Gateway," said Max, "And even if we do, as Sean said, we don't know what it will take to move Earth."

They were silent. This was always at the back of all their minds.

After a while they all agreed they were warm enough, wet enough and relaxed enough to move on to their next adventure.

They stood on the platform. "No, we are not taking the SloT again," Anne said. "Let's just take the Mini Train," and she started to walk over to the Mini Train Platform. They all followed.

They had a compartment to themselves and soon were at the Artists Enclave.

Chapter Twenty-Six

At the center of the Artists Enclave, a hologram of Earth glowed high in the sky—surrounded by worlds they had built. The worlds rotated and sparkled in magnificent color and detail.

"Spectacular," said Max.

"And there are your worlds," pointed Miranda. "How clever you are, Ariel."

"And Max's worlds," said Anne.

Ariel felt the magnificence of Life rise in her as overwhelming awe and gratitude. These holograms said everything. Who they were as humans, what they'd accomplished. She fervently hoped her Argos endeavor would only enhance this magnificence. The new humans had so carefully guarded against repeating the disasters of their past.

They were silent for a while, looking up in awe, then Max broke the silence, "Let's eat!" and looked around, deciding which way to go.

Packed clay paths radiated in all directions from the center of the enclave, leading to the entertainment district. Beyond the entertainment district lay professional buildings and artists' studios. Farther out were residential areas.

"I'm hungry," said Sean. "Can't wait to try one of these artist meals everyone travels here to eat." He looked at Anne, "Any recommendations for a place?"

"No, let's just walk around and find something new," said Miranda.

"I like the Remember," said Anne. "They have great dishes, and the atmosphere is enchanting."

I'd rather not remember, thought Ariel. For the moment, she just wanted to forget. The Remember was named after their demise and meant to remind them, as were many other places on the New Earth.

"Yes. Let's just walk around," said Ariel. "It will be fun. It's such a beautiful night. Besides, there will be heaters throughout, so it will be nice." She looked around and started walking, and the others followed.

Art was everywhere: statues, small holograms, installations of every sort, old-style paintings, performers of every kind, stages with ongoing plays. Scattered groups of musicians played a variety of musical styles. Cooking smells wafted from numerous food stands along the path. Hanging lights floated gently, illuminating the lively atmosphere. Small heating spheres rolled near the ground, keeping them warm.

"This is wonderful," said Miranda.

"Yes, fabulous idea coming here, Anne," said Ariel.

"What are they doing over there?" pointed Max.

A large group of people stood around a performer who wore a red top and purple hose. He had long brown hair that hung in waves to his shoulders.

"All right, here are the rules," he shouted, "In case you've not seen my performance before. First, I will give you clues to the time period I will be traveling. Then I will give you the category of objects I will be bringing back. Then I will teleport, get the object, and then you will guess what I brought back. If you guess correctly, the object will be your prize." He looked around, "Is that clear?" Affirming shouts came from the crowd. "Now, no using psychic perception!" He pretended to look hard at them.

"All right, here's the first clue," and he gestured a crown on his head, pretended to sit in an austere regal fashion, looking haughtily at them.

"Old Earth Elizabethan period," someone shouted.

"Got it!" he shouted back. "All right. Now, the category." He pretended to cut something, then moved around as if reaching for something, then he was stirring.

"Cooking utensils," came a new shout.

"Correct! Now I'll be gone for just a minute. When I'm back, you get to guess what I've brought back. All right?" He paused. Then vanished.

Excited chatter broke all around.

"He must be an excellent teleporter to be doing this trick," said Ariel.

"For a fact," said Max.

"Wonder what he'll bring back," said Miranda.

After a while, he was back, holding something behind his back. "What did I bring?" he asked, a big smile on his face. "No using psychic perception!"

"A knife," someone shouted.

"A spoon," someone else called out. And so it went until someone from the back yelled, "Wooden bowl."

"That is correct!" said the performer. "Come on up and claim your prize."

"That was fun," said Sean, "Not all that difficult to guess, I suppose."

"It's getting the time period right that's hard, I think," said Miranda, "Though this particular round it wasn't that difficult."

"I think he has to make it fairly easy otherwise it would be nearly impossible to guess, given the options," said Max.

They continued their leisurely stroll down the path, enjoying a variety of music and chatting. A silent open-air passenger vehicle drifted by, issuing merry laughter.

"What about this place?" said Anne.

They turned to look.

Heart's Desires, said the sign in big pink letters. Two large holograms in the shape of hearts stood on each side of a brightly illuminated door.

"I can go for some fulfillment of my heart's desires," said Max and headed for the door. They all followed.

"Wonder what they mean by that name," said Miranda, sounding a little suspicious.

Like the pub, Heart's Desires was crowded and noisy with conversation and music. Holograms of pink and red hearts were everywhere. Tables were in the shape of hearts. The restaurant itself was in the form of pink heart chambers.

They ended up at a large heart-shaped table.

"I think they overdid the heart thing," said Max.

"A little," said Ariel.

"I feel like I'm in some bizarre world," said Miranda.

"Yes, well, it is the Artists Enclave," said Sean. "I hope the food is good."

Anne gave him a look, her lips compressed.

After a while a young man appeared wearing a tight green jacket with an enormous green plume for a collar. He carried a stack of thin boards. His shoulders were pushed way back, and he held his head high and straight.

"Good evening, good evening," he shouted. "You've not been here before?" He looked around at them, and they shook their heads.

"You will have an experience you will not forget," he smiled. "What does your heart desire today?" he looked at them. "Here is the list of ingredients," and he handed out the boards. "Choose the ingredients and we will create something unique for you, something you've never had before." He straightened himself out, standing taller, his green jacket tightening across his chest. "One you're unlikely to ever eat again." He smiled a smug smile. "So, pick the ingredients, and we'll do the creating."

They nodded, and he continued, "The drinks, unless you have a strong preference, will be a surprise, made especially to match the dish the chef will create." He looked around, and when no one said anything, he added, "Very good. I'll be back shortly," turned on his heel and took off.

"An officious sort of fellow," said Anne.

"Really, they should have named the restaurant, Stomach's Desires," said Max. "My heart wants something different from what's on this list here."

"Such as?" asked Anne, and everyone looked at Max.

Max mumbled something and pretended to look hard at the ingredient list.

No one pressed him to answer.

"Look," said Miranda.

They looked at her, then looked where she was looking. A holo projection of a fairy was floating toward them.

"How very beautiful," said Ariel.

The fairy glistened and sparkled in a long pink and yellow

gown, her blond hair coming down in waves to her waist. She held a long wand embedded with jewels. She was smiling the most beatific smile.

"Hello, my friends," she said in a soft melodious voice she somehow managed to project above the clamor. "I am Gwendolyn, your fairy godmother. I am here to fulfill your heart's desires."

They stared in disbelief. Ariel looked at Max, who was looking at her. His brows went up.

"I will hear your heart's desires and, in time, you can expect them to be fulfilled." She smiled the most beautiful smile. "Is that all right with you?"

There was silence for a second, then they all shouted their agreement.

"A psychic transmission, if you please," she said and turned to Miranda.

One by one, they transmitted their desires to the fairy. She closed her eyes and after each transmission nodded and waved her magic wand, which emanated brilliant sparkles with each wave.

Ariel thought about her heart's desires. Easy. She just wanted successful completion of the Argos experiment.

"My dears, blessings upon you," said Gwendolyn, "Keep in your heart your beautiful desires. Watch for their fulfillment." She smiled that angelic smile, slowly turned and drifted away.

They were all silent, looking at each other.

"I guess that's the reason for the name of the restaurant, not the food," said Max.

"How absolutely amazing," said Anne.

Miranda and Sean were looking at each other.

"What a beautiful fairy with beautiful work," said Ariel.

"She must be working out of a studio nearby," said Max.

"That was wonderful," said Miranda and bent her head to look at the ingredient list.

They debated, discussed and argued over the virtues of having certain ingredients come together. Ariel, having experimented with spices, declared herself the spice expert, though no one took that very seriously. Max declared himself the meat expert, having a propensity for very early human history, and no one took that seriously either. In the end, they all conceded that Miranda was to have the final say in the matter because it was her birthday. That decision included some form of synthesized meat that promised to be better than any real meat, orange rind and lemon grass. Ariel made Miranda quit at these ingredients, saying that too many ingredients would simply cover up each other and make it taste like nothing. And besides, the chef would throw in other things if he decided it would help with the taste.

"Wonder if our heart's desires will really be fulfilled," said Anne. She was looking at Max.

"No doubt the fulfillment will follow its usual path of manifestation," said Sean, "But having her show up like this sure makes a difference."

"What a lovely lady with a lovely idea. I'm glad we came here," said Miranda. She was looking at them, smiling. "And on my birthday!"

"Very fitting," said Max.

Their drinks arrived, a feast in color and form, and they sat back and listened to the four musicians crowded on the small heart-shaped stage.

"So, when will we be able to vacation on Laurus?" Anne asked and took a sip of her blue drink.

Once the world they built was established, they could vacation there. Resorts were built in a way unnoticeable to the natives, but provided unique experiences for the visitors.

"Not for some time," said Ariel and took a sip of her own drink. It tasted fruity with a touch of a liqueur she couldn't identify. She liked it. "We're still in the phase where we're stabilizing the world."

"Won't it be fun," continued Anne, "To travel to a world of color?"

"I think so," said Ariel. She turned to look at the musicians. They were dressed in frilly red outfits, playing a cheerful tune.

"I'd love to travel to a world that is all light," said Anne, her voice dreamy. She had snuggled up next to Max, who didn't appear to mind. He was drinking his drink, watching the musicians, with a smile on his face. Ariel thought, he's as relieved to be away from the ship and away from the projects as I am. Only too soon we'll be back hustling to get things completed in time. Richard's serious face appeared, and she pushed him aside, a ripple of sadness moving through her.

When the food arrived, it came on a massive platter that was hoisted a foot above the table. It was a grand affair simply serving it onto their individual plates.

"He was right," said Max, "We will not have anything like this again. Absolutely divine!" Everyone agreed. The spices were perfectly balanced, the orange rind making a discrete but undeniable presence. They moaned and groaned and, after the plates were gone, sat and ate small fruit desserts sprayed with liqueur and dashed with chocolate rinds.

Sean and Miranda were enjoying a languorous kiss, and Anne looked hopefully at Max, who was too preoccupied with his fantasies, probably a new world, to even notice. Well, if Max ever had a mate, she'd really have to be special. Poor Anne. Tonight would not be her night for romance. But soon enough, she did get Max's attention, and he put his arm around her, and they seemed to be having a nice chat.

When they came out into the chilly night air, it was late. They sorted out their various modes of transport and headed home.

Chapter Twenty-Seven

It was dark in the barn. Ariel just barely made out Richard. He was standing next to Mistre, lifting the saddle, then stopped, still holding the saddle, turned in her direction and she materialized. His eyes darted, looking for people. Mistre whinnied and shook her head. Richard turned and put the saddle back on Mistre.

Ariel sensed alarm, then images came from him: meet down the road away from the house. She dematerialized, teleported to the location and found herself standing in a clearing in a forest. A thin pale light from the moon illuminated a narrow path. She shivered, pulled her cloak tight around her and waited for Richard, inhaling the raw smell of the earth. It was still except for the occasional rustle of dried leaves.

It seemed she'd waited a long time before she heard hoofbeats. She saw him move through shadow and light and come beside her. He extended his hand, heaved her up behind him and they were riding away at a trot from the house, the mare's hoofs pounding into the darkness.

The cold air burned her face, but she welcomed it after the agonizing struggle with herself before she finally broke and came to see him. The cover of the night was right for all she felt and all they were doing.

The hoofbeats slowed down, and Richard twisted around and glanced at her, "I would have come to you first if I could have."

She tightened her arms around him.

"It seems our fates are somehow intertwined. And we can't go against it," he said.

Ariel tightened her grip around him in response.

They were deep in the forest now. They steadily moved through dark shapes of trees down some path both Richard and Mistre knew. Occasionally the squeal of a bat erupted. Ariel shivered.

"It goes against all our New Earth laws for me to come and see you. Yet, I have to see you. Resisting seems impossible."

"And I am tethered to someone I can't even go see if I wanted to." She felt him exhale. "We're in quite a predicament."

Ariel felt all dark inside, all tangles. "Yes. An impossible situation."

Richard halted Mistre. "Let's walk."

He helped her down then dismounted himself.

"This way," pointed Richard, and took her hand.

In the thicket beside the road, a narrow path appeared. They threaded through the trees to a small clearing with a scattering of large boulders and a fallen tree.

Richard tied Mistre, and they sat next to each other on the tree trunk. Long black shadows fell around them. Richard's face appeared as if he had come from another world himself.

He looked around, looked at her, as if to say something, but it seemed hard for him, then it came out, "I apologize. I am sorry I pushed you away. That was cruel," he paused, "I thought I'd spare us both pain. It was the wrong way to think about all this. I gave in to my feelings forgetting the larger truth."

Ariel took his hand. "I know. I tried to stay away—"

"If I could have, I would have come to you first and apologized."

Ariel squeezed his hand.

They sat in silence for a while.

Ariel sighed. Her shoulders drooping in resignation, "I am breaking every New Earth law there is, being here with you like this, building the Argos prototype—"

"Argos?"

"The world I'm building because I have no choice."

Richard tilted his head, "You're building a world?"

"Yes."

She waited for Richard to take that in.

After a while he asked, "How?"

"I know, hard to believe sitting here right now, but humans have evolved to where they have become creators of worlds." She went on to explain how all of earth took part in this process.

He was silent for a while, taking this in.

"What is your work in this?"

Richard's face was in dark shadows, but his eyes glistened now and then as he moved his head.

"I am a New Worlds Designer. I design worlds."

"You dream it up?"

"Yes."

He looked away for a while, then turned back to her, "Like those other worlds I saw when I was away from my body."

"Yes," Ariel smiled. "And I've gotten myself into trouble."

Richard waited.

"This world I designed, Argos, they found flaws and it will not be built. But here is the problem. Deep within I know it must be built."

Richard was quiet, paying full attention, his eyes wide.

"So I'm building a small model. Which is not allowed," she shook her head, "That's what I mean. I'm in trouble in both worlds. Breaking every law and rule."

Richard exhaled a big loud breath, put his arm around her and pulled her to him, "You do know how to stir things up, don't you?" He tried to laugh, but didn't get far.

Ariel nestled into him. It felt good to tell him all this, felt good to have at least one person know all the truth about her and her life.

A small breeze rustled leaves. An owl hooted.

"Has this ever happened before?"

"Proposed worlds have been rejected, and legitimately so. But no one tried to build a prototype." Ariel sighed, "And certainly there was no one that revealed herself in another time," she paused, "On the other hand few people travel in time..."

"And you're doing both." Richard stroked his chin. "Hmm. Something's definitely brewing in your world."

Ariel pulled back to look at him. "Brewing? What do you mean?"

"With that many unusual things happening, well, it usually means a big change is coming."

Ariel thought about it. "I suppose it's possible."

"For certain. These things don't just happen for no reason."

"I've not thought about the whole situation that way."

He was looking at her, waiting for her to continue.

"In the Old Earth, change only came after great discontent and violent upheaval. In the New Earth, we've learned to consciously evolve. In constructive directions. We've been stable since the Reconstruction."

Richard kept looking at her.

"Reconstruction?"

"Yes. That's when we had a big change on Earth. In any case, if you're right, it would be the first major shakeup in our world." Ariel could hardly breathe at the thought of it.

Richard nodded.

"If you're right, it could mean there is a whole new level of evolution that's about to happen..." Ariel's voice trailed off. "No one thinks there could be a major shift in our world. A whole new level of evolution. A whole new kind of evolution." Ariel felt her brain shatter into a million pieces. All she'd known was stability. She couldn't even imagine a new direction of evolution for the New Earth. She shivered.

A small breeze swirled dried leaves breaking into the silence. Ariel shifted on the tree trunk, unsettled. The cold night air felt good on her hot face. Her mind was in shambles. As Creators they were supposed to be in tune with the creating process, learn and unfold. The Elders tracked that. The painful, violent growth and evolution of Old Earth humans had not been their experience. They believed it never would be again. Were they wrong?

She breathed in cool long breaths.

Richard caressed her hand, "A lot to consider."

Ariel nodded, took a breath and looked up. The tiniest crescent of a moon rested in a dark sky. The owl hooted again into the night.

After a long while Richard said, "I wanted you to come back, wanted to see you, talk to you."

Ariel turned to look at him. "I tried to follow your orders."

"Didn't want us to get hurt," he shook his head.

"We're learning." She slid her arm around his waist, felt the solidity of him.

She listened to his breathing.

Then they were breathing in rhythm.

After a while, it was just one breath. No body. No boundaries. Just space expanding into infinity.

A breeze picked up dried leaves and swirled them in frantic possession. Squeaks burst into the night.

Ariel opened her eyes, tried to focus.

Silence again, as the leaves settled back on the ground.

Richard stirred, turned toward her.

His eyes glistened. He reached up and touched her face.

Ariel breathed full easy breaths.

The night was deep. The air colder now.

An owl hooted.

Richard stood up and pulled her by the hand. "Let's go to the hut. I've brought food."

Chapter Twenty-Eight

Richard built a fire. It crackled, hissed and finally settled into a steady dancing flame. They sat on stools and watched. The hut began to warm up. Ariel relaxed. It felt good to have told Richard about Argos.

Richard smiled a crooked smile. "You know, I've never told you how beautiful you are." He tilted his head, his eyes soft, "You are beautiful."

Ariel stopped breathing for a second then smiled. He'd taken her by surprise.

He put his hand on her knee, "Are you hungry? I've brought some bread and cheese. Was going to eat when you appeared."

"Yes, I am. Love your bread and cheese."

Richard brought everything to the fire, and they ate.

"A time when humans will be creators of worlds," said Richard, his voice filled with wonder. "And here now we have every struggle, endless wars, even the church is fighting battles with its Crusades." He shook his head.

"Yes, hard life here. And more horrible times came before everything settled down and we began to build a peaceful world a long way into the future."

Richard tossed a stick into the fire and stood up. He walked behind Ariel and stopped.

Then Ariel felt him touch her hair.

"Your ornament. You wore it before." Her hair clip. "It's very pretty."

She heard it click open, and her hair came tumbling down.

"Pure gold," he said. He ran his fingers through her hair, "Silken gold."

Ariel's eyes widened with surprise, then she relaxed, mesmerized by the gentle touch.

He was quiet for a while, and Ariel turned to look at him. He was holding the hair clip, his brows gathered, "Just like before, it reminds me of something, but I don't remember what."

"My sister, Miranda, made it for me for my birthday."

"Your sister?"

"Yes. She lives on Earth and makes jewelry."

"Lovely," said Richard and handed her the clip.

He walked away and came back with two goblets, handed her one, "Sweet wine."

Ariel took a sip, "Thank you, delicious."

Ariel looked at the crimson wine. Should she tell him everything? Finish the whole story. It would feel so good. She took quick glances at Richard until he finally asked, "What is it?"

Ariel took a big breath and blew it out loudly through her mouth. "There is more. There is more to the story, Richard."

He nodded, "All right. Tell me."

"We've built quite a few worlds since we've become Creators."

"Creators," repeated Richard and looked off to the side, considering this, then nodded. "Incredible for humans to have developed in that way."

"Yes. It took a long time for us to develop all the abilities necessary to build worlds. Anyway, the overall energy in a system needs to remain in balance. By building worlds, we've generated tremendous energy. Because of that, we have to move Earth to a new dimension, and also because we don't want to become known as the Creators."

"What?! Move Earth, but how?" Richard's voice got louder.

"I know this is a lot, but we have a lot of power." Then she explained the Gateway.

"My parents, Vivian and Andreas, were Gateway researchers. They went missing, well some part of them, but not their body, on that last mission which seemed promising."

Richard looked at her, his mouth open, "Your parents."

"Yes. They're at a healing center," Ariel exhaled.

Richard put his hand on her knee. "Must be difficult. But you say they may have found the Gateway so you could move Earth?" Richard picked up a stick and poked the fire, all agitated. "This is unbelievable."

"I know," Ariel said again, "And I've been looking for my parents..."

Richard took her hand.

Ariel felt sad, sad that they as a people hadn't succeeded in finding the Gateway, sad she'd made no headway. She felt crushed. "Everything's a big mess."

Richard blew out a long breath, "Yes, I see. And us here." He shook his head, turned toward the fire and was silent.

Ariel shifted on the stool. Now that she was telling Richard, all the feelings came to the surface in full force. The urge to build, the defiance of the system, the potential consequences. And most of all, the urgency to be here with Richard.

"Yes, all a big inexplicable mess," she mumbled, "It feels good to say it all."

"Yes, I see," said Richard.

They watched the flames dance, finding a little peace after the harrowing conversation and time apart.

"And you don't know what will happen with your Argos model?"

Ariel shook her head. "No. I've just had this push to build. I'm doing it. It's supposed to yield some answers, but I don't know what will happen. My friend Max is helping, so he will have ideas."

"Your friend Max?"

"Yes, a colleague, another New Worlds Designer."

Richard nodded.

After a while she turned to him, "What's it like being a physician?"

He picked up a twig and slowly broke one little piece after another, throwing each piece into the fire. "All right. But after what I've seen, I know there are better ways to heal." He leaned forward and stirred the fire. The hut filled with light. "It's what I'm working on."

Ariel remembered the pile of books on the table in his bedchamber.

"Trying to make it all add up. What I've seen when I had my accident and all this," he motioned with his hand, "Around me. This world." He glanced at her. "I suppose you don't even have disease where you come from."

"No. Not really, nothing like here."

He was quiet, waiting for her to continue.

Vivian and Andreas came to mind. "There are still things for which we have no answers. Not yet, anyway."

Richard nodded.

It was warm in the hut. Except for the crackle of the fire, it was quiet. Absolute stillness of night.

Richard turned, looked into her eyes, reached out and put his hand behind her head, leaned over, and Ariel felt the soft warmth of his lips.

Chapter Twenty-Nine

Ariel brushed her arm across her forehead, wiping sweat, then stood on guard waiting for the next signal. She was working out at the Platt, Palladium's workout sphere, designed to work out all aspects of the human being, physical, mental, emotional and psychic by sending signals to which the trainee responded.

A tremendous force pushed Ariel down. She pushed up with all her might and threw off the packet of energy. No sooner was she on her feet when she sensed something behind her. What? What? She made an accurate identification of a life form, and it vanished. She took a big breath, at the ready for the next signal.

Something grabbed her from behind, she threw it over her head and was at the ready again. Then blackness. Silence. Nothing. Then an explosion of signals. Ariel worked furiously to discern the critical one. An energy beam heading her way unfolding into an image of a large animal. She checked her fear, and it vanished.

She glanced at the monitor. The sequence beeped three times and went into a pause.

She stopped, hands on hips, breathing hard. Her short yellow unitard drenched. She reached behind her for the towel tucked in her belt, wiped her face and watched the monitor.

Suddenly she was flat on her back. She'd missed the signal. She was gasping, couldn't move, was about to scream, then focused, identified the fine net of energies holding her down and was free. She jumped up and was at the ready again.

Lights flashed orange, green. The cycle swooshed to a halt, and immediately she heard the intercom beep.

She stepped off the platform, wiped her face, and took big breaths.

At the intercom, Miranda's face appeared. "You working out?"

"Just finished," gasped Ariel. "How's it going at the ranch?"

"Had a good workout?" Miranda smiled. Her blond curls shiny in the sunlight.

"Yes. Had to take a sweat break after all the work." Ariel focused. "Mom's not doing well this time?"

"Neither is doing well. Mom especially." Miranda frowned.

Ariel's heart sank. "What's happened?"

"Same as before with Dad. Weakening for no obvious reasons." She pushed aside a strand of hair. "I just came in from riding and found the message from Melrose." Her eyes glistened. "I am sorry. I don't know what to do." Her voice had a mild squeal of exasperation.

"What did Melrose say?"

Miranda shook her head, "As before, they could not explain it. What do you think we should do?"

"Let me clean up and I'll call you back," said Ariel.

"I'll be here," said Miranda and did a little twirl with her fingers.

Arie ran the towel over her face and neck. Years relatively stable, then problems. Why these vacillations? Why now?

In her quarters, she washed up quickly and called Miranda back.

"What do you think is going on?" said Miranda.

Ariel shook her head, shrugged her shoulders.

"Why suddenly these vacillations? And not before," said Miranda.

"Was wondering the same thing," said Ariel.

"Maybe they'll improve soon, like the last time with Dad." She waited for Ariel to agree.

Ariel nodded. "Let' hope," she mumbled. She had no answers. Just frustration. These days everything around her was a mystery, an unknown.

"I hope we don't lose them," said Miranda, biting her lower lip.

They were silent for a while. To lose both of their parents. Ariel felt something in her drop to the bottom of some horrible deep dark pit. That just can't happen. She'll try again, a gateway run.

"Let's not think that way, Miranda. It's just a little setback, I'd say."

Miranda nodded.

Ariel changed the subject. "How are things with Sean?"

"He is at my place a lot. I've been teaching him to ride." She laughed, "Can you believe he's actually never ridden?"

"Does he like it?"

"Yes, and you know," she paused, "He's quite good."

"Wonderful. You can go riding together," said Ariel.

"I'm not sure about that opal idea of his, though," Miranda's face tightened. "Actually, to be honest, he has all kinds of strange ideas."

"What kind of strange ideas?"

"He has ideas about jewelry and everything else, but I already know what I'm doing." She paused. "I don't know why it interests him so much."

"He's interested in you, that's why," said Ariel, "Isn't that obvious?"

"Hmm."

"Why don't you just have fun with his ideas?"

"I don't know. I guess I like things the way they are."

Why didn't that surprise her? She sensed into Miranda. Her shields were up. Now what is she trying to hide? Ever since Sean entered Miranda's life, she'd become unpredictable and secretive. She hoped Miranda didn't get hurt in some way.

"Explore a little, Miranda. Have some fun." She couldn't keep the slight impatience out of her voice.

Miranda looked at her, her lips compressed, but said nothing.

She'd learn whatever she needed to learn. She decided not to worry about Miranda and let her figure it out on her own.

"What do you think we should do?" said Miranda.

Ariel was quiet for a moment. "Let's give it some time. I think it will be all right."

"I want to believe that," said Miranda, a small smile on her face. "I'll go see them." She waved and was gone.

Ariel swiveled to look at the time. She needed to get on with work, but she'll try another gateway run first. Maybe she could find something, anything that would help. The thought of losing Mom and Dad was unbearable.

She took a big breath, closed her eyes. Richard came to mind. She'd seen him several times since he kissed her. It was good to have someone to talk to about everything, at least one friend in whom she could confide.

She'd let her heart love him and all the days were better because of it, the edge of constant anxiety softened. She felt new strength. So much to do, but a little easier now. Unless she started thinking. She exhaled. She tried not to think.

Got to get moving. She pushed out of the chair, picked up the console and headed for the studio. Maybe afterwards...

Chapter Thirty

Richard stood at the far end of his bedchamber, farthest from the door, his hands on his hips. He watched her materialize, shook his head, walked up to her and put his arms around her. "I like the way you travel."

Ariel melted into his embrace. "No one around?" she whispered.

"No one around. You can relax." He looked her up and down, "Wearing the local garb, are you?"

"Wasn't sure where I'd find you, and this is safer."

A dull afternoon light seeped through the windows, painting gray shadows. It was chilly and damp in the bedchamber. The fire in the hearth burned down low.

"Come sit," said Richard, and led her to the chair by the hearth. "I'll get the fire going."

Flames burst forth. Richard looked at it for a while, then came and sat opposite her.

"Just found out my parents are not doing so well. Again. I did another search for them with same results. Nothing."

Richard leaned toward her. "Difficult to see your parents like that."

Ariel nodded, felt it in her throat, the impulse to cry.

Richard put a hand on her shoulder briefly.

"We seem to be getting nowhere with that," said Ariel, "But at least Max and I are making progress on the Argos model." She looked at Richard. Her heart felt warm.

He sat thinking, chin in hand finger on lips, then announced, "Time to forget your troubles!"

He leaped up, pulled her out of the chair, and planted little kisses on her hair, cheeks, then stopped, took her face in his hands, looked deeply into her eyes and placed his lips on hers.

Ariel opened up to the softness.

Then he moved to the wimple, tugged lightly with his teeth, and Ariel pulled it off. And he planted small kisses on her neck. Then his hands moved to the back under her veil and into her hair and the veil came off. His eyes were open as his lips softly caressed hers. He looked at her a steady even calm look of certainty and knowing. Then she was lifted and carried and they sank into softness of pillows and blankets, tugging at each other's clothes until there was nothing but skin between them.

He wrapped his arms tight around her and rolled them until he was on top. "I love you so much." His eyes blazed a fiery blue. "The infinity of your being." His lips were on hers again.

Ariel moaned. Then there was only light, boundless space and ecstasy.

Then Ariel saw it. First it flashed by so fast she barely noticed it. Then it happened again, the image of a hot dusty street in brilliant sunshine.

Gently, she pulled back from Richard.

"What?" he said.

"Did you see that?"

"Images of a crowded street?"

"Yes!"

"What is it?"

"Don't know, but let's see if we can see more."

They lay quietly.

"Camels!" said Richard.

"Geometric mud houses. Palm trees. Where is this?"

"Somewhere very hot."

"What language is that?" Ariel said. "I can almost understand it."

"Yes. Strange."

They were silent, absorbed in the vision.

Ariel watched the street milling with people. The sun was brilliant. The street dry and dusty. Low cream mud houses lined each side. Dark-skinned people. Women in sheath dresses. Men in short skirts.

"Wonder if we're creating this or if we've activated a memory," she said.

Richard said nothing for a while then, "Feels familiar."

Ariel looked at the street, then worked on changing her perspective. Slowly she lifted above the street. It was a city. Crammed houses. Narrow winding streets. She lifted higher, looked around. Soft dry tan hills shimmered under a blazing sun. "Pyramids!" she gasped. "Richard, do you see the pyramids?"

"What?"

"Change your perspective. Pull up higher, above the houses. You'll see the pyramids."

"Incredible," whispered Richard.

She let out a breath. "Old Earth Egypt! The Nile."

"It's so hot and dry here."

Ariel felt Richard move beside her.

"I remember this place!" he said.

"What?"

"I remember it."

Ariel was back at street level. Children stood in a circle singing, playing a game. Ariel looked closer. They were playing a board game. Then they started running, pointing up the street, their voices rising in excitement.

Ariel looked in the direction they were running. A procession was approaching.

"Do you see that?" She tuned into Richard's perspective. "Down by the street."

She felt Richard scanning. "Yes. They're carrying an official."

Eight men carried a large covered litter. It was elaborately decorated. Two people sat inside.

Ariel focused. A man and a woman wearing crowns. The woman's face was placid except for the tiniest hint of a smile. A contented smile, noted Ariel. The man's face was serious, as if he had a lot on his mind. They were holding hands, their fingers intertwined. A large blue topaz ring was on her middle finger.

The woman turned to the man and smiled a smile of incredible radiance. His face softened.

People scrambled out of the way to let them pass and stopped to look. Others called out to them. Then the litter was out of view.

Ariel opened her eyes and looked at Richard.

His eyes were wide open. "The ring. Her ring. It's the same as what was in your hair."

Ariel watched Richard, hardly breathing.

Outside chickens cackled. The light had dimmed with the passing of the day.

Ariel felt back into the scene. For sure the man and the woman were familiar.

Then Richard said it, "They seem so…" He was looking for the right words.

"Like we know them," finished Ariel.

"Yes. But how could that be?"

They each considered this.

"What was it we saw? A vision? What?" He scratched his head.

"I don't know. Maybe. But no. Don't think it was a vision."

"No?"

"Because of the way it came to us," and she smiled, feeling shy.

He pulled her closer to him and kissed her on the forehead.

"I think we were there," said Ariel.

He looked at her, his eyes questioning.

"We could easily have time traveled spontaneously. Not with our physical bodies, of course… spontaneously broken through time."

"Hmm."

"It's normal. Happens often. Spontaneous travel to another time or place," she said.

"Yes. I've not thought about it, but I think you're right." He considered for a moment. "Yes, I've had similar experiences. Thought nothing of them."

"I think that's how it happens with most people. We spontaneously travel to other times and places in our current life, and we also travel to times and places in our other lives. Most people just don't notice, or don't pay it any attention."

Outside, the horses nickered. Bennet barked.

"Do you think that was us? We stumbled on us?!" said Richard his voice incredulous.

"Could be." Ariel shivered. They had been lying in a trance for a long time, and she now noticed she was freezing. She sat up, "Let's get some logs into the fire. It's cold in here." The day had moved on. The bedchamber was in near darkness.

Richard pushed back the covers and stumbled to the hearth. "I'll have it going in no time."

He poked embers, and the room lit up. Then he piled several small logs, waited, then placed a large one on the top.

He came back to bed and crawled under the covers and took Ariel in his arms.

Ariel shivered. "Oh, cold."

He stroked her hair, kissed her cheek. "Let's tune in again and see what else we can find out."

They became still and were back on the hot, crowded street.

After considerable scanning and tuning in, it looked as if the man and the woman were rulers of a small province, both trained at the mystery school. Masters of their craft.

"How do we find out...? he said but didn't finish.

Going deeper and expanding, they each sensed it.

"They're us!" said Ariel. "I feel it. Her energy is me." She felt this like a distant memory, as if the woman was someone she knew but could barely remember. Yet she felt the woman close to her, overlapping her own being.

She exhaled, a smile on her face. "And it's you, the essence of you is the same." She felt her heart beating faster.

The quality of Richard was the same quality she saw in this man. She recognized him. And other memories were stirring, rising to the surface. Formidable will, determination, sheer amazing power. Ariel was in awe.

"That would explain a few things," Richard laughed.

They were quiet for a long time, absorbing the implications.

Ariel looked around. The room was dark except for the fire. It was getting warmer.

Then Richard leaped out of bed, "Time for some food. I'm hungry."

He dressed, then placed a small table in front of the hearth and two chairs on either side, left the room and was promptly back with a tray—a loaf of bread, a wedge of cheese, a big slice of smoked fish, and a small bowl of dates and nuts. Two cups filled with mead.

Ariel had dressed and sat by the fire. "Wonderful. I'm so hungry."

She tore a chunk of bread, chewed, then took a sip of mead. "I love mead." She leaned forward and put a hand on Richard's arm, "Thank you."

Richard looked at the window, "It seemed like no time passed, but it's evening already." He sliced large pieces of cheese and handed one to Ariel.

"Time travel does that. Can create some confusion," said Ariel.

For a moment outside there was the sound of bleating sheep, then a bark. Then distant thunder.

Ariel looked up, "Rain coming."

Richard nodded, "It's probably why you were in my dreams." He spoke with a piece of bread he'd just placed in his mouth. He swallowed. "And why you looked familiar when I saw you at the market."

"And probably why you could see me when I first came." Ariel looked at the fire dancing on the wooden panels. It was mesmerizing.

"Yes, the mystery school." Richard stopped chewing. "I wonder how much I can remember."

"Probably everything." Ariel was excited.

Ariel looked at Richard and allowed herself to feel the familiarity she'd always felt, but always resisted. She let that knowledge spread through her body.

"The mystery school." Richard lifted the cup to his lips and took a sip. "If I could remember everything I'd learned there..." He brought the cup down. With his other hand, he rubbed his chin.

"Certainly had to be masters of leaving the body," Ariel said. That was one of the main teachings at the school, if she remembered correctly. She'd need to do some research. And remember herself.

Richard nodded. "That would explain those other things I was telling you about before."

He stood up and stirred the fire. It crackled loudly, illuminating the wool tapestries of hunting scenes on the wall.

For a long while they sat quietly sipping their drinks.

Then Ariel thought about needing to get back, and Richard heard the thought.

"You need to get back?" He looked at her and kept looking at her.

Ariel tilted her head puzzled, "What?"

"Teach me to teleport." His face was solid determination. "I should be able to come to you like you come to me. Don't you think?" His eyes challenged her. A small smile showed mischief.

It began to rain, a soft pitter-patter on the roof.

Ariel froze. "What?" She put the cup down and stared at Richard, then slowly around the room. Brown leather books piled high on the table by the window. Crumpled bedding. Leaping flames in the hearth. Then back at him, "I guess it makes sense," she paused, "In some strange way."

She heard him exhale.

He stood up, walked to stand behind her. He ran his fingers through her hair. Then he bent down and kissed her neck, "Don't be afraid."

Ariel felt so light she wondered if her body might disappear.

The rain beat harder on the roof, a gale bashed swaths of rain against the windows, drowning out the silence.

Chapter Thirty-One

riel studied the flashing Laurus statistics on the big screen, her lips tight with concentration. Sounds of violins, flute and harp filled the studio. The crystal transducer flashed and hummed.

She leaned forward, inspected the energy output of Laurus and nodded satisfied. She yawned, leaned back, raised her arms and stretched. Good work. Then felt a tug and sat up straight, alert. It was Max. "Meet. Now!" he transmitted.

Ariel swiveled away from the workstation, hands on thighs. Had to be Argos. "Be right there." She shut down the screens, picked up her console and hurried to Max's studio.

The hallways glowed yellow. She breathed deeply and took in their healing energies. Whatever the problem, and obviously it had to be a problem, she hoped it had an easy solution. She walked faster.

The second the door closed behind her, Max announced, "We've got a problem," his psychic shields firmly in place. He wore his usual white robes and was running his fingers through his hair, looking more disheveled than usual.

"What kind of problem?" Ariel placed her console on the table.

"Come, look." He whipped around and headed for the Argos dome.

Ariel followed, pushing aside strings hanging from the ceiling and with her foot pushing aside what looked like packaging material.

Max pointed to the data screen next to the dome, "We need Bronelven."

"What?" Ariel bent forward and looked at the equation. "For what?"

"Enlivening."

She straightened up and looked at Max. This was a big problem. Bronelven was a rare mineral and difficult to obtain. They could make a lot of things, but not Bronelven. They had to mine for it.

"Can't be... how?" Ariel shook her head puzzled. "You're sure? How is that possible? It was not part of the design."

"Of course," Max waved his arm impatiently, "I've checked and rechecked." He exhaled, pushed his hair off his forehead, "Didn't think we'd run into anything this serious."

"Tried substitutes?"

"Of course." He didn't bother to explain further.

Ariel looked off into space searching for any explanation that might give them a way out. She became aware of the smell of alcohol and vaguely looked around for the source. Something gurgled and swished.

"I've been designing and redesigning, trying to do without it, and there just isn't any way, not the way you've designed the species with early sentience."

Ariel stepped around Max and headed for the table.

Max followed, "Plenty of it on Altima."

Ariel turned and glanced at Max, "Yes in another solar system with raging winds and sand and temperatures so cold..." She shivered just thinking about it.

She pulled out a chair and sat at the table. Max grabbed his console from the workstation and sat across from her. He looked down at the console. After a while he said, "Nope. No new Bronelven mines."

"What options do we have?" Ariel sat slumped in her chair. She felt incredibly tired.

Max drummed his fingers on the table for a while, then pushed his chair back and walked to the food dispenser. After a swoosh, the smell of coffee wafted through the studio. He stood with both hands around the cup, looking at Ariel, brows raised.

"Nothing thank you." She felt heavy like an enormous weight had suddenly been placed on her shoulders. "Well, our secret little team does not have earth miners specially equipped to send to Altima to excavate."

"Oh, that's too bad," Max made an exaggerated sad face.

"But seriously, teleporting is out of the question. Way too dangerous. Besides, what do we know about excavating Bronelven?" She blew out a loud breath.

Max strolled back to the table, sipping coffee. He swayed his head side to side, "Well—"

"What about Earth? Is there any way we can get it there, get what little we need?"

Max shook his head, "Not a chance. Security's too tight because of the volatility. The quantity of sensors around that room... no psychic shields could protect against them."

Ariel tapped her console with the stylus. "What can we do?" She wondered if there was a way for her to get to Altima to get what they needed.

Max read her thoughts, "You can't go! You have no mining experience and you don't know what you're looking for."

Ariel looked at him. "And of course, you have mining experience." She shook her head.

"I've worked with Bronelven."

She raised her brows, "And that makes you a mining expert? You're no more equipped than I am." She paused, "You have? You've worked with Bronelven before?" hope rising.

"Yes, a small experiment a while back."

There was a loud beep. Max put the coffee cup down and rushed to one of the machines, checked the screen, pressed buttons, then came back.

She sat straighter in her chair looking at Max, "How'd you get it?

"As usual. Signed out for it. Approved."

She sank back in the chair. "That doesn't help us."

"In any case, I know what I'm looking for." He twirled his cup. "I'll figure it out."

"No. It's too dangerous."

"But you were thinking of going yourself!"

"That's different. It's my project. And besides, I am a better teleporter than you."

"Oh, you think so?"

Ariel gave him a look and said nothing. She turned in her chair and straightened out her legs. What to do?

"We can't do the prototyping without Bronelven," said Max.

"There has to be a way."

Something splashed on the table. They both jumped. Ariel looked up. A vine of sorts hung from a pipe that was wet. She looked at Max. He shrugged.

"Let's think about it. We'll come up with something," he said.

"We don't have time," she muttered.

The equipment whirred and buzzed.

Max scratched his head, "We try Altima and don't come back, Argos doesn't happen. We don't try Altima, Argos doesn't happen. A fine predicament indeed."

Chapter Thirty-Two

Ariel found him in the kitchen talking to the cook. She hovered just long enough for him to notice her then vanished. Soon after, Richard left the house riding Mistre. She followed for quite a distance. When it seemed safe, she materialized.

"My beauty has arrived!" Richard called out cheerfully. He was wearing a black cloak, a linen shirt and black breeches.

He dismounted and wrapped his arms around her. "How's my Egyptian ruler?" He kissed her forehead.

"Oh, thinking about my provinces, naturally."

"Of course, of course," Richard laughed.

With his left arm still around Ariel, he turned slightly and pointed with the hand holding the reins, "A little further there is a large meadow with a lot of trees. We'll go there."

The hills danced in bright sunlight and autumn colors. Everything had dried out, and Ariel was glad they didn't have to trudge through mud and wet grass.

Richard looked her up and down, "You're wearing your work clothes."

"I was somewhat in a rush."

Richard kept looking at her.

At last she said, "Ran into a big problem."

They pushed their way up a small hill, then down to the

clearing.

Richard looked around and pointed, "Over there. The big oak."

He tied up Mistre, and they sat leaning on the old oak tree.

"Such a beautiful day," said Ariel. She breathed in the fresh sweet air, listened to the hum of insects. So peaceful.

"Yes," said Richard, and twisted to look at her, "What's happened?"

"We need this mineral, Bronelven, for prototyping. We can't do without it. But it's hard to get. Max wants to go mine for it, but it's very dangerous. I worry he'll go after it anyway. I tried reaching him earlier to discuss it again, but couldn't find him."

"You're worried he's gone after it?"

"Yes. And it's dangerous…"

"You're worried he might not come back…"

"Yes. That would be a disaster. Losing Max. Couldn't proceed with Argos without Max and Broneleven." Ariel felt thoroughly miserable.

Richard put his arm around her and was quiet for a while looking at the scraggly dry grass in front of him. Then squeezed her shoulder and said, "If he's gone for it, he'll be back," he paused, "I am certain. He has to. How could that impulse to build be so strong without the certainty of success?"

Ariel sighed, "I want to believe it will all work out."

She put her head on his shoulder. It all felt heavy and full of foreboding. "I wish I didn't need to do all this in secret. It's tormenting. And seeing you… everything's chaos, nothing makes sense."

"Yes. Difficult right now. Have to give it time. It will all come together."

A raven flew by squawking loudly. Ariel watched him land on

a branch, where he stood watching them.

"Yes. Of course, you're right." It was nice to be reassured, but the worry knot in her stomach remained.

She searched for something lighter to talk about and said, "My sister had a birthday party a while back."

"Yes?" Richard looked at her.

"Yes. She lives in the Horse and Buggy Enclave.

"Enclaves?"

"Oh, yes, enclaves. They were set up on the New Earth at the time of Reconstruction. It was a way to accommodate the many human interests and natures, a way to facilitate creativity and growth. Its main purpose was to sustain human expansion and evolution, to ensure we didn't repeat the past. Hence the Horse and Buggy Enclave, which Miranda loves."

"What's it like?"

"Horses and buggies," laughed Ariel. "It has basic technology, but no advanced technology. It's very quiet, slow and peaceful."

"Technology?"

"I, yes. You call it mechanical arts. There have been many innovations," and she went on to explain.

"Fascinating. Many advancements. But this enclave is not too different from here, then."

"Right. But a lot more comfortable."

"What are some of the other enclaves?"

"There are all kinds—resorts, artists, engineers, agriculture. Lots of them. They're fun to visit."

"Where do you live? What kind of enclave?"

"It's a present-day enclave. No specialization. All present-day amenities."

"And you like it there?"

"Yes. It makes living easy."

Richard twisted a blade of grass. "So much freedom. So much is possible."

"Yes. It has to be. It's what we've learned from the big devastation of the Old Earth. It's where all the energies are now channeled, into creative expression and constructive action."

"Some time you'll have to tell me about what happened that the Earth was destroyed. If it's like it says in the Bible."

Ariel nodded, "It's not a pleasant story."

She inhaled the sweet scent of dried grass and enjoyed the warm laziness of the day. She noticed she had relaxed despite recent troubles, grateful to be away from Palladium and to have this small bit of rest with Richard.

"And how was the birthday celebration?"

"It was a very nice evening," and she told him about Sean. "Miranda is having a hard time adjusting. I think she's been alone too long, used to having things her own way. Not very flexible."

Richard nodded, "Hopefully with some time..."

Mistre nickered. They both turned to look. She thumped her hoof, her tail swishing away flies.

Richard pulled his legs up and put his elbows on his knees. "I've been remembering." He turned to look at her, a smile on his face. "The school in the temple. I'm remembering."

Ariel sat up straighter, "You have?" She looked into his eyes and saw the knowing.

"There is so much we knew back then. I remember being able to leave my body and travel wherever I wanted to go."

Ariel nodded, "And now we can take our bodies with us, if we choose."

"And do you know what else I remember? I remember healing

people just by touching them. No wonder I've been trying to heal my patients in a different way. I once knew a different way."

The sun was moving toward the horizon, shadows getting longer.

"Hmm," said Ariel. "Never thought about my other lives before. No need, I suppose. Now I am curious to remember what we have known."

"A whole new world." Richard's voice was low, thoughtful.

Ariel looked beyond the grassy field to where trees swayed in the breeze. If Richard remembered so much on his own, it would be easy to teach him what she knew.

Then she leaped up and ran, "Catch me if you can!"

She turned and took a quick look at Richard. His face crinkled in puzzlement, then a smile, then he leaped up and was running after her.

She zigzagged and evaded him, making sure she didn't enter hyperawareness and teleport out of his reach.

Finally he caught up with her and deftly pinned her to the ground. "You think you can escape me?" he laughed, pressed her harder to the ground and kissed her.

"The lessons are officially started: developing your psychic abilities. And we'll build from there."

"Ah. If this is the beginning, I can't wait for the rest!"

They sat up, breathing hard.

Ariel moved to sit directly in front of Richard.

"What am I thinking now?" Ariel said, laughing.

He was quiet, then laughed too.

"All right, let's synchronize our energies. See if you can locate the energy flow inside me."

Richard took both of her hands.

Ariel sat up straight, "As you do that, I'll track your energy."

It took a while, but she felt Richard's focus clearly on her. They were tied together through this attention.

"Good. See if you can even out your breathing."

Richard straightened up a little, and she sensed his breath moving throughout his entire body.

"All right, be ready to receive," and she slowly rode over his thoughts and introduced the New Earth language.

His eyes flashed open in surprise as he felt it.

She nodded, and he closed his eyes again. To all the subliminal thoughts that he had, Ariel added New Earth vocabulary. They continued in this way until Ariel sensed he had reached a saturation point. Then she stopped, opened her eyes and waited for Richard.

"I felt it going inside me, like water or food. Amazing." Richard shook his head, his face lighted up with surprise.

Ariel nodded, "It is amazing, isn't it? It's one way we learn a lot fast."

They held hands and looked into each other's eyes, felt the warmth and closeness and knowing.

After a while Ariel stood up and pulled Richard by the hand, "Let's walk."

A soft breeze rustled the dry grass.

"It changes the brain," said Ariel.

"Hmm." He was looking off in the distance.

A wave of fear swept through Ariel. What was she doing here teaching Richard this stuff? She turned to look at him. He was so beautiful. Her heart softened. She pushed the fear down. The decision was made. It was the right thing to do. Even if it looked all wrong, like everything else in her life right now.

"Ready? Let's try something else. I will think of an object and you guess what it is."

They stopped walking and stood under a tree facing each other. Ariel quieted her mind then sent images, strong ones so it was easy for Richard to see. She watched his face. It was still with concentration. She followed his energy as he tried different ways of focusing to locate her image. She was impressed with how swiftly he shifted. If one focus didn't work, his energy instantly changed as he tried another approach.

"The more you relax, the easier it will be," Ariel said, and Richard's shoulders let go and his concentration deepened.

Again it took him a while, but he started to receive the images she broadcasted. They continued with this exercise until Richard's accuracy became consistent.

"Enough!" said Richard and walked off energetically. "Makes my head hurt." He waved his hand to sweep away the whole exercise.

Ariel followed, enjoying the gentle warmth of the sun. He was a fabulous student.

"Do you remember the time we went hunting?" said Richard.

Ariel looked at him puzzled, "Hunting?"

He smiled, then opened up to her with images of the hunt.

"Oh," said Ariel.

They continued walking slowly, exploring this image more deeply. It was another memory from Old Earth Egypt, from when they first met and courted. One of the first things they did was go on a hunt together.

The memory was similar to this very moment. They were walking, holding hands, smiling at each other, savoring being alone, looking into each other's eyes as if nothing in the entire world was more fascinating. A tiny touch was enough to send endless ripples of bliss.

Ariel squeezed Richard's hand. In this moment they were themselves, Richard and Ariel, and they were also the selves they once were. Richard let go her hand and pulled her to him, holding her tight. "We're together again."

Between her skin and his skin Ariel felt no separation, just a vast oneness.

After a while Richard pulled back. "Soon I'll know your slightest thought." He raised his eyebrows in challenge.

"To be so known by someone I love..." Then she had an idea. "Let's play hide and seek!"

He raised his brows, "Really?"

"I'll teleport to a hiding place, and you use your psychic powers to find me."

"Easy! The easiest thing for me to do. Find my love."

"Let's go to where all the trees are," Ariel said and vanished.

She could feel Richard's energy searching for her. He was good. He was sending it out in the right way. It was just very weak and lacked focus. She focused her own energy, amplifying his, helping him find her.

After a while he walked around the tree where Ariel stood, laughed and wrapped his arms around her. "See! Easy."

They continued in this way until Richard called out, "Enough! My head is starting to hurt again." He pulled her to the nearest tree, and they sat down.

Ravens protested, loudly screaming their displeasure that they were sitting under their tree.

They quieted down after a while and Ariel said, "Let me see you psychically scan the area."

"Hmm," he considered. "All right. But this is the last exercise for today."

They shifted to face each other, and Richard focused, scanning her thoughts, scanning the area, alert for what was there.

Ariel monitored his process and assessed the way he was using his energy. "Now, turn your attention and look closely at where that power and energy is coming from?"

Richard nodded and focused.

Ariel tracked him, searching around trying to locate the power she was talking about, and when he hit upon it, Ariel called out, "That's it," and he stayed there feeling it for a second then lost it. It was hard for him to stay focused.

"It's that energy you need to amplify, focus it more sharply." She was going to say like a laser but then remembered he would not know what a laser was.

He nodded again and focused.

Ariel sensed him make a note of the energy and the feeling and the location.

"Good!" She was pleased.

"I want to teleport."

Ariel stopped.

"You take us. Just a short distance." He looked at her face and laughed. "Scared?!" and laughed again.

Ariel came out of her shock and shook her head, "Not scared," she stammered, "You just always amaze me."

"With an amazing woman I amaze myself!"

Ariel tried for a smile. She was afraid. Taken off guard. Suddenly confused about what she was doing, but nodded anyway, "All right."

She took his hands, "You don't need to do anything." She

focused carefully and leaped them a small distance from where they were standing.

Once they were solid, Richard said nothing for a while. His face was still with concentration. "It's like standing in a summer breeze, teleporting is. Like being blown by a gentle wind."

Then he put his arm around her, turned and they started walking. When he came to a tree, he sat down. "Come sit with me for a little longer before you go back." He opened his arms, and Ariel lowered herself into bliss.

Chapter Thirty-Three

She could not find Max. She had tuned in psychically and found no traces of him. He had his psychic shields up firmly.

She tightened her lips. More and more it looked as if he'd gone to Altima for Broneleven. Or maybe he was just involved in a project and had all communication shut down. She hoped that was it.

She stepped over to the garment dispenser and pressed buttons.

She had difficulty breathing. She put her hand on her chest. Just too many problems. She shook her head. What was she doing teaching Richard to teleport? She'd gone way beyond breaking New Earth laws and rules. She'd been living in a world of her own laws. She shook her head again. How could her life have become such a mess? The fear was back, gripping her with merciless steel fingers. The secrecy tormented her. The unknown felt like a big black hole into which she was falling deeper and deeper.

Her entire body was frozen with tension. She forced herself to take a slow deep breath. She had to regain composure, regain balance, regain trust, somehow believe again that all this led to something good.

The garment dispenser beeped, and a white oxygen suit emerged, then a blue backpack. She picked up the backpack and headed for the kitchen, ordered sandwiches and water and stuffed them in the backpack. She looked around, thinking. What else might she need? If she decided to stay on Xarinda a while, she would need an oxygen bubble.

She heaved the backpack and headed back to the sleeping quarters. She tapped buttons on the garment dispenser, and an orange oxygen bubble emerged. She took the sandwiches out, stuffed the oxygen bubble at the bottom of the pack, then placed the sandwiches on top. She inserted the water bottle into a separate compartment where she could hook it up to the suit.

An escape to Xarinda. She felt her spirits lift a bit.

She pushed her legs into the suit, then arms, fitted the headgear and set up the water dispenser. In one heave she had the pack on her back. She adjusted the straps and focused.

She landed in a darkling world of red dust and black rubble, a breathless gloomy emptiness. A big red valley spread before her. In the distance, black sharp cliffs jutted malevolently towards a mottled yellow sky. Just beautiful.

She turned in a circle looking for a place where she could start the climb.

Xarinda was a bleak barren world. It offered nothing to humans. Not minerals, not growing possibilities, not anything. It turned so slowly on its axis, the Xarinda sun came around to the same spot once every twelve Earth days. Ariel had carefully avoided both the illuminated side, which would have been too hot, and the dark side, which would have been too cold.

She found a face of a mountain where there were enough footholds low to the ground where she could start the climb. She reached around and checked her pack, making sure it was on securely. She adjusted the oxygen flow and started toward the cliffs. Red dust instantly billowed about her and she slowed down, stepping gently.

No one came here. That's why she did. She had the entire planet to herself. To say it was quiet would have been an understatement. In aesthetics, it lacked everything. In distraction, it offered everything: none. Which was exactly why she was here.

She stepped around rubble and rock, heading toward the mountain, looking about her as if expecting to see something other than red dust and black cliffs. "There is no one here," she said out loud.

Images of Old Earth Egypt and Richard drifted through her mind. They were together at one time. She felt warmth rush through her. To teach him to teleport. The most natural thing to do. And the craziest thing she had ever done in her whole life.

She changed direction when she saw a low set of rocks that led to steeper cliffs.

She thought back to how quickly he learned. It was possible that in no time he'd be able to teleport on his own. But to what end? She sighed.

She had let herself dream of having him by her side. But when she stopped and thought about it, how could that ever be? She'd let herself fantasize about him being on the New Earth, working with her, contributing his wisdom and power, but that was ridiculous, and she was somewhat embarrassed by this teenage fantasy. He was a man from long ago and though once they had a life together in Old Earth Egypt where they had special knowledge and special powers but, if she was honest with herself, this amounted to nothing. For so many reasons nothing was possible for them.

She stopped and looked at the black boulders in front of her, then looked up planning a climbing path. She turned and looked at the vast red lonely valley, then started toward the big boulders.

Soon she was right up against the mountain. She looked up and found the first handholds. She had to be careful. It was hard to see in the twilight, and the rocks were brittle. She put her whole attention on placing her hands and feet on solid rock. Her full weight on one of these rocks, if it were to crumble, would have her falling back to the valley floor, tumbling on the jagged peaks all the way down before she had time to enter hyperawareness and teleport to safety.

She climbed steadily for a while and came to the first ledge. She pushed herself up on hands and knees, then turned around to face the valley. She rested, breathing hard. She adjusted the temperature of her suit and took a sip of water. It felt good to be alone in this vastness, even if she had to wear the oxygen suit.

Andreas and Vivian came to mind, knotting her stomach with worry. She talked to Miranda earlier. No change with their parents. She wondered how long they could remain as they were. And she couldn't find Max. And he might be trying to get Bronelven on Altima. This horrified her. If he went to Altima... What if he didn't come back? What if they couldn't continue with Argos?

She took a breath, pushed herself up, dusted her suit and faced the mountain, looking up. She was halfway to the top of this face. Behind it was another peak. She wanted to get up there.

She climbed for a while, giving her full attention to synchronizing her arms and legs, breathing hard, feeling delicious relief through powerfully moving her limbs and pushing her lungs to expand to their fullest.

She was almost at the top. With a few more pushes, she stepped onto a narrow ledge, breathing hard. She turned around slowly. Bleak. Utterly bleak. Why do I come here? She shook her head. Small sharp black peaks. The dull light revealed them as ominous harbingers of an indistinct future. The sky was dead still. She took a few good breaths then turned around and started up again.

Soon she was where she wanted to be, a ledge big enough to set up her oxygen bubble. She took off the pack, pulled out the bubble, set it up, sat inside, pulled off the breathing mask, crossed her legs, took out her sandwich and ate, looking at the desolation through the clear face of the oxygen bubble.

Andreas and Vivian. She'll have to try looking for them again. Obviously she was approaching the research from the wrong direction. Yet, as many times as she'd gone over their collective research notes, she found no indication of any other approach. Nor did she have any significant new ideas. Yet there had to be a way. At some point, something would give. She hoped. But will it be in time?

She noticed she was eating too fast, stopped, took a breath, and continued slowly. She had gotten hungry climbing up the mountain. When she teleported here, she had deliberately scanned for a place to land at the bottom so she could have a nice long hard climb up.

She chewed and thought about Bronelven. She hoped Max didn't try to mine at Altima. Neither of them could do that safely. They simply wouldn't survive it. Entire special teams were trained for months before being sent to Altima to mine. As good as she and Max were, they didn't stand a chance. The only solution would be to redesign Argos. But if she did that, it would be inaccurate. The Argos the Earth Council rejected is the one she had to prototype. And anyway, there was not enough time. Ariel felt she could explode with all the dead ends she had slammed against.

How could so many things be so intractable?

She was now cold, having cooled down from the climb. She adjusted the temperature and took a drink of water. She was anxious to get back and try to find Max.

The ground was hard, and she shifted position. And all the secrecy. She thought about all the things she was lying about to so many people and felt sheer misery.

Was she even going to pull it off—Argos? She shuddered. What if she didn't? Panic swept through her. She had to. She sensed dreadful consequences with failure. That was not an option.

She stuffed the sandwich wrapper in the pack and saw her hands shaking. Stop. Take a big breath. Relax. "I will relax. I will rest. I will come up with solutions," she said out loud.

A little calmer, she laid down and enjoyed the silence. It was quiet. Peaceful. I have to persist. There is no other direction to go than forward. Have to follow this through to the end. I have to be strong. I have to trust. I have to stay on course. With that she closed her eyes, focused on the peace and began to breathe nice long deep breaths.

When she opened her eyes again, it was slightly darker, but not too dark for her to climb down. She felt a little better, calmer. She put her suit back on, deflated the oxygen bubble, threw the pack on her back and started the climb down. She would find answers to everything. Including Richard. She was determined. As Richard said, this is not meaningless. There was a purpose. She just had to keep going until answers revealed themselves.

After a while of gripping rocks, her fingers hurt and she stopped to rest. She opened and closed her right hand to take away the cramp and held on to the rock with the other. Then she switched hands. She glanced down. Her stomach lurched. She turned away quickly, regained her balance and continued the descent.

Chapter Thirty-Four

Ariel sat at the counter in the kitchen and ate the last tardpolane. A glass of milk sat on the side. It was sweet. The combination of ingredients and spices gave it a pleasant unique taste. I love this! She wished it wasn't such a project to make otherwise she might make it often. She drank some milk. A nice breakfast and a nice change from the usual eggs and oats and such.

She finished eating, took the dishes to the recycler, and headed to her sleeping quarters. Standing at the door, she saw the green message light was on. Her chest tightened. She held her breath and took a slow step to the workstation and played the message. "Gone hunting," Max's voice announced cheerfully. She heard loud jungle noises, squealing monkeys, snarling panthers and squawking birds.

Ariel froze. Did he really go to Altima?! She listened again, then jumped out of the chair and ran to Max's studio, stood psychically announcing herself. No response. She tried again and again. Nothing. She stood for a minute considering whether she should enter. She had the codes. Decided against it.

She ran to his quarters. Not there. She pivoted away from the door and stood thinking. Palladium shimmered blue. Should she enter? She also had codes to his quarters. No. She'll wait.

Oh, Max, what have you done? She exhaled and hurried back

to her quarters.

At the workstation she listened to the message again. It was sent hours ago. He wasn't responding to all her calls earlier because he was preparing to go.

Ariel held her head in her hands. Why did he do that? She was filled with dread. What if he didn't come back?

She pushed away from the desk and stared into space. How long will it take him to mine? She'd no idea if he'd warped in time or just teleported. And no idea what was involved in mining on Altima. Where did he get the equipment? She should have made sure he didn't try this.

What to do, what to do? No. She had to wait. Hope he came back. And quickly. And in one piece.

She set to work but couldn't focus. The knot in her stomach would not go away. Every few minutes she stopped and scanned for Max, hoping he'd returned, trying not to think the worst. It would be a disaster if he didn't come back.

Ariel inhaled, mouth compressed. She couldn't think in that direction. But the worry kept churning in her stomach.

A single bright thought crossed her mind. What if he did come back in one piece and with Bronelven? They could speed forward with Argos. For a second her spirits lifted.

Again, she marshaled her attention, tried to work. At the edge of her consciousness, she sensed Miranda wanted to talk. She pushed that to the back. It will have to wait.

It was very late when she finally picked up a weak signal from Max. She was instantly alert, pushed up her psychic shields and focused carefully trying to locate him. He was in his quarters. She jumped up and ran down the hallways, announcing herself way before she was anywhere near his door. She felt a weak signal in response and picked up her pace, coming to a momentary abrupt halt at his door, used his codes, and was in.

Max lay sprawled on the floor, arms and legs thrown in every direction. Several containers lay scattered about him. He wasn't moving. Ariel was down on her knees. His eyes were wide open but not focused.

"Max!" She shook him gently. "Max! Come back!"

The vacant stare remained. He groaned.

She touched his forehead. Cold. She took his hand. Ice. She entered hyperawareness and scanned his body. His life force was weak. She scanned further, found a few bruises, but they were minor and not contributing to his overall absence of life force. All his organs were functioning at a bare minimum. After scanning for one more second and finding nothing, she sat beside him and focused on giving him energy.

Then she crawled around to his head, slid her hands under his armpits and dragged him to his sleeping quarters and onto a thick layer of furs, which constituted Max's bed. She piled more furs on top of him. She got the transducer going. Then she set about adding her energy to warm him up and boost his life force. She went around him, rubbing his hands, his feet, sending healing energy through her hands. Soon she felt his body temperature rising and his life force increasing.

He moved his head from side to side, groaned.

Ariel continued rubbing his hands and feet.

His eyes opened. "Ah, everything hurts."

"You're doing fine, Max. You'll feel better in a little while."

"My head. Feels like I've pounded it against a wall."

"I'll get you something to drink." She got up and brought back a strong cup of hot coffee.

He was pushing up with his hands trying to sit up. Ariel walked around and helped, pulling him up to lean on the rock that was his headboard.

"Ah, now I'm dizzy." Max closed his eyes. "I feel perfectly horrible."

"It will pass. Just give it a little time."

Max opened his eyes, and Ariel handed him the cup.

He took it, his hands shaking.

"Breathe a bit. More deeply."

Max's chest rose slowly, and he brightened up. "I got it. I got our mineral."

Ariel made sure the psychic shields were firmly in place and nodded, "Good work, Max."

"It was worse than I thought." He took small sips of coffee. "I couldn't get the coordinates right." He shook his head and looked at Ariel. "I don't understand why that was so difficult."

They were silent for a while as Max drank his coffee and Ariel continued to monitor his body temperature and life force, both of which were slowly returning to normal.

Ariel wanted to scream at him, "Why did you go? Why did you take such a risk? Why didn't you tell me?" but held back.

"I know what you're thinking, so don't try to hide it." He had a smug weak smile on his face.

Ariel tilted her head, "That was way too dangerous, Max."

"I know. But, you know... it was worth it just to have your hands on me like that."

"Max!"

"All right. I felt pretty certain I could do it."

"How are you feeling?" She touched his forehead. It was warmer.

"I'll go again if you promise to do all that all over again."

"Oh, Max." She tucked the furs tighter around him. "How did you do it?"

"Accessed Altima mining training manual and trained myself in short order."

She shook her head, "Max, Max, Max. You are a wonder!"

"Ahh." Max was basking in her attention.

"Are you hungry? Shall I get you something?"

"In a minute."

"What are all those containers?"

"Ah, yes!" Max shifted under the furs. "Yes. Well. While researching Bronelven, I discovered Altima had some other very interesting minerals." He looked away. "It was actually those minerals that almost messed up the entire mission."

Ariel groaned.

"For my next world... what?"

Ariel was scowling.

"I was already going..."

She couldn't believe Max.

"All right, I forgive you because you managed to come back. Now, you really need to eat something and get your strength back."

"Anyway, we could have done nothing without Bronelven," he exhaled. "I'll have some beef stew." And he handed her the empty cup.

Ariel came back with a tray and placed it on Max's lap.

She looked at Max, a smile on her face, then bent over and kissed him on the cheek.

"He looked up, "As I said..." and he winked at her.

Chapter Thirty-Five

Ariel materialized in the darkness of Richard's bedchamber, inhaling sharply as her feet hit the cold wooden floor. The fire was out, the bedchamber frigid.

Richard laid in bed having been asleep, and turned toward her, "I felt you coming," he whispered. "Come, get in." He pulled the covers back and scooted backward to make room for her.

"I didn't wake you then?"

"I woke up just before you came."

Ariel put the boots down, pulled off her blue suit shivering, placed it at the foot of the bed and got under the covers with Richard.

He wrapped his arms around her and pulled her to him.

"Mmmm. You're so nice and warm."

Richard kissed her forehead, then her ear, then her neck. "Welcome."

Ariel moaned.

They snuggled and cuddled and made love and it seemed to Ariel she was given life again after all the anxieties and worries on the ship. When she started to drift off to sleep, she noticed she was smiling.

When she opened her eyes again, white light was seeping through the cracks in the closed shutters.

"Did you sleep well?" Richard asked and pulled her to him.

She snuggled up against him, "The best sleep in the world." Apparently he had been awake a while and had waited for her to wake up.

"Something to eat?" He pushed the cover back, walked to the table, lit a candle, then started to get dressed.

Ariel stretched, "I don't want to get up. I want to stay here all day," she pretended to whine, then turned, propped herself on her elbow and watched Richard get dressed. He moved quickly shivering, putting on his warmest woolens.

He looked at her and smiled. "I won't light a fire since we'll be leaving soon."

When he was dressed, he bent over and kissed her. "You just lie there. I'll be right back."

Ariel pushed herself up on the pillow, pulled the cover all the way up to her neck and watched the candle flame dance on the wooden paneling. This was bliss.

He was back with a tray in no time. "Apologies for the cold meal. I think it's best we not linger here." He placed the tray on the bed and sat down.

"Thank you," Ariel sat up and touched his hand for a second.

He smiled, tore a chunk of black bread and handed it to Ariel. She took a bite. She loved the earthiness of the dark bread.

"How's Argos coming along?"

Ariel nodded, "We're making good progress now that we have Bronelven."

"You're on track then. Good man, that colleague Max."

"Don't know what we'll find, but we're on track. Yes. Max is special."

More light streamed through the shutters, though not much.

"Looks like we'll have a wet day practicing. More teleportation today?" Richard looked up from slicing the cheese, then handed Ariel a slice.

Ariel nodded.

They've had quite a few lessons since they started. Richard was learning quickly. Though of course that had a lot to do with the training in Old Earth Egypt. Yet his ability to remember it so easily amazed her.

"Yes. More teleportation today." Something drove him to understand. No, Ariel corrected herself, not understand, but master. He wanted to master the workings of her world. She was in awe. At the same time, it made her feel uneasy. She pushed away the worry.

"How does it work to look for the Gateway?" he asked. "How did your parents do it?"

"They teleported together in search of an opening to other dimensions."

Richard nodded, "Yes? They have to be able to hold their positions for long periods of time?"

"Yes. It's one of the reasons it's so hard."

Richard nodded again.

They ate in silence, each in thought, then Richard took away the tray and Ariel reluctantly got out of bed, slipped into her suit and pulled on her boots. Soon after, they were in their training grove.

It was gloomy and wet from the night's rain. Puffy morning mist sat suspended on the hills. The golden autumn warmth had turned to biting winter cold.

"Great day for training," mumbled Ariel. She'll get wet yet again. Should have worn her thermal suit.

Richard looked at her, "Yes, beautiful," he said wistfully. "Let's get started." He paused then cheered up, "Maybe afterwards we can go to the hut and warm up."

Ariel nodded. "Good idea."

After training for a while, it was time to explain teleportation in more detail. Richard listened with complete attention, studied her face, his eyes focused with concentration. Periodically he nodded. When Ariel had gone through all the steps, she once again demonstrated by teleporting both of them. She told Richard exactly what to look for so he could duplicate her steps. Then she teleported both of them again.

"Difficult to think of disassembling myself," Richard said in frustration and started walking.

Ariel followed. "Many New Earth humans cannot do it, Richard, so of course it will take you a while to master it."

He continued walking, his neck stiff.

"Let's do it again," Richard said, swinging round towards her.

They went through another series of teleportations. Richard asked more questions and listened closely to answers.

They rested by walking. It was too wet to sit anywhere.

It started to drizzle, the clouds lower and now gray.

Richard wiped the rain from his face and turned to look at her, "I've been using my deep seeing to see into my patients. I see weakness and sluggishness, but I'm not sure what to do about it. The herbs I use are inconsistent in their results."

Ariel saw the first signs of trouble in teaching Richard what she knew. Soon she will have created an unhappy man. He will know too much and be stuck in this place. As unhappy as he was before, he'll be unhappier yet.

She looked up at the expanse of gray sky, "It's too cold here, let's go to the hut," she said and teleported them.

As soon as they materialized Richard said, "That was different. Hmm." He stroked his chin, looking down at the dirt floor. Then he looked up at Ariel, turned and got twigs to start the fire.

It was dark, cold and damp in the hut. She shivered. But soon it would cozy warm. She followed Richard, "Different, how?"

She sat down on the stool by the fire and watched Richard layer kindling.

He turned and glanced at her, "The other ones were smooth. This time there was a drag for an instant, a place where the teleporting seemed to stretch." He blew on the fire so it would catch.

"Hmm. I didn't notice anything." She had never noticed variations in the many teleportations she had done, but then she wasn't particularly paying attention.

"Is it possible that because the two of us are teleporting there's some kind of drag?" He fanned the fire with his hand, and flames shot up. "It's going," he said, turned and pulled a stool next to her.

"I don't think so, but then I almost always travel alone. It could be you're just getting used to teleporting."

Richard shrugged.

The hut soon felt friendlier with the crackling glowing fire. They watched it dance, mesmerized.

After a while Ariel said, "What you said about your patients, there is something different you can do."

He looked at her, brows raised.

She wasn't sure how much she should tell him, what was good for him to know or not know. What she was sure of was that she wanted to tell him everything, hold nothing back. Ever. That was her impulse.

The blue eyes were fixed steadily on her, and Ariel felt him gathering out of her the said and the unsaid, and she felt waves of thrill coursing through her entire body. His abilities were growing at an amazing speed.

She finally said, "You could use your concentration and that power source we identified the other time and simply add to their energy to strengthen them."

She watched his face, his eyes slowly moving around with thought, his lips tight with concentration, until he looked at her and nodded, having understood.

He turned his gaze to the fire, "Yes, I remember from the mystery school, but only now that you've reminded me." After another long pause, he looked at her, "I'm quite the barbarian, aren't I?"

Ariel exhaled. What to say? The contrast between his world and her world was so dramatic it would make anyone feel small and insignificant. And whatever his unhappiness before he knew her, it was now hugely exacerbated. What have they gotten themselves into? She can't let him feel this way. She focused hard on him until he looked up at her and into her eyes and began to understand.

Embarrassed he looked away, "You're right, it's just self-pity. Not good for anything." He reached for her hand. "I shouldn't forget I'm a man blessed to have an angel appear to teach me all that I have forgotten. And so much more."

"Yes, that's right," She laughed, pretending smugness. "But seriously, look at all that you've learned and remembered already." As good as that sounded, they were both instantly reminded of just how much even less he fit in this world.

He stood up and got a log from the pile and put it on the fire.

Nothing about being together was safe. At any moment it could all end. She felt uneasy and automatically scanned their future for any information that would give her some assurance. She saw absolutely nothing. It was blank. It was always blank. She'd scanned before trying to see where all this was leading. Never an inkling of information. But somehow, this moment was right. This moment was perfect. And that made it all the harder to bear. Yet, she had committed to keeping her heart open, being true to the moment, committed to trusting, committed to walking the length of this path. Time would reveal. But what? Now Ariel sat deep in inner gloom. All this uncertainty. It was unbearable.

Suddenly she felt Richard put his hand on her forearm.

"What am I thinking now?" he asked.

"Clever you!" Ariel said, surprised, sensing strong shields.

He had a lopsided smile on his face, daring her to break through his shields. How did he learn this?

She tried without success. "Hmm. What *are* you doing, you minx?" In teaching Richard, it seemed shields were easiest for him to learn. She tried again without success.

He laughed. "Try again," he said, "What am I thinking now?" He was looking hard at her.

Ariel scanned, ran into thick shields, she looked for cracks, weak spots, found none.

"I can't see, but I can imagine," she said, throwing a small twig at him. He quickly threw a twig back. That started a small twig war that got Ariel scrambling off the stool, trying to get out of Richard's accurate aim with no success and finally resorting to small teleportation jumps, at which point Richard stopped and yelled, "Not fair!"

He stood still for a long time, then made the effort to teleport, keeled over, and caught himself just in time so he wouldn't fall on his face. Soon they were looking at each other, screaming with laughter.

Ariel bent over put her hands on her knees, breathing hard, trying to catch her breath, then felt Richard's arms around her.

"I am caught! I am caught!" screeched Ariel.

This brought about another round of laughter.

"You're mine!" he exclaimed, pretending to be victorious.

Chapter Thirty-Six

Ariel poured boiling water over the coffee grounds, stirred and waited. The wonderful smell wafted up to her nose. She wanted a good cup of coffee, nice and strong.

No doubt Richard will soon be able to teleport on his own. She felt warm inside when she contemplated that. Then fear. She exhaled. Her shoulders slumped. Where to go with that? She felt the craziness of it all rising in her. She shook her head. No! Can't let that happen. Can't let that feeling overtake me. Not now. Just have to live with the unknown.

She looked down, stirred the grounds, and poured the coffee slowly through a dense sieve into a big mug, added cream and sugar, tasted it. Delicious! She placed a lid on it, got her portable console and hurried to the studio.

Lights went up, soft music started. She powered up the workstation, then stood and looked at her worlds on the big screens. She smiled. Her creations. Beautiful. The transducer hummed. She took a big gulp of coffee. So good. Nothing like a good cup of coffee to start the day right.

She turned back to her workstation and took a big breath. All right, let's get to work, get this done, and get it to Max. She sat down, pulled up all Argos prototyping data. Enlivening day. One more look to make sure everything was accurate then to Max's studio.

Step by step she went through all aspects of the Argos prototype. Looks perfect. But what if it isn't? What if she'd made a mistake? She'd worked fast, and it was quite possible. What if it failed altogether, yielded identical results as before? What if they were right after all?

She felt her body tingling all tight. She blinked. Can't think about that right now. Only one direction to go: forward.

She worked methodically through the design, carefully checking everything. Then it came up again. The terror. She'd been working on the very strong assumption that they were wrong. All of New Earth was wrong. But what if they were right? She felt anxiety like ice move through her whole body, heart beating fast. If there were any mistakes, any oversights, with same results as before, what would she do? She would put herself in the position to wonder about trusting this powerful force that made her go against so many people, against sanity. What would that imply? Andreas and Vivian. At least they had stabilized, but still the endless waiting, anxiety. The Gateway. She'd made no progress there either. Everything just hung in suspense.

Stop! She stood up, shook her arms, shook her legs. She didn't dare succumb to all these thoughts. Not now.

She sat down and faced the transducer, closed her eyes, took more deep breaths, opened to receive calming energies. Just get done. Enliven. Be finished. Know. Nothing she could do now to safeguard her venture. It had to happen one step at a time, each step revealing the next.

She swiveled back and continued working. Her body felt all tight, brittle, as if it could break any moment. It just looked too good. Looked too much like it looked when she first designed Argos, a world and species almost too good to be true.

She inhaled a big breath. Max was waiting. She pulled together all her energies, forced her attention to the screens and finished.

She powered down the equipment to accept minimal incoming data, gathered the Argos information into a cube, secured psychic shields and walked to Max's studio.

He was sitting at his workstation. Enormous design screens lit up in a repeating series of pulsating lights. Max was working on his own new world.

She stood and waited, looking around the usual clutter, shifting from one foot to the other.

Max swiveled around, stood up, looked at Ariel, "Ready?! Let's get this baby born. Come on," and swooshed toward the Argos dome.

Ariel followed, feeling dizzy unsteady, her legs trembling, weak. She pushed through Max's clutter particularly annoying just now.

"All right. What have we got here?" Max activated the Argos control panel. Lights flashed rapidly in a cycle then steadied. He watched, rubbing his hands together. "Give me the cube." He held out his hand, then looked up, "Scared, huh?"

Ariel nodded. "What if it was all a crazy lark?" She felt miserable with fear.

"Could have been. But nothing will be lost. Come on."

Ariel handed over the cube. She felt her heart pounding in her chest.

"All rightie." He inserted the cube.

A rapid display of drawings and calculations appeared, then miniature versions of the main species, the Argonians.

Max watched, his face illuminated with delight. "An amazing

species, truly amazing."

Ariel watched eyes wide wet palms together in front of her chest.

"At your signal!" Max said, his finger on the start button that would begin the enlivening process.

When she didn't say anything, he looked up.

She stepped to the panel and checked everything again. Looked at the Argos data. Everything looked fine. She double checked the Bronelven flow. Fine. She paused. This is it. She took a big breath, "Let's go!" And exhaled. "The sooner we get started, the sooner we'll have results."

"Happy birthday baby!" said Max and pressed the button.

Soon, energy currents trickled in, and then the entire platform was illuminated in semi-solid holo images. Bioorganic particles undulated.

Ariel felt small flutters of thrill in her chest. No matter it was a prototype, the children of her dreams, her fantasies, her love, were coming to life, breathing a certain kind of breath. She felt small trembles of fear that it would end soon, that in truth they had no life, no real life, ever, that this was as far as they would live, before being aborted forever.

She bit down on her trembling lip, squeezed her impulse to cry and continued to watch Argos.

"They are stunningly beautiful," said Max.

"Mmmm." Ariel was mesmerized.

After a while Max said, "Let's hope for the best." He looked at Ariel. "Don't worry, I'll keep an eye on them."

But she didn't leave. For a while they both stood and watched, enchanted.

"I'll check in later." She left reluctantly, all weak, barely able to walk, taking in the comforting golden glow of the Palladium hallways.

Chapter Thirty-Seven

The sun shimmered just above the horizon. Puffs of fog floated lazily in the valleys. Dogs barked. Carts wheeled by going to market. Men and women bustled about starting the day, feeding livestock, chopping wood, lighting fires, carrying water to kitchens.

She couldn't sense Richard anywhere. "Richard, Richard," she called out psychically and waited. No response. Puzzled, she remained in pre-material form and roamed around looking for him. She found him in the dim light of the stable adjusting the saddle on Mistre. He let go of the saddle, put his hands on his hips and watched her materialize, a big grin on his face.

"You heard me, but you didn't answer," Ariel said in a loud whisper, incredulous.

He stepped up to her, put his finger under her chin, leaned down and kissed her, "In the grove," he whispered and led Mistre out of the stable looking back at her over his shoulder, a self-satisfied smile on his face.

Ariel watched him walk away, then came out of her trance and teleported to the practice field. It was wet, but the sun held promise for the day.

Richard had heard her and used his shields so she couldn't find him. He had deliberately shut her out! It came as a revelation that he now had a lot of power, especially after all the recent lessons when he'd learned to teleport. Her lips tightened. Was she right to have taught him, given him powers? Was she right to have trusted him? She paced, trying to calm down, her stomach tight with fear. She loved him, believed in him. But...

She heard swishing, looked up and saw Richard approaching. He had the same self-satisfied smile on his face. He jumped off Mistre and before she knew it, had her in his arms and was twirling her around. Ariel squealed and held on tight, her hair flying wildly about.

"Today I will be the best student you have ever had or will have." He put her down.

Ariel brushed her hair back. "What's happening? Why all the excitement?"

"Ah, yes." His eyes twinkled. He took her hand and pulled, "Let's get started with the lessons."

Ariel let herself be pulled, wondering at Richard's unusual behavior.

Then, as they started practicing, he continued to be hidden, mysterious. He told her endless silly bawdy jokes that made her laugh with gusto. She had never seen Richard like this before. And when she commented on it, he gave her a wink and said, "There are always surprises in life," and teleported away from her, forcing her to dash after him. And not find him!

Not only had he successfully teleported away from her, but had also successfully put up shields, making it difficult to find him.

Ariel stood in wet boots in wet grass feeling perfectly miserable. She had hesitated just long enough in her pursuit that it caught his attention, and he was back looking at her closely. A soft comforting knowing murmur issued from his lips. He took her in his arms, kissed the top of her head, stroked her hair. Out of nowhere, tears. He held her closer. She could feel him feeling into her and let tears flow, worry and anxiety finally finding release.

"You're worried about the enlivening aren't you?" he said, having picked this out from her thoughts.

She nodded into his chest, where all was damp now.

"And you don't know what will happen," he said, and she nodded again, a hiccup issuing among the sobs. "And you're worried about your mother and father," he continued, "and these lessons with me."

Ariel felt the heavy weight of everything and let Richard hold her.

He stroked her hair. "It will all turn out all right."

After a while he pulled away, held both her hands, his eyes full of love, "Let's sit for a while."

Sitting under the tree, Richard held her tight.

It felt good to cry. She breathed, let everything drain from her.

The sun was making its way up the sky. The air was fresh. The trees crystal with water droplets.

"A little too much," said Richard.

Ariel nodded.

"But everything going well? Enlivening going all right?"

"Yes. Everything looks good at the moment, but I can't help but worry about the results. What if I was wrong? What if they were right? And all this crazy secrecy..."

"Yes. A lot at stake. But you have to stay the course," he said in a firm voice.

Ariel groaned, "Yes."

"Of course you did the right thing. How could you not pay attention to such a powerful inner directive?" There was a long pause. "If we cannot be true to our noblest impulses, our highest sense of truth, what is life worth living for, who are we really?"

Ariel nodded, "You're right."

"It will turn out all right. Just be patient. Soon it will all be over, and you will have your answers."

"Yes. But what will they be?" She shivered.

After a long while, Richard patted her knee, "Let's not worry about that now. It won't help," he paused, "You ready to practice some more?"

He was up pulling her, "Let's go. You'll feel better if we're doing something."

She followed. She felt better and worse all at once, but determined and focused on the lessons.

The sun was high up now. The sky a vibrant blue. Birds were busy with excited chatter. It had turned out to be a warm beautiful day.

"All right. This time, let's incorporate all three. But let's keep it going until either you can't keep going any more or I catch up with you."

Richard would teleport, simultaneously terminating psychic communication with her, putting up shields, and disguising his location. At her go, he was off. On the first two tries, Ariel found him. After that, she could not track him.

Then he appeared in front of her, a crooked smile on his face. "I'm good, huh?" He strutted around her, his shoulders back, his head high. Then he stopped. "And I'm exhausted," and his shoulders drooped.

He took her hand and pulled her under the oak to rest.

"It will get easier. You'll be able to keep going for longer periods of time without getting tired." She took his hand and sensed a lowering of life force. Good to rest and replenish energies.

"I've been improving the strength of my patients. Just a little, so no one could get suspicious. Thank you for showing me how to do that."

She squeezed his hand.

After a while she heard him say in a voice that was more to himself, "I would like to see the New Earth." He put his arm around her and kissed her forehead.

She kissed his chin, put up her face and felt his lips soft and slow.

He pulled back, "I want to see where you live. If I wanted to come to you, how would I do it?"

Ariel took this in, surprised. "Hmmm."

They looked at each other for a long time, saying nothing. This was new territory.

"If I wanted to come and see you, how would I do that?" he asked again.

Ariel's mind raced. Teleporting from tree to tree was simple compared to teleporting in time. How could she even explain? Should she even teach him? Images of the Earth Council flashed through her mind, and she knew with absolute certainty she should not. And yet, and yet, something deep inside her said it was all right, it was the right thing.

"All right, I will show you," she said at last.

He moved to sit across from her, his legs crossed, his face tight with concentration.

First Ariel explained the basic process and made sure Richard understood. They practiced for a while, then rested.

Richard took her hand, "Oh, my fair maiden, and how do I come to you?" His eyes glistened full of love.

Ariel smiled, "Don't you need to get back?" She was trying to delay, afraid. Once she showed him, there would be no turning back.

"Aahhh, you are right! I should be getting back."

Ariel let out a sigh of relief.

"But," he continued, "I don't really need to." He had a big grin on his face.

She shook herself internally, "Richard, are you sure? Are you sure you are ready? Are you sure you want to... separate yourself so much from your own time, your own life here?" She looked into his eyes, searched for the truth of what he really wanted, what drove him to these extreme acts, and what she found was power and determination and conviction. And love. Love for her. Her heart softened. "I will show you."

She spent a long time explaining how to determine the coordinates, then how to focus and find the place and how to generate energy. After he had mimicked her processes, he said, "The New Earth then?"

Ariel looked down, scared, hesitant, then nodded a slow yes, lips tight. "Let's do it next time I see you. All right?"

Chapter Thirty-Eight

"We can't stay long," whispered Ariel and looked around. Her whole body was tight with anxiety. She'd gone back to see Richard and after more lessons, kept her promise and brought him to the ship.

They stood in low light in Ariel's sitting room. Richard was looking down at the floor hand on chin, then looked up, "Did you feel that?"

"Feel what?"

"I felt it again," said Richard and looked around the lively room with luminous walls of yellow and green, down at the ruby carpet. "Comfortable," he smiled, "You live here?"

"Yes. My home when on the ship," she paused, "We can't stay long," Ariel said again, then quickly transmitted, strong shields!

Richard nodded, then looked closely at her. "Don't worry. A quick look around and we go back."

"What did you feel?" asked Ariel. "Are you all right?" She did a quick scan, checking for irregularities. He seemed fine.

"The little drag as we teleported here. It was there again. You felt nothing? Nothing unusual?"

She shook her head. "No, nothing unusual," she paused. "Wonder if teleporting is affecting you differently." She looked around, worried they'd be noticed. "Can't talk about it now."

She felt breathless, jittery, now fully aware of what she was doing. She'd brought someone from another time to the ship! She was anxious to leave. Again, she looked around as if expecting someone to pop up and find them.

She watched Richard's eyes move to the window. He looked out of the ship into the blackness, then took a careful step forward as if he might be walking on something that wasn't solid under his feet. He put his hand on the sofa and kept looking into the vast blackness.

Ariel stepped over, put her arm around his waist and looked out with him. She scanned his body again. She was worried teleporting might be hurting him in some way, but found nothing out of the ordinary, just the expected lowering of body temperature and faster heartbeat.

He turned his head briefly, the corner of his mouth pulled up, "Don't worry, I'm fine." He stepped back and put his own arm around her. "When can we see something out there?" He pointed at the window.

"Not until we're closer to Laurus. Let's go." She pulled him by the hand, "I'll show you the rest, then we go back."

In the kitchen, she explained the fireplace and the food dispenser.

Richard nodded and kept nodding, an amused smile on his face. "Ah, that we could have that where I come from!" he chuckled. "How? Same as teleportation?" He looked at Ariel.

"Yes." Then she led him to the sleeping quarters.

He looked at the huge bed, gauzy drapes and fluffy pillows, the amused smile again on his face.

"We can't stay long," Ariel said, feeling more and more anxious.

"Just a little longer. What's that?" asked Richard, pointing to the transducer?

She sensed him sensing into it to see how it worked.

The intercom buzzed.

Ariel jumped. Richard looked at her.

"That's somebody calling me."

"Just a minute more and we go back."

He nodded, looked around. "So much innovation."

Ariel was biting her lip. What did Richard think of her home on the ship, her, her ways? So many new things. He was here, against all... well, against everything that was normal. Or allowed.

She looked back at the station. Did anyone leave a message? Then looked at Richard, "How do you feel?" She was still on guard for any adverse reactions.

"Could not be better!"

Ariel noticed he was continuing to use his psychic shields and let out a small sigh of relief. If he was present enough to do that, he must be doing all right.

He continued, "How would any man feel if he found himself in a lady's chambers?" He put his arms around her, planted quick kisses all over her face. "Alone with that lady."

Ariel relaxed a little, thought back on the many nights she was here alone dreaming of him. She leaned into him for a moment, daring to accept the wonder of his presence in her world. Then she pulled away, sobering up, "We have to go back."

"How big is the ship?"

Ariel sent quick images of Palladium. Richard nodded, his eyebrows lifted a little.

"Big." He paused. "Argos. Show me Argos."

"What?" Ariel felt knots tighten in her stomach, "All right, come," and stepped over to the workstation connected to Max's studio where they could view the prototyping dome.

"It's in Max's studio. We can't go there, but you can see it here." Myriad of lights danced, data screens flashed. Small holo images of residents hung suspended above the model, as yet inactive.

"Not much to see just yet, but it will develop."

Richard had his hand on the back of her chair. "Fascinating. Images! What extraordinary technology. And this will become an entire world?"

She nodded, "Yes. In model form, of course."

"And later become a world, like Earth?"

"Yes."

"How?"

"Later," she said. "I think we'd better leave."

She shut down the station, then sent her awareness out through the ship, checking for anything unusual. Everything seemed all right. She tracked Max. He was in his quarters at the long table along the windows, deep in work.

"Let's go," she said, "Back to the house."

Chapter Thirty-Nine

Ariel stood outside Richard's house in pre-material form, filled with dread. She could not find him again. Where was he? Why was he making himself untraceable? Was he teleporting on his own? He shouldn't be teleporting on his own. He could make mistakes. He could hurt himself. He might be lost. He could die! Oh, Richard, where are you?

Another gloomy day with a low gray sky. Mud everywhere. Must have rained overnight.

She checked the hut, the practice grove. No Richard.

Where else might he be? She pushed down the anxiety that he might have accidentally teleported out of this world.

Where else could she look?

Then again, he might simply be practicing with his psychic shields. And that was all. They were excellent now. Nothing to worry about, she told herself. But she didn't believe herself.

What have I done? She groaned. He could teleport and he could hide. He might get hurt. All this was new to him. Was she right to have trusted him with all this power?

She dashed between the trees in the grove, hoping he was hiding behind one of them, playing with her as he'd done before.

Richard, Richard, where are you? She called out psychically. But he'd successfully shut himself off.

Then, a dreadful thought entered her mind. Maybe he didn't want to see her anymore! Maybe he was thinking again, and decided there was no future for them and decided to stop it now, like he did before. Simply vanish instead of confronting her. Ariel froze. She could barely keep her transparency. What if that's what it was? Except this time, she would not be able to find him.

Ariel worked to calm herself. She was thinking the worst. It could easily be something simple, a simple explanation as to why he made himself untraceable. Some good reason. She relaxed a little. Yes, it could be that. She tried to convince herself.

What to do?

After a while, it came to her to ask Marion. Maybe Marion would know. But how could Marion know? It didn't matter. She had to do something before she did something dreadfully wrong herself.

She forced herself to organize her mind. She'd have to visit Marion and somehow casually find out if Marion knew anything about Richard. She couldn't just appear asking about Richard. With luck, Marion would volunteer the information before being asked since she was fond of him and somehow managed to keep track of him.

Near the cottage, she scanned for Marion and found her behind the house, wiping her hands on her skirts, having just fed the chickens. The hood of her brown cloak was drawn over her head.

Ariel went down the road a ways, calmed herself and materialized. She would walk as if she were simply passing by, going to town.

A distance away she called out, "Oh, Marion, Marion."

Marion came from around the house, "Lizzie!"

She sloshed through the mud toward her. "Are you going to

town?" Her eyes sparkled with excitement. "Come and see baby. He's growing so fast. He'll almost be too big for his little shoes."

"It would be lovely to see little John. Has he been a good baby?" Ariel asked and followed Marion to the cottage. Then she realized she had nothing for them and groaned.

Elisabeth was at the fire stirring morning porridge with baby John on her hip. "You surprised us," she called out. "Good morning, sit yourself down. I'll have this ready in a bit."

It was warm and cozy in the cottage, a comfortable refuge from the gloom outside.

Ariel sat down, "Something hot would be good now on this chilly day." She pulled her damp skirts away from her. "How have you been?" She looked at baby John. He was smiling and gurgling. His color was good. He was doing all right.

"We're getting by," said Elisabeth. She handed the baby to Marion and brought the porridge to the table.

"No one wants to see him anymore," exploded Marion. She sat on the stool next to Ariel and rocked the baby. "They say he's been seen with the devil. Did you hear?" She crooned to the baby.

Ariel forced herself to keep her face neutral. "What's happened?"

"The townspeople say they've seen him walking around with a blue devil, jumping around and flouncing." Her eyes were wide.

Someone saw them teleporting! Icy shudders ran through Ariel. How? They were careful. She thought.

"They think he's a heretic. There's talk he should be burned at the stake," said Elisabeth. "Wouldn't be surprised." She placed a bowl of steaming porridge in front of Ariel. "Good to have you visit Lizzie."

Ariel looked up and squeaked out, "Thank you." She stirred.

"How unfortunate about the physician."

They must have been so involved practicing or, probably more accurately, one of the moments when they were playing around and their psychic shields were not up, someone noticed them. Oh, the carelessness. This was a basic shield lesson, and not even Ariel had succeeded at it.

She forced herself to keep sitting on the stool when she wanted to bolt. She stirred the porridge. Her throat tight. Her stomach tight. How was she going to eat this? She inhaled a slow breath. Calm down.

Elisabeth sat down opposite her, "He's always been strange, thought himself better than others, I'm sure. And all those experiments you hear him doing with gold and herbs." Elisabeth shook her head. "Not a surprise he would come to this end, burned at the stake."

"He didn't think himself better than others," said Marion with energy. "That's why I like him. Besides he helped Father."

How quickly people changed their minds about someone. She took small spoonfuls of porridge and discovered she could swallow. And how could they speak so casually about someone being a heretic or being burned at the stake? Then remembered. Of course, these were times when such things were not that unusual, and felt another surge of urgency to dash out the door and try to find Richard. Maybe he was already dead. Maybe the townspeople had already gotten hold of him. Maybe they'd already burned him. Ariel forced herself to keep her face pleasant.

"He's hiding in the ruins of that old fort," said Marion. Ariel choked on the porridge and started to cough.

Marion looked at her.

"Went down the wrong way," she croaked. And not wanting

Marion to stop talking, she said, "What's he doing there?"

"I saw him there, walking in the ruins, talking to himself when I was out with the sheep."

Oh Richard!

Carefully modulating her voice, she said, "He's probably just doing some thinking. It's just gossip about the blue devil, I'd guess. People say all kinds of things."

"What are you getting in town today?" asked Marion. She was bouncing little John on her knee. He was smiling, making baby sounds.

"Ah, just some supplies."

"There will be lots of mud." Marion made a face.

"Yes. If I'd known it would be so muddy, I'd not have started out. But now that I'm halfway there, I'll go on."

Ariel looked for a way to leave, but they had to finish their porridge. Meanwhile, she had to be a polite guest. "Chickens behaving?" She looked at Marion.

"Yes! Lots of good eggs. I'll be going to the market to sell soon."

Finally, Elisabeth stood up and picked up their empty bowls, "People never liked him much," she said, obviously having continued to think about Richard.

It went from Richard being the savior of the poor to people not liking him. How unfortunate.

"Well, people talk," Ariel said and stood up, "I better get going while it's still early. Got work to do."

"Come back soon," Marion followed her out.

"Yes, visit, any time," said Elisabeth.

It was drizzling. Ariel pulled her hood up, forced herself to walk at a normal pace until she was away from the cottage and on the path in the woods leading to town, then she dashed to the ruins of the old fort.

He wasn't there.

Ariel kept turning in circles hoping to see him. Nowhere in sight.

Chapter Forty

Ariel pulled off her soaked garments and stuffed them in the recycler. She shivered. She was cold outside and cold inside. Numb. She stepped over the mud and went to stand under hot water for a long time. After that, she dressed in a warm peach sweater and cream pants. She cleaned up the mud and dried the wet spots.

Where was he? Why was he hiding from her? The possibility that he no longer wanted to see her, that she might never see him again, kept sneaking into her mind, filling her with dread.

And he had all those powers now. She should have thought this through more carefully, considering the potential consequences of those powers. Her body ached all over from worry. Have to calm down and think clearly.

In the kitchen she got a fire going, got a mug of hot chocolate, pulled up a comfortable chair, sat down and watched the fire. It crackled and hissed, and she fed it more logs, and it crackled and hissed and she sipped the sweetness of the hot chocolate and felt the flames warm her face.

She was exhausted. She closed her eyes. The warmth of the fire felt good. She was sure she'd feel something later, but right now she felt nothing. Solid static reigned in her head.

Yes, she should have thought this through more carefully,

considered the consequences. She looked around. So quiet. Everything seemed far away from her, nothing to do with her. So very alone. Even the crackles from the fire seemed to fall into the loneliest silence.

The console buzzed and startled her. She focused to see who it was. Max. She'll call him back later.

The truth was, she could not have done anything differently with Richard. They'd both agreed things weren't an option. And here she was. Completely confused. Nothing made any sense. Numb.

The fire made her warm and sleepy. She relaxed, then sat upright. Argos. Maybe Max was calling about Argos. She shifted uneasily on the chair. She should call and find out. She braced herself and walked over to the workstation.

He was in the Garden, the ship's large growing facility that also held experimental stations throughout. One look at him told her something was on his mind. Not good, not bad, just something there. She pulled on her boots and went to see him.

Max was moving lasers around a large dome, tapping in new configurations on his portable console. Minuscule vegetation grew inside the dome. "No progress," he pointed with his chin to his devolution experiment. Then he hefted his shields and Ariel followed suit, expecting the worst.

The Garden was huge, warm and steamy. It was dimly lit, with spotlights here and there. Every imaginable plant grew here. In the center, the tallest plants. Three levels rose around it. She stood with Max on the third level with a good view all around.

"Got the first results," Max said, "It's the same as what they found. Energy output way too high," he paused, then quickly added, "But I'm not done yet." He scratched his head.

Ariel exhaled, nodded, "All right." There was nothing left in her to care.

"Got the results a while back." Max looked closer at her, "Are you all right? Did you hear what I just said?"

"Don't feel great. But that can't be right."

Max kept looking at her.

"Just tired, I think. I'll be all right."

"Hmm," Max continued to look at her. "I'll run other configurations. It's not over yet."

Ariel brushed sweat from her forehead. She wore too many clothes for the Garden. "I'll come to your studio later to look at everything."

"There's still a good possibility we'll find something," said Max. He stepped up to her, put his hand on her shoulder and squeezed, "Get some rest if you need to."

"Thank you Max."

She took her time getting to the studio, absorbing the amber light, breathing deep breaths, synchronizing her walking to her breathing. Then, like an avalanche, thoughts of Richard tumbled down on her, burying her in pain and confusion. She pushed back hard. Then Argos calculations spun in her head, starting from the top and to the end and starting again. She felt dizzy. Weak. She stopped, put her hand on the wall, waited for the dizziness to go away. After a while, she continued walking.

In her studio, she got a big strong mug of coffee and sat, drank, and waited for the light-headedness to go away. She was drooping in the chair and tried to push herself up to sit straight. She felt weak, discouraged. It was hard to keep trying. After a while, with a sigh, she powered up the workstation and got to work.

She didn't expect to find anything new, but went through

everything nevertheless. All dead ends. Nothing had changed since the onset of this madness.

Her feet and hands were cold. Her body felt wilted. Slowly, she pushed herself out of the chair. Took a breath. If they hadn't overlooked anything then why, why, why the urgency to build? Why the maddening dictate to proceed? Why the urgency to prototype? Why?

She walked around the transducer. Was she simply crazy? Fallen off the mental track and didn't even know it. How could this possibly be so nonsensical?

She clenched her jaw, determined to find answers. Determined to look deeper. Search for whatever she might have overlooked, again and again and again until she knew. Until she understood.

She sat down, faced the transducer and opened to receive calming, healing energies. Afterwards, she got herself a cup of hot chocolate and commandeered herself back to work.

She was deeply buried in numbers and energy projections when she sensed a pulling, a tugging on her awareness. At first she pushed it aside, but it persisted. She stopped and paid attention. Darius was approaching her studio.

Ariel pushed her chair back in surprise. Why would he personally be coming to her studio? A wave of fear washed over her. She walked toward the door, attempting to perceive the nature of his intent. His energy was intense, full of determination and conviction. She gave quick permission for him to enter. When he walked in, Ariel saw it on his face before he spoke. It was about Richard.

Darius read her mind and knew that she knew why he was there. "Come with me," he said, turned around and walked back out the door.

Ariel felt as if her entire body had suddenly sunk to the bottom of the deepest pit. She closed down her screens and followed Darius. It was all over. All of it. She knew what this meant. She should never have brought Richard to the ship.

She forced her legs to follow Darius to his office.

"You don't need me to tell you why you're here," Darius said. He was sitting behind his desk looking at her and, Ariel sensed, holding back his own confusion, anger and incredulity. His face was all sharp angles.

"I don't have to ask why the Earth's lead New Worlds Designer is breaking all the most sacred rules of the New Earth."

They looked at each other.

There was very little they could say to each other.

Ariel did want to say, "But Darius, you *must* understand this feeling, this feeling inside me that propelled me forth despite all I know," but she couldn't say it. It was against regulation and there was nothing to say.

Darius waited.

"It felt right," Ariel said, just to say something.

"I am sure," said Darius, his voice clipped like a sharp knife chopping. "You know the rules."

And Ariel sensed that he meant it. He saw she had her own consistent logic within the framework of her perceptions with Richard and that it was valid for that time and that place. Nevertheless, it was unacceptable. Of course, all New Humans were allowed to make mistakes, and they did, and there were remedies. But this was outside that scope.

"Of course you must not continue," said Darius, as if Ariel did not know this.

"We've checked. No harm has been done. We'll have to find

him, of course, make him forget all that he knows, all that you've taught him. But that's a simple matter."

Ariel felt her face burning with shame. She was sorry she had hurt Darius personally. She knew how much he admired and cared about her. She said nothing.

"You too will forget," he said, "As you know." And he got up. "Please come with me."

They had a room on the ship that was essentially a sickroom. It wasn't used much but occasionally, when someone needed something, that is where they went. Alec, the ship's health scientist, would sort it out. For Ariel the cure would be to erase her memory of Richard.

Ariel followed Darius at a distance, her legs heavy. Then she became completely alert. She had to remember! She had to remember, no matter what they did to her. Quickly she made calculations. How much cure would they need to administer to make her forget Richard?

Oh, Richard, Richard.

Darius turned his head and glanced at her, "Best forget him, Ariel."

The crying inside her was deafening. No tears. Just the screaming. All lost. It didn't end up in sense. It ended up in chaos. Once out, she would not remember him, would not know that she had ever met an incredible man named Richard.

Then she snapped to total alertness once again, threw up shields and quickly, frantically, deliberately filed information about Richard into parts of her brain where it would normally not be stored. She built associations with as many things as fast as she could, associating him with flowers, and spices and ale and her worlds, so that when he was erased from the main part of her brain, hopefully, maybe, some part of him would remain. Oh, she wanted to remember. She wanted him in her heart forever, even if only as a memory.

She pushed her sluggish brain, pushed against the gooey substance of her turbid emotions, making connections. She may never see him again, but she wanted to remember. He was a beacon of something that could have been, something vaster than herself, vaster than her imagination could have created. He may be gone, but the memory of that miraculous potential she wanted to keep forever.

By the time they reached the sickroom, Ariel's eyes were large and luminous with exertion and will. She felt sharper than she had felt in a long time.

Darius pointed to a chair, "Alec will be here momentarily." He stood in front of her a moment, looking at her, mouth and eyes drooping. Then he turned on his heel and left.

Ariel sat down and ran through her repertoire of associations again.

Chapter Forty-One

Ariel opened her eyes and winced. A sharp pain in the back of her head froze her. She breathed shallow breaths and waited. It settled into a dull ache.

She looked around. Her morning light had come on, but she didn't wake up. Strange. Then she focused on the peach ruffle at the top of her bed. She stretched. Drowsy and lazy. She found the ruffle indeed fascinating.

She smiled and pulled the covers all the way to her chin. She felt a childish satisfaction in being warm and snuggled in bed with nothing to do but get up whenever she felt like it. Except she realized with a start, it wasn't the weekend and of course she was not a kid any more.

She pushed the covers down and sat up. Something had happened. What? She could not remember. After a little effort, during which her head ached more, she concluded it really didn't matter. She was happily ensconced in her sleeping quarters with no need to hurry to do anything.

When she opened her eyes again, she realized she had fallen back asleep. She must have been tired to have done that. She couldn't remember the last time she had been in bed, had woken up, and had gone back to sleep. All that work on Laurus and Argos. Argos! That must be why she was so tired. It had caught up with her. Quickly, she raised her psychic shields. She had almost forgotten! All that work. She must be exhausted, more exhausted than she let herself admit.

She breathed out a big sigh and slid down into the pillows, feeling happy for some reason. She didn't know quite why, but then she decided it didn't matter.

Then she remembered everything was not all right. In fact, all quite wrong. She remembered her conversation in the Garden with Max. The prototype was not yielding new information. Ariel mentally kicked that thought aside, turned over, laid on her side and now found fascinating her garment dispenser, which was directly in her view. She must design some new gowns, and speaking of, well, thinking of gowns, she must take some new excursions into Earth's distant past. She had not done that in a long time. They were always a great source of new designs for her wardrobe. Yes, she must do that very soon. Images of huge tropical flowers and great big ferns filled her mind.

The next time she opened her eyes, she was puzzled that she had slept again, and this time made a concerted effort to push herself to a sitting position. Leaning back against the pillows, she heard her stomach rumble. She wondered what time it was, but before she could find out, she shuffled to the kitchen and pressed buttons on the food dispenser. An enormous omelet appeared, followed by two biscuits and a huge mug of steaming coffee. She put it all on a tray and took it to the sleeping quarters. She crawled under the covers, put the tray on her lap and savored the omelet. The coffee was good and strong.

She noticed there was no psychic input from anywhere. Strange. But then she got busy enjoying the tasty eggs with mushrooms and cheese and onions. She was so very hungry.

She psychically got the music going, and the room filled with velvet strands of violin and harp.

She leaned back, closed her eyes and listened. Occasionally she took a sip of coffee.

Intruding rudely into this peaceful reverie was a call. From Miranda. Ariel started to send psychic messages of "leave me alone," then stopped herself, thinking not only was that rude, but she hadn't spoken to Miranda in a while and really should take the call. She put the tray on the side table, got out of bed and went to the workstation.

"You're not up yet!" came Miranda's incredulous voice, her eyes wide.

"Yes, so?" asked Ariel, becoming aware that she was still wearing her sleeping gown and that her hair was a mess.

"Nothing. Nothing," said Miranda. "How's it going there?" she asked, and Ariel noticed the controlled, quick way in which Miranda had changed the subject.

"Just fine. I guess I was tired. I slept a long time."

Miranda nodded and looked at her closely. After a while she said, "Sean and I are going to a play at the Actors Enclave tonight." She was smiling and bubbly, and her curly blond hair was reflecting small diamonds in the morning sun.

They made sure they said nothing about their parents, which meant, from Ariel's perspective, that they were probably about the same as before. It was hard this morning to think about them, to think about taking one more trip to the coordinates, so she pushed that aside and continued to listen to Miranda to see if there was any particular reason she called or just to say hello.

In the end she concluded it was a hello call. They switched off, and Ariel lumbered to get dressed and go to the studio. She was so sluggish this morning.

In the studio, she walked directly to the food dispenser and got herself an extra-large mug of coffee. With the mug securely in her hands, she walked to the workstation and turned on all the screens. She yawned, did not feel like working. She strolled around looking at her worlds, daydreaming, lazily tuning into them psychically, not to see how they were doing, as she usually did, but just to enjoy being part of their life. She became one of them, and for a while lived their life.

It was tugging at her, though it felt at a great distance, that she had to urgently get back to work. But as imperative as this seemed, she ignored the feeling. She continued to roam the studio, enjoying her worlds.

Again, that sense of something niggling at her, something forgotten. How strange. Can't be that important, she told herself, otherwise she'd remember it right away, so she smoothly pushed it aside and, when it really came right down to it, continued playing with her various creations.

For the next hour she daydreamed and drifted.

She finally came around to her desk with Laurus in front of her and the decision that she indeed needed to get at least some work done today, even if she was starting at noon. What came of that decision were doodlings of a new world she'd been thinking about designing. She looked at them in frustration and realized she had not done one tiny amount of work, but then the new sketches intrigued her and she transferred them over to a new screen and continued to play with them.

The feeling of something tugging at her persisted. Annoyed she pushed it aside.

A little after two, she sauntered over to the Knife & Fork to have lunch, after a thoroughly unproductive time in the studio. She looked around trying to find someone to talk to, but nobody else was there. They probably all had their lunch already. Ah, she remembered, lunch was served between noon and two. Too bad. It would have been nice to talk to someone.

She got a prepackaged ham sandwich and looked closely at the pink and blue holo flowers in profuse bloom all around the Knife & Fork.

Then she took herself to the promenade outside the Knife & Fork, occasionally pausing to look at the holo flowers, as if they were real.

The tugging feeling was back. It was persistent. She stopped and paid attention. Hmm, what could it be? Probably nothing though. She continued her promenade. She really was not interested in tracking the psychic footprints of anybody. If they weren't here to talk to and have a pleasant lunch with, she would not waste her time tracking them down psychically.

She toyed with the idea of going for a very small workout at the Platt, but decided it was too much of an effort. Maybe teleport and visit Miranda. That too seemed too much of an effort. She settled on going to the Garden and making a tour of all the plants, and if Max was there, visiting with him a little and seeing how his project was coming along.

Steamy warmth enveloped her when she walked into the Garden. She stood for a minute trying to decide how to make her tour. She psychically called out to Max and found out he was indeed in the Garden, up on the third level with his devolution project. She shook her head at that. Max would always surprise her with his creations. She communicated she would be up there in a little while and started her tour of the ground plants. Her enjoyment was continuously disrupted by the tugging. In fact, as she sauntered through the vegetation, it grew more persistent, at last forcing her to stop and focus.

The face of a man rose to the surface, intense. His eyes fierce. He was saying something urgently to her. His mouth moved rapidly, his hands gesticulating in sharp movements. She shook it off. How rude to intrude like that. Whoever he was. She resumed her stroll.

She inspected closely plants that caught her interest, going deeply into their structure, experiencing their life force, only to find the face of the man rising to the surface again and this time other sensations—familiarity, recognition, warmth. Puzzled, she continued her tour but more slowly, trying to remember.

The more she walked, the more sensations she had of this man touching her. At first, each time she felt it, she almost jumped, but then she saw they were always gentle touches and she calmed down to feel more. As she was standing in front of a giant purple blossom the size of a big pumpkin, she was certain that she knew the man, had known him. Where had she seen him? Who was he? After a while, she realized she wasn't looking at the plants any longer, and took the lift to the third level to see Max.

"How's it coming along?" asked Ariel, walking up to Max.

She saw him put his psychic shields up, closing to her. "I've run several different configurations, and we're at the same place we were yesterday." He stopped and looked at her.

"What configurations?"

"Argos!" He looked around, his face tight with anxiety.

"Oh," she moved closer to look at Max's devolution experiment. "Yes, well, it couldn't be helped." When she heard no response, she turned to look at Max.

He stood very still looking at her.

"Hmm." He reached over and rubbed his earlobe, then pointed at his project, "I think I will get the right chemical balance in the next round."

Then he stopped, turned, and looked at her again.

"What? What are you looking at?" asked Ariel, puzzled. She had felt his psychic shields go up and found that strange. He rarely put up shields to keep her out.

"That hurts, Max," she said, not used to being summarily dismissed from Max's inner world.

"Sorry," he said, embarrassed. "My thoughts aren't always chaste, you know." He turned to the control panel, and Ariel knew that his response was a glib improvisation. What was going on?!

She uttered a loud, "Hmm," turned and left.

He didn't say anything. And that too was strange. Going down in the lift, Ariel concluded that it was indeed an odd day this day. Perhaps with a little more rest, things would return to normal.

Chapter Forty-Two

Ariel hummed as she strolled to her quarters. Perfect rose light in the hallways. She stopped, frowned. No tugging. Hmm. It had passed apparently. How strange, so intense, then nothing. She shook her head and kept walking.

Her head still ached a little and felt stuffed with fog, but not as bad as before. Maybe it's all the work. She would rest and after that she would probably be her old self. She felt satisfied with that plan.

The door to her quarters swooshed open. She stepped in, gasped and jumped back. Sprawled on the floor was the man whose face she'd been seeing.

He wasn't moving. His long black hair was spread around his head. A cloak twisted around him. His left leg was bent at the knee. He looked as if he had been flung into her sitting room.

Ariel stood, her hand covering her mouth. Who is he? What was he doing here? She took a step forward. He was completely still. She kneeled beside him and scanned for any psychic output, then remembered and quickly put up shields. Until she found out what this was about, she would rather no one knew.

His face looked like plastic. But he was breathing. She hesitated and then took his hand. Ice. She ran and got a blanket, covered him, then scanned his body for issues. Found drastic depletion. If it was any worse, he would not be alive.

She sat on the floor, crossed her legs and put her hands over his body. She concentrated on boosting all his energies.

Who was he? Why was he here? What a striking looking man. Old Earth Middle period from his clothes.

She maintained a steady augmenting of energy, watching him closely. After a while he began to improve. She continued to boost his energies.

His vital signs strengthened little by little. He was recovering.

Ariel breathed out a sigh of relief. She sat back her arms around her knees. She waited for him to come around, then realized she herself was cold and gave a voice command to turn up the heat. Then waited. It was better not to move him until he was awake.

Images came. Feelings of pleasure, fondness. She could not understand where they came from or why.

After a while he moaned and moved his head. Ariel straightened up.

"Ariel, Ariel," he mumbled.

Ariel pushed to her knees. How does he know my name?

His eyes opened and looked directly at her. "Ariel," he said, his voice weak, but full of relief. His hand reached toward her, then dropped. He was too weak.

"You know my name." Ariel was puzzled. "Who are you?"

"Ariel." He pushed with his hands trying to sit up, then slid down, holding his head. "Oh, my head," he moaned, "Like someone hit me with an axe." His eyes were closed, his face contorted in pain.

"It will be all right. It will pass." She closed her eyes and sent more energy his way.

"I can't move. I'm like a rock."

"There is nothing wrong with you. You're just weak because you've been depleted of energy. You'll be fine. But how did you get here? Who are you?"

"Ariel," he tried to get up again, gave up and laid back down, but continued to look at her, "That drag in teleporting! I've been thinking. It may be the Gateway!" he rasped, his voice urgent.

Ariel looked at him. "What? The Gateway? What are you talking about? How do you know my name? Who are you?" She moved slightly away.

She saw the sadness in his eyes and knew that something was very wrong.

"No time. Have to hurry."

"Hurry, why?" She was shaking her head.

"Take my hand. Try to remember." He put out his hand.

Ariel looked down at his hand. Who is he? She hesitated.

"Please." He looked at her. It took a lot of energy for him to plead with her. "Have to hurry."

Ariel hesitated, but then it was a quick way to find out who he was, and she took his hand.

Images flooded in. When they first saw each other, conversations, lessons, time in Egypt, time in bed. Love, passion, understanding. Kindred souls.

She held on to his hand. After what seemed a long time, with tears streaming down her face, she regained all her memories with Richard, including the last time she had seen him and the moment Darius had walked her to the sick room for erasure.

She sobbed, huge uncontrollable sobs, understood why today was strange, why Max looked at her in that funny way, why Miranda called, why Argos didn't seem to matter. She cried harder and at last slowly let herself embrace Richard, hold him tight.

"It's all right. It's all right," whispered Richard, "My queen, it's all right."

All of that wonder she had almost forgotten. She cried harder, then in shock pulled back, "You teleported here on your own!" Her hands flew over his body again, scanning for anything that might be wrong with him.

"Listen." He waited for her to focus on him. "I think I know where the Gateway is."

She moved away and searched his face. "Why teleport here? Why take the chance? You weren't ready!"

"The Gateway."

Ariel heard him say this, but her brain worked slowly to understand what he was saying.

He waited, looking at her, holding her hand.

"The Gateway?"

"Yes. We have to hurry."

"Hurry?"

"We have to see if I am right. We both have to do it together." He pushed himself up on his elbow, grimacing in pain. "I feel like I've fallen off a horse again. Everything aches."

"Let's get you to bed. I think you can walk." She stood up and pulled on Richard.

"No. No bed. We have to check if I am right about the Gateway."

"We can't do anything until you're stronger." She tugged at him again. "And until I'm clearer."

He tried to stand up but couldn't. He held his head in his hands and groaned.

"You have to rest and recover."

He said nothing. Then they tried again and got him to the sleeping quarters.

"Lie down. Rest."

"How long?" asked Richard, laying down slowly.

"I'll get you something to eat, then we'll work on strengthening us," and she was off to the kitchen. She heard Richard calling after her, "Hurry."

While she prepared a tray of coffee, toast and jam, she strengthened psychic shields. She wondered how they had found out about Richard. They were here for only minutes. She hurried. She'd have to get him out of here as fast as possible. It seemed that Richard had teleported here while they were searching for him in Eventon. Her hands started to shake. I have to get him out of here. I have to get him somewhere safe until I can figure out what's happening.

She spilled some of the coffee carrying it back. "You're right. We have to get you out of here as fast as possible."

Richard sat up, and she set the tray on his lap and walked to the workstation, sat down and activated the transducer. "See if you can add to the psychic shields," she said and activated healing and energy-boosting sequences. The transducer hummed and sparkled.

She aligned herself with its frequencies and synchronized her energy functions, allowing it to augment them. Simultaneously, she sent the same energy to Richard.

"They're looking for you." She held his eyes for a minute.

He stopped chewing. "Why?"

She told him they were discovered. She told him about the erasure. "They want to erase your memory, too. We have to get you out of here. Find you a safe place."

He nodded and winced. "Makes sense." He picked up the coffee and took a swallow. "All right. I'll be ready to go in a minute here."

He held up the cup, "What is this? It's good."

Ariel smiled. "Coffee. Very popular." She watched him, sensed him gathering his energies. Good, he's activating his own healing capabilities. That will expedite things. She watched him a little longer. She loved him so much. Then she turned to the transducer, all her energies focused on strengthening both of them. They had to get strong fast.

She had to ask, "I looked for you everywhere. Couldn't find you. Where were you?"

Richard looked down. "My apologies. I had all shields up trying to figure out what to do. You know they'd seen us?"

"I went to Marion's. She told me."

He nodded. "But this Gateway problem was on my mind, and I kept noticing the drag when we teleported. That does not happen when I teleport on my own."

Ariel looked at him, her brows together. He was teleporting when she wasn't there.

"And your parents worked together, right?"

Ariel's heart raced.

"We have to try, see if I'm right about the Gateway."

Ariel's brain was moving fast. The Gateway. They had to get somewhere safe. "Richard!" she was over to him instantly, her lips on his then pulled back, "You're amazing!"

Richard's face was bright with joy, "I love you."

Ariel kissed him again, "And I love you."

Richard took a breath. His face became serious, "I think that lag is an anomaly. I think it's there we need to look for the Gateway." He paused, then said softly, "Maybe it's not too late to find your parents."

Ariel's heart leaped. "We will look."

She went back to the transducer and continued to build up their strength. To find the Gateway and Vivian and Andreas! All of her exploded with hope. Maybe. She glanced over at Richard.

His eyes were closed. He was focusing, strengthening his energy and simultaneously strengthening the psychic shields. His face had shades of pink now and was luminous with concentration. Her heart warmed.

He opened his eyes and looked at her.

She didn't want to say this now, but had to. It was too strong in her. "Richard." She paused. "I think I was wrong about Argos."

His eyebrows went up.

"The prototype shows nothing new." She looked down at her hands. "I think that's the end."

Richard shook his head, a mysterious smile on his face. "No, no," he paused, "No, not the end, just not done."

Ariel snapped to attention, her eyes wide, "Not done?! How not done? We've all checked, double-checked and triple-checked the data from every direction, and now the prototype shows the same information. I can't see what else can be done."

"No," he shook his head again. "No," he said with finality.

Ariel said nothing, wondering about his certainty. How could he know?

"You have to follow through."

"But it's impossible," said Ariel. "All the data shows it's impossible."

Richard shook his head, "When the heart is pure, anything's possible." He held her eyes, powerful intensity in his face.

Ariel nodded. Felt his strength coming into her.

The crystal transducer hummed and flashed. They were quiet, focused on becoming stronger.

After a while, Ariel opened her eyes, took a big breath and turned to Richard, "How do you feel? Are you ready to move?"

Richard swung his legs to the floor. "Where to?"

"Xarinda. It's a world where I sometimes go to get away from things."

Richard nodded and smiled, "You have many places you go to escape, don't you?"

Ariel's brows went up, "Busted! Anyway, there is nothing there. A good place to hide."

On Xarinda he'd be safe until she had time to figure out what to do. Then she transmitted the Xarinda information.

Richard stood still, receiving. Once in a while he nodded. His eyes were hard with concentration.

She sent a visual of the spacesuit, then the life-support dome. His eyelids flickered, and he looked up at her.

"They don't have air on Xarinda like here. We need all this to breathe and survive."

He nodded and looked off into the distance, taking this in.

It's the only plan she could come up with. She had no idea what to do after that, but it was far better than Richard going back and having Darius find him. She could regain her memories, but she wasn't sure Richard could. Yet. At some point, he would learn, would be strong enough, but not now.

She quickly gathered everything they needed. For a moment, they stood looking at each other. One side of Richard's mouth went up.

Ariel smiled.

"Watch for the rift," Richard said.

Chapter Forty-Three

"The small drag," said Richard when they arrived on Xarinda,

"Did you feel the small drag then a subtle bump?"

Ariel shook her head. "No."

Richard looked around slowly at the black peaks, at the red dust at his feet, then back at Ariel. "Not very cheerful," he smiled, then his face became serious. "Let's do it again. Teleport a little distance." He nodded. "You'll feel it. Pay attention." He was thoughtful for a second. "Your focus is completely on where we are going. Leave some of your attention, sequester a small part of your consciousness and monitor the actual transport."

Ariel looked around, considered the craziness of their situation. Here she was on Xarinda with Richard. He'd teleported to Palladium—by himself! Now he wants to look at the rift. She shook her head. If things were unreal before, now they were way off the spectrum of normal.

"All right. Let's go." Nothing to do right now but go with what is. She took a deep breath.

They teleported a short distance.

Richard looked at her, his eyes focused on her closely.

"I see." She did notice. "Wonder why."

"You see how it's all smooth and then there is this drag followed by a slight bump, this very sharp slowing of time, then back to normal?"

She focused back on what she'd felt and nodded. It was as if they were hurled along with a nanosecond interruption. Definitely something there.

"If we could stop at that moment and explore it..."

"Yes. An interesting irregularity. It's amazing you noticed." She slid the pack off her back and looked around for a place to set up the dome.

"We have to explore it," said Richard.

Ariel spotted a flat area with a semicircle of rocks and started toward them. Richard followed.

"We can't do it now. I have to get back to the ship before they start to miss me." She dropped the pack to the ground, squatted and started pulling stuff out.

Richard looked around, set his pack down, "Let's see if we can find out more."

"I don't think we're strong enough yet, Richard. We should wait. Anyhow, we don't have time right now."

"We're fine. One short jump with one quick up-close look."

Ariel unpacked the dome and in a moment it unfurled, glistening silver in a sea of red.

Richard looked at the dome. "I am to stay in there until you're back?" He did not sound happy. "With all there is to do, I am to wait?!"

"I am sorry, I shouldn't be long. Anyway, it will be good for you. You can rest and get all your strength back." She smiled. "Think about all we'll be able to do then."

He picked up a small pebble and threw it at her. "We'll see about that, milady. One more. Let's do it. One more jump. Nothing to worry about. That way you'll have more information and can start to work on it."

Ariel hesitated, shrugged, "All right." If he felt that strongly, was that confident, she was sure it would be all right.

She focused on the destination coordinates. She watched very carefully for the irregularity. When it came, they both stopped.

It took all her energy to isolate the precise moment in which it occurred and to hold there. But without a doubt, the area around them wobbled and was unstable.

"It's as if it goes in all directions," Richard said when solid again. His eyes were closed, and he had his hand on the helmet.

"Head throbbing still?"

Richard nodded. "Don't worry, it will go away. Much better than before."

Ariel thought about what just happened. "Interesting. I've not encountered anything quite like it. Worth exploring."

"Exactly!" said Richard. He looked around and reached for his pack. "At least we've made a start."

Ariel crawled into the dome, "Come."

Richard followed with his pack.

"And it will be easier once we have all our strength back." She started to pull out the supplies, packages of food, water, cooking equipment, emergency kit and sleeping roll.

Richard looked at the laid-out packages, "I hope I don't have to stay here that long to use all this stuff."

Ariel put a hand on his shoulder, "I'll be back as soon as I can." She felt anxiety move throughout her whole body, a small electric wave.

He nodded, looking around the spacious dome, "At least it's nice and roomy."

She stepped out, and Richard followed.

"Rest. Don't go anywhere. Don't try to reach me. All right?"

"Sure. It will be good to rest," Richard said, his voice unconvincing.

Then she saw he was thinking of practicing teleporting and said, "Only if you feel strong enough. Please don't take any risks."

"Nothing to worry about. Didn't I make it to you?" He stepped over and wrapped his arms around her.

"Not the best hug I've had," she said. The suits and helmets created a big barrier.

Richard stepped back. "If we can just hang there long enough to see what it is."

Ariel nodded. "Listen, just in case, the coordinates to get back, if I can't come back for you." They looked at each other but said nothing about what that might imply. They stood silently as she transmitted the coordinates to him. First coordinates to Palladium, second coordinates to his house. Her throat tightened. She didn't want to leave him.

"Don't try anything…" She looked deeply into that blue flame of his eyes. She didn't continue, didn't believe he'd listen. He would do whatever he believed was right.

"You have to regain your strength. I have to get back." She swallowed. To leave Richard. Just as she had gotten him back. Her stomach tightened.

She stepped forward and wrapped her arms around him. Can't kiss him. She stepped back, her lips compressed, determined not to cry.

"Come back for me." The right side of his mouth was curled up in an amused smile.

She nodded and stepped back, looked at him, a white bundle in a vast gloom of red.

His hand came up in a slow wave.

Chapter Forty-Four

Back in her quarters, Ariel scanned the ship. Was anyone looking for her? Had anyone found out? She held her breath, lips compressed, and scanned. Anything unusual? Her heart thundered.

Nothing. She let out a loud breath of relief and sat back in the chair. But for how long?

She checked for messages. How long had she been gone? A few

hours since she'd found Richard. Everything appeared normal.

She tore off the bulky suit, recycled it and slid into her blue work suit. She combed her hair and pulled it back with the topaz clip. Her face was tight with anxiety. Muscles rigid, ready for action. She stood still for a minute. Breathe, breathe. Everything will be all right, she tried to convince herself.

Something to eat. That will help. In the kitchen, she ordered a turkey sandwich from the dispenser and sat in front of the fireplace to eat, even though there was no fire.

She chewed and wondered. If Richard hadn't teleported, when would she have remembered him fully? If at all. Erased. All her decisions, all her faith in the two of them, erased, obliterated. Her life, her choices, shaped by someone else, determined by someone who believed they knew better. Her body hardened into a determined resistance. They won't take my life away from me! I will see this through!

She ate the sandwich with determination, tasting nothing. She will regain all her strength. She will persevere. She will find answers.

What to do with Richard? She swallowed. How long will Darius persist in looking for him?

She took another bite of the sandwich. Her hands shook. She will have to stay alert, stay ahead of them, be ready with options depending on what unfolded.

She was cold through and through and called for a higher temperature, then got a mug of hot chocolate. The warmth felt good. After a few swallows, she started to relax.

She considered the irregularity Richard discovered. Could it possibly be the Gateway? It was hard to believe, but maybe. She laughed at the irony of the possibility. The new humans searching for the Gateway for years, and the forbidden man from the forbidden past finds it.

She swallowed the last bite and quickly cleaned up.

In her sleeping quarters, she straightened the bed cover, then stood in the middle of the room and scanned to see if any tracks remained of Richard and cleared the slight remaining energetic patterns. It hurt her to do it, but she had to. They would have plenty of time together, she told herself, once all this was over. Then she wondered if that was really true. She pushed that thought aside and sat by the crystal transducer. She had to equalize, can't let them know she remembered. She took her time making inner adjustments. The transducer ran through a cycle of tones and light emissions then settled into a steady hum.

Feeling solid, she walked to her studio. No sooner had she activated her equipment when the console toned and Miranda's face appeared.

"No. Not good." Her eyes were red, and her mouth drooped at the corners.

"What?" Ariel searched her face to find out what was going on.

"No good news," said Miranda.

Ariel waited. She noticed the careful shields Miranda had up.

"If I could see you..." Miranda said, her voice a whisper, her lips compressed as if she was trying not to cry.

Ariel sensed the longing, the need. She felt her own exhaustion. One more teleportation. She glanced at the Laurus screen. She looked at the time. If she went for just a little. She clenched her jaw.

"I'll be over as soon as I finish this," said Ariel and ended the call.

She quickly moved through work, spent some moments boosting her energies with the transducer. She had to be careful. She could not afford any energy loss. Not right now. No mistakes of that kind.

She found Miranda sitting on the sofa looking out the window. She wore gray riding pants and a white blouse.

The sun was setting. The great room had the stillness of dusk, of timelessness, painted with splashes of amber light and shadow.

Miranda turned to look at Ariel when she appeared, then turned back and continued to look out the window.

Ariel sat next to her. Whatever it is, she could not stay long, and she transmitted that to Miranda, including images of the approaching Laurus.

"Yes, I know," said Miranda. "I am just glad you are here," she said in a small voice. She twisted and hugged Ariel, then pulled back, "Sean and I ended it all." She looked down into her lap.

Ariel was taken aback. All this just because she and Sean had a fight? She exhaled loudly. "What happened?"

"I'm so confused. I don't know what to do." She was twisting the tissue in her hands.

Ariel waited.

After a while Miranda said, "It's not just that. Mother and father are not well. They never fully stabilized as we both thought they would." She let out a sigh.

Ariel jerked back in surprise, "What? They're not better?"

Miranda shook her head. "I tried calling, but you weren't there." She blew her nose. "Anyway, I was still hoping it would pass, like the other times."

Ariel felt her entire body tighten. She had to get back to Xarinda. They had to investigate the rift. She checked the time.

Miranda continued slowly, "I just feel this dreadful empty feeling and I can't think what to do about it. I've not had my lessons for days, and I've not made a single piece of jewelry." She turned to look at Ariel; her face was pure misery.

"Because of Sean?" Ariel closed her eyes. It was hard to listen. She was anxious. She had to get back. She had to get to Richard.

Miranda nodded.

"What happened?"

"He just kept wanting to do these things. He kept having all these ideas, like the idea he had about the opal he gave me for my birthday. Remember?"

Ariel nodded.

"I felt like I was always running to keep up with him, and it was never fast enough."

Ariel remembered the opal and the freshness and novelty of his idea. She had liked it tremendously, but she knew Miranda wouldn't.

"I think that was it more than anything," she continued, "He was always pushing me to do things I didn't really want to do." She sat thinking. "But I miss him." She was looking out the window again.

"But why, why not try the new things?" Ariel said, exasperated.

Miranda jerked her head, looked at her frowning.

"Never mind." Ariel took her hand, "You miss him."

"I do." She paused. "That's what I can't understand." She let out a sigh, her shoulders drooping.

Ariel got up. "You want something to drink? I'm getting a juice." Then froze. Darius was tracking her, transmitting that it was urgent she come to his office immediately. Ariel could hardly breathe. Why urgent? Why his office? What did he want?

She transmitted she was off the ship and would be back shortly. She took a big breath and exhaled. Everything inside her was churning. She had to get back. She had to listen to Miranda. Just calm down, calm down. Everything will be all right. I can handle whatever comes my way, she was convincing herself.

She took a breath and turned her attention back to Miranda. "What did you say, want anything to drink?"

Miranda shook her head. "I wish I didn't feel so miserable."

Sometimes it was hard to be patient with her. Miranda liked routines. She liked predictability. So that meant one thing: go back to doing what she had always done. Even though she said she wanted to do something new.

"You have to get back to creating jewelry and giving lessons," Ariel called from the kitchen.

She poured some raspberry juice, came back and handed a glass to Miranda and sat down. "Drink, you'll feel better. Doing a little work will put things in perspective quickly enough. Just start."

"You think so?" said Miranda, hope in her voice.

Ariel nodded. "Yes. Did they have anything new to say at Melrose?"

"No. They just sounded less certain than ever about their ability to continue. I'm going there later today."

Ariel put her hand on Miranda's shoulder, "Thank you for carrying the main burden of our parents. Let me know how they are doing when you get back."

Miranda nodded, "It's not a burden. I am here. I know you're doing all you can to find them."

They were quiet for a while. Everything felt dark and heavy. Ariel could hardly breathe. Finally, she forced herself to get up. "I have to go. I have to try one more thing."

Miranda also stood up, looked at her, questions in her eyes, but said nothing.

"Just get back into your routine. And don't worry about Sean. With a little time, that will sort itself out." She waited to see if Miranda took this in.

"All right," Miranda said, her voice a weak resignation.

"Just... have too much to do right now to stay longer."

Miranda nodded. "Don't worry." She hugged Ariel. "It helped you coming, even if for a little while."

Chapter Forty-Three

"The small drag," said Richard when they arrived on Xarinda, "Did you feel the small drag then a subtle bump?"

Ariel shook her head. "No."

Richard looked around slowly at the black peaks, at the red dust at his feet, then back at Ariel. "Not very cheerful," he smiled, then his face became serious. "Let's do it again. Teleport a little distance." He nodded. "You'll feel it. Pay attention." He was thoughtful for a second. "Your focus is completely on where we are going. Leave some of your attention, sequester a small part of your consciousness and monitor the actual transport."

Ariel looked around, considered the craziness of their situation. Here she was on Xarinda with Richard. He'd teleported to Palladium—by himself! Now he wants to look at the rift. She shook her head. If things were unreal before, now they were way off the spectrum of normal.

"All right. Let's go." Nothing to do right now but go with what is. She took a deep breath.

They teleported a short distance.

Richard looked at her, his eyes focused on her closely.

"I see." She did notice. "Wonder why."

"You see how it's all smooth and then there is this drag followed by a slight bump, this very sharp slowing of time, then back to normal?"

She focused back on what she'd felt and nodded. It was as if they were hurled along with a nanosecond interruption. Definitely something there.

"If we could stop at that moment and explore it . . ."

"Yes. An interesting irregularity. It's amazing you noticed." She slid the pack off her back and looked around for a place to set up the dome.

"We have to explore it," said Richard.

Ariel spotted a flat area with a semicircle of rocks and started toward them. Richard followed.

"We can't do it now. I have to get back to the ship before they start to miss me." She dropped the pack to the ground, squatted and started pulling stuff out.

Richard looked around, set his pack down, "Let's see if we can find out more."

"I don't think we're strong enough yet, Richard. We should wait. Anyhow, we don't have time right now."

"We're fine. One short jump with one quick up-close look."

Ariel unpacked the dome and in a moment it unfurled, glistening silver in a sea of red.

Richard looked at the dome. "I am to stay in there until you're back?" He did not sound happy. "With all there is to do, I am to wait?!"

"I am sorry, I shouldn't be long. Anyway, it will be good for you. You can rest and get all your strength back." She smiled. "Think about all we'll be able to do then."

He picked up a small pebble and threw it at her. "We'll see about that, milady. One more. Let's do it. One more jump. Nothing to worry about. That way you'll have more information and can start to work on it."

Ariel hesitated, shrugged, "All right." If he felt that strongly, was that confident, she was sure it would be all right.

She focused on the destination coordinates. She watched very carefully for the irregularity. When it came, they both stopped.

It took all her energy to isolate the precise moment in which it occurred and to hold there. But without a doubt, the area around them wobbled and was unstable.

"It's as if it goes in all directions," Richard said when solid again. His eyes were closed, and he had his hand on the helmet.

"Head throbbing still?"

Richard nodded. "Don't worry, it will go away. Much better than before."

Ariel thought about what just happened. "Interesting. I've not encountered anything quite like it. Worth exploring."

"Exactly!" said Richard. He looked around and reached for his pack. "At least we've made a start."

Ariel crawled into the dome, "Come."

Richard followed with his pack.

"And it will be easier once we have all our strength back." She started to pull out the supplies, packages of food, water, cooking equipment, emergency kit and sleeping roll.

Richard looked at the laid-out packages, "I hope I don't have to stay here that long to use all this stuff."

Ariel put a hand on his shoulder, "I'll be back as soon as I can." She felt anxiety move throughout her whole body, a small electric wave.

He nodded, looking around the spacious dome, "At least it's nice and roomy."

She stepped out, and Richard followed.

"Rest. Don't go anywhere. Don't try to reach me. All right?"

"Sure. It will be good to rest," Richard said, his voice unconvincing.

Then she saw he was thinking of practicing teleporting and said, "Only if you feel strong enough. Please don't take any risks."

"Nothing to worry about. Didn't I make it to you?" He stepped over and wrapped his arms around her.

"Not the best hug I've had," she said. The suits and helmets created a big barrier.

Richard stepped back. "If we can just hang there long enough to see what it is."

Ariel nodded. "Listen, just in case, the coordinates to get back, if I can't come back for you." They looked at each other but said nothing about what that might imply. They stood silently as she transmitted the coordinates to him. First coordinates to Palladium, second coordinates to his house. Her throat tightened. She didn't want to leave him.

"Don't try anything…" She looked deeply into that blue flame of his eyes. She didn't continue, didn't believe he'd listen. He would do whatever he believed was right.

"You have to regain your strength. I have to get back." She swallowed. To leave Richard. Just as she had gotten him back. Her stomach tightened.

She stepped forward and wrapped her arms around him. Can't kiss him. She stepped back, her lips compressed, determined not to cry.

"Come back for me." The right side of his mouth was curled up in an amused smile.

She nodded and stepped back, looked at him, a white bundle in a vast gloom of red.

His hand came up in a slow wave.

Chapter Forty-Four

Back in her quarters, Ariel scanned the ship. Was anyone looking for her? Had anyone found out? She held her breath, lips compressed, and scanned. Anything unusual? Her heart thundered.

Nothing. She let out a loud breath of relief and sat back in the chair. But for how long?

She checked for messages. How long had she been gone? A few hours since she'd found Richard. Everything appeared normal.

She tore off the bulky suit, recycled it and slid into her blue work suit. She combed her hair and pulled it back with the topaz clip. Her face was tight with anxiety. Muscles rigid, ready for action. She stood still for a minute. Breathe, breathe. Everything will be all right, she tried to convince herself.

Something to eat. That will help. In the kitchen, she ordered a turkey sandwich from the dispenser and sat in front of the fireplace to eat, even though there was no fire.

She chewed and wondered. If Richard hadn't teleported, when would she have remembered him fully? If at all. Erased. All her decisions, all her faith in the two of them, erased, obliterated. Her life, her choices, shaped by someone else, determined by someone who believed they knew better. Her body hardened into a determined resistance. They won't take my life away from me! I will see this through!

She ate the sandwich with determination, tasting nothing. She will regain all her strength. She will persevere. She will find answers.

What to do with Richard? She swallowed. How long will Darius persist in looking for him?

She took another bite of the sandwich. Her hands shook. She will have to stay alert, stay ahead of them, be ready with options depending on what unfolded.

She was cold through and through and called for a higher temperature, then got a mug of hot chocolate. The warmth felt good. After a few swallows, she started to relax.

She considered the irregularity Richard discovered. Could it possibly be the Gateway? It was hard to believe, but maybe. She laughed at the irony of the possibility. The new humans searching for the Gateway for years, and the forbidden man from the forbidden past finds it.

She swallowed the last bite and quickly cleaned up.

In her sleeping quarters, she straightened the bed cover, then stood in the middle of the room and scanned to see if any tracks remained of Richard and cleared the slight remaining energetic patterns. It hurt her to do it, but she had to. They would have plenty of time together, she told herself, once all this was over. Then she wondered if that was really true. She pushed that thought aside and sat by the crystal transducer. She had to equalize, can't let them know she remembered. She took her time making inner adjustments. The transducer ran through a cycle of tones and light emissions then settled into a steady hum.

Feeling solid, she walked to her studio. No sooner had she activated her equipment when the console toned and Miranda's face appeared.

"No. Not good." Her eyes were red, and her mouth drooped at the corners.

"What?" Ariel searched her face to find out what was going on.

"No good news," said Miranda.

Ariel waited. She noticed the careful shields Miranda had up.

"If I could see you . . ." Miranda said, her voice a whisper, her lips compressed as if she was trying not to cry.

Ariel sensed the longing, the need. She felt her own exhaustion. One more teleportation. She glanced at the Laurus screen. She looked at the time. If she went for just a little. She clenched her jaw.

"I'll be over as soon as I finish this," said Ariel and ended the call.

She quickly moved through work, spent some moments boosting her energies with the transducer. She had to be careful. She could not afford any energy loss. Not right now. No mistakes of that kind.

She found Miranda sitting on the sofa looking out the window. She wore gray riding pants and a white blouse.

The sun was setting. The great room had the stillness of dusk, of timelessness, painted with splashes of amber light and shadow.

Miranda turned to look at Ariel when she appeared, then turned back and continued to look out the window.

Ariel sat next to her. Whatever it is, she could not stay long, and she transmitted that to Miranda, including images of the approaching Laurus.

"Yes, I know," said Miranda. "I am just glad you are here," she said in a small voice. She twisted and hugged Ariel, then pulled back, "Sean and I ended it all." She looked down into her lap.

Ariel was taken aback. All this just because she and Sean had a fight? She exhaled loudly. "What happened?"

"I'm so confused. I don't know what to do." She was twisting the tissue in her hands.

Ariel waited.

After a while Miranda said, "It's not just that. Mother and father are not well. They never fully stabilized as we both thought they would." She let out a sigh.

Ariel jerked back in surprise, "What? They're not better?"

Miranda shook her head. "I tried calling, but you weren't there." She blew her nose. "Anyway, I was still hoping it would pass, like the other times."

Ariel felt her entire body tighten. She had to get back to Xarinda. They had to investigate the rift. She checked the time.

Miranda continued slowly, "I just feel this dreadful empty feeling and I can't think what to do about it. I've not had my lessons for days, and I've not made a single piece of jewelry." She turned to look at Ariel; her face was pure misery.

"Because of Sean?" Ariel closed her eyes. It was hard to listen. She was anxious. She had to get back. She had to get to Richard.

Miranda nodded.

"What happened?"

"He just kept wanting to do these things. He kept having all these ideas, like the idea he had about the opal he gave me for my birthday. Remember?"

Ariel nodded.

"I felt like I was always running to keep up with him, and it was never fast enough."

Ariel remembered the opal and the freshness and novelty of

his idea. She had liked it tremendously, but she knew Miranda wouldn't.

"I think that was it more than anything," she continued, "He was always pushing me to do things I didn't really want to do." She sat thinking. "But I miss him." She was looking out the window again.

"But why, why not try the new things?" Ariel said, exasperated.

Miranda jerked her head, looked at her frowning.

"Never mind." Ariel took her hand, "You miss him."

"I do." She paused. "That's what I can't understand." She let out a sigh, her shoulders drooping.

Ariel got up. "You want something to drink? I'm getting a juice." Then froze. Darius was tracking her, transmitting that it was urgent she come to his office immediately. Ariel could hardly breathe. Why urgent? Why his office? What did he want?

She transmitted she was off the ship and would be back shortly. She took a big breath and exhaled. Everything inside her was churning. She had to get back. She had to listen to Miranda. Just calm down, calm down. Everything will be all right. I can handle whatever comes my way, she was convincing herself.

She took a breath and turned her attention back to Miranda. "What did you say, want anything to drink?"

Miranda shook her head. "I wish I didn't feel so miserable."

Sometimes it was hard to be patient with her. Miranda liked routines. She liked predictability. So that meant one thing: go back to doing what she had always done. Even though she said she wanted to do something new.

"You have to get back to creating jewelry and giving lessons," Ariel called from the kitchen.

She poured some raspberry juice, came back and handed a

glass to Miranda and sat down. "Drink, you'll feel better. Doing a little work will put things in perspective quickly enough. Just start."

"You think so?" said Miranda, hope in her voice.

Ariel nodded. "Yes. Did they have anything new to say at Melrose?"

"No. They just sounded less certain than ever about their ability to continue. I'm going there later today."

Ariel put her hand on Miranda's shoulder, "Thank you for carrying the main burden of our parents. Let me know how they are doing when you get back."

Miranda nodded, "It's not a burden. I am here. I know you're doing all you can to find them."

They were quiet for a while. Everything felt dark and heavy. Ariel could hardly breathe. Finally, she forced herself to get up. "I have to go. I have to try one more thing."

Miranda also stood up, looked at her, questions in her eyes, but said nothing.

"Just get back into your routine. And don't worry about Sean. With a little time, that will sort itself out." She waited to see if Miranda took this in.

"All right," Miranda said, her voice a weak resignation.

"Just . . . have too much to do right now to stay longer."

Miranda nodded. "Don't worry." She hugged Ariel. "It helped you coming, even if for a little while."

Chapter Forty-Five

Ariel and Max sat at the table facing Darius. Darius's face was tight with anger. "I am waiting for an explanation as to why the two of you decided to build an Argos prototype when you know perfectly well that's not allowed."

Except for the hum and occasional click of the equipment, the silence was thick.

Darius looked from her to Max, waiting. He sat in his white robes, hands on the desk, fingers intertwined.

Ariel said nothing. She tried several times to come up with an acceptable explanation about Argos, but everything that came to her sounded infantile.

She sensed Max shifting in the chair next to her, but he said nothing.

At last she said, "I was certain I was right."

Darius nodded.

Ariel knew it didn't matter what she thought or felt. Breaking New Earth laws was forbidden. That's all there was to it. And here she'd broken more of them. She sat still in her chair. The hum of the equipment droned on.

So close and to be found out now! She felt the tightness in her chest. I can't get to Richard now. The rift. She closed her eyes and sensed Darius watching her. Her psychic shields were tightly up.

She didn't care what he thought. She didn't care that he saw them firmly in place.

She opened her eyes and gazed directly into his eyes. You don't know, she thought. You don't know and you never will. Her body felt rigid with the effort of maintaining the shields.

Darius' eyes went to Max.

Ariel heard the psychic communication going to Max. How could you have colluded on this, Max? What were you thinking you would accomplish? Why do you think we, as the people of the New Earth, do not know what is best for all of us?

"Darius, I saw no harm in experimenting," Max said quietly, yet in a firm voice. His clasped hands rested on Darius' table.

Darius raised his eyebrows, shifted his weight and transmitted, "You know very well that is not the issue."

The tiny hum of the transducer sounded volcanic.

Darius continued to look at them and continued his telepathic transmissions. He ran images of all of Earth's history, the reasons why things were the way they were, why they did what they did now, as if Ariel and Max didn't know. They knew.

He underscored the danger of losing everything the New Humans had worked so hard to have: peace, stability, and most of all boundless freedom to create, no longer troubled by destructive human emotions that led to destructive acts of all sorts, led to wars.

She wanted to scream; I had a powerful intuition! but knew it would sound ridiculous. Especially now that the prototyping showed nothing new. Did she really jeopardize the New Earth just by building a prototype? Did she really do that? How could they know for sure? What if she was right? They would never know.

She looked around the room, studying the way the lights illuminated the equipment, the way the readouts flickered.

She tightened her shields. She just wanted this to be over. She groaned, thinking of what all this might mean. And Richard. Alone on Xarinda. How long would he wait? Before he realized she wasn't coming back. Ariel felt black inside.

At last, Darius was done running them through the history and the New Earth's directives and prime directives. He pushed his chair back, sighed and said, "It is not my decision alone. The Earth Council will be informed. They will make the decision." He stood up. "You're both relieved of all your duties for the time being."

Ariel felt as if her head had been thrown into a pot of boiling water.

She heard a small gasp from Max, then. "Darius, is this really necessary? I have a lot of work to do?"

Darius looked at Max. "You will wait in the sickroom until the Earth Council has made a decision." He headed for the door, motioned for them to follow.

Ariel forced her body to stand up, to walk. She felt as if she was being slowly lowered into the final darkness.

She turned to Max, "I am sorry."

"It was my choice," said Max. "No need to apologize." He smiled and patted her on the back.

Ariel walked but didn't feel her body. Everything seemed unreal, as if she was looking through thick glass.

They stopped by the first sickroom, and Darius motioned Max to go in. He led Ariel down the hall and into the second sickroom. Ariel stepped in and heard the door shut behind her.

Here she was again.

The room was small with light green walls. The lights were low. A bed, cabinet, food dispenser, table, two chairs, and a door going into the washroom.

She walked across the room and sat on the bed.

All gone. All a big waste. She bent over and put her elbows on her knees and held her head. She'll never know. Never know if any of these powerful drives were real—about Richard, about Argos, about any of this.

And Richard. What will happen to Richard? Even if he teleported back to Old Earth, Darius would find him. If not right away, eventually. His life will be the same nonsensical mess that hers had become.

She stood up and paced the small distance of the room. And the rift. What if Richard was right? What if it was the Gateway? What if Vivian and Andreas were there, stuck? Now they couldn't even look. She groaned.

She sat back down. And the humiliation. She could hardly breathe from it. Having enjoyed the undisputed, coveted position of lead New Worlds Designer, she couldn't bear to think that she was now a simple old-time criminal. She closed her eyes, her body hurt all over.

Unable to stand the chaos in her mind, she got up again and paced. How long will she need to be here? When would the Earth Council convene? Certainly not immediately. And they would need time to review the situation and time to make a decision.

She was glad her parents were not able to witness this humiliation. She shook her head in disbelief at the turn her life had taken.

She walked to the food dispenser and got a glass of water. She was hungry, wanted to eat, but her stomach felt twisted shut.

Apparently through all this business she had simply not enforced her psychic shields enough, had been sloppy with her thoughts and work. She laughed. Just that little omission. Why, oh why wasn't she more careful, more methodical?

She put the glass on the table, pulled out a chair and sat down. Her head hurt from exertion.

And what did it matter anyway? She sighed. It seemed that her hunches about Argos were wrong. The prototype showed that. Whatever those powerful driving intuitions were that forced her into unprecedented New Human disobedience were wrong, wrong, wrong. She was wrong to follow them.

And this was possibly the worst of it: she was somehow flawed!

Then she stopped pacing. But, but not yet, not yet, she screamed inside. I wasn't done! I wasn't done! Richard said that. Richard said that. What if he was right?

She knew there was nothing she could do to stop her mind, and she didn't care if she did. Even if it drove her crazy. There was no more reason to remain sane. Richard. But even Richard was probably a mistake too. She was bitter through and through.

She stood up and walked around the room. Teleportation was out of the question. All the security systems were in place that would interfere with any effort to teleport out of here. She would have to stay here until they came for her. What will they do to finish up Laurus?

She reached out telepathically to Miranda and found shields in place around the room to prevent psychic output. She knew there would be, but she instinctively wanted the comfort of Miranda's presence.

After a while, when the pain had become more bearable, she cried. All the weeks of effort. All the weeks of fear and doubt. The torment of not knowing if she was doing the right thing or not, the agony of her intuitions, the doubt about all her decisions, hours and hours and hours of work. All done. All for nothing. All misguided. And the exhaustion complete. She'll never see Richard again. And she sobbed harder. This time she was sure all the traces of him would be gone if they decided on erasure as a way to bring her back to normal.

She cried and cried until she could cry no more. Then she laid down on the small bed and felt a dreadful peace. At least it was over.

It was nighttime by then. She pulled off her boots, pulled the covers over her and released herself to oblivion.

Chapter Forty-Six

Ariel opened her eyes, turned over on her back, and started to remember. And anguish spread through her entire body. Then pain. Excruciating pain. Her face contorted in unnatural angles. It was all over. She lay motionless. Still. The stillness of resignation.

She did not want to get up. Why? What for? Everything that had any meaning for her was gone. She wondered when they'd let her know their plans for her. Not for a while, she didn't think. Maybe it's good to be alone, get used to this new reality. She sniffed. Hardly.

It was quiet in the sickroom. The ship hum unusually loud. She breathed and listened.

Will she be sent back to Earth, taken off her post as lead designer? This had never happened before in New Earth history, so she didn't know what they would do.

She pulled the cover up to her face and held it there with both hands. Did Richard suspect something by now? What would he do? Where would he go? Would he even be able to teleport from Xarinda?

So many things unfinished, unanswered. She groaned.

And Max, poor Max. She had involved him in all this. Maybe they'll be easy on him, allowing for the passion of the creative impulse. But she doubted it. His career may be ruined just like hers or worse.

She lay there. At least she didn't have to get up, do anything, go anywhere. She could be in her misery all alone, uninterrupted.

Then Richard's soft smile floated before her. She welcomed it. She imagined his arms around her. Heard his voice urging her to look closer at the rift. The sense of his presence comforted her. She vaguely wondered if there was something she could do to change the course of this devastation, but it was just a passing hope in a thick gloom.

A mug of coffee. That would help. She pushed back the covers, shuffled to the dispenser and got a large mug, then sat down at the table.

There was no communication equipment in the sickroom. She was by herself, completely cut off. She was grateful for the coffee. It tasted better than it ever had.

After a while she got a peach pastry, ate it and felt better. What could she do? Maybe there was something, though she had no energy to even think about what it could be. She sat with elbows on the table, head in her hands. She wondered whether she could access any reading material. She got up and walked to the small workstation. Looked like quite a good amount was available. She tried reading various things, finished nothing. She gave up and went back to lie on the bed. Stared into space feeling numb.

Somehow it got to be night. She washed up and went to bed.

She was warm and comfortable and numb. The exhaustion from the effort of these weeks was over. It had all settled into a quiet stillness inside her, and she was grateful. She could rest. She closed her eyes, hoping for deep sleep.

Images of Richard flickered through her mind. He was smiling at her as they teleported together. He says, "See!" and takes off. The Gateway... energy, forming and dissolving, forming and dissolving... "I think Miranda could experiment with the opal," says Sean, a big bright smile on his face as he hugs Miranda... Argos is huge, a planet in its own right. Ariel gasps in delight, zooms in to take a closer look. The Argonians are moving about purposefully. They are beautiful. Ariel's heart feels like it will burst with love... "When the heart is pure, anything is possible," says Richard and smiles, walking toward her... "He just wants me to change too much," says Miranda, her face contorted in misery... Vivian and Andreas. Ariel is looking up at them. "Careful with the transducer," says Mom and bends down and kisses her cheek. Ariel shrieks with delight and bounces up and down. They are out the door... the key, Andreas extends his arm, the key in the palm of his hand.

Ariel tossed and turned... Miranda holds out her hand, the topaz clip shimmers in her palm. She smiles. "Take it, take it"... the azaleas, big beautiful blossoms... the large topaz on the finger of the Egyptian ruler...

Ariel gasped, opened her eyes, breathing hard. Her heart was pounding. What? What?

She scrambled up into a sitting position. She looked around. The hum of the equipment. Nothing else. She rubbed her head. What was all that? Everybody is talking to me all at once.

The images started again, flashed by one after the other in explosive frenzy. Ariel tried to follow, tried to assimilate, but they moved too fast. She was breathing hard. She sat up straighter. What was going on?

A small hum. She listened. Louder. Then louder.

She jumped out of bed. In her solar plexus she felt a swirling of energy, like a wind picking up before a tornado.

She was taut with attention. It swirled faster and faster, the hum louder and louder. Then it was outside of her, all around her, a swirling mass of energy and sound. She was swept up and tossed, her insides thrown in all directions. She gasped, held her stomach, tried to breathe.

Then, in the center, it got still. Quiet. Then an explosion of light. It grew, spread wildly from the inside and out. Brilliant light. Illuminating her mind. And she could see clearly. All of it.

She was right! Right about everything!

The light became thick, dense with power. Slowly spread throughout her entire body. Solid. Intense. Then stillness. Then it started up again, intensified. Ariel gasped for breath. She felt like she was on the edge of a precipice, about to topple over into something from which she would never return.

She took a strong stance, legs apart, head up tall, breathed it all in. Big breaths expanded her entire being. She floated her awareness on it, expanding it, reaching out to the perimeters, to the security shields, to the static that would interfere with teleportation, to the barrier of psychic input and output.

The energy inside her grew, magnified. Ariel took it in, hungry for it, breathed it in greedily, expanding fiercely. Her arms and legs huge. Breathing big breaths, as if she could inhale the entire room out of existence.

She stood straighter, her chest high, her head tilted back, taking in the heady power.

And before her swirled images of the Gateway, a cavernous opening, eating everything in sight, then spitting it out in a furling, slithering mass of raw energy.

Then a voice. Ariel froze. "It's the love!" it rumbled.

The voice swirled, howled like the wind, "The two of you.

Together."

Again the power expanded, and the voice rode on the power, "Creating the Gateway."

Then, quickly, images, one after another... Miranda's fear—contracting energy. Sean's creativity—expanding energy. Miranda resisting change. Love always required change. Ariel swayed with giant waves.

The hum again, loud, shook her like an earthquake.

She saw Andreas and Vivian. The two in a big white light of love. Bonded. Strong. Exploring the Gateway. Love stronger than any other energy in the universe.

The Key that unlocks the Gateway!

Ariel breathed. Her legs shook. But she was solid on particles of light.

Again images. Andreas and Vivian entangled in a web. Richard waiting for her by the Gateway. Numbers streamed by. All the calculations of Argos accurate.

Then, juxtaposed: the Gateway and Argos. Between the two, an equal sign.

Ariel gasped.

She understood.

If they had the Gateway, the excess energy Argos would produce would be the energy they would need to move Earth!

Her body felt like it would shatter into a million pieces. But the energy held it together. And grew.

And then she was outside the sickroom, through the security boundary, fixing her coordinates toward Richard.

Chapter Forty-Seven

Red dust and rock whipped around in mad chaos. A hellish windstorm raged on Xarinda. The life-support dome flapped furiously, threatening to tear apart.

Ariel held suspended, aghast at the fury around her. She looked for Richard. Not inside the dome. Nowhere near it. He'd left. She was glad. It would have been difficult to stay in this pandemonium. Then fear gripped her. Was he safe?

She thought for a second. Back home. Where else could he go? She set coordinates for Old Earth.

Richard wasn't in the great room or in his bedchamber. She looked in the stable. Mistre was gone. A wave of relief washed over her. He was here! Somewhere. She scanned for psychic traces. Nothing. Where could he have gone that she could not sense him?

She tuned into the hut. Nothing. But then he would have the shields up; he was a wanted man by all. She had to find him fast.

She teleported to the hut. No Richard. What to do? She stood thinking. How could she penetrate his psychic shields? They had never discussed this, never agreed on a signal just between the two of them.

Where was he likely to be? She automatically scanned the surrounding area. And why? He had to be expecting her arrival, on the lookout for her. So he'd be scanning, at least periodically.

If she was right about this, then all she had to do was open up and wait. All right, she'll wait.

She breathed out a sigh of relief now that she had a plan, such as it was. She looked around the hut. She was cold. She looked down at her bare feet. She hadn't had time to change being blown out of the sickroom like that. She stood for a moment in total amazement at what just happened. And now here she was in a ridiculous sleeping outfit.

She looked around for anything she might wear and took one of the blankets and wrapped it around her.

She looked at the fire pit. Did she dare light a fire? She closed her eyes and scanned for anybody near the hut. Safe enough, she decided. She layered the kindling and had a small fire going quickly.

She was exhausted. Yet strong. She felt the new power inside her, inside her body. A wonder.

The sound of the crackling fire comforted her. She warmed her hands and went over the events in her mind, reviewing the images. There was hope, she concluded. If they could work out these last few pieces, everything could change. A small part of her relaxed: she wasn't crazy, and she wasn't imagining outrageous things.

The voice that had spoken to her, who or what was it? She remembered it echoing in every atom of her body. Who had spoken to her? She remembered clearly the presence, and inside her, as if it wasn't separate from her, but a part of her. She felt herself expanded beyond who she knew herself to be. Gigantic, with a vision far larger than she knew herself capable of. She was amazed. She discovered she had a big smile on her face. She enjoyed this new sense of herself.

And why did it all happen? The urgency of the New Earth

situation certainly. Richard's presence and his awareness of the rift, the final catalyst. It all came together, and the Great Light gave her a helping hand.

But why didn't it all go through the Elders? They were the receivers of new directions. They had their set ways. Nothing had changed with them since the beginning. And what just happened—she didn't think it could have happened through the Elders. This was too dramatic a change.

Ariel breathed and took that in. The synchronicities, coincidences, all planned by the Great Universal Being working through. The reason the voice was so powerful and insistent.

They had to do this last part carefully. There couldn't be any mistakes. She made the effort to calm down and settle into clear thinking.

She took deep breaths. Adjusted the blanket around her. She was warm and comfortable, then jolted out of her reverie. Richard? Where is he? She opened herself up to see if he was transmitting. No. No traces yet.

She glanced over at the fire, got up and stacked a couple of small pieces of wood. Flames leaped and hissed. She hoped she wouldn't need to be here much longer.

She heard her stomach rumbling and walked around looking for food. Did not expect to find any, though she did find the water bucket. It was filled with water. She dipped in with the metal cup and drank.

She felt much better, calm, clear and hoped Richard would make contact soon.

Just as she was about to put another log on the fire, she sensed him reaching out to her. Richard! They connected. He sent a quick image of his location. In town delivering a baby. "I'll be done soon," he transmitted.

What was he doing delivering a baby?!

She looked around the hut. She placed the blanket back on the bed, then snuffed out the fire.

When Ariel appeared in near-solid form, Richard was standing at the foot of the bed packing his bag and talking to the merchant whose wife just had a baby. His head jerked slightly as she arrived, but he didn't look in her direction.

The room was on the second floor, with little light coming through. It was small and crammed. The young woman laid on the bed propped up on big pillows. She was smiling, her black hair tangled and moist from perspiration. The baby was asleep in her arms.

Richard looked happy and, Ariel sensed, relieved. Must have been a difficult delivery. That was why he came back. Her heart softened.

"Wait for me outside," Richard transmitted and walked down the stairs, calling out his congratulations as he walked out the door.

"What took you so long?" His head turned slightly in her direction.

Out on the street, Ariel followed in pre-solid form.

"They found out about Argos. I was back in the sickroom."

Richard faltered in his stride, "What?"

"We have to hurry," she said and sent a few images of what took place.

"I am sorry. I had to deliver the baby. Made a promise."

He made a promise. Ariel's heart warmed.

They were moving at a quick pace down a narrow street with houses squeezed together on each side. Periodically Richard nodded at a passerby.

He looked in her direction and quickened his pace.

"Where are we going?" Ariel asked.

"Apothecary," he pointed with his chin, "Just up here," and they proceeded up the street, Richard stepping around dumped trash. "Have to order herbs to be delivered back there."

"We have to hurry," she transmitted.

"Won't take long," and he walked faster.

Then she saw the apothecary sign of mortar and pestle.

A step led into a large room and a powerful earthy smell of herbs. On the counter sat jars, bowls, sieves, mortars and pestles of various sizes and a weighing scale. Behind the counter, shelves were lined with tall jars. On one side stood a large wooden table. Drying herbs hung from wooden beams on the ceiling.

A slight man with wispy gray hair sat on a stool by the table, a large mortar between his legs. He was working the pestle with vigor, grinding something into a fine powder. Next to him, a boy with long blond hair poured liquid into jars.

"Rowan! Good morning."

"Ah, Master Richard! Good morning to you!" He put aside the mortar and pestle and stood up. "How can I be of service today?"

"Busy at work, I see."

"Oh, ay, people don't stop being sick, do they now?"

"Or you and I would be out of a profession," laughed Richard. Then he gave orders for herbs.

"I'd appreciate it if they were delivered to William, the merchant. His wife just had a baby boy."

"Blessings on the little one, may he live a long life," nodded Rowan and walked over to a bundle of herbs and called to the boy. "Edmund! I'll get these herbs ready, and you can take them to the merchant."

Rowan nodded and mumbled something unintelligible.

Once back on the street, Richard transmitted, "I'll meet you in the training field," and was off to get Mistre.

Ariel teleported to the field and carefully sat down under their tree, feeling each leaf and twig under her bottom and feet and the rough bark of the tree on her back.

She looked around. Beautiful day. The sky a clear blue, the dried grass fragrant. And cold. She took a minute to raise her temperature.

She inhaled the fresh air and thought about the rift, felt her body full of energy, ready to surge forward, explore the rift, full of hope and an agonizing wish that somehow Vivian and Andreas were there, that they could be found, that they could be brought back. All assumptions, but she fervently hoped they were accurate. This is the first time there was even a possibility they might find them. Oh, Richard, hurry up!

She turned inward and felt that new power and strength, felt the expanse of it. Her energy field was huge. And it was solid in its cohesiveness, in its integrity. Ariel explored it and breathed it in, gathering in this new reality that she had been presented. Then she turned her attention to what they had to do.

Hoof beats! Richard! She stood up.

"The people are talking," Richard called out and slid off Mistre.

"Richard!" She ran into his open arms.

"My queen," he whispered.

Ariel instantly felt perfect peace. Nothing else existed except Richard, the solidity and warmth of his body. His perfection.

He stroked her hair. "It's nearing completion, isn't it?" He stepped back, "Listen," then he looked her up and down and laughed: "Your welcome-Richard regalia?"

"My very best. Hours to get ready."

"We'll find something for you to wear at the house." Then his face was serious again. "People are talking. The blue devil story has spread."

Ariel nodded, "Yes, and Darius. We have to move fast."

"What's happened?" he asked.

"All right. I think I've got some answers. Open to receive."

Richard nodded his head and closed his eyes.

Ariel transmitted images of what had transpired and all the images and information she was given.

His eyes opened wide in surprise. "We have all we need!" He was jubilant. "Let's go." He started toward Mistre.

Ariel followed. "It seems it's our energy together that makes the difference in finding the Gateway."

"Clearly."

"It's why Andreas and Vivian made progress and other researchers didn't. No other couple worked on the Gateway."

"And the love," he called back. "Don't forget the love," he turned and glanced at her.

"Of course."

He stood beside Mistre, right hand on the saddle. "Can't stay here much longer." He lifted his foot into the stirrup. "They'll be coming for me."

Ariel nodded and stepped away.

He sat, reins in hands, "I'll meet you at the house, then we look at the rift," and urged Mistre into a canter.

Ariel watched Mistre's tail flying. She'll give him time to get back.

She shivered. Her feet were cold. If they found the Gateway, all their problems would be solved. Well, most. Maybe.

She looked around their grove of trees and open blue sky. It was so peaceful.

Most likely, Darius had put off looking for Richard, having been busy with her. What a piece of strange luck. Had they found out yet that she was missing, she wondered. If not, they would soon enough. They could find her, though it would not be easy. But not before she had her answers.

Chapter Forty-Eight

They halted at the instability, strengthened their position and started to scan. After a while they intertwined their energies and deepened their concentration. The thick gray mist that was all around them began to undulate and thin. They watched and maintained focus. It was smooth and light now. They continued a systematic scan. No opening. No crack in the field. Nothing.

What now? She sensed Richard wondering.

"Maintain," she sent.

"Can do only for so long."

She knew. They continued to hold and scan.

Then Ariel felt Richard's concentration waver. The connection was broken. She snapped and picked up the energy loss, and they were again working as one.

"Sorry," he sent.

After a while Richard stopped scanning. His focus intensified.

Ariel turned her attention to where he was focused. A narrow ripple in the space beneath them.

They both concentrated. It opened up, widened. A wave separated. They strengthened their focus.

An opening! What is it?

"Let's go," Richard transmitted and rushed forward.

They passed through a series of small ripples, then blackness.

"What now?" she asked.

"Nothing here," Richard sent.

No barriers of any kind. Just smooth liquid blackness. All calm, steady.

Ariel probed more deeply. They were in some kind of neutral zone, with paths going in different directions. And it seemed like there were infinite directions one could go. At a distance, she sensed several irregularities. Beyond them, different energy systems.

"Like a platform of a station with routes going to different destinations. Except this station leads to different reality systems. Could this be the Gateway?"

She could feel Richard's excitement.

"Do you think this is where they came, then went on looking for a good location for Earth?"

"Possible."

"Where do we look first?"

They probed in every direction looking for traces of Andreas and Vivian, anything that would tell them where to search.

Ariel sensed Richard's energy draining. He could not hold out much longer. Had to hurry.

She boosted his energies and sensed his impatience.

"Any idea which opening to take?" Ariel asked.

"No. But let's try this way," and he took off.

After trying a few different directions, it was clear there was no way to choose one direction over another. They just had to keep looking.

Again they passed through small waves that opened into an energy tunnel. They entered without a problem and continued through. It was a long tunnel. Ariel noted coordinates.

"Looks like we're coming out," Richard transmitted.

The tunnel widened and became brighter. Then blackness with millions of stars.

"An entire universe!" gasped Ariel.

She turned to Richard. He was looking around him.

"An entire system."

Ariel was mesmerized by the vastness and the seeming perfection. "Looks that way."

The rift was the Gateway. Leading to the neutral zone. From the neutral zone, paths led to other universes.

Ariel was in awe.

"We've got to hurry. I don't think Vivian and Andreas are here. Let's go back and try another direction." She took off and transmitted back to Richard. "Can you keep going?"

He didn't respond, but she sensed him following.

Back in the neutral zone, they tried to decide on a new direction.

"Can you pick up anything at all?" Richard asked.

All directions looked identical. Energy the same. No distinguishing features. Ariel focused more deeply, trying to pick up traces of Andreas and Vivian.

"Nothing. Let's try this way."

They went through another tunnel. Vast blackness and stars. Just like the other direction.

"Another system. Pick up anything?" Richard sent.

They held steady, sensing in all directions.

"Let's go back and try a different direction."

Ariel wondered how many different universes led from this node. It looked impossible to figure out where Vivian Andreas went. There were just too many paths to explore. And no indications of any kind, no signs of Vivian and Andreas.

"One more, then we go back and rest. Come on, this way."

Richard followed.

They came out of the tunnel and were slammed by psychic winds and catapulted through space.

Ariel fought to maintain position but was hurled along like a feather.

She saw Richard tumbling after her. What kind of energy was this? She couldn't operate in it.

Richard started to drift away from her. She fought to stay with him, then saw him pull apart like a rubber band, then pull back together.

She increased her energy to help him keep himself together, but it was no use. They were buffeted about, carried helplessly by some strange force.

Ariel fought, using all her power, all her energy, but it was like being a tiny fly fighting a hurricane. She desperately held on to her awareness, fighting to keep track of coordinates, trying to stay with Richard as he alternately tried different things to keep himself together.

In between the blasts, she furiously searched to identify the source, but there was no time. Just as she started to analyze, she'd go tumbling again. Then Richard was swept up by another wave and sent tumbling in another direction.

She followed, but the force of the wave pulled him away faster. He stretched and gathered, then vanished.

"Richard!"

She struggled in pursuit, but it was useless. All her strength was powerless in this massive storm. Richard, Richard.

She tumbled, then in a tiny calm she leaped in the direction he'd disappeared. Did not see him. Then was hurled again. When calm came, she didn't see Richard anywhere. Weak, she struggled.

She tried to get herself back to the neutral zone, but only tumbled and tumbled, being taken who knows where.

Then there was a split-second break in the storm, and in that small instant she focused all her energy and was back in the neutral area.

She was exhausted. Richard! Where did he go? What was this power? She forced herself to calm down. She willed some strength and energy.

If she went back to look for Richard, she didn't think she'd make it. She was too weak to fight that force, whatever it was. No choice. Got to go back and rest.

Can't go back to the ship. No way she could maintain psychic shields feeling so weak and shaken. Besides, they'd be on full alert looking for her. Even with shields, they would find her. The hut? No. Xarinda. Safer.

Chapter Forty-Nine

She had to be precise. Had to have the exact coordinates to land directly in the life-support dome. She pulled together the last of her energy and teleported.

The dome was gone! She jolted to a halt. For a split second all went blank. She panicked. Then focused. Reset coordinates for Old Earth. The hut.

Landed, knees buckled, arms flew out to grab something, nothing. She sprawled on the dirt floor. Laid there, head spinning, shivering, breathing hard. She tried to push herself up and collapsed back down. Everything was spinning. She groaned, closed her eyes, waited for the nausea to stop.

Psychic shields! She tried. Sensed nothing come up. She felt she might throw up, took deeper breaths. Waited. What if they were here looking for her? Tiny needles of fear prickled through her body. She had to get better fast.

She lay breathing ragged breaths, waiting to feel better. Richard. She had to get back to Richard. What if...? No. No.

She became aware of the earth smell, strong, sobering. She breathed it in, letting it revive her.

The wind had swept the dome away. She barely escaped becoming solid on Xarinda, otherwise that would have been her end.

She opened her eyes. The hut walls weren't moving. She pushed up on her left elbow. Spinning began. She fell back down. Had to wait. She groaned. Cold. I have to get back there. Richard!

She tried again. She was shaking, but could move. On her knees. Nausea, again. She closed her eyes, breathed. Waited. Then slowly started to crawl toward the pallet. She put her hands on it, put her head down, waited for the spinning to stop. One last push. She was on the pallet, pulling at the blanket. She groaned, sank into the straw. Everything spun wildly. She breathed hard. Just keep still. Rest. You will be all right in a minute.

Richard. She had to get her strength back. Lie here, get better, fast. That's the only thing you have to do right now. Concentrate.

How long was she gone? Where was Darius? Was he looking for her?

She opened her eyes. All was a moving blur. She closed them quickly. Have to get myself together.

Richard. Where was Richard? Waves of anxiety coursed through her body. I have to go back, find him. Her body jerked up, wanting to get going. Then nausea. She fell back breathless.

Rest, just rest.

The next time she opened her eyes, the brush walls were not moving. She was hungry.

She focused on accelerating her healing. Stitching herself back together. She had to go back. If Richard was lost, all was lost. Would the New Humans ever find the Gateway? Without it, they were doomed. Pain seized her body. No more humans. Stop! She screamed. Focus on healing!

She evened out her breaths and started repairing herself. The more she strengthened, the more energy she had to get even stronger. She monitored her levels. She needed just enough to get back and find Richard. Then she'd decide what to do next. What they would do next! She stopped herself from thinking beyond that. Richard had to be alive! Somehow.

She persevered in strengthening herself. Then, feeling like she could, she stood up. Her legs trembled, but she walked and drank a cup of water, felt it carve down her chest, a cold track. Delicious water.

It was tedious building a fire. Her hands moved in slow motion, uncoordinated, robotic. Finally, the flames hissed alive. She watched for a minute, then crawled into bed again. It crackled and threw comforting blades of light on the brush walls. She was feeling stronger. Just a little more time.

Richard, she had to get to Richard. If they could be sure of the Gateway, the rest would be easy. She forced herself not to think further.

She attempted to secure shields, and this time she succeeded. Whatever good they might do, but saw the pointlessness in thinking about it further. She closed her eyes.

The little fire warmed the hut. She dozed.

When she next opened her eyes, she felt clear enough to analyze the energies of the storm. She set herself to discerning the differences, the minute nuances in those energies. How could she navigate through those energies without being swept away by them? There had to be a way. She was certain.

She continued the analysis. She needed a laser-like method to move through that psychic storm. To push against it, obviously did not work. To travel through it in the usual way did not work. She needed another means.

She explored possible methods. Eventually she found a path. It was a way of going underneath all that psychic energy, bypassing the storm. Moving at a different frequency. She was pretty sure that would work. A change of focus, a pathway beneath the other existing pathways.

Chapter Fifty

She teleported to the neutral zone, stabilized, set her course and proceeded to where she'd last seen Richard.

She entered the storm, stopped, maintained the frequency and waited. Will she be swept away again? All around her, the storm raged. Frenzied swooshing and whistling. Nothing happened. She maintained position. She waited a little longer. Nothing. Relief.

She turned her attention to Richard. She scanned for energy traces, sifting through masses of information. After a while, she sensed him. Weak. The signal came and went. But definitely Richard. Her body filled with energy. Richard! She waited. When she picked up his signal again, she leaped in his direction. Then the signal was gone. A second later it was back, and she leaped again.

After a series of leaps, she saw him. He was bouncing up and down in a small vortex of energy. Richard! She was overwhelmed with relief. Richard! Was he alive? No movement. Richard! No response. Don't panic! Don't panic! She forced herself to stay focused.

She examined the edges of the vortex from a distance, then moved in closer. Fine strands of energy. Short frequencies. A whole mass of them moving rapidly. An intricate fine web, swirling and pulsing rapidly.

"Richard!"

She saw him move.

He's alive! Ariel filled with joy.

"Richard!"

Toward her came love, so much love, it made her stumble in surprise.

"Hang on," she transmitted and began to examine the energies inside the vortex. She needed to know how to move in and then get them both out.

"I'll get you out, just hang on," she transmitted.

"I love you so much," came from Richard.

Her heart warmed. She continued to examine the energies. The vortex operated on the same frequency as the other waves that had buffeted them about, just in a more concentrated form. Relief. All right, she knew what to do.

"Richard, you need to change frequencies. That will get you out."

"Ready," came from Richard.

"Here it comes, the new frequency," she transmitted. "Richard, mark it. Then hold it. I'll come in, get you."

She sensed him struggling to change his frequency, changing his focus, then changing again.

"Send again," he transmitted.

Ariel sent again and continued sending. Come on, come on, Richard. Get it, get it. Tune in.

After a while, she saw him make a move. He was gaining control. All right, all right, just a little more to go.

"Maintain that focus! Maintain! I'm coming in!" She leaped into the swirling mass of moaning, howling energy, grabbed Richard and pulled.

They were out!

He wobbled, faded out, faded in.

"Maintain the frequency! Maintain!" She screamed. She couldn't lose him now!

"Nothing like a screaming welcome," Richard responded.

"Are you all right?" She scanned quickly. She was relieved to see him, relieved he was all right.

"Fine. Took no energy to stay there. Just couldn't get out."

"All right. Ready to teleport back to the hut?" She transmitted coordinates.

Then a gigantic wave slammed them, and they were tumbling.

She sensed Richard swear and was surprised.

"Let's get that frequency back!" she screamed.

She used all her energy to focus on the frequency they needed to get out. But they kept tumbling further and further away from the exit portal.

She was losing sight of Richard. She couldn't focus. Something gooey was clouding her mind. Richard!

Suddenly they were in perfect calm.

What? What happened? Ariel looked around, waiting for the waves to pick her up again, but nothing happened. She looked toward Richard, felt his exhaustion and fear.

"A wild ride, no doubt," he muttered as if in utter surprise. He was stabilizing and looking around.

"No time! Quickly, let's get back before the waves come again."

"No!"

She snapped her head in his direction. "What?!"

"Wait!"

"Focus!" he commanded.

"What?" Ariel scanned about trying to discover what Richard

had noticed.

Images came from him that Andreas and Vivian could have been trapped in the same way.

"Possible, but we've got to get out of here." It was too hard to sustain focus.

"A quick look, then we go back."

Ariel hesitated, then agreed.

It seemed that this universe was these waves of energy. This was a world. The psychic winds carried all sorts of information, on many levels. There was order, stability, meaning, purpose.

"Fascinating," she communicated.

"Sense any traces of them?" Richard asked.

At Richard's question she began searching for traces of Vivian and Andreas, sensing in all directions, probing. "No. Nothing."

They continued their search.

After a while, Richard transmitted, "We have to try something different."

They brought their energies together and focused in various ways to see if anything would open up. Nothing. They rested.

"Let's try again."

They followed the waves in different directions. After a while, everything changed. The quality of energy became more refined, smooth, peaceful.

"Amazing!" transmitted Richard.

"A new universe?" Ariel was incredulous.

Boundless expanse of placid stable energy.

"Beautiful," Richard sent.

They investigated further. A few planets with simple life forms. That was all. Basically empty. Waiting to be populated! The perfect place for Earth! They could create here, build here for thousands and thousands of years.

Could it be? Could it really be? Ariel looked in Richard's direction.

"Ideal," he transmitted.

Ariel was filled with joy. A new home for Earth? Might they be spared from doom?

"We'll need to investigate further later," sent Richard. "Now your parents." He continued to move and scan.

"Wonder if they came here just like we did."

"Don't think so," delivered Richard. "I'd guess they got entangled the way I did."

"I think you're right."

"Go back, rest. Search again in the area you found me?"

Ariel agreed. "Back to the hut?"

"No, the house."

Chapter Fifty-One

Richard put a finger on his lips, "Shhh. The cook's still here, but she'll be leaving shortly."

Ariel nodded, closed her eyes and exhaled. They were here. Solid. Together. Then she felt his arms around her.

"It's all right." He kissed her forehead. "We're almost done. One more exploration and we'll have all we need."

Ariel held him tight, relief rippling through her. Then she pulled back, "Amazing you held steady in that awful vortex."

Richard nodded and pulled her to the chair by the hearth, then sat opposite her.

"Exhausting, that storm," said Ariel.

"Just one more exploration."

They sat in silence for a while, thinking of all that just happened.

"I'm so grateful I could find you, that we're back here and not dead."

Richard murmured agreement and stood up, leaned over and kissed her, "Can't believe how my life has changed since I met you." He shook his head.

Ariel exhaled, "Glad we're back here." And they sat in silence again.

After a while Richard moved, "I'll get us some food," and

headed for the door.

"Shields!" She sent after him and heard a loud whisper of assent.

The room was cold and gloomy. She shivered, rubbing her arms. The morning sunshine had left, and a white overcast enfolded everything into a suffocating uneasy quiet.

She tiptoed to the hearth to get the fire started. Layered twigs. She felt sluggish, as if she hadn't slept in days, but also exhilarated. They were finally getting some answers.

The fire started to take, shooting vigorous flames. She held her hands up, felt their life-giving warmth.

Had they really found the Gateway? She thought so. She hoped. Now Vivian and Andreas. Did they really have a chance of finding them? Whatever was left of them. That they could integrate back into their whole selves after all these years—it seemed more a big fantasy than reality. Yet she hoped.

How long had she been away from Palladium? Darius. Was he looking for them? Anxiety overwhelmed her. Where was Richard? They had to eat quickly and get back out there, then think about what to do next.

The fire crackled, giving the room a warm comforting glow.

The door opened, and Richard walked in carrying a tray. He kicked the door closed behind him and walked toward her, efficacious and lively in his movements.

"We did it!" He placed the tray on the table and looked at Ariel.

Ariel looked up at him, smiling.

"We've found the Gateway!"

Ariel looked around, afraid they'd be heard.

"Oh, the cook was done and left, so we can talk." He smiled that crooked smile she loved.

"Without you, it couldn't have happened." Ariel looked at him, her eyes soft.

"Without us. Without us!"

"How do you feel?"

"Here," he handed her a cup. "Mead."

She took it. Blessedly hot. Just what was needed to revive her.

"I feel fine. Really. But we do have to hurry. Just heard again from the cook—the blue devil story." He chuckled, "If they only knew."

He looked at her open mouth and nodded. "Yes. Let's eat and go."

When she didn't say anything, he continued. "Don't worry. It took no energy at all to sustain myself. I just couldn't get out. I tried. All it did was make me weak. So I waited for you. I knew you'd be back." He smiled and winked.

"Richard." Ariel felt her heart fluttering. Silly me, but he is so very beautiful.

Richard sliced ham, tore pieces of dark bread. A couple of apples were on the tray, a dish of walnuts, a big chunk of cheese.

"Eat. We must be strong. Moving Earth and such." He shook his head in disbelief. "How?" He looked at her with narrowed eyes. "How could anything like that be accomplished?"

Ariel reached for a piece of bread. "It takes tremendous amounts of energy, of course. But now we have it."

She chewed. "If it all works out, Argos will provide it."

She stuffed a piece of ham in her mouth. "After that, it's mountains of work calculating all sorts of energies."

She looked at his incredulous face and smiled. "It's the next stage of human evolution. Not only possible, but necessary. If we can't accomplish it, we can't evolve. If we can't evolve, we perish."

Richard lifted the cup of mead to his mouth, thinking, then nodded.

Mouth full of ham and bread, she mumbled, "It's as if I've not eaten for a week." She drank from the cup. "Good stuff, mead."

"Feeling better?" Richard asked, amused by her hearty eating and drinking.

"Mm," she nodded.

She looked at him a smile on her face. He was adapting quickly to all that was at hand. She was in awe. But shouldn't be, really. He always adjusted quickly. When all this was over, she'll have to find out a lot more about him, what in him made him able to do what even most New Humans could not do. It couldn't possibly be only the mystery school and that early experience.

"I have a feeling we'll find them." He stuffed a piece of bread into his mouth. "They can't be far from where I got tied up." He chuckled, turned, looked at the hearth, got up and placed a log on the embers.

A soft slow drumming—first drops of rain. The room darkened with the gathering clouds. The flames grew brighter in the gloom.

They were each thinking their own thoughts. Where to look for Vivian and Andreas? What will it take? What exactly would they find—if any aspect of Andreas and Vivian could be saved, if they found them at all.

Then he asked, "Tell me more how you got out of prison."

"The sickroom," Ariel said. She didn't like to think she was in some anachronistic prison. Though if she was to be honest, she was. How new were the New Humans, really? How different from the old? Troublesome thoughts.

She frowned. "Maybe you're right, maybe it's not so different in the world in which I live from this world here," she said, "Or any other time in Earth's history." She looked down. Perhaps there was much more for the New Humans to learn than they knew. A startling thought. They had been so confident.

"Perhaps," said Richard. And was silent. Though the silence was thick with implication.

"The power became so strong, it automatically propelled me out of there. To you." She answered his question, feeling a little shy.

"Why am I not surprised?" He spread his arms mocking surprise.

"Feel different?"

How to describe it? "Yes. I have access to much more than before."

Richard waited.

"More information. More power. More understanding." She was amazed. But yes, that's just how she felt.

"Good," Richard said, his eyes pools of something deep, some unspeakable knowledge.

Ariel looked at him puzzled. What did he know that he wasn't saying?

It was raining hard now, a steady loud pounding. Flames jumped around erratically. Blasts of wind whipped through crags hurling packets of cold air.

She leaned toward Richard so as not to shout over the tumult. "Have you marked that frequency?"

Richard nodded, "Wondering if that's all we need, or if they're somewhere else and we might need a different method."

"I know. No time for a different method." She bit into the apple.

"You're thinking of going back to where you found me, right?" he asked, then went back to concentrating on his food, deep in thought.

I'd say the likelihood is high they went through something similar to us. Yes. So, likely to be where you had ended up. Don't you think?"

Richard nodded, chewing. "We go there. They're not there. Then what? Where do we go?"

Where could they look? With infinite options. She chuckled and shook her head.

Richard looked up and smiled. "Yes, with everywhere, where do you look?"

"Let's hope we pick up traces. Some sign."

"That's what we hope for, otherwise it's going to be a lot of work." He sat back. "Rest another minute, then go?"

Chapter Fifty-Two

Ariel and Richard stabilized in the Gateway, oriented themselves, established the frequency they needed to maneuver the storm, and headed for the location where Richard was trapped.

They searched for Andreas and Vivian all around the area.

After a while Ariel sent, "I'm not picking anything up. You?"

"Negative," came from Richard.

"Let's keep going."

They continued the search in expanding circles.

Something, anything, even the tiniest of traces would be enough. At least they'd know they were searching in the right area. But there was nothing except undulating energies of varied frequencies. She wondered what those energies really were. Were they traveling through life forms? Perhaps another time she'll have a chance to explore it more closely.

After what seemed a long time, Richard called out, "Over here!"

Once Ariel was beside him, he transmitted, "Very strange, don't you think?"

Ariel scanned. A huge drop of mixed erratic energies. "Looks like a tiny black hole."

"Another opening into a different energy system?" Richard transmitted. "Go in?"

They stayed at the edge, considering what to do, then simultaneously gathered up their strength and went in.

The energies thinned and thickened, became clear then dense. It was slow moving through the dense parts, but nothing like the storm where they were hopelessly tossed about.

They searched methodically, then Ariel picked up weak signals. "That way," she sent. "I'm picking them up!" Could it really be? She hurried, following the signal.

"I got them," called out Richard.

They pushed through the sludge, working hard in the dense energies and whipping through the thinner sections.

"There!" Richard indicated.

They both leaped in the direction Richard was pointing.

Andreas and Vivian. Thousands of strands of thin opalescent threads held them in place.

Then, a call! Muted, but clear. It was Andreas.

They moved in closer. Vivian and Andreas faded in and out.

"Here!" Andreas transmitted.

"Dad!"

She heard him transmit, but garbled. Then again a fragment, loud, distorted, then nothing.

"Can you make out what he's saying?"

"No," came from Richard.

They maneuvered to get a different view. The strands were woven throughout their essence.

"We're trying to find a way to get you out," Ariel sent to her parents. A short garbled response came back.

"How the hell do we get them out of there?" Richard erupted.

"What are those strands?" Ariel tried to discern.

"Parasites of some kind." Richard sent. "Look at the way

they're entangled."

It was a strange arrangement, to be sure. Andreas and Vivian looked vibrant, yet paralyzed.

"What do you think? If we tear it, could they be severed permanently from their bodies?" Ariel transmitted.

Again, something from Andreas.

"Can't make out what he's saying," Richard emitted in frustration. "Hang in there. We'll get you out," he sent strongly.

Ariel moved in closer. "Give me a minute. I'll run scans."

After a while she said, "Life forms. Peaceful. Symbiotic. They're living off their energy and simultaneously giving them energy." Makes sense. It's why Mom and Dad looked so vibrant. What kind of life form was it? If it wasn't intertwined through Vivian and Andreas, she'd say it was beautiful.

"Can we destroy it?"

"Don't think it would be difficult," Ariel responded. "But what would it do to Mom and Dad?"

They considered.

"Can we try simply pulling them away?" He paused. "On the other hand, that many strands? To pull them all apart?"

"Too interwoven."

"Is it a single organism?"

"I think so."

"Destroy it, then," Richard sent.

Ariel felt horrible revulsion. To destroy was not the New Earth way.

"Don't know that we can. They've been this way too long. Maybe they can't survive the withdrawal of this being's energy."

"What other choice do we have?"

"Give me a moment. Maybe I can find something that will help us."

"What about a simple thing like pulling on one strand? Maybe the rest will follow automatically?"

"I doubt that. If they're that intertwined."

"Let's give it a try," Richard sent, and moved to the cocoon.

He reached out and gently touched one strand. The whole web trembled. He pulled his hand back and looked toward Ariel, then reached out and took a strand and pulled slowly. The entire web swayed. He stopped.

"It's all of a unit." He came back beside Ariel.

"A single organism," Ariel transmitted.

"A single organism," Richard echoed.

They contemplated in silence.

Then before she could do anything, Richard leaped, grabbed a strand and jerked with great force.

Ariel gasped.

A dreadful shriek emanated from the web. Blue liquid squirted from the torn strand and sprayed in all directions.

Richard jumped back.

The mass of strands undulated, convulsed, shuddered, then started to shrivel and turn gray. The shrieks repeated, weaker this time. It thinned and started to float apart, the blue gel sloshing about the flaccid strands.

Vivian and Andreas lay exposed. Faded, appeared, then were gone.

Richard was at Ariel's side.

She couldn't speak.

"They'll be all right," he transmitted. "Let's go back."

Chapter Fifty-Three

In the sickroom Max lay on the bed, head propped up on pillows, hands steepled on his chest, feet crossed at the ankles. He was humming, his fingers tapping in rhythm. At the sight of Ariel, he leaped out of bed and stood staring at her, his mouth open.

"No time to explain," sent Ariel. "Psychic shields up. Now!"

He held his hands palms up, shaking his head in question.

"Let's go!"

"What?" he squeaked.

She sent a picture of the hut. Again the hand gesture, questioning.

"Later. Teleport. Here, the coordinates," she transmitted.

"I can't get out of here," he hissed. "You know that."

"I'll get you out. Let's go."

He straightened himself up and closed his eyes.

They landed in the hut. Max ducked quickly so he wouldn't hit the brush ceiling. "What in the world?!" He looked around, then kept looking at Richard.

"Welcome," Richard said, his arms open in welcome.

Max looked at Ariel.

"This is Richard," she said.

Richard stepped up and bowed, "Max. An honor. Truly."

Max did a short quick bow and looked at Ariel, "What? Who's

this?"

"Have a seat," said Richard, and pulled a stool next to the fire.

"It's alright, Max." She put a hand on Max's arm. "I'll explain." She patted the stool for Max to sit, "We don't have much time."

Richard pulled a stool for Ariel next to Max, and she sat down.

Richard stood looking at Max, an amused smile on his face. Max wore his usual white robes which were particularly wrinkled right now, and his hair stuck out in every direction.

"Where am I?" Max looked around the hut. "You drag me here. .. this better be good, Ariel, or hey, how am I going to explain this to Darius? We've already given him plenty of trouble. So where am I and why am I here?"

Ariel started to explain when Max interrupted, "And who are you?" He was looking at Richard. "Nice hut, though. My style." He smiled.

Richard laughed. "Ariel spoke highly of you, Max. I am truly pleased to meet you. A lot has happened. But we must hurry."

"Psychic shields up, please," Ariel interjected.

"We're pretty sure we've found the Gateway," said Richard and sat on a stool opposite Max.

"And probably the place where we can move Earth," said Ariel.

"You sure know how to take a man out of a pleasant sedate contemplative repose with a bang," said Max.

When they came back, they talked it over and decided to have Max present their findings to the Earth Council. It seemed safer, more likely to guarantee a fair reception. And so here was Max, all confused and baffled.

Richard poked the fire. The flames shot up. "We knew you'd understand."

Max finally seemed to register the gravity of the situation, "The

Gateway?! Are you sure?!"

"Here," said Ariel, and swiftly transmitted images of their findings, including Vivian and Andreas.

"Ah, that's wonderful," said Max.

"Don't know yet—" Ariel started to say.

"You don't know if they've survived it." Max put a hand on Ariel's shoulder briefly. "You want me to present this to Darius? It's why I'm here," Max paused. "But how were you able to penetrate the security shield to my room? How did we get out? How did you get out?"

"Quite something, isn't it? Yes, all that energy that was there from the very beginning that I couldn't explain—it just exploded and I broke through."

"She came back a mountain of power," said Richard.

Max looked from Richard to Ariel, then back and forth again and again.

"We think it's the bond, the energy, the combined energy of the two of us that allowed the perception of the Gateway. Vivian and Andreas were a team." She paused to let Max realize no other research had been done by a couple as a team.

"Incredible!" Max slapped his knee with enthusiasm. "What else?"

"If we're correct and have found a dimension for Earth, then we have a reason to build Argos. All the extra energy generated from Argos would be used to move Earth. This was said at the meeting, if you recall."

Max nodded.

"In other words, we *have* to build Argos, so we can move Earth," said Ariel.

"Amazing!" said Max.

"So we need you to go back and explain to Darius what happened," said Ariel.

"You're our emissary," said Richard, "Our man."

Max made as if to go, "Can't wait."

"No wait, Max. Richard's part in this has to be made clear." She told Max about Richard, what had happened with them, and about what she'd taught him. Told him they were looking for Richard to erase his memory.

"Ariel," was all Max could say. After a while, "And you never said a word." He was hurt.

"It happened so fast... and I was so unsure. I am sorry. But really it was probably best you didn't know."

Max nodded. "I wish you'd told me at least something." He frowned. "But go on."

"Anyway, they have to accept that Richard's part in this is unique and vital. Furthermore, he will have to move to our world."

"What?" Max's eyebrows went up.

She explained the danger Richard was in if he stayed. "But that isn't the main point. The main point is Richard is an essential part of the project."

"But no one ever was moved from another time..." said Max and stopped, "Yes, I see. This is different, utterly different. Anything else?" Then he looked at Richard with admiration, "Picked up our ways pretty quick, didn't you?"

"All part of a greater design," Richard said, his eyes glowing and mysterious in the firelight.

Max stood up and ducked quickly. "All right. I go back. I present these... these incredible findings." He turned and looked from one to the other. "Where will you be?"

"Here," Ariel motioned with both hands. "We'll wait here."

She stood up. "Mark the coordinates."

Richard walked up to Max, put his hand on his shoulder.

Max looked into his eyes, very still, "Yes, I see," he mumbled, then stepped back, looked down at the ground, then looked up quickly, "I'll be back as soon as I can."

Chapter Fifty-Four

The Palladium conference room was hot and heavy with coffee smells and loud conversation.

Ariel and Richard sat at the table. Periodically, a head would turn to look at Ariel, then Richard. Some would smile. Mostly faces looked with eyes full of questions.

Ariel shifted in her chair, wanting the meeting to be over once again, but this time for a different reason. All this attention was disconcerting. She was hot all over and unbuttoned her jacket to cool down. She tried not to fidget and look nervous, though she was.

She turned and looked at Richard sitting next to her. He wore a nice black jacket and white shirt. He had a smile on his face and was calmly looking around at the Palladium crew. Once in a while he'd nod at someone. *He's actually enjoying this.* She was surprised, then glad. *It will make the meeting easier for everyone.*

Max had arranged the meeting, and now they were waiting for the Earth Council to arrive.

Darius sat at the head of the expanded triangle table. He was looking down at his portable console.

Richard leaned over and whispered, "This should prove interesting," then continued looking at the people gathered at the table.

She looked for Max. He was sitting close to the door, twirling his stylus, his hair clean and combed back. He looked up at her. She interpreted his look to mean, let's hope for the best here.

Finally, the first council member arrived in holo form. Richard looked at Ariel, eyebrows raised at the sight of the holographic image. Ariel transmitted a quick explanation and he turned his head to look back at the holo form.

When all the council members were present, Darius started the meeting.

It was hard going telling the story, starting with her powerful intuitions and meeting Richard. Hearing herself talk, she sounded juvenile. Worse yet, it was a flagrant display of disobedience of all New Earth laws. She was hot with embarrassment.

Then came the harder part: her relationship with Richard had to be explained in detail so they could understand why the two of them could find the Gateway.

Darius looked at her. "And you were rulers in Egypt? This is a past life you remembered that was seminal to the Gateway discovery?"

"Yes. But that isn't all of it. It was the training we both received at the mystery school that gave us incredible power," said Ariel. "It's why Richard was able to learn so quickly what I taught him." Then, they had to explain in detail their training at the mystery school.

"It wasn't until Ariel appeared that other similar experiences I had finally made sense," said Richard. Then he explained in detail his accident and what transpired.

When he was done, he looked at Ariel, and she saw the weariness in his eyes. They were both made to drag out and make public something that was private.

"Yes, it was when Ariel started to teleport with me that I started to notice the differences between teleportations and an unusual momentary drag. By then I knew about the search for the Gateway and one night it came to me that this might be the way in." Richard went on in detail about the differences in his observations.

"Why would Richard have noticed the rift when none of our explorers did?" asked one of the Earth Council members.

"Synergy between a couple creates a unique energy," explained Ariel, "There is more power and clarity than a single individual has. It's why Mom and Dad, I mean Vivian and Andreas, were able to find the Gateway. The love between them created a synergy that amplified their abilities and exponentially increased the work they could do."

"And we've had no couples working on the Gateway?" asked another council member, a woman.

"That's correct," said Darius, "I looked into it." They were all silent for a while and then began the questions about Argos.

Ariel and Max listed the configurations they had tried and their conclusions.

"They add up to our original conclusions. Is that correct?" asked Darius.

"That's correct," said Ariel.

Ariel felt Richard's leg press against hers. Her head automatically turned to him, but she stopped herself from looking directly at him.

She noticed the silence. All the faces were turned to her, waiting.

She continued. "Originally, Argos was not feasible, as previously concluded. However, if we have the Gateway, it's not only feasible, but necessary."

There was a stir. People shifted, talked, jolted out of a daze.

Max took over, and the mathematics flashed on the screen.

"Now that we have the Gateway—" Max said and was interrupted.

"That will need to be confirmed," said Darius, and Max continued.

"If this dimension proves to be the appropriate new home for Earth, then we would need the Argos energy to move Earth to the new dimension. The amount of energy generated by Argos over time will be approximately the amount of extra energy we would need to move Earth to the new dimension," he pointed to the numbers.

Another stir in the room. Ariel noticed she was holding her breath and exhaled. She glanced at Richard. He was looking closely at Max, his hands on the table, fingers intertwined.

"We'll need people to run these calculations again," said Darius. "And if we could have you and Richard stay for a while to identify the perimeters of the energy required for the Gateway, we'll send people to look into that." Once the energy that was required to find the Gateway was identified, others could find it. Ariel and Richard's work was done.

Ariel nodded, "Certainly."

Then a long discussion followed, where Ariel explained how she broke out of the sickroom. Sounds of surprise and questions followed, concluding with an elder council member saying that she will need to come to the headquarters for a complete energy exam and report. "Excellent work, Ariel. This will change much for the New Earth going forward."

Loud applause followed. Ariel smiled. Richard put his hand on her arm.

Ariel was pleased. All that early craziness was not craziness at all, but this incredible opportunity. Her expansion meant the expansion of all New Earth. It meant they were moving into a higher cycle of creation. It meant they would have new knowledge and new abilities to move Earth.

After the applause died, there was silence. Left to discuss was whether Richard would be allowed to stay on the New Earth.

Ariel's stomach was in knots. It was strange to feel, on one hand overwhelming relief that the mystery was solved, relief that Mom and Dad were back—news Max brought with him when he came back to the hut—and at the same time the nerve-wrecking possibility that they may not let Richard stay. They may have found the Gateway, they may be able to move Earth, Argos may be built and she, she might lose Richard! She wanted to touch him so badly, but held back.

The oldest council member opened with: "We have laws about time travel…" and he left the sentence open, suggesting that we don't just import people willy-nilly from other timeframes.

Ariel's jaw tightened.

She looked at Richard, found him looking at her, his eyes soft, full of love. She smiled.

Then he turned to Darius, "With all due respect, sir, councilmen, councilwomen and crew."

Everyone turned to look at Richard.

Richard looked around at all of them and when he had their attention, he proceeded, his voice strong, clear, precise: "I have not been a part of your world, but I believe I understand your Prime Directive well. And again, with all due respect, I would like to present you with a new way to think about your Prime Directive. I would suggest that there is a real possibility that, with Ariel and my experience, the fundamental structure of the process of your evolution may have changed. That your Prime Directive—to create and expand—may now include energies from other realms. That inclusion would, so to speak, add to the gene pool of creative possibilities. I believe I am your first such inclusion. I believe others are to follow, and that would be the new way going forward. I would like to propose that this new level of evolution include the creativity of the freedom of time—not only linear and local as has been the case, but spontaneous and inclusive of all dimensions, as is the case with my presence."

He finished, his hands palms up. There was perfect silence for a second, then excited gasps and smiles.

Darius cleared his throat, "This is quite a proposition. Definitely worth considering."

He was immediately backed up by some of the council members, one saying, "Yes. Excellent. We'll explore this and run mathematical projections."

Another added enthusiastically, "This would expand our creative possibilities infinitely."

Ariel looked at Richard, her mouth open. This was simply brilliant. If they could include influences such as Richard from another time, their creating potential would become boundless.

Richard continued, "If you accept this model as a viable next phase of the New Earth evolution, you can see that for me to stay here would be the natural result of such a next phase. Therefore, I respectfully request permission to join the New Earth as one of its permanent citizens. I believe I have a lot to contribute to your society. And," he looked at Ariel, "I would like to remain with my beloved." He touched her arm briefly, then turned to look at all of them. "Furthermore, I don't believe our work, Ariel's and mine, is finished. I believe that together we have much more to offer the New Earth."

All was quiet for a minute again, then Darius said, "Thank you, Richard," and other thank you's emitted from the group. Then loud applause.

"My honor," Richard bowed his head slightly, "I thank you for your attention."

Ariel felt all light inside, filled with joy. She turned to Richard and sent, "You've held this back from me, you minx."

Richard leaned his head to one side and sent back, "It took a while for that to brew to the surface."

There was talk among the group, then the elder councilman said: "We will take everything under consideration and will notify you of our decision regarding Richard." He paused, "Meanwhile, please remain available for further questions, in case we have any."

Ariel and Richard gave their acknowledgment to be available.

A general festive air filled the conference room. Voices rose in excited conversation. Smiling faces all around the conference table. They called out, "Good work, Ariel. Good work, Richard!"

Ariel and Richard looked at each other, smiling.

"It may turn out all right," said Richard.

Ariel put her head on his shoulder. Maybe it will turn out all right after all.

Chapter Fifty-Five

"I love this place," said Ariel.

It was a warm night at the Lotus Enclave. The fragrance of plumeria drifted on the air, mixed with smells from restaurants, bakeries and ice cream parlors. Once in a while, a breeze blew in from the ocean, enveloping them in the briny ocean smell.

Richard was looking around. Amber lights, set on low, floated around them, illuminating the path. Music spilled from restaurants. People came in and out, talking and laughing. "A happy enclave."

"It's good to be here after everything." She inhaled deeply. "I love how it smells here." She turned to look at him, "Just one more thing and the whole thing will be over." She was relaxed and comfortable in a sleeveless shimmery sky-blue dress, though the tension in the back of her being remained.

"Just one more thing." Richard walked in a loose way, as if he, too, felt finally free. It was a long journey getting here. "We need a plan in case they don't approve my transfer."

Ariel looked up at the stars. So many. A big universe. Many possibilities. "Hard to think about that possibility. Yes, I've thought about it. We could leave Earth, live someplace else." She felt an empty hollow feeling saying that, but they had to consider it.

His brows went up, "That's an option?"

"Yes. Many options." She exhaled and asked, "Would you be willing to leave Earth? I know that's difficult to consider, but would you leave Earth?"

They were strolling toward the ocean. Bright lights of various establishments poured onto the path. Laughing groups stopped to decide on the next entertainment.

"Where could we go?" He looked into the distance, turning over that possibility, to no longer live on Earth.

"I've done some research. There was a time in early New Earth history when we were part of the Galactic Union. In those days, there was a lot of trading between various cultures. There is one planet, Vamion, that might be a good place for us."

"Yes?" His face was sad. "Never even imagined living anywhere else but here." A loud wave came crashing in, and he raised his voice, "But everything has changed. So much."

Ariel nodded. "I know. For me it's a lot. For you it's even more strange." She looked to see where they were, if she hadn't missed the restaurant. They had a little farther to go. "I've visited a few times. It is a thriving, advanced, well-organized society. All manner of beings from everywhere live there in harmony."

Richard's eyes were big.

"They have an interesting, simple entry policy. They check the individual's vibration and either they qualified for entry or they didn't. If they didn't, it was impossible for them to enter Vamion. What they look for are evolved thoughts and feelings. So very clever, don't you think?" Ariel smiled. "We'd have no problem gaining entry."

Three children ran by squealing and laughing.

"They're a little exuberant tonight," the mother called out, smiling.

Ariel and Richard smiled back.

"What's it like?"

"Very beautiful with many of Earth's features plus its own unique characteristics. Overall, a very good place."

Richard nodded.

"We'd find work, start a new life. It would take time to adjust, but..." Ariel shrugged, "That's all right. There will be many opportunities there for us."

Richard looked around, "Smells good, whatever they're cooking... you would leave your family?"

Ariel hesitated. "It would not be easy, especially since Mom and Dad are back. How about you?" She felt her chest tighten at the thought of leaving her family.

Richard shook his head, "You know the answer to that. I've never fit it. Now they're looking for me... besides the only way my life makes any sense is if I am with you."

Ariel pulled him to a stop and wrapped her arms around him, "It's the same for me."

They stood with arms around each other for a long time, then Ariel pulled back and they continued walking.

In the distance, the ocean glistened and rolled in the moonlight. A yellow hover cycle swished by with a couple talking loudly. The enclave was bustling with laughter and music.

They stopped in front of a beige stucco building illuminated by floodlights. Big ferns stood on each side of the entrance. A profusion of flowers grew in the front and all the way to the path. Music and laughter issued forth.

"Here we are, Heavenly Delights."

"Mmm, heavenly smells promising a heavenly repast."

A blond girl in a strappy flowery dress led them through the restaurant clamor and out to the back deck where the ocean roared and tall water fountains of various heights sparkled in the mid-distance. On top of each fountain sat a dining table with diners.

"Spectacular!" said Richard.

Ariel squeezed his hand.

They stepped onto an open-air lift and soon were seated at their own dining table at the top of their own fountain.

"What a place," said Richard, talking louder to be heard above the splashing water and music.

"Perfect for our celebration," said Ariel.

Richard looked around, "Are you sure it's solid? We're not going to drop down into the ocean, are we?" He was half mocking half serious.

Ariel shook her head, "Of course not."

Water fountains splashed. Ocean waves came crashing in. Lively guitar music broke through the roar now and then.

They ordered drinks, dinner and dessert from the menu on the tabletop.

"It's hard to believe they wouldn't approve your transfer." Ariel sat thinking, "If they approve, we could be living in a renaissance. It would be an exciting time to be alive." Ariel looked at the glistening ocean. "If they don't approve, I'm not sure I would want to stay here. It would be living in a world heading toward death."

"You think that's what would happen?"

"I think so. If we're not evolving, we're dying."

Richard shook his head, "A world ending. An entire world, not just a civilization." He shook his head again and looked around at the many diners on glistening fountains. "Humans are humans any place, any time. No matter how open-minded, there is always that belief that you are the one who has the ultimate truth."

Ariel sensed him thinking about all the battles fought for some truth, and nodded and said, "Same motives, different stories. We were sure we had transcended this very thing." She took a big breath. "And after thousands of years, we ourselves may have become the very problem we once solved." She shook her head. "And all our effort may not have been enough." Ariel bit her lower lip.

Richard leaned toward her and took her hand in both of his, "Don't feel bad. You know. Every civilization has its rebels. Sometimes they change history and sometimes they die trying. Then the world waits for another rebel who finally succeeds."

"If there is anything even left of Earth." The thought Earth would no longer exist wrenched her gut. "Hard to imagine such horror."

Richard squeezed her hand. "Yes. An unimaginable possibility."

She thought about that inner power that drove her, how right it was. "They all probably had visions like me. That inner light pushing to be expressed. The inspiration irresistible."

Richard nodded, "Obviously you were right to trust it."

"And you helped." Ariel thought back on all the times Richard had told her to trust, to follow through.

The waiter appeared with their dinner, prawns in light white sauce on a bed of rice with a side of grilled papayas, pineapple and mangoes on a skewer.

Richard looked at the silverware, then up at Ariel.

"Ah, yes, the fork," said Ariel, "You use it instead of your hands," and showed Richard how it all worked. The fork was not yet in use in Richard's time.

"I really am a barbarian," said Richard, laughing.

"And I love my barbarian."

Ariel looked around, "It's a beautiful night. This is a beautiful place. We are together. We have a plan. Let's enjoy our dinner."

The prawns were large and fresh. The zesty white sauce a dream. The fruit caramelized perfectly. Truly a playful joy for the senses.

Excellent," said Richard.

The music changed. A mellow tune now. Ariel could barely hear it, but loved the way it rode on the waves.

They both turned their heads as the lift brought a couple of new diners, a man and a woman, wearing simple tops and pants.

A waiter came right after them, collected their plates and placed a dessert in front of each of them—a big ball sprinkled with ground walnuts and chocolate.

"My favorite dessert." She took a forkful, "Mmmm." White cake with cream filling and orange liqueur.

Richard took a bite, "Delicious."

She paused, fork in hand, closed her eyes, felt the breeze warm on her face, listened to the rhythmic crashing of the ocean waves, caught the scent of plumeria between the ocean smells. A perfect moment. Her heart was full. She breathed nice easy breaths. She filled up with hope. Maybe everything will turn out all right.

"That was divine," said Richard, and she opened her eyes.

He pushed away the dessert plate. "Slightly different from our usual recent grub," he laughed, then became serious. "Let's decide what to do in case we have to leave."

Ariel put her napkin down. "My favorite dessert in the world. Yes. Let's meet at the hut," she paused. "There would be no coming back, you know, once we're gone. It would be permanent."

Richard nodded. "That would be all right. I would not want

to come back. I would not want the memories. I want to move forward into a new life."

They were quiet for a while.

"All right. We go back take care of things and be ready to go in case we need to. Hopefully, we won't need to. Difficult to think about leaving Earth."

Richard nodded, "Yes." Ariel watched him take a big breath and exhale.

So much to get in order. She couldn't get everything done. She'd have to focus on what was most important and just let the rest go.

Richard pushed back his chair and stood up.

Ariel called for the lift, and soon they were down on the beach walking in the sand, the half-moon illuminating their path.

The waves sparkled and danced and roared in foaming. Periodically a breeze brought laughter and music from the restaurants. In the distance lights of the enclave twinkled. They held hands and walked in silence for a long time, both deep in thought.

Chapter Fifty-Six

Ariel searched the garment dispenser, a finger on her lips. What to pack in case they had to leave? Images of Miranda, her parents, her friends, her house, her life... raced through her mind. To leave all that! Her chest felt like it had a giant boulder on it.

She sighed, chose a few essential garments, then stepped to the workstation and wrote goodbye letters. Tears ran down her face. She tightened her lips, made no sound, breathed deep slow breaths and opened to receive healing energies from the transducer.

Finished, she lumbered to the kitchen. Everything felt heavy. She got a cup of chamomile tea from the dispenser, sat at the counter and took small sips.

If they had to leave, Vamion was a good place—happy, upbeat, with advanced technology and boundless opportunities. Living there would be easy. They'd find work, start a life together. It would take time to adjust, but a worthwhile effort for the peace they would have.

Into her reverie boomed Darius' voice, "Attention, please. Good news. Laurus is in view. All welcome to come on deck."

She jumped in surprise then was off the stool and running.

"Ariel!" called out Darius as she entered, "Just look at your world!"

The deck was loud with excitement. Everyone was talking at once. There were many slaps on the back, laughter.

Laurus. Billions of strands of pulsating color. Luminous. Constantly changing, forming new patterns. Beguiling.

Ariel put her hand on her heart, mesmerized.

"A sight to behold," Darius whispered, his voice full of awe.

Max appeared beside her, "Ariel, that was some good design work."

"Max! It's beautiful!

There was something about Laurus that was beyond beautiful. It had a wonderful regalness, as if unconcerned with the rest of the universe. It was going to shine its own brilliant light, even if it eclipsed all else in existence. All the love she felt in creating it was evoked again in beholding it. They would develop, evolve, attain sentience and, hopefully, at some point in the future, become Creators themselves, looking for a new dimension to move to, as now they themselves were doing, because they, too, will have populated this side of the universe with their own brilliant creations.

They stood and watched. Then the loud talk began to subside and turned into occasional comments. They were transfixed by the shimmering, glimmering lights, the pure brilliance of Laurus.

Darius broke the spell, "All right, about six hours before we're in orbit. Let's get ready."

There was shuffling toward the door, excited voices commented about going to the surface. Slaps on Ariel's back, and appreciative smiles.

Chris showed up beside her, his face aglow, "I can't wait to be working on Argos!"

Others overheard. Heads turned. It hadn't even been decided, so no one was inclined to talk about Argos just yet.

But not Chris. He continued, "I'm curious what building a very evolved sentient species would be like."

Tom stepped up, "Yes, we've just built worlds that have a ways to go before reaching sentience. Building a world with high sentience... there would have to be some interesting effects, besides the fact that we have to get the heck out of this dimension faster."

"The timing on that will have to be rather precise," said Ariel.

"If it's approved, we'd all suddenly be very busy," Chris continued with his enthusiasm and walked off a bounce in his step.

They scattered to get ready for the landing and maintenance work on Laurus.

Ariel moved with the rest of them, planning what she had to do.

In the hallway, Max was back at her side, and they walked together to their studios, "It's fantastic, isn't it?" He looked her up and down, "Ha! Look at you! All lace and frills. In your fancy wear!"

Ariel wore a creamy lacy blouse, blue slacks and periwinkle boots.

"Yes. Finally had a little time to think about something else besides..."

"Good to see the old Ariel back. No more deadly face." He frowned. "I will miss that if only for the jokes."

Ariel gave him a look.

"Exactly what I mean," said Max, "But seriously, how are you taking the waiting for the decision on Richard?"

The Palladium hallways gleamed rose today. Ariel was particularly fond of rose and enjoyed the glow.

"It's been all right. Went to see Mom and Dad, getting caught up on lots of things."

"How are they?"

"Surprisingly well and getting stronger every day. It was so good to see them awake." Ariel thought about the joy of all of them being together again as a family. She hoped for many more years of that. Unless she and Richard had to leave.

"Yes. After all these years..." said Max.

Ariel nodded then asked, "Max, have you ever heard of a whole workstation failure?"

"What? Workstation failure? Hmm. No. Never happened. Never heard of it happening. Why?"

"I'm still trying to figure out why I showed inaccurate results with Argos."

"You checked again, and are still getting the same results?"

"Yes. And now that I can think clearly, that's the only thing I can think of as the problem. That my station is flawed."

Max rubbed his chin. "I suppose it's possible. Are you going to call it in?"

"I will. Strange I didn't think of it before."

Max shrugged, "Who would have? Things like that don't happen."

"Just Argos data flawed."

They stopped and faced each other.

"Hardly a coincidence," said Max.

Ariel nodded.

At that moment, a rarefied energy started to form around them, wrapping them in intense love, shutting all else out.

"Feel that, Max?"

She felt herself in the presence of the most sacred, that safe harbor of all life. She could hardly breathe.

"Oh, definitely," Max whispered, "Affirmation of its guidance."

Ariel nodded, took deep breaths, felt all tension leaving her, filling up with lightness of being.

Footsteps echoed down the hall.

They unfroze and started walking.

In front of Ariel's studio, they hugged, not saying a word, feeling the wonder of the moment, then Max continued to his studio.

Ariel sat for a long time feeling that wonderful, beautiful presence, feeling assured, renewed, breathing deep easy breaths. Her heart was full. And just one more thing would make it fuller.

Chapter Fifty-Seven

riel laid in the lounging area on Blossom, looking up at the stars, hands behind her head.

She had the ship transmissions on low, tracking all communications, waiting for news about Richard.

It was nice to be away and relax, wait for whatever happened next. She had found a calm about Richard. At least for now. She hoped they'd approve his transfer. She preferred not to leave her home, her family, her friends. But she would if she had to. She was ready to do so. No doubt Richard was also prepared.

At last it came. Darius announced the meeting would start in half an hour.

Ariel leaped and got Blossom going. Just enough time to get back to Palladium and make herself presentable. She braced for whatever was to come. She and Richard would continue here or elsewhere, and that's what mattered.

When she walked in, it's Richard's eyes she caught first. They said, we have our plan, nothing to worry about. He turned to look at Darius, and Ariel followed his gaze.

Darius stood at the head of the table, "Have a seat, Ariel," then sat down. "The Earth Council will be here momentarily."

The table was opened to accommodate the holo forms of the Earth Council. The slender rose columns warmed up the meeting room with their glow.

Ariel walked by Max, patting him on his shoulder.

He looked up, "Ariel," and put his hand on hers. He looked calm in his white robes.

Ariel made her way to Richard. He stood and pulled a chair out for her.

She smiled, "How are you doing?" she whispered. She noticed her voice was breathy, felt her heart beating.

Richard met her gaze, tightened his lips and nodded, but said nothing. He wore black hose and a linen tunic, his hair combed, beard trimmed. Ariel saw dark circles under his eyes and a line between his brows.

She sat down and exhaled. It hadn't been easy for him either, of course. She wondered what had happened, if the gossip had died down or if he'd been approached about his exploits with the blue devil. She looked over at him, but he was turned in on himself and inaccessible.

Quiet chatter filled the room. The food dispenser buzzed, dispensing coffee and coffee smells drifted in the air. Darius was looking at something on his portable console. Max was twirling the console stylus and humming.

At last the Earth Council members appeared. They looked lively. Ariel was hopeful.

After pleasantries, the Earth Council Chairman said, "We'll get right to the point. We've examined the entire situation. The Gateway really is the Gateway!" He looked at Richard and Ariel as he said this.

Instantly, loud cheers and applause erupted.

Ariel felt a warm sense of pleasure. She looked at Richard, who was looking at her, a smile on his face that said, see I told you. He reached over and put his hand on hers.

"The dimension you found is indeed the place where we can move Earth."

More loud applause and cheers.

The chairman nodded and looked around at everyone. "Soon we'll make it known to all on Earth."

More applause and cheers.

"And, most importantly, the Earth Council welcomes Richard!"

Ariel jumped up, clapping her hands. She pulled Richard up and hugged him, half laughing, half crying into his shoulder, felt his arms tight around her, heard him whisper, "My queen."

Whistles, laughter, and more applause. Chairs scraped back. They came, hands extended, to congratulate them.

Richard smiled a slow lazy smile, shook hands with everyone, "Thank you, thank you!"

After a while, they sat back down. The joy in the room was explosive. After all these many years, they finally found the Gateway.

The New Earth had entered a new phase.

The chairman continued, "At the ceremony we'll say more about this decision. Yes, we're having a whole Earth celebration ceremony." Council members looked at each other, grinning and nodding.

The entire room was now in uproar. Applause, laughter, congratulations all around to everyone, didn't matter who. It took a while for everyone to settle down.

The Earth Council departed, but everyone else remained, throwing comments and implications around about the recent developments. The efforts of Earth will now be turned to building

Argos and the move.

"There is the matter of Richard's transport," Darius said, his voice energetic. He seemed very pleased with the decision. "If the two of you can come to see me tomorrow, we can plan this out and also Richard's orientation."

"Of course," Ariel said.

Richard nodded his agreement, his face bright, eyes shining.

Ariel thought about the work on Argos that had to start again and realized that she and Max were quite far along with the prototyping.

Just then Darius said, "We'll reactivate the prototyping. Max, if you can help with that, it would be appreciated."

Max jumped on that, "Will do!" and leaped out of his chair.

Everyone else stood up.

Max turned and said loudly, "But before we do that, how about my quarters for celebratory drinks?" He rubbed his hands together, his face aglow with enthusiasm. "I know we can't all fit, but of course there is always the hallway."

"You go on without me. I need to finish that report," said Darius.

Others declined, suggesting a small celebration the next day at the Knife & Fork, so the three of them marched off to Max's quarters talking loudly and slapping each other on the back.

"Maddening little world you've created," Max teased about Argos.

"Working on the devolution of a species does not qualify as maddening?" Ariel laughed. She felt like she wasn't walking at all, but floating on an invisible cloud of energy.

"She's quite the creator," said Richard, ambling along as if walking on Palladium was the most natural thing in the world.

Ariel felt a soft warmth in her heart. She took Richard's hand.

"Hmmm. I'd like to see that devolutionary species sometime," Richard continued, and Ariel felt a small squeeze on her hand and love coursed through her entire body.

Outside Max's quarters he said, "You'll have to please excuse the disarray."

Just in time, Ariel remembered to brace herself for anything, but didn't have enough time to warn Richard and so they found themselves standing on snowy mountain peaks, that old disturbing sight.

Richard, who was looking at Max, at first didn't notice, and when he did, his body jolted a little, and then he smiled. "Striving for a different perspective, hah, Max?"

Max chuckled. "Come in, come in. I'll change it." He walked over to the console. "Ariel doesn't like it, but thanks for appreciating it yourself. Please go on through."

"Max! No more surprises. I thought my surprise for you would give me a break from all your surprises."

They seated themselves in Max's cave.

Richard looked around and nodded, "Pleasant."

Max exhaled. "And that was some surprise you gave me! A whole man hidden from my knowledge. Suddenly to be manifest. And all the rest..." his voice trailed off. He shook his head.

Ariel smiled, feeling smug.

"I will try," said Max and bowed slightly, a white waiter's cloth draped over his left arm. "And what may I bring you to drink?" His voice was slightly nasally, his pronunciation exaggerated. He was aiming for haughty obsequiousness.

"Your friend is quite a character," said Richard.

"For a fact. It's why he's my best friend," said Ariel.

"Feels good to be appreciated," said Max, handing them drinks, then started a small fire.

And the stories began. Ariel told Max about how she met Richard. And Richard talked about the locals and their intention to hang him. And Max told them about his journey to Altima and how he was using some of the minerals for his new experiment.

Then Max served an improvised dinner of food-dispenser venison, which they pronounced surprisingly delicious indeed.

They sat and chatted late into the night, relaxed after all the recent excitement.

Max raised his glass: "A toast." He waited while Richard and Ariel did the same. "To the New Earth."

To the New Earth!" came the enthusiastic cheer from Ariel and Richard.

Chapter Fifty-Eight

Richard's bedchamber was in half shadows. Pale light seeped grudgingly through the windows, the day burdened with heavy silent overcast. The dank acrid smell strong in the wet chill.

Ariel watched him walk around his bedchamber collecting things he wanted to take with him. He was quiet, his face tight.

A leather sack sat on the bench. Next to it his medical bag. He'd gathered a few items—books, scrolls, ink, quill.

He turned and glanced at her. "I know I am leaving a world where I never felt at home, but…" he held his hands palms up, "It's hard leaving."

Ariel nodded. Then as an afterthought, "We can always come back and visit."

He continued to look at her, his eyes hardened, "No. No, I will not come back," the finality in his voice caustic. "It will only be a dream. This world. Very soon." He moved the bowl on the table, then moved the candle holder. He walked to the windows and pulled the shutters closed. Now it was dark in the room, except for narrow strips of light that pushed through the cracks. "My strength and my nemesis, this world," he said, almost as if to himself, and dropped into a chair by the cold hearth.

Ariel watched and listened. They needed to hurry, get out of here before someone came to look for Richard. But Richard was caught up in his own world, memories having taken hold of him.

Then barking. They looked at each other. Ariel caught her breath. Richard squeezed his eyes shut. "Bennet."

"It's best we go, Richard. No use protracting this."

He pushed himself up slowly, shoulders drooping. He reached for the sack when vigorous pounding on the door jerked him to a stop.

"Marion," said Ariel.

Richard dashed to the door and clattered down the stairs.

Ariel tuned in and listened.

The door opened. Marion stood looking up at Richard. She was breathing hard, her face pink from running. "They are coming for you!" she said and started to cry.

"Come in, Marion." Richard took her by the shoulder, guided her inside and closed the door.

He squatted down and brushed her hair back. "No need to cry, dear Marion. It will be all right. Now tell me what happened."

Marion took a quick look around. "I was at the market and heard talk. They said they were getting people together to come find you, that you are siding with the devil and need to be burned at the stake." Her eyes were round with fear.

"You know that's not true, don't you?" Richard said in a soothing voice.

"I know!" Marion protested with energy. "But what will you do?" She exhaled a big breath.

"No need to worry, little Marion. Now listen. I am joining the Crusades. I am packed and ready to go."

A pout appeared on Marion's face, and she looked ready to cry again. Her true knight was leaving. A small oh escaped her lips.

"It's best that way, don't you think?" Richard's voice became light to reassure her.

She didn't say anything, the pout deeper.

"How about you take Bennet and take care of him while I'm away?"

Marion brightened a little, "I'll take Bennet."

Ariel heard the door close as Richard and Marion went out to get Bennet.

"You go on, walk back home. If you see them along the way, tell them you heard the physician has gone to the Crusades. All right?"

Marion nodded. "To the Crusades. You're going to the Crusades." She nodded energetically. "I know I will see you again. I just know it! You'll be back!" She turned to Bennet, "Come on, Bennet."

"Godspeed, Marion." He patted her on the head.

She looked up with that enchanting Marion smile and deep blue-violet eyes and waved.

Richard walked back into the house, closed the door and took two steps at a time up the stairs. "Ariel!"

Chapter Fifty-Nine

Ariel opened and closed cupboards in Miranda's kitchen looking for champagne glasses. They had gathered for dinner to celebrate, and the kitchen was hot and smelled wonderful. Ariel wore a long aqua gown embroidered with golden flowers.

"Ah, here they are." She held one up, "Use these?"

"Yes," Miranda nodded and handed her the bottle of champagne. She wore a long gauzy gown in periwinkle.

"You look so happy," said Ariel.

"I am. Finally," said Miranda.

Sean peeked around the corner and stepped into the kitchen. He wore a loose green sweater and gray pants. His face was radiant, "If I may be of service..." he wrapped his arm around Miranda.

Miranda snuggled up against him. "You can pour. Being the expert at anything mechanical."

"I don't argue with truth," he kissed Miranda on the forehead and took the bottle from Ariel. He poured, set the glasses on a tray and carried them to the great room.

"You go out there, Ariel, I'll be done here in a minute."

It was early in the evening. The sun was setting, throwing long shadows on the distant mountains. The great room was studded with lit candles that flickered as they moved around.

Ariel stood and looked at her parents. They sat together on

the sofa. She had a big smile on her face. Her parents were here at last!

"Our daughters," Vivian said, "Andreas, our daughters may have grown up better without us," she pouted a little in pretense. She looked at Ariel with mother's eyes.

"Ah, Mom," Ariel shook her head, leaned down and kissed Vivian.

Vivian's face was alive with energy, her cheeks rosy, her brown hair shiny. She wore a flowing blue dress. She put her hand on Ariel's cheek briefly, "Sweetheart."

They had regained their strength quickly at Melrose and were back in their home and rapidly catching up on all that transpired since they left.

Andreas smiled and pulled Vivian to him. His hair was sleeked back. He looked elegant in a navy knit sweater and cream trousers. "Ah, yes, our child here disobeyed all the laws, Vivian," he said with mock shock.

"Seems, if I recall correctly, she's done similar things before," said Vivian, "So, why would we be surprised?" And she told the story of Ariel and the transducer.

Richard looked at Ariel, a big grin on his face.

"Hmm," was all Ariel said.

"Well, well," said Sean.

"That's our Ariel," said Miranda and wrapped her arm around Ariel.

Sean having successfully distributed the champagne, they settled in the great room, perched on various chairs. A jovial light-hearted atmosphere prevailed.

"So, Richard, tell us," said Andreas, "What do you like best about your new home?"

Richard sat a few yards from the sofa looking at Vivian and Andreas. He wore a linen tunic with ties and black hose. His hair was pulled back in a ponytail. He pretended to think about the question in earnest then said, "The privies." He nodded, "Uncommonly comfortable." Everyone laughed.

"Where *did* you find such a barbarian?" teased Vivian mercilessly. "Please do tell us what you found so appealing about our here soon-to-be son-in-law."

There was silence. Everyone waited, surprised by this proposition.

Vivian looked around, "Well, of course, you will marry, yes?" Some more laughter. "But tell, please, what was the appeal?" She had a mischievous smile on her face.

Ariel laughed, "His mare, I think. Her name was Mistre." She looked fondly at Richard. "And he makes excellent pottage." More laughter.

"As soon as you're settled, you'll have to make us some authentic pottage," said Vivian, "That would be a treat."

"It would be my honor." Richard bowed.

Ariel sipped champagne. She thought of the fairy at Heart's Desires. She wasn't sure about Max, but believed all their desires were fulfilled. She was happy. The long ordeal was over. She could relax. Richard was here with her. They had a future together. And Miranda. Here was Miranda with Sean. She was thrilled. She had been so busy herself she didn't know things had taken a good turn until she and Richard arrived and found them laughing in the kitchen.

Sean was walking around holding up the bottle of champagne, "Refill anyone?"

"Glad to see the two of you have come to an understanding,"

said Ariel.

"My Miranda is a courageous woman," said Sean.

Miranda twisted her mouth and shook her head.

He continued, "As it turned out, I've been pestering her about too many things." He looked down. "But somehow she came around, saw the error of her ways." He backed away laughing as Miranda extended her arm to punch him. "No. I figured it out and stopped pushing so hard. But Miranda was curious... and here we are."

"Well, can't say it was easy." Miranda was serious now. "I'm glad Sean persevered with his ideas otherwise I would never have known such a fascinating area of jewelry making," she paused, "Besides other wonderful new things."

They all waited for Miranda to explain more. She looked at their faces, "Another time I'll show you all."

"To the couples," said Max, who until now had somehow managed to stay in the background. He wore his usual white robes, but they were fresh. His hair was combed and he looked happy.

He had been under great stress, too. Now all that being gone, Max looked his normal jovial self and rather handsome. She was pleased.

Max raised his glass: "To love!"

Glasses clanked, loud cheers erupted, the seriousness of this toast clear to all of them.

"All right! Anyone hungry?" asked Andreas and started to rise.

Then they were all in motion. They pulled the table away from the wall, placed it in the middle of the great room and threw a tablecloth over it. They gathered up the chairs. They carried plates of chicken, sausage, asparagus, kale, and potatoes and placed them on the table. Wine was brought out, and soon all was ready and they were seated. Then there was silence. They looked at each other.

"Gratitude," said Andreas. "We have a lot to be grateful for being reunited in this way." He was silent for a while, and everyone thought about how fortunate they were. So much was almost lost.

"May the gods of all time and all space protect us and honor us with long life and great happiness," said Richard.

An enthusiastic yes resounded all around.

Then there was toast after toast, to the new home for Earth, to Argos, to Vivian and Andreas, Richard and Ariel, Sean and Miranda. To Max's courage for helping Ariel. And finally the clanking of silverware as they started to eat.

After a while Miranda asked, "Mom, Dad, what was it like?"

Everyone paused slightly. Andreas and Vivian looked at each other.

Ariel was curious. They hadn't had a chance to hear their entire story. "Yes. What happened while you were away?"

"Well," Andreas paused, fork in his hand, "Hmm. Like being in a comfortable dream."

"Were you aware of being trapped in the web?" asked Ariel.

"We were aware of being there, but there was no urgency to leave. It was as if time didn't exist," said Andreas.

Vivian nodded, "Yes, like we were away for a split second only, and that split second was magnificently comfortable." She shook her head slightly, in disbelief herself.

"So many years, yet, it was as if no time passed at all," said Andreas.

They were all silent for a while.

"I am sad about how much we missed," said Vivian. She looked around at all of them.

"Of course," said Andreas, "And the research we could have been doing all that time. If we didn't get trapped, we would have had the answer to the Gateway years ago."

"How did you get trapped?" asked Max.

Andreas was thoughtful for a minute. "We had traveled through that same portal that Ariel and Richard traveled, many times. We weren't certain it was the dimension to which to move Earth, so we kept coming back, looking, checking, exploring. We weren't going to reveal any of these findings until we were certain. As you know, we only left the coordinates," Andreas paused and took a sip of his wine. His elbows were on the table, and he looked deep in thought.

Then continued, "What made us unsure were the breaks in the space. It seemed to be perfect except for these places where the energy changed in unpredictable ways. This is what we were exploring, to find out if these cracks in the fabric had some kind of regularity. If so, then we had found our place. If not, then we had to keep looking."

Ariel looked out the windows. The sun was almost down. Only the tips of the mountains were illuminated in amber light. The candles in the great room shone brighter. She was glad Andreas and Vivian did not suffer while away. Her heart was full. There was plenty of work ahead, but all exciting work. And with Richard at her side, life had attained a deep rich meaning and purpose unlike she had ever known. She felt content and at peace.

"It's when we stopped to explore one of these irregularities," picked up Vivian, "That we ran into problems." She was twisting her napkin, remembering.

"Andreas wanted to go in and look," she turned and looked at Andreas, "And I wanted to go back and organize teams. You can see who won," she laughed.

Everyone had stopped eating and was listening closely, enthralled. A soft hum of a spacecraft in the distance heading for the station was the only sound.

"The energy of this particular irregularity was, well, the best way to describe it is, welcoming," said Andreas. "It practically beckoned us. Inside, it felt peaceful, steady."

"And we just got lost in it," said Vivian. "Really didn't even notice it." She shook her head, surprised at this.

They were all quiet.

Then Ariel said, "The teams that have gone in are finding that these energy irregularities are fountains of new energy that we can utilize."

"It will be magnificently exciting," said Max, "To explore the area." He had pushed his chair back and sat with his arms crossed.

Eager assent and comments as to the possibilities came from every direction.

"Mom, Dad," said Miranda, "Did you think of us, try to send your location?"

Ariel told them how she had picked up clues.

Vivian looked at Andreas, "Yes. I did. Had you both in my mind, but not to reach you, just love."

Andreas nodded his head, "Yes, like that. Just love."

The love reached her. And the great universal power helped.

"You're shining," sent Richard and smiled, "You're beautiful."

Ariel's heart felt big and warm.

"I'm feeling it," sent Richard, "I love you, too."

"Richard," said Vivian, "A lot of new things to get used to for you here with us. How are you doing?"

"That is the truth," said Richard. He had a smile on his face.

He was sitting back in his chair, one arm on the back of Ariel's chair. "As much as I know already, I know there is far more to learn. I look forward to it," he nodded.

And he did look forward to it. He was finally on a path that was truly his own, his true calling—in another time and place. It's something she would never have imagined possible. With New Earth rules, there wasn't the smallest chance anything like this could ever happen.

Miranda got up, lit more candles, got the music going and came back carrying a large cake. The sight of the cake elicited cheers and light applause.

Sean cut slices, and soon they were all commenting on how delicious it was, sponge with buttery chocolate cream with hints of coffee and rum.

"So, Mom, Dad, how did you meet?" asked Miranda.

Vivian and Andreas looked at each other, then Andreas said, "How do you think?" as they all waited, "In a research lab, of course. There is no other way we could have met otherwise because neither one of us went anywhere else!" He laughed and they all laughed. "It was love at first sight," he continued. "Vivian was the best researcher I had ever known. She was also the prettiest." He looked at Vivian. Vivian blushed, looked down at her plate.

"She was dedicated, thorough, innovative, what more could a man ask for," he finished, looked at all of them, a big grin on his face, evoking peals of laughter.

"It felt fated," said Vivian more seriously. "When I saw Andreas, I felt I had found something I had been searching for, without knowing I was searching." She put her arm around Andreas and leaned into him.

"Did you know it was your combined energy that was allowing

you to see the Gateway," asked Ariel. She knew that most likely they would not have known, after all they always worked together, so there was no basis of comparison.

"We didn't know, as such," said Andreas, "Though we did think that working together we were able to do much, much more than if either one of us worked alone or with someone else."

There was silence. Richard and Ariel were looking at each other, and everyone else looked at them.

"To love," said Max, and held up his glass.

"Yes!" said Vivian. "May our journey into the future be filled with success and ever-expanding love." All glasses went up with loud cheers.

Chapter Sixty

Ariel wore a diaphanous white dress. Golden lights shimmered six inches beyond the fabric. Her hair was swept up and held by the blue topaz clip. She was a cloud of white amidst golden sparkles.

Richard took a step toward her, waved his hand through the golden lights, shook his head and pulled her into his arms. "You are the most beautiful woman in all time and all space."

Ariel could barely breathe she was so happy. "You look very handsome yourself." Richard wore a navy blazer and a white shirt.

He smiled, took a small bow and took her hand, "Where to?"

Ariel transmitted coordinates and in a flash they appeared on the top-most tier of a dance platform.

"Quite a breeze up here," said Richard, raising his voice to be heard above the ocean roar, voices and music.

The sun was low on the horizon. A silver half-moon rising quickly. The North Star twinkled.

"It will be calmer when we go down," Ariel shouted back.

They looked around. Miles and miles of platforms, nine feet above the ocean, spread as far as they could see, for the Whole-Earth Celebration. In the center stood the amphitheater.

"This is grand!" shouted Richard.

Food courts from every period of Earth's history were

everywhere. Games of every kind were set up, many of them involved participation. Dance platforms rose high above the main level. Music blasted from every direction.

"We've never had anything like this before," said Ariel. She felt giddy with excitement.

People arrived in all manner of transport. Some in space shuttles. Good teleporters materialized in seats or hovered in pre-material form. Others came in holo form.

"Let's go down to the amphitheater," said Ariel.

Darkness was descending quickly, floating lights became brighter amongst strategically spaced transducers. A lively warm breeze tossed about refreshing salt air. Groups of musicians played, inspiring enthusiastic dancing on multi-tiered stages. Delicious cooking smells floated on the breeze.

Down in the amphitheater, Vivian, Andreas, Sean, Miranda, Max and Anne were already seated.

Vivian and Andreas held hands, their heads close together in conversation. Then Vivian looked their way, "Hello, darlings." She blew kisses. "What a beautiful couple, Andreas, don't you think?"

Andreas smiled, "Glad to be with my family again."

Max nodded quickly and turned back to Anne. They were arguing about the precise time they would start moving Earth. Anne, after being neglected by Max for quite a while, and after giving him a hard time about this, had agreed to accompany him to the event and was now in her element challenging Max to the max. "Even after Argos is built," she was saying, "It would take time for the Argonians to evolve. None of this will happen in our lifetimes."

"No. You're wrong," said Max. "Ariel has designed the species already superbly evolved. It will hardly take any time."

Miranda and Sean were seated farthest away. They waved.

Once seated, Richard put his arm around Ariel, "How about we take time off after all this is done?"

Ariel warmed up at his touch, his closeness, amazed again that they were together after everything. "Can't imagine anything better," she whispered back.

"Old Earth Ancient Egypt?" said Richard.

"Old Earth Ancient Egypt," agreed Ariel.

He looked at her a little longer, twisted a strand of her hair, touched the topaz clip, smiled.

Ariel felt all cozy inside.

The musicians quieted down, stopped playing, and music from the main sound system started up. The crystal transducers livened up, communicated softly with one another, emitting gentle sounds and healing energies encapsulated in brilliantly composed musicality. The roar of voices slowly died down. Those in semi-material form came closer to the podium, others still milling around found seats. All eyes were on the center stage in the amphitheater.

A smiling young woman wearing a long gown with red and yellow flowers walked on stage. "Welcome, welcome! As you all know, we are here to celebrate the discovery of the Gateway."

Thunderous applause broke out from the crowd, with whistles and cheers that went on for quite a while.

"And to honor our first Gateway researchers, Vivian and Andreas. We are most grateful to have them with us again. And of course, Ariel, Richard and Max." More applause and whistles.

"And to celebrate the commencement of the building of Argos." More applause.

"Most importantly, I am here to announce a change in our Prime Directive." A commotion at this news, then more applause.

"Here is Darius to tell you about it and to hand out awards for highest achievement in research and innovation." The excitement floated in the air, almost tangible, solid.

Darius walked on stage with alacrity, a big smile on his face. He wore white robes with beautiful gold trim, his long hair pulled back. When the applause subsided, he led them in the usual unity and remembering, then was silent for a while before he started to speak.

"Our Prime Directive is to create, to expand. We have learned from our history. However, it appears we had forgotten and had to be reminded again."

Ariel squirmed, wondered how much Darius would reveal. She hoped he wouldn't go into embarrassing detail about how things came about. She squeezed Richard's hand. He gave her a quick look with his knowing eyes and squeezed back.

Darius continued, "Today we are reminded that no matter how evolved we think we are, we are always learning, expanding and the Great Universal Consciousness is greater, bigger than anyone of us could ever imagine," he paused and looked around.

"We are in the process of expanding our Prime Directive. Going forward, it will include, as Richard had suggested, resources from all time and space, such as Richard's transport to our world. This will give us infinite potential for creativity and expansion." The crowd was on its feet in thunderous applause and piercing whistles.

After the cheers subsided, Darius continued with information about Argos and finally the awards. "Vivian and Andreas, please come up to receive the highest achievement award in the area of Gateway research."

The girl who had announced Darius appeared with a beautiful

plaque for Vivian and Andreas.

"We are grateful to be here," Andreas looked around, "And thrilled to continue our research together."

"Thank you, all," said Vivian and held up her plaque.

The crowd was on its feet honoring the couple.

Darius stepped up again, "If Ariel and Richard can please come up to receive the highest achievement award in the area of Gateway research."

The girl was back with two crystal pyramids.

Ariel and Richard walked to the stage to wild applause, whistles and cheers. The energy of joy, excitement and gratitude reverberated through the crowd.

"For your courage and innovation," said Darius and handed them the pyramids.

Richard spoke first, "I am grateful to be part of your world, my world now." Huge applause. He bowed, "Thank you, thank you." He turned to Ariel, "And none of this could have happened without Ariel." More applause. "I stand in respect of your courage and your love." He bowed to Ariel. Loud applause again.

Ariel had a big smile on her face. She held the pyramid to her heart, "Thank you all. You've just made up for all the long months of unbearable anxiety and frustration." More applause.

Richard put his arm around her. They bowed lightly to more applause and cheers.

Darius took center stage again and talked briefly about plans for the future. Then called out cheerfully, "Enjoy yourselves! As you see, drinks and food courts are everywhere. Partake please! And dance! If anything is needed, just announce it. This is truly a day of celebration. Have a good time!" More applause and then everyone started moving. Music started up. Some of the folks in semi-material states found a place to land further from the stage.

Ariel and family were up, hugging, laughing. "Let's see if we can get some drinks," said Andreas, and they all followed him to one of the long tables loaded with bottles and glasses.

After a drink with the family, Richard and Ariel toured the area.

They stopped and watched two teams play air dodgeball. The objective was to materialize, throw the ball, then de-materialize. Of course to dodge the ball, the player had to quickly de-materialize. The team with the least amount of hits won. Facility in teleportation, materialization and de-materialization was critical.

Richard watched, mesmerized. "Do they play this regularly somewhere?" he asked, turning to Ariel.

Ariel smiled. "Of course. We'll go one day, and you can see. Plan to be on the winning team, don't you?" she teased him.

He had a big grin on his face.

They roamed around, then heard the rebec and lute. Richard looked at Ariel, and they followed the music to discover a circle of men, women and children holding hands dancing a nice, slow dance. They joined the circle, and Richard pretended to be the teacher, though he didn't know the dance. They ended up bumbling along, laughing a lot, but soon had the simple steps down and enjoyed dancing.

The moon was now high up in a perfect sapphire sky. The crystal transducers sparkled. The ocean water lapped steadily.

Ariel had her arm through the crook of Richard's elbow. He had his hands in his pockets a smile on his face. They watched an ancient court dance for a while.

Then Richard said, "Want to go home?"

Ariel nodded, took Richard's hand and started toward the

temporary transport station.

"I've never been to your enclave before." His voice had a quality Ariel could not name. Excitement, wonder, curiosity maybe.

It was slow going through the celebratory crowd. And loud.

"I think you'll like it. Lots of variety," Ariel turned back and smiled.

"And your house."

"Our house now."

Ariel felt the squeeze of his hand.

They made it up to the dancing platforms, where it got too crowded to get through.

Ariel leaned over, "Let's just teleport."

Richard nodded.

She sent coordinates.

Then they were standing at the bottom of the footpath leading to Ariel's house, a two-story butter-colored stucco surrounded by palm trees and thick shrubbery. Floodlights illuminated two fuchsia azaleas, one on each side of the door.

Ariel watched Richard look around. In the distance flickered lights of a few scattered houses. It was very quiet. The air was fresh. Millions of tiny lights twinkled. He looked at Ariel, took her hand and they started up the path. "Filled with amenities, I am sure," he jested.

Ariel felt her heart pounding. Good to be home at last.

The End

Tardpolane Recipe

From *Daily Life in Medieval Europe* by Jeffrey L. Singman (pg. 245), who got it from Hiett and Jones, "Two Anglo-Norman Culinary Collections," 864

Take flour and sugar and put them together, and let the dough be mixed with almond milk; and make pie crusts with this dough two fingers high; and then take pears and dates and almonds and figs and raisins, and add liquid, spices, and mash them together, and cast in the yolk of an egg, and a piece of good soft cheese, not too old, and a few eggs; and then put it on the fire and coat the top with the yolk of an egg, and serve it fourth.

Translation: Soak ¼ cup ground blanched almonds and 2/3 cup water for 5 minutes to make almond milk. Mix 2 cups flour with 2 tablespoons sugar. Strain the almond milk through a cloth, then stir into the flour and sugar. Kneed the mixture into of dough and roll it out to about 1/8 inch thick. Cut into 4 inch circles and form into small tart shells (this will be much easier if you use a muffin pan). Mix ½ cup chopped fresh or dried pear, ½ cup chopped dates, ½ cup chopped almonds, ½ cup chopped fresh or dried figs, and ½ cup raisins. Add ½ cup red wine, 3/4 teaspoon cinnamon, ¾ teaspoon ginger, ¼ teaspoon cloves, stir together, then mix in 1 egg yolk, 4 oz soft cheese (e.g., farmer cheese), and 2 eggs. Bake in a preheated oven at 350 degrees for 20 minutes. You may wish to omit the egg yolk coating in deference to modern concerns about salmonella. Makes 12 tartlets.

Acknowledgments

I am very grateful for:

My wonderful beta readers: Elle, Sam Chapman, and Brian William Jewell, who provided valuable feedback in the last stages of writing.

My friend, Athena Marshal, who gave me excellent feedback in the early stages of the novel.

My niece, Katie Wolfe, who offered insightful comments in a very early draft.

My sister, Jasna Gojkovic Sekovski, who read the very first, very, very rough draft—when I wasn't sure I even had a novel—and said: "This is better than most published books." Being well read, I trusted her opinion, was encouraged, and kept on writing. And here we are.

Also by Zorica Gojkovic

Nonfiction:

The Workings of Energy in the Human Energy Field: A Psychic's Perspective

Manifesting: A Planning System for Visual, Creative & Spiritual People

About the Author

From the author: "Ever since I could read, books were my love, comfort and inspiration. My deepest desire is to give readers the same experience; for them to enter a world of wonder and pleasure where they can rest and be renewed."

If you've enjoyed *Ariel* and would like to know about the next release, please sign up to be notified at zoricaauthor.com

9 781947 168046